ABSOLUTE POWER

THE PANTHEON SAGA BOOK 5

By
C.C. Ekeke

Absolute Power © 2020 by C.C. Ekeke

C.C. Ekeke
www.ccekeke.com

Cover Art: Carlos Cabrera

1st Edition

ShatterHouse Press

To the readers.

This series wouldn't be possible without your continued support.

PROLOGUE

The fierce, seesaw battle lasted thirty seconds. And Hugo Malalou had lost.

Correction, he *pretended* to lose. Wearing the head-to-toe royal purple costume with black lining, hood and half-mask on, he was dressed as his alias, Aegis. "Wow, Reg!" He fake-grimaced, speaking in modulated tones. "When did you get so strong?"

On one knee, elbow on a coffee table, Hugo fake arm-wrestled eight-year-old Reggie Palmer. Small and worryingly thin, Reggie needed a heart transplant. He also was Aegis's biggest fan. Hugo had learned about this brave boy thanks to his own mother, who worked at San Miguel Mercy Hospital where Reggie was being treated. His new management services had then contacted Reggie's parents to connect.

For weeks, Hugo had visited as Aegis to buoy Reggie's spirits. And arm wrestle.

Hugo slammed the back of his own hand onto the table, clutching Reggie's smaller one. He feigned defeat, while Reggie raised both arms in triumph. "YAY!"

Hugo rose, shaking out his arm theatrically while sneaking a look at the clock. Friends and teachers assumed he'd missed fourth period French for a doctor's appointment. But Hugo would be back by lunchtime. "You destroyed me! Clearly the wrong person's protecting San Miguel."

Reggie shook his buzzcut-haired head and smiled. "You're the right guy, Aegis."

Those words gripped Hugo's heart. "Thanks, Reg."

Beating up supervillains and rescuing people was awesome. But visiting fans or even having fans exhilarated Hugo like nothing else. He wouldn't take that for granted.

Early afternoon sun spilled through the window, warming the sterile space. Still, it bothered Hugo how Reggie shivered in his hospital gown even with a blanket, never able to get warm. He masked any worries for Reggie's sake.

Then Hugo's superhearing caught two women outside the room, and he grinned.

Reggie's mom entered, pudgy yet pretty, mousy-brown hair in a sloppy bun. "Thank you, Nurse Lina," she gushed, holding the door for a nurse. "You've been so helpful."

"Of course, Mrs. Jarrett." The smiling nurse was Samoan, swarthy-skinned with broad features and a flat nose. Beautiful inside and out. "Anything you need." The nurse eyed Hugo with maternal pride before leaving.

Hugo watched his mother go, forcing his expression into blankness. *Love you, Mom.*

Then Mrs. Jarrett approached, gaping at him as if not believing he was real. "Mr. Aegis? May I take pictures?" She sheepishly pulled out her phone.

"Sure." Hugo crouched and draped his arm around Reggie's thin shoulders. Pictures always brought him mild anxiety. He gave the threat of a smile but never a full one. Aegis wasn't a smiler, while Hugo was. God, thinking in third person was weird.

As Mrs. Jarrett took pictures, Hugo vibrated his face with enough superspeed to appear slightly unfocused. Another deterrent to protect his identity.

"Public appearances are the easiest way to out yourself," Lady Liberty had once said, "You have to create a different walk, cadence, and facial expressions anytime you're in costume." Her lessons still guided Hugo, even though he couldn't forgive Lady Liberty.

He shrugged off the unpleasantness. "What's the latest on Reggie's transplant?"

"He's high on the list," Mrs. Jarrett said. Her smile was forced, the toll of her son's ordeal etched on her face. "But they've said that for months."

Reggie clutched his mother's hand. "It's okay, Mama. I'll get the new heart."

Hugo couldn't hide his broad smile. This kid was living sunshine, like his friend Jen Thomas.

Mrs. Jarrett looked to her son with genuine love. "I hope so, sweetie." Her eyes fell.

Hugo advanced, placing a hand on her shoulder. "Don't lose faith," he said quietly. "Reggie's story is far from over." He would've willed Reggie a new heart if possible. But all he could offer was friendship to someone spending his childhood in and out of hospitals.

Mrs. Jarrett's eyes sparkled with unshed tears.

Troubled, Hugo searched for something to say. Then more footsteps caught his ear from outside, a girl addressing someone while opening Reggie's room door.

Hugo stepped back from Mrs. Jarrett, annoyed. "We have company." *Do Not Disturb* instructions had been given while he visited Reggie.

The door opened, and a teenage girl walked in, supermodel tall and slender. Except that her pupil-less eyes shined like emeralds, her long green mane resembling a churning smoke cloud. The girl's costume, a red crop top with short-sleeves and matching short-shorts, left little to the imagination.

Hugo gulped, recognizing her.

So did a gleeful Reggie. "Starchylde!"

"Greetings, young earthling—" The Extreme Teens' resident "alien" saw Hugo and gawked. "Omigawd," Starchylde gasped very humanlike and bolted.

Hugo stared. That was unexpected. Starchylde seemed terrified of Hugo. *Or was that something else?* He gestured to the Jarretts for a moment and strode after Starchylde.

This floor of the children's wing was irritatingly packed. Ignoring stares from patients, nurses, and doctors, Hugo rounded a corner and found her several rooms down the hall. Starchylde's eyes blazed as she berated her dapper assistant. "You didn't tell me *he'd* be here," she whispered heatedly.

Hugo didn't care much about the Extreme Teens, the poster children for nine-to-five heroics. But Starchylde seemed level-headed…and hot in an otherworldly way. *AJ's gonna freak when he hears this.* "Starchylde," Hugo called out in his Aegis voice, and approached. "Hello." He held out a gloved hand.

Starchylde had a deer-in-headlights look. "Hi." She accepted his handshake, any alien mannerisms gone. She was a nervous teenager with a crush.

On me? Hugo almost laughed at such an absurdity. He settled for a warm smile and clasped her hand, never breaking eye contact. "How are you?"

"I'm well." She regained that alien poise after her assistant cleared his throat. Yet her heartbeat thudded in Hugo's ears. "I'm visiting young patients for the Extreme Teens. Apologies for interrupting."

Hugo waved the apology off. "No worries." Realizing they were still holding hands, he let go. Starchylde's brief dismay gave him a small thrill. Since going public as Aegis, Hugo understood the craziness Titan had dealt with in his career.

"Want to meet Reggie?" Hugo pointed down the hallway.

Starchylde nodded, eyes never leaving him. "Definitely."

As expected, Reggie was bouncing on his bed when Starchylde entered. She entertained him with stories of her "arrival" from the planet Vimvarii. Then she took numerous goofy photos with Reggie and Hugo.

"You two should date," the boy decided after the two heroes posed together for a photo.

Hugo choked back laughter. Starchylde reddened, her fiery mane burning brighter.

Mrs. Jarrett nearly dropped her phone. "Reggie!" She watched Hugo apologetically.

Reggie folded his arms in defiance. "You're both strong and have muscles and can fly!"

Hugo chuckled. "Solid argument, Reg. But we're different ages." Actually, Starchylde was a year older. But that wasn't the biggest issue. Hugo was spoken for, somewhat.

He eyed Starchylde, who'd adopted that familiar stony expression from her show *Extreme Dreams,* when her team jumped into battle.

Hugo sobered and approached. "What's wrong—?" His work cell buzzed. Excitement jolted through him. *Is it San Miguel PD?* Geist had linked him with police contacts before departing San Miguel. Now Hugo had a direct line to crimes or rescues requiring his help. A top priority for San Miguel PD was catching Vincent Van Violence. The murderous powerhouse had narrowly escaped Justice Jones months ago. Hugo had a massive score to settle with that asshole.

To his chagrin, the ping wasn't about V3. "Code Zero at Avila Beach." Hugo's eyes nearly popped out of his mask. "Code Zero" was police talk for attacks on San Miguel between Defcon Level 2 and 1.

Starchylde met his gaze. "A kaiju just reached Avila Harbor."

Mrs. Jarrett gasped.

"A kaiju?" Reggie crowed.

4

Hugo felt no such excitement. "In San Miguel??"

Years ago, the criminal mastermind Doctor Know-It-All had fashioned ginormous monsters straight out of a Godzilla film. He'd dumped dozens of eggs into the ocean before getting captured by his archnemesis—Lady Liberty. The problem was that hatched kaijus hid in the ocean's abyss until adulthood, reaching sizes of two hundred and fifty feet or larger.

The Vanguard had worked with superhero teams across the globe to exterminate each kaiju discovered. But no one knew if there were more until another kaiju swam ashore to terrorize another coastal city.

"I thought the last ones attacked Auckland and Miami," Hugo said.

Starchylde shrugged. "Obviously not. Shall we?" She nodded toward the door.

Hugo eyed the wall clock. Fourth period class was halfway done, followed by lunch. Hopefully, this wouldn't take long. He faced the Jarretts, feeling remorseful. "Sorry to leave early."

Mrs. Jarrett scoffed. "It's fine. We know you're busy."

"Get 'em, Aegis!" Reggie cheered.

The encouragement buoyed Hugo's heart as he and Starchylde dashed out of the room.

CHAPTER 1

San Miguel's skyscrapers and crisscrossing boulevards rushed past Hugo, drenched in golden sunlight. The cityscape shifted into the residences and waterfronts of Avila Beach, home to Central California's largest port.

Starchylde flew beside Hugo, her long hair blazing a smoky green trail behind her. Neither had spoken since leaving the hospital. Hugo's mind churned with excitement and terror. How big was this kaiju? Could he and the Extreme Teens stop this monster? Even Titan and Lady Liberty had needed help against kaijus.

Already, bone-shivering booms sounded in the distance, almost like footfalls.

Simon Han's name flashed across Hugo's eyescreen, indicating an incoming call. Hugo tapped the left side of his hood to accept. "Yes?" he answered in his Aegis voice.

"Dood!" By the background chatter, Simon was in Paso High's Quad. "A fucking kaiju's attacking Avila!"

Another boom rippled across the glittering sea ahead.

"Heading there." Hugo glanced at Starchylde on his right. "Not alone."

Simon got the hint. "Got it. Don't get eaten."

Hugo almost laughed. *Motherfucking Simon…* "I'll do my best."

A louder boom shook the streets, followed by another—again like footfalls.

Hugo sobered quickly. "This might take a while."

"I'll grab you lunch," Simon promised. "See ya at school."

Hugo and Starchylde reached the sparkling blue seas. His superhearing caught screaming crowds and a deafening roar echoing across San Miguel's coastline.

The pair hung a sharp right, and Starchylde's eyes bulged. "By the stars above!"

Shock ran through Hugo. "That's one big, ugly motherfucker." Videos of Godzilla-sized monsters wreaking havoc worldwide, most recently Miami, flooded the Internet.

None of that prepared Hugo to see a kaiju up close, easily clearing three hundred and fifty feet. He shuddered to guess its weight. Foaming seawater spilled off the kaiju wading toward Luis Pier with its bistros, carnival rides, and dozens of civilians. This kaiju didn't resemble other Godzilla-like creatures. To Hugo, it looked like a VFX designer had slapped a kraken together with a T-Rex and a tarantula, then tripled the size. The kaiju's four impossibly long tentacle arms flailed, each fortified with nasty webbed pincers. Its half-submerged legs were five redwoods wide, each footstep causing tremors.

The beast's scales were different shades of grey, glistening like burnished steel from water and sunlight.

Nearly stopping Hugo mid-flight was the round, gaping mouth ringed by rows of huge, sharp teeth.

Simon's warning about getting eaten filled Hugo's thoughts. It wasn't like those teeth could seriously harm him. Still, the visual wasn't pleasant...

This, like every other kaiju, came from the twisted mind of the imprisoned supervillain, Doctor Know-It-All. In his delusional crusade to save Earth, the evil genius had planned on conquering it with his designer super predators.

"It's like the kaiju that attacked Auckland," Starchylde detailed. "A Tiamat."

The name clicked in Hugo's memory. "The one that vomits electricity?"

Starchylde nodded, fiery mane fluttering.

Hugo frowned. *Fuck.* Concentrated lightning could hurt him, like when he fought the Elite. And the Tiamat's electroplasma could liquefy steel.

Another worry seized Hugo. *If that beast attacks Diablo Canyon Power Plant nearby...*

As Hugo and Starchylde reached the pier, civilians were screaming and fleeing. The PCH within a mile of the Tiamat had become a parking lot.

"*Starchylde. TheTeensareinAviladoingevac,*" someone spoke in her earpiece so fast his words ran together. Definitely a speedster. "*AlmostdoneinPortSanLuisPier. Whereyouat?*"

"Almost there, Blur." Starchylde eyed Hugo and grinned. "I'm with Aegis."

Blur's tone shifted and slowed. "The more the merrier. Tomorrow Man's coming too."

Hugo rolled his eyes. Blur had been trashing him for weeks on interviews as a Titan rip-off. An actual Titan rip-off, Tomorrow Man, had taken shots too, still salty over Aegis stealing his "spotlight" or whatever. "Just Tomorrow Man? We're going to need more help to stop that!" He gestured at the Tiamat blotting out the sun. For a heartbeat, Hugo feared it would smash into Port San Luis Pier. Instead, the kaiju waded past the Pier toward landfall.

Thankfully, Blur and his teammates had almost fully cleared the pier.

"*ChillAegis*," Blur said. "*LibbyBattalionandtheHollywoodBombshellsarecoming.*"

Hugo floated down with Starchylde amid screams and panic, internally recoiling at the prospect of seeing Lady Liberty. But he was more curious about why two LA superhero teams were in town. "Why are Battalion and the Bombshells in San Miguel?"

Starchylde gave him a sidelong look. "They're judging candidates for San Miguel's new superhero team."

"Oh." Not that Hugo wanted to be on *any* team, but receiving an invite to decline would've been polite.

The Tiamat's roar shook the whole pier.

"Right. Superheroics," Hugo murmured, working with Starchylde to guide civilians from the pier.

He supersped the citizens he rescued as far inland as possible. The rest of the Extreme Teens soon converged near Port San Luis Pier. Cyberpunk, his body covered in cybernetics; Sunrider, a tanned and beachy blonde riding her energy surfboard. Roadblock stood eye to eye with Hugo but was burlier and cased in granite. Bald and copper-skinned Vendetta crouched like a panther. A whoosh of motion heralded the arrival of Blur, his wild hair windblown. He puffed out his chest and smirked.

The other Extreme Teens were friendly. Blur studied Hugo with unveiled disdain.

Cyberpunk announced another issue. "The Tiamat is emitting some dampening field. It's why cars on the PCH are stuck in Avila Beach."

"Are we waiting for backup?" Sunrider sounded excited.

"Hell no!" Roadblock bellowed. His "don't give a fuck" attitude amused Hugo.

The Tiamat stepped one gimungus foot onto shore, sloshing water over the boardwalk. Mouth wide open, it doused one building in thick, electric energy.

The structure exploded. Chunks of wood, metal, and stone flew every which way.

The Extreme Teens recoiled. Hugo shielded his eyes, waves of intense heat wafting at him.

"On it!" Blur rushed toward the ruined structure.

Hugo breathed easier after a sweeping glance confirmed the pier and boardwalk were empty.

The skyscraper-sized Tiamat swiveled its bulbous head, searching the shoreline.

Hugo was drawing a blank on strategy. *I have to do something.* He floated off the ground, fists clenched.

"Stand down, Aegis!"

Hugo grimaced, a familiar reaction to that voice.

Several figures touched down around the teenagers, ripped straight from the superhero movies.

Hugo recognized everyone but hadn't met most.

Battalion approached first. The powerhouse Hyperion flew beside Blast-o-Lantern, who sported a flaming head and a furnace-like chest. Viva la Volt issued electric forks from his fingers to float his other teammates on metal plates: statuesque Masada, Arachnaut with his four spider legs, the vigilante La Noire, dinomorphing Raptor, and medieval Man-of-War.

The Hollywood Bombshells came next. All female. All stunning. Merry Mayhem, the petite leader, landed first. Malibu, with her sky-blue hair, carried Thunderosa and Stiletto.

Hugo was stunned seeing Tsunami, veteran from The Vanguard's Sensational Seven roster. She rode a foamy wave in her iconic bikini costume.

But Hugo's attention landed on the hero who'd spoken. Lady Liberty hovered a few feet above, majestic in presence with beautiful and stern features. Her leggy red costume clung to her statuesque build with a silvery diadem on her head.

The stare-down was intense and uncomfortable.

Hugo forced out a professional greeting. "Lady Liberty."

Her expression was steely as she addressed everyone. "This Tiamat swam from the Gulf of Mexico, where Know-It-All dropped the last of his kaiju eggs."

Acrimony aside, Hugo was relieved by Lady Liberty's presence. And standing among this caliber of heroes, the Samoan knew in his soul that he belonged.

Hyperion's movie-star good looks scrunched up in aggravation. "I thought every kaiju got destroyed. What special kind of asshole makes sea monsters?"

"Evil man-babies wanting attention," Merry Mayhem dismissed. "And to punish the world for ignoring their intellect."

Another whoosh marked another arrival: Tomorrow Man, barrel-chested and blond, in his orange-and-black suit with his cape fluttering. "Have no fear. Tomorrow Man is here," he said unironically, hands on hips.

Hugo guffawed, and Tsunami giggled. Everyone else ignored Tomorrow Man. The superhero community and general public had considered him a joke after his humiliating defeat on Black Wednesday.

The Tiamat gave another quivering cry and bathed San Luis Pier in scalding electricity. As the famous pier burned, the kaiju turned its eye toward the shipping port farther up the coast.

"Your city, Libby," Raptor remarked. "What's the play?"

Lady Liberty took charge. "Evacuating surrounding buildings is the priority. Medical vehicles are blocked until the Tiamat's energy drain is disabled, so we get injured civilians to them." She pointed to the gigantic Tiamat wading toward the shipping port. "We keep the Tiamat here and kill it. Blur, sweep the nearby buildings. The Extreme Teens except Starchylde can help anyone trapped in their cars."

Blur dashed off while every Extreme Teen save Starchylde ran normally toward the frozen PCH.

Lady Liberty turned to Battalion. "Hyperion," she addressed the handsome powerhouse. "Battalion can evac the port with Aegis." She turned to her former teammate. "Tsunami, kill those fires."

Tsunami nodded, raising both hands and circling them. Ocean waves swelled up, drenching the blazing pier. Hugo found the former teammates' solidarity comforting, given their previous feud.

Steam from the boardwalk reached skyward in knotty curls.

When Battalion got moving, Hugo almost questioned Lady Liberty's plan for the Tiamat, now a gigantic shadow behind the steam wading up the coast.

But he watched Lady Liberty give Starchylde, Viva la Volt, and Tomorrow Man instructions.

"Draw the Tiamat's attention, but be careful," she warned. "Those electroplasma blasts killed half a dozen superheroes in Miami." While that trio took off, Lady Liberty huddled with the Bombshells for further strategy discussions.

Only then did Hugo soar toward the Port of San Miguel. Occupying San Luis Obispo Bay's west end was a small city of cargo terminals, container cranes, rows of color-coded containers, and miles of dock rail. Those rails of the port were on half-artificial land to accommodate the cargo exchange in and out of San Miguel.

Hugo dreaded the damage the Tiamat could do. Port police were already evacuating workers.

"We've redirected all freighters to the Port of Los Angeles," one female officer said, harried but proficient. "But three freighters haven't docked yet."

"I got one!" Hugo stated, flying ahead of Hyperion. "You get the second. We'll do the third together."

Farther away, the towering Tiamat broke through steam and smoke, stomping toward them. Starchylde, Malibu, and Viva la Volt's tiny forms buzzed around the kaiju's round head like angry bees, blasting away with energy attacks. Tomorrow Man launched himself into the Tiamat's torso, shoving the kaiju back. These attacks stalled the beast but hardly damaged that scaly hide.

Hugo's heart leaped anytime the Tiamat puked out jets of electroplasma, then relaxed when his fellow heroes kept buzzing unharmed.

He focused on pushing a massive red-and-black freighter into the port, careful not to damage the hull. Despite weighing several tons, Hugo was pleased at how easily he moved the vessel. His strength continued to increase.

Hyperion, however, was struggling. Hugo flew over to slow his ship before it docked. Members of Battalion directed everyone off.

"Big sea monster wants to eat you," Arachnaut ordered, sounding twelve. "Run." That sent every passenger scrambling as soon as they touched land.

Hugo moved toward the third freighter, strong currents already steering it into the dock. Tsunami stood atop a frothy wave, pushing the ship with her hydrokinesis.

She'd retired in 2005 when Hugo was a toddler, but he'd become a fan via YouTube videos and modeling photoshoots. In her late forties with four kids, this enduring beauty still wore her white bikini-styled costume flawlessly.

She caught Hugo staring and teased him with a flirty look. "Hello, Aegis. Big fan."

Hello! Hugo's eyes widened beneath his mask. Something else widened down south.

"Thanks, Tsunami." He waved, almost forgetting his Aegis voice.

"It's Margarita." Tsunami winked and dove backward off her wave into the sea.

Meanwhile, the Tiamat roared, swatting at the heroes circling its head.

Hugo noticed Hyperion hovering nearby, staring after Tsunami with sex-glazed eyes. "What a fox!" he noted. "She can still get it."

Hugo barely kept a straight face. "No comment."

"Aegis," Lady Liberty annoyingly interrupted over coms. "Are the container cranes clear?"

Hugo scowled and scanned about with telescopic vision. "Yes—wait." His heart lurched. "Stragglers." Swearing heatedly, Hugo rocketed toward the red crane. Two wiry and weathered men tried working the machine's controls with no luck. There was *always* someone.

"Hey!" Hugo landed on the platform beside the duo, startling them. "Let's go!"

The taller, dark-skinned man shook his head stubbornly. "We have a job to do!"

His coworker nodded.

Hugo felt the searing heat before seeing it, memories of Thor's lightning leaving him paralyzed.

But those two dockworkers' terrified faces illuminated by looming death snapped Hugo out of it.

"I have a job too." Hugo rag-dolled both men over his shoulders and dove. A split second later, a jet of yellow electroplasma sheared the crane in half.

The top of the massive crane fell. But Hugo couldn't catch it while holding these dockworkers.

Luckily, Hyperion sped through the air, grabbing it in time.

Hugo exhaled and floated toward the docks. "That was close."

The dockworkers scowled. "Now we don't get paid," the taller man huffed. "Thanks, asshole."

Hugo almost shoved him into the water. Instead, he dropped them on their butts. "Get outta here."

Once they fled, Hugo flew toward Port San Luis Pier. He arrived as Lady Liberty detailed the critical point of her plan. "Tomorrow Man, drive that pylon with all your strength through the Tiamat's throat. Then Malibu, Starchylde, and I will superheat it with a combined energy attack."

Tomorrow Man somehow found a large metal pylon five times longer than himself. He sneered at Hugo and the Extreme Teens. "Watch and learn, children." He raced at the Tiamat, pylon hoisted overhead.

Currently, the kaiju had been blinded by a combo of Lady Liberty's crimson optic blasts, Starchylde's flame bursts, and Tsunami's water spouts. With the Tiamat distracted, Tomorrow Man accelerated to ram the pylon through the kaiju's throat.

The Extreme Teens, Battalion, and the Bombshells cheered. Lady Liberty hung in the air, riveted.

Despite any personal dislike, Hugo was rooting for Tomorrow Man. "C'mon. You got this—"

The Tiamat wildly flailed. A tentacle smacked Tomorrow Man out of mid-air.

Everyone cringed. Tomorrow Man went skipping across the sea like a stone.

"Tomorrow Man got knocked into next week!" Thunderosa jeered. Despite being six feet, two hundred seventy pounds, thick-bodied and irresistibly strong, the Filipina hero laughed like a bubbly tween girl.

Hugo had to laugh. Every Extreme Teen laughed. That was, until the pylon twirled in another direction and impaled the Port San Luis Pier with a solid crunch.

Hugo's heart sank. "Oooph!"

Lady Liberty recovered from the setback, weaving around another swing of the Tiamat's tentacle. "Grab him, Sunrider." She looked to her former teammate, who pounded tidal waves against the Tiamat. "Tsunami, keep distracting. We'll drop cars in its mouth, then ignite them."

In its mouth... Hugo instantly recalled that Jonah and the Whale Bible story. Getting anywhere near that Tiamat's mouth scared the shit out of him, until a somewhat bonkers plan came to mind.

"Where are you going?" Lady Liberty demanded as Hugo flew past.

"To pick a fight," he called back.

The Tiamat's throat glowed, about to vomit another electric blast.

Hugo came sailing in with an axe-handle blow to its jaw.

The Tiamat got rocked sideways, shaking its mammoth-sized head.

Realizing his plan needed firepower, Hugo turned to Starchylde hovering nearby. "I need you."

Malibu and Lady Liberty floated forward.

"What?" the latter remarked.

Starchylde glanced reluctantly at her team.

The Tiamat trained its gleaming eyes on Hugo, who now felt ridiculously tiny.

He needed Starchylde's answer now.

"Yes," she blurted out.

"Let's go." Relieved, Hugo dove down the length of the massive kaiju.

"Aegis, no!" Lady Liberty protested.

Hugo ignored her. "Keep distracting him."

The Tiamat glared down at him and lifted a foot as large as a city block.

Starchylde hovered just above the ground, like him. Her pupil-less eyes bulged in understandable worry. "Where do you want me?"

Hugo clenched both fists. The kaiju bared its teeth and stomped its foot down. "Follow me."

"Hey!" Blur barked from several feet away. "You don't order around my team."

Hugo blasted skyward, uppercutting the Tiamat with both fists. The blow hit like a thunderclap, and Hugo hissed at his stinging knuckles, even in shock-absorbent gloves. "Motherfuck!"

The Tiamat's head snapped back, the beast stumbling several dekameters, but didn't fall.

A sustained sonic scream to the Tiamat's face knocked the beast off its feet.

The colossal splash shot several miles high. Everything and everyone around Port San Luis Pier got drenched. The kaiju sank. Hugo floated higher, waiting.

Beneath the rippling surface was a massive silhouette covering three football stadiums.

Two demonic red eyes stared up at Hugo.

"Aegis!" Merry Mayhem cried. "It's tracking you!"

Hugo grinned victoriously. "Exactly." He flew away from the pier slow enough for the Tiamat to see him. "Everyone but Starchylde stay!" he bellowed.

Starchylde pursued him, a thick vein of green smoke trailing her.

"Lady Liberty—?" Blur whined.

"Do as he says," she said, openly seething.

Now miles away from the shore, Hugo turned to Starchylde. "Stay higher than me. And when I say dive, you follow me full blaze."

Starchylde nodded, never questioning him. "Done."

Hugo slowed and pulled several feet higher. Avila Beach and the San Miguel coast looked so tiny this far out. His attention fixated on what lay beneath the deep blue. "C'mon. C'mon." Heart racing, Hugo was scared that he could die, exhilarated by this insanity, worrying if the Tiamat would take the bait.

Soon, the deep shadow moved with frightening nautical speed.

When the underwater shadow reached them, Starchylde tensed but didn't flee. "Now?"

Hugo shook his hooded head. "Not yet." Fear dominated his thoughts. What if this got him and Starchylde killed? He pushed that thought aside, the moment arriving.

A foamy eruption breached the ocean surface, the Tiamat jumping up at Hugo. Its mouth opened wide to swallow him, ringed with too many teeth to count.

"DIVE!" Hugo plunged into the Tiamat's stinky, fathomless gullet. Descending into darkness, he sensed Starchylde's heat washing down behind him.

Hugo unleashed a sonic scream, shredding apart this creature's esophageal tunnel.

Barreling down the beast, Hugo saw and smelled Starchylde's flames scorch away mucus-lined tissue. Convulsions and tremors intensified the deeper they burrowed into the Tiamat's digestive tract. Upon entering the stomach, Hugo angled up with a burst of speed and punched through the Tiamat's midback.

An explosion of scales and bowels trailed him, along with a fiery green flash marking Starchylde's exit.

Hugo, flying too low, went skidding across the water until finally sinking. He quickly surfaced, gasping, covered in ichor and kaiju guts.

His worry shifted as the Tiamat's swaying corpse pitched backward.

"Shit!" Hugo blasted up and away, just missing the Tiamat's body flopping into the ocean. Another massive fountain splashed miles high. Hugo grinned and soared higher, arms spread triumphantly.

Once he was high above the ocean, a sudden fear spurred him to turn and check if the Tiamat was truly dead.

The ocean roiled around the kaiju sinking into the depths with twitching limbs, never rising again. A quick listen with superhearing confirmed the Tiamat's heart slowed to nothing.

Starchylde seared the air as she flew to him. "That was amazing!" she gushed.

Hugo brushed gooey Tiamat slime off his costume. "And gross." He'd definitely need a few showers.

When he and Starchylde flew back to Avila Beach, power had restarted. Emergency services arrived with blaring sirens. Cars were moving again. Throngs of civilians swarmed the outskirts to catch sight of the superheroes at the port. There was considerable damage, especially to Avila Beach's famed pier. Quite a few buildings had been torched by the Tiamat, no longer burning thanks to Tsunami. Even sweeter, Hyperion reported zero casualties.

"Well done, Aegis," he remarked.

The Extreme Teens, the Hollywood Bombshells and Hyperion's own team echoed his compliments while clearing debris. Getting acknowledged by his fellow superheroes felt weird but meant a lot.

But Blur rolled his eyes in disgust while Lady Liberty glared at him.

Sunrider reappeared on her gleaming surfboard, carrying a drenched Tomorrow Man. "That creature will pay." He swiveled his head, soaked blond locks flying hilariously. "Where—?"

"Dead." Merry Mayhem gestured at Hugo admiringly. "Aegis and Starchylde took him down."

"It was Aegis's idea," Starchylde corrected.

Hugo's cheeks warmed.

Tomorrow Man bristled. "*You* again?"

Hugo shrugged, unapologetic. "Me again." Not his fault that Tomorrow Man kept dropping the ball.

"You're a teen, aren't you?" Starchylde asked a little later while she and Hugo floated above to give EMTs and firefighters space to work.

Hugo stiffened but managed to play dumb. "What are you talking about?"

Starchylde smiled knowingly. "Your verbal reactions betray your adolescence."

Shiite. Hugo really needed to watch his sarcasm.

Then Starchylde reached out and clutched his hands, her pupil-less eyes filling his world.

"Blur is aging out of our team soon," she intoned gently.

Hugo blinked. "You're inviting me to join the Extreme Teens?" No way was Starchylde serious…

She squeezed his hands. "We make a great team." Her husky whisper oozed with naked intent. "Think of what you could do on the Extreme Teens with OWE's resources."

"I…" Hugo forced his brain out of the fog, remembering his rule about teams. "I don't mind team-ups, but I normally go solo—"

"Aegis."

Hugo pulled away from Starchylde like the kid caught stealing from the candy jar.

Lady Liberty came boiling forward. "We need to talk."

Starchylde paled and flew back to her team below.

Hugo sighed and folded his arms. Best get this lecture over with. "Yes, Mother-May-I?"

"Your powerset may be vast." She pointed in his face. "But common sense didn't come with the package."

Hugo barely kept his cool. "Here we go—"

"*I'm* talking!" Lady Liberty steamrolled over his quip. "You went rogue with a reckless stunt—"

"—that worked," Hugo cut in. "The Tiamat's dead. A few damaged structures. No casualties except Tomorrow Man's dignity." The last remark cracked him up.

Lady Liberty turned brick-red. "You think this is funny?"

"I think you're full of shit," Hugo smiled through gritted teeth, sick of this conversation. "And I'm done listening to you." Right then, Hugo felt countless eyes watching. Several heroes and a gathering gaggle of news crews. That was press he didn't need.

Lady Liberty was barking a rebuttal when Hugo glimpsed a nearby digital clocktower.

Sixteen minutes until lunch ended.

Hugo gulped. Battling that Tiamat had felt like ten minutes tops. Jesus. He feigned indifference. "Whatever. I'm out." Hugo whirled and rocketed back to Paso Robles High at top speed.

INTERLUDE

Rodolfo Sanchez had much to celebrate. Next month, he'd be sworn in as Argentina's new president after a landslide victory. His citizens loved him. Lovely wife. Three lovely children. Very lovely mistress…

Sanchez also had much to stress over: his obligation to forty-five million citizens, working with Congress's various factions to pass his agenda, and keeping his affluent supporters happy.

That was why he'd accepted this impromptu morning meeting despite today's back-to-back transition meetings. Sanchez now sat in a private jet on the tarmac of Buenos Aires's Aeroparque Jorge Newbery.

"Your gratitude and support are appreciated." Sanchez adjusted the coat of his crisp navy-blue suit. He put on the dimpled smile that had won millions of votes. In truth, his nerves were stretched tighter than a drum. "The in-person meeting, even more so."

The woman sitting across from him smiled back, showing off pearly-white teeth. "Of course, President-Elect," Riva de León spoke in flawless Argentine Spanish, despite being a Mexican native.

At a glance, she was just *una bombón*—eye candy. Barely above five feet, Riva with her beauty and trim figure was hypnotic. Her black hair in a tight knot, paired with a sleeveless white turtleneck dress, flattered her caramel complexion. But in their year-long professional relationship, Sanchez had learned that Riva was far more than eye candy. Anyone who'd amassed a multibillion-dollar empire before age forty should be valued.

Sanchez crossed his legs. "Why aren't we meeting at La Casa Rosada?"

Riva steepled her fingers and sighed. "My time's limited, so I'll be blunt."

Her grave tone alarmed Sanchez. "You've been my oracle since I announced my candidacy. What is it?"

"Argentina is on the verge of its largest economic crisis since 2001," Riva stated evenly, as if discussing the weather. "Which will trigger violent revolts from various radical groups."

Sanchez sat up at full attention. "My advisers haven't—" The president-elect stopped himself from asking how Riva had learned this. Her knowledge of opportunities and obstacles before anyone else had won him the presidency. "What should I do?"

"Simple." Riva's beady brown eyes twinkled. "The agroindustry deals with your mega-donors in the northeast?" She gave a terse headshake. "Those cannot proceed."

Sanchez practically swallowed his tongue. "Excuse me?"

Riva continued merrily. "The augmented supers you intend to sell on the black market? That also stops. Once resolved, so will your pending problems."

Sanchez worked through several moments of bald-faced shock, followed by volcanic anger. "How *dare* you," he growled. The nerve of this arrogant bitch with her eight-hundred-dollar shoes. "Threatening me? In *my* country?" Especially with his security detail just outside.

Riva's smile lingered. "Argentina isn't yours yet, President-Elect," she reminded curtly. "Our agreement was based on trust. Yet you downplayed how many extra unregistered supers were seized, all which I was promised." Riva's face became a tight, severe mask. "For what? So Argentina can take Amarantha's place selling designer supersoldiers for your personal profit?"

How the fuck does she know? Sanchez began to stammer out a reply.

Riva raised a silencing hand. Sanchez blushed at his automatic subservience.

"You'll honor our agreement," she continued, "and follow instructions. Or, Argentina's economy will crater days after your inauguration. Uprisings will consume this country. You and your lovely family won't make it out of Buenos Aires. Then I'll be speaking with your successor in two months." Riva's smile returned, this time barbed and sinister. "From Congress or your cabinet." She waggled her hand cheekily. "The details are still murky. Do you understand?"

Riva's ironclad certainty speared through Rodolfo Sanchez's soul. He knew Riva's predictions always came to pass, like she was some *bruja* who could divine the future.

And he, president-elect of Argentina, had no say.

Sanchez nodded in acquiescence, disgusted.

Riva's demeanor warmed. "Good!"

Someone new entered the passenger cabin, a pale and leggy American with wavy brown hair and steely eyes. Despite the chic black pantsuit, something about her feline movements petrified Sanchez. She moved like a *killer*.

The American walked up beside Riva to murmur something in her ear, handing over a tablet.

Riva's expression shifted. "We'll discuss Operation: Dom Pedro with your incoming Intel Secretariat chief before your inauguration. I'm needed back in the United States."

She began reading the tablet. "You can see yourself out," Riva added as an afterthought.

Shaking all over, the Argentine president-elect rose. He then marched out of the jet as fast as possible without further embarrassing himself.

CHAPTER 2

Hugo reached Paso High in under two minutes. Once in his gear-stash spot, an unused storage unit near the gymnasium, he undressed and raced to the gym bathrooms.

Five minutes under a boiling shower blasted the Tiamat guts and seawater off.

Superspeeding back to the storage unit dried him off quickly. He threw on his Outlaws baseball jersey and jeans with pristine Chuck Taylors, back in civilian clothes.

Still irked about the San Miguel superhero team, Hugo dialed his publicist—yes, he had one—on an encrypted line. "A new San Miguel team?" he asked peevishly after exchanging pleasantries, mussing up his spiky hair with product. "Why didn't you tell me, Mrs. Sherwood?"

"For the umpteenth time, it's Annie." Annie Sherwood spoke buoyantly despite the late time in Berlin. "And what did you say about joining any team?"

"On the thirty-second of Nevuary," Hugo repeated. It had been his biggest request when he'd hired Annie.

"Exactly," she stated. "There've been nonstop offers from American teams, including the San Miguel tryouts, since I became your PR Goddess. I've rejected them all."

That deflated Hugo's argument. "Oh." He slumped against a wall, smelling faint traces of putrid Tiamat guts. He should've taken three showers.

"Everyone *loves* you," Annie went on blithely. "And after fighting that Tiamat, endorsements will rise."

Hugo felt better knowing Annie had his back, forever grateful that Quinn Bauer connected them. Annie and her husband, Johnny, were handling Aegis's business and media so Hugo could focus on superheroing. "Is Seneca International behind this?"

"Seneca auditioned to bring a superhero franchise to San Miguel and got rejected," Annie said. "More cities are pushing for traditional Emergency Response Action teams after the Elite disaster."

Hugo pushed off the wall, reaching in his backpack for deodorant. "Huh."

"Tryouts are being hosted in cities that don't have official or any teams." Annie sighed. "San Miguel has solo heroes like you, Lady Liberty, some C-listers. But not having an official team is just bad optics."

Hugo couldn't disagree with Annie there. Cities with exclusive superheroes or superhero teams was like getting a sports franchise. This included endorsement deals, merchandise rights, agents, and support staff, especially if corporate-sponsored. The Vanguard and Extreme Teens operated nationally. But both were considered unofficial San Miguel teams. However, The Vanguard, the former gold standard, had disbanded. And like most teen teams, the Extreme Teens weren't taken seriously due to age limitations, mediocre villains, and caring more for fame.

Why would I join them? Hugo shuddered. Yuck.

"So joining any team is still no?" Annie asked.

"Yeah," Hugo replied briskly.

"Good." Annie's tone became gleeful. "Focus on establishing yourself as San Miguel's new protector since 'professional fail person' Tomorrow Man is now a punchline."

Hugo laughed at her open scorn. Poor Tomorrow Man. "Let's talk tomorrow. And tell Quinn and Therese hello." The call ended. Hugo checked his cellphone clock. Six minutes until lunch ended.

Crap. He slid his slime-slathered costume into its hiding spot in the ceiling. That would need serious cleaning after school. Luckily, Hugo had several spares in his lair. He gathered his backpack, did a quick listen making sure the coast was clear, then slipped out of the storage unit.

He quickened his pace through a half-empty parking lot. The sound of Paso High students across campus grew closer. He reminisced over collaborating with Tsunami and the two LA-based superhero teams. His life was crazy!

The Hollywood Bombshells and Battalion, two of Los Angeles's five official teams, fit their city perfectly. The all-female Bombshells had formed at the peak of #TimesUp three years ago.

Battalion started as a popular show loosely based on The Vanguard, casting superpowered leads to reduce VFX costs. Everything changed in season 2 during a bombing at a Boston fan event. The cast had leaped into action, saving countless lives before any New England heroes arrived. OWE, who produced the show, immediately capitalized on the publicity. After months of combat training and replacing any actors uninterested in real-life crimefighting, Battalion became LA's biggest superhero franchise. And they still shot seven-episode seasons each year.

The show had jumped the shark for Hugo after the Atlas name change, done for legal reasons when Battalion became real superheroes. Story-wise, the Titan-esque character Atlas got killed off mid-season 4 and reintroduced as his alternate universe doppelganger Hyperion (played by the same actor/hero).

Yet Hugo still hate-watched the *Battalion* show, now on its eighth season.

He turned a corner around the gym building, now seeing students spread out in groups.

Simon Han waited for him against a rusty fence near the football field's edge, unusually dapper in a polo and slacks. His girlfriend's influence, clearly.

Hugo waved and approached. "Hey."

"Hiya." Simon, his best friend, had finally returned to his Bruce Lee bowl cut. "Here." He handed over a Beach Bum Burger plastic bag.

The smell of burgers and chicken nuggets had Hugo salivating. "Thanks!" He snatched the bag. "Killing kaijus made me hungry." He fished through the bag, popping nuggets in his mouth as they walked.

Simon watched him eagerly. "That battle was EPIC. Check this." He whipped out his cell, revealing headlines on *Herogasm* and *Avngr* about Aegis slaying a Kaiju.

Hugo smiled, starting on his double-double cheeseburger. He kind of enjoyed seeing his deeds recognized. "As long as I don't become a meme." He lowered his voice further. Someone could always be eavesdropping. "BTW. Do I smell like kaiju?"

Simon leaned in and sniffed Hugo's torso, drawing stares. He drew back. "Nope. Just seawater."

Hugo bucked his teeth. "Shit."

The pair kept walking toward the Quad, the lunch crowds growing more condensed. Listening around campus, most of Paso High gabbed about Aegis vs the Tiamat. Some thought it was a PR stunt, irritatingly. But the Coast Guard currently removing the kaiju's corpse disproved that flat-earther nonsense.

"Also saw the Lady Liberty confrontation," Simon muttered, shouldering his backpack.

Hugo bristled. "No comment." He changed topics. "Tsunami is way hotter in person. Like *nuclear* hot." He made a mushroom cloud gesture to emphasize.

"I love your life." Simon's words carried a sliver of envy. "Speaking of sexy heroes…Starchylde?"

Hugo gaped at him. "Hell to the naw-naw!" he snapped. "She tried to thirst trap me into joining the Extreme Teens." Starchylde was hot, but not hot enough for him to join those famewhores.

"Which you're not joining, right?"

"The only team I'd join," Hugo remarked, "is the Sensation Seven era Vanguard, which will never happen." Not without time travel. They weaved through a maze of crowded tables as he inhaled his burger. The briny taste on his fingertips made him gag.

"My professional life is staying girl-drama free. There's enough of that in my personal life." He'd broached going exclusive with Jordana Buchanan before school had started last month. No answer yet. Hugo sighed, tossing his empty Beach Bum bag in a nearby trashcan. "Glad I kept my options open."

Simon looked ahead and squinted. "If you say so."

Hugo followed his gaze, and his heart grew light.

A beaming redheaded skipped toward them from the edge of the Quad, tall and lean and athletic. Her freckled skin retained its light summer tan, complementing her green henley and blue jeans.

"Hey!" Jen Thomas stopped right before Hugo, hugging him fiercely.

"Hey!" Hugo returned her embrace with delight. They'd grown close these last few months. One, J-Tom protected his secret identity like Simon. Two, Hugo had been training J-Tom to be a hero. She had no powers but possessed reverse-engineered battle armor crafted from two of Dynamo's practice droids.

At first glance, J-Tom might be considered unremarkably pretty. Until she serenaded you with that contagious laugh or her irresistible smile. J-Tom's positivity alone could light up a city block. And Hugo couldn't get enough.

She pulled back with an ear-to-ear smile. "I need help with better excuses for my bruises," she whispered. These bruises had come from unarmed combat training with Blackjack and Domino, two of Geist's street-level proteges. "I can only use the volleyball excuse so much."

A grin gushed out of Hugo. "Then stop getting bruised."

"Jerk!" J-Tom gasped and playfully smacked his cheek. "Training tonight?"

"After my evening patrol." Hugo enjoyed training J-Tom, loved her enthusiasm. But deep down, he wasn't sure if she could actually become a hero. For starters, her makeshift armor belonged to Dynamo. What would happen when he found out someone was using his tech? But Hugo had more immediate worries. "How do I smell?"

J-Tom sniffed his neck and wrinkled her nose. "Like saltwater."

"I just told you that!" Simon whined.

"Girls know what smells good," Hugo disputed.

Simon grumbled something in Korean. With five minutes left in their lunch period, the trio moseyed through the sundrenched Quad toward their group. Today was warm and cloudless, vestiges of summer lingering even as fall began.

Hugo's clique occupied two round tables under a shaded area. Most were present, with new satellite members. Wale stood near the tables, dreadlocks flying while showing aggressive dance moves to Groban and John Torres.

Grace Misawa lounged back on the table seat like she owned the damn place, in a funky polka-dot getup, black locks styled in a retro updo with a bandana. She chatted with Marin and Karin, the strawberry-blonde Stanley twins. Grace spotted Hugo and pursed her lips in disapproval. "Here come the three amigos," she murmured.

Hearing that from afar, a pang throbbed in Hugo's chest. But Grace was all smiles for her boyfriend, Simon, and J-Tom. Hugo expected that from her now. The next table over, Raphael Turner had his arm around his girlfriend, Karlee Danvers. They were chatting up a curvy girl with silky brown skin and cornrows reaching her waist. Sneaking up from behind, Hugo slipped his arms along her waist and leaned down to kiss her throat.

"Mamacita..." he crooned in her ear.

Jordana shivered with passion, twisting around to smile up at him. She barely reached Hugo's chest in height, looking like she'd been poured into those peach-colored jeans and matching button-down shirt. "Papi Hugo…" They shared a passionate kiss. "Doctor's visit go well?"

"Very." Hugo hated being dishonest. But for Jodie's safety and his promise to her cousin, lying was necessary. Ugh… Hugo eyed Raphael and Karlee, greeting them blithely.

Simon sidled beside Grace, slipping an arm around her waist.

J-Tom parked atop the table near Jodie to share fries and kisses with the willowy Melinda Wang, a fellow varsity volleyballer. They were cute together. Hugo enjoyed seeing J-Tom happy. But this was probably another casual fling…like her previous ones.

He approached as Wale instructed Groban and JT like a drill sergeant. "What are those for?"

"Dance tournament," Wale answered, chest puffed out.

"Bakersfield Battlerama this weekend," Groban remarked.

"Ah." Hugo held Jodie closer, masking his disappointment. He'd expected the Fab Phenoms to move on after his departure. But the reality stung. "Good luck."

Grace watched him. "We'd invite you, but you're always busy, so…yeah." She made a lazy hand gesture.

Jodie stared up at him expectantly. JT's, Groban's, and even Wale's faces said *Please come back*.

But with his superhero responsibilities, Hugo couldn't promise anything. "We'll see."

Grace turned away to hide her disappointment. "Whatever."

Hugo's stomach tightened. The gulf between him and Grace had become a river. *But can she forgive me and accept my half-truths?*

"Anyone see the rest of my tacos?" Groban asked, searching around the tables. "They were here a minute ago…"

Raphael thankfully filled the tense silence. "Did you hear about Aegis slaying a kaiju?"

"Half-Man, Half-Amazing," Groban added.

"Who hasn't heard?" Hugo scoffed. *I was there.* His friends jabbered on about Aegis while he tried not to smile too proudly.

"I'm curious," J-Tom stated, eyeing Hugo pointedly. "Why are Battalion and the Hollywood Bombshells in town?"

Wale looked disturbed. "I'm more worried about a Godzilla beast barbequing my neighborhood."

"I heard that's the last one," Hugo remarked honestly. "But who knows?"

"If another shows up, Aegis and Lady Liberty will protect us," J-Tom declared decisively.

Simon glared down her exuberance. Hugo's cheeks warmed. No pressure.

"Don't forget Tomorrow Man," Groban added.

Simon snorted. "Too late!" Barking mirth erupted around their group.

"Speaking of losers…" Raphael pulled out his phone. "There's video of the Tiamat whacking him into next week."

Jodie rolled her eyes. "Raph's watched like ten times."

The Stanleys and J-Tom gathered round the cellphone video showing drone footage above the Avila Beach battle.

Hugo gulped, shocked anew by the Tiamat's size. Wow. It swung a ginormous, tentacled arm and smacked Tomorrow Man so hard, he landed with a frothy splash all the way in Pismo Beach miles away.

Hugo guffawed watching this new angle. "Next week called, Tomorrow Man, and they're sick of you. Just like we are today." Both tables roared with laughter.

"He's a loser," Karin Stanley said.

"And a liar," her sister Marin added.

"Tomorrow Man is so uncool," the twins said simultaneously.

Hugo felt guilty laughing at his counterpart's expense but just couldn't stop. Superheroes without their peers' respect or that cool factor which kids emulated usually didn't last long.

The bell ending lunch rang. Students swarmed for their fifth periods. As his friends departed, Jodie led Hugo by the arm to move around Raphael and Karlee.

"Check this…" She gestured at one of their friends passed out, folded arms pillowing her face.

Hugo grinned, whispering an idea in Jodie's ear. She cackled mischievously and scurried to the other side. Hugo raised a hand, silently counting to three.

J-Tom, Melinda, and Simon cringed in anticipation.

"WAKE UP, BRIE!" Hugo and Jordana shouted.

Briseis El-Saden sat bolt upright, fully awake. She glared at Hugo and Jodie, pushing bouncy, shoulder-length locks of auburn from her face. "Ass and hole," she mumbled, stretching her arms catlike.

Hugo smiled cheekily. "Hello right back, Briseis."

Brie's simple attire, white t-shirt with a little black strappy dress, flattered her slim yet filled-out figure. What hadn't changed was Brie's *ridiculous* face, more beautiful than ever in Hugo's opinion.

Also unchanged—her vanity. "Omigod, is my lipstick *everywhere?*" she whined, brushing at her lips. "Do I still look glam, boobs?"

"*Always,* wife," Jordana teased, tilting her head cheekily.

Brie turned to J-Tom. "Any thoughts, Jenny?"

J-Tom, snacking on Skittles, froze. "I like peanut butter?"

Hugo burst out laughing with Jordana and Melinda.

Brie smacked J-Tom's arm. "Real helpful, buddy—" She paused and frowned. "Interesting." Her fingers groped up the length of J-Tom's arm. "Didn't know the gun show was in town."

Hugo stiffened. Simon gulped. Brie wasn't the first to notice the lean muscle J-Tom was putting on. The regular combat training with Blackjack and Hugo was paying dividends.

J-Tom covered quickly, flexing her left arm and pointing across the Quad. "Down that way in Pismo!" While Brie and Jodie laughed, Hugo sighed in quiet relief. J-Tom's improv was better than she realized.

"You're corny as fuck, J-Tom," Jodie teased.

Simon shook his head in disgust as everyone else scattered. "See what you've infected our group with?"

"Pipe down, friend police," Hugo snapped. His BFF remained leery of the three popular girls hanging with their circle of artsy dance geeks and superhero aficionados. And Simon certainly didn't approve of Hugo befriending Brie again. Those two still *loathed* each other.

But last year had changed Hugo and Brie for the better. Shedding that mutual animosity and forgiving each other had been…liberating.

After Simon and J-Tom departed, that left Hugo with Jodie and Brie.

"Dinner at the Promenade? After your tennis practice?" Jodie asked Brie.

"Totally," she agreed.

"Sweet." Jodie twirled to gaze up at Hugo. Her brown eyes gleamed, melting his heart. "Talk tonight?"

Hugo drew her closer. "My breath's bated."

"My body's calling."

The sexy retort raised more than Hugo's eyebrows. "Freak."

"Fuckboy."

Hugo pulled her into another kiss. Jodie made a contented noise. Her fingers caressed the nape of his neck, and Hugo's toes curled.

Brie cleared her throat. "While we're still young, people."

That sent Jodie scurrying off to class, blushing and giggly.

Hugo turned to see Brie's eyes widen while she forced on a smile. Strange. He sneered at her, and they headed to Advanced Placement Biology 2.

"Question," Brie inquired. They'd entered the steel-and-glass Science building, countless students racing around them. "Is Grace taking friendship applications? I'd kill to hang out with her."

Hugo shrugged. Grace's invite-only dance parties and oddball charisma had made her quite popular. "You try talking to her?"

Brie's gaze fell. "My Spidey sense is saying she's not a fan."

Hugo cringed internally. He and Simon had told Grace many unflattering stories about Brie last year. But she didn't need to hear that. "Ask her about fashion." Two minutes until class began. Hugo strode faster. "She makes lots of her own clothes."

Brie whipped her head around. "For serious?" Her pale green eyes gleamed with possibilities. "I'm just…I'm *shooketh* by her awesomeness!"

Brie was still figuring out her new normal after a very public fall from grace. Jodie and J-Tom joining Hugo's clique had gone smoother. J-Tom was literally a sunshine human whom everyone fell in love with. And Jodie was always unfiltered, always fun to be around.

"Is Easy Breezy fucking him, too?" someone asked when they entered the Science building's second floor.

Hugo flinched and watched Brie's reaction. She'd schooled her face into a blank, beautiful mask. But her eyes revealed lingering pain from the crass reminder of the video that destroyed her reputation.

Abby Dunleavy strutted by with legs for weeks, flanked by friends. "Easy Breezy Cover Girl!" she cried.

While her minions howled, Abby shot a nasty look at Hugo.

He ignored her. Those secret summer hookups had been a *huge* mistake.

Brie, fuming, whirled around to unload on Abby.

"No!" Hugo spun her back around by the shoulders. "Not worth it."

Brie sighed and let him steer her forward in resignation. "There's a lot of them to ignore."

Hugo squeezed her shoulders in support. "If you don't mind, they don't matter."

Brie coughed out laughter. "My therapist said the same. I shouldn't be shocked after what a monumental bitch I've been."

"You're not that girl anymore." Hugo wouldn't have rekindled their friendship otherwise.

A weary smile pulled at Brie's mouth as they neared their classroom. "Recovering mean girl. Totally de-bitched."

Their Biology 2 classroom had rows of tables facing before the front of the room, most of them full. "How's therapy been?" Hugo inquired quietly, nodding to a few classmates he knew.

Brie shuddered, sitting down beside him. "Had a joint session with Daddy and Mumu." Mumu, aka her mother, aka Ms. Universe of the Mentally Unstable. *"Pure* torture."

Hugo felt for Brie, whose parents were amid an ugly divorce. "What happened?"

"I called out Mumu for causing my eating issues," she stated. "Like whenever she'd bash my weight or meal sizes, I'd take that as a punishment and exercise myself to death. If she said nothing or gave her approval, I took that as a pat on the head. Mumu *didn't* react well."

"Glad you finally told them," Hugo encouraged, studying her. "Mumu deserves to get owned."

Brie's shoulders sagged. "She's been trying since then."

During their many talks this summer, Hugo had seen how deep Briseis's scars went. "That convo got dark," he remarked dryly.

"Sorry."

The bell rang for fifth period to start. Their Biology 2 teacher, Mr. Saito, hadn't arrived.

"You've been through a lot," Hugo soothed, tapping his desk. "And survived."

Brie grinned and poked his arm. "No thanks to you." Her eyes warmed.

"Well, excuse my friendship," Hugo snarked. "Did you watch Aegis fight that kaiju?"

Brie's mirth turned to meh. "Some of it. Then I dozed off."

That annoyed Hugo. She had this "meh" face anytime Aegis was discussed. "Still a hater?"

Brie prickled. "It's been three months. People need to chill the fuck out with calling him the next Titan."

She wasn't wrong. The glowing press and high expectations since his debut scared Hugo sometimes.

Brie wasn't done, flipping through her textbook. "But if Aegis hooks up with that handsy alien whorebag from the Extreme Teens, then he's CANCELLED!"

Hugo wanted to crawl under his desk from the alarmed stares watching them. "One, you're crazy. Two, Starchylde isn't a real alien."

"I know that," Brie snapped, then softened. "Therapy helped me see that the Extreme Teens, whom I used to love, represent everything wrong with superheroes. Aegis joining them would prove he's another famewhore nine-to-fiver."

Hugo felt the same way. But why he cared about her liking his alter ego mystified even him. "We'll find out in his *Newsworthy* interview Thursday." Quinn had interviewed Hugo as Aegis weeks ago before leaving for Germany. "Watching that might *Aeg-just* your opinion."

Brie stared at him. "You're a *child*," she declared, shaking her head scornfully.

Hugo winked. "There's the Brie we know and love."

Briseis blushed and smiled, quickly averting her gaze.

Hugo's work cell buzzed, and he checked under his desk.

Doc Freeze: Got target details for tomorrow night's mission.

Excitement scorched up Hugo's body. His and Dr. Michelman's war against Paxton-Brandt continued. He slid his phone back into his pocket when Mr. Saito arrived to begin class.

CHAPTER 3

Six past ten o'clock at night. The gloomy skies were bucketing rain.

A lone costumed man crawled across the flooded street. Mandrake, one of Laredo's superheroes. His dark-grey outfit bore slashes from battle, skull-shaped helmet cracked.

"C'mon…" He fought up to a knee. "This isn't over."

"Actually, it is."

Mandrake turned around. His eyes, exposed by that cracked helmet, bulged. Greyson Hirsch approached unhurriedly in a rain-soaked trench coat and light armor.

Mandrake, a rookie from that do-nothing team called Squadron, had been on patrol. Greyson had been doing some business with the Delgado Cartel. The opportunity was too perfect to pass up. Greyson clenched a fist in anticipation, rivers of energy coursing through him.

Mandrake coughed. "Fuck you." He raised his arm, the purple glow of his fist illuminating the street.

Greyson smirked and waggled his fingers, increasing the weight of Mandrake's arm.

The hero cried out and crumpled, unable to lift his arm off the pavement.

Greyson strode closer. "Stay down." Rain dribbled down his beard and thick hair. "It's a shorter distance to fall." Tonight, he had a taste for torture. Maybe because of how…easy this was.

Mandrake thrashed and strained but couldn't escape.

Greyson smirked. "Still fighting?" He reached out. Gravitational energy swirling around his hands distorted nearby raindrops. "Wouldn't want a one-sided fight."

Mandrake actually chuckled. "About that…"

His confidence alarmed Greyson. "Eh?"

Footsteps splish-splashed from behind.

EKEKE

Greyson swore and turned, sheathing himself in gravity fields.

A lanky man dressed like Mandrake stood several feet away, energy rippling around him.

He thrust out both hands, despite his distance.

An invisible wall slammed the breath out of Greyson, breaking his hold on Mandrake and nearly breaking him in half. He landed on wet pavement with a hard smack. Greyson coughed as the dark skies spat down rain. His sternum throbbed. That attack would've done more damage if not for his shields.

"Got him!" the young man exclaimed.

"Stay on him, Suerte," Mandrake warned. "We don't know how powerful he is."

Greyson forced himself into a seated posture. "You're right."

Mandrake was catching his wind. Suerte, beside him, advanced to attack again.

Despite aching muscles, Greyson reacted faster.

Suerte froze in place. "Can't…move…"

With two opponents, Greyson had to end this fight quickly. "Time's up." He raised a fist and closed it, magnifying the gravitational pull on Suerte's bones.

The hero screamed, then imploded within Greyson's forcefields, spraying it bright red.

Greyson withdrew his forcefield, and Suerte's crushed remains splashed to the pavement.

Mandrake stumbled upright. "NO!"

Greyson shrugged, feeling nothing. "Self-defense."

Mandrake had murder in his eyes. "You're dead!" His body lit up, rain sizzling off him.

Greyson beckoned the hero forward. "Try."

Mandrake cocked both fists and charged.

Greyson lazily swept his hand left, tethering Mandrake's gravity to a nearby car.

The hero got yanked sideways, sailing into the dark. A crack was followed by several crunching ribs.

That stirred Greyson somewhat. "How…disappointing." He shivered theatrically and then walked to where Mandrake was now pinned. "Oh well."

The hero's rangy body was trapped against a Suburban SUV, limbs splayed like a starfish. Blood wormed down his lips, indicating internal injuries. But with Greyson altering his gravity, Mandrake was trapped.

"Why…" he demanded feebly. "Why are you helping the Delgados? They're…monsters."

Greyson bristled at this man's hypocrisy. "As are you."

"Me?" Mandrake gawked. "I'm…keeping the borders safe…"

"You hold the line," Greyson corrected with a laugh. "Capturing or killing your quota of drug dealers yet making no actual change."

"Untrue." Yet doubt crept into Mandrake's pained eyes.

"Is it?" Greyson moved closer, arms behind his back. "You could've destroyed these warring cartels smuggling drugs into our country." He grabbed Mandrake's throat. "Yet you don't."

"Not our jurisdiction," Mandrake blurted out, as if scripted.

Greyson scoffed. Always an excuse. "Meaning you and your ilk are lazy cowards."

To his credit, Mandrake remained unafraid. "My team will stop you," he rasped.

The empty threat stirred a sliver of excitement within Greyson. "I welcome it." He tightened his grip, watching the life fade from Mandrake's eyes.

An hour later, Greyson lay shirtless and dry in bed. The TV's pale glow spilled over a dim hotel room.

Connie Ishibashi-Hirsch, his wife, knelt beside him. Her pink lingerie was a welcome distraction, sleek raven-black hair up in a ponytail.

"You're hurt," she fretted, pressing ice wrapped in a hand towel on his purple-bruised sternum.

Greyson tensed from the icy touch, then relaxed as the soreness ebbed. "They put up more fight."

Connie searched his face, frowning. "Yet you aren't satisfied."

Wifey knows me well. Another reason why he loved Connie. "Squadron aren't who I want."

Understanding filled Connie's features. "The Shield of Justice."

Aegis, in San Miguel, had made quite a splash since defeating those fraudulent Elite months ago. Since then, he'd beaten several threats to his patron city. There were also rumors that Aegis helped stop some undisclosed international crisis weeks ago. But a random cape appearing out of nowhere and becoming an instant press darling? Something felt wrong, and Greyson had to stop this new false god.

Connie sat next to him, hand on the icepack. "Remember what Paxton-Brandt said," she recited.

Greyson rolled his eyes. "Aegis is off-limits. Which I don't understand." He'd taken occasional Mexico visits to help the Delgado Cartel fight superhuman drug lords. But Greyson had started hunting US-based superheroes, C-listers that mainstream news barely covered. All because Paxton-Brandt wanted to cripple a corporate rival. "They're playing a game of chicken with Seneca International. Not sure I like being a pawn."

"It's an outlet to sharpen our skills," Connie suggested. "And Seneca's brand of heroes represents the worst." She looked like she'd smelled bad cheese.

Greyson knew the feeling. His lip curled. "Corporate nine-to-fivers." His attention glided back to the TV, and he smiled. "Our message is trending."

Connie watched the screen and beamed. "I'm sure people are hearing us loud and clear."

Placing the compress on the floor, she straddled Greyson with a hungry look and nibbled along his collarbone.

Greyson appreciated her ministrations. But he was fixated on the visual of Mandrake's body nailed to the front of El Paso's Plaza Theater by his wrists.

Written in Suerte's blood above the dead hero was following:

DAMOCLES FOUND THEM UNWORTHY.

Greyson's loins stirred. Damocles, his codename. That triumph turned him on more than Connie.

He flipped his wife over and had his way with her.

CHAPTER 4

Hugo loved every second of flying, especially for leisure.

Tonight's all business, Hugo mused, *with one desired outcome.*

Destroying Paxton-Brandt. Hatred seared Hugo's bones as he recounted the lives this malignant corporation had ruined—including his friend Quinn Bauer. Even though Paxton-Brandt was wounded, they weren't dead. Hugo would do his part to finish them off.

He hurtled through clouds, arms thrown back, heart racing. A million twinkling stars freckled the night.

Hugo narrowed the focus of his hypersensitivity to what lay below.

Three navy blue capsule-shaped drones flew several feet lower, each larger than Hugo's six-foot-four-inch frame. He recognized the Khamber-Statham military drones in triangle formation high above his target. The five-vehicle transport peeled off the freeway onto an access road, headlights blazing their route ahead.

All from Paxton-Brandt. The three drones matched the transport's movements.

Hugo veered left with them. Blessed with night and telescopic vision, he kept the caterpillar of lights below in sight while it snaked through unlit terrain.

For that, Hugo felt such relief. The last thing he wanted was to fight Paxton-Brandt on a packed freeway.

"Almost go time." Hugo tapped the side of his hood, activating his suit's phone system. He spoke a name and heard ringing.

"December to Aegis. Are you in range?" Ezra Michelman asked.

Hugo had strong, conflicted feelings about Dr. Michelman, aka December. He'd worked at Paxton-Brandt as a top scientist for years. Michelman had secretly turned on his overlords after they'd unlocked the powers of his daughter, Spencer, aka Hugo's evil ex-girlfriend. For weeks, he'd helped Dr. Michelman target Paxton-Brandt's US black sites to gather data on their illegally captured human test subjects. The enemy of Hugo's enemy was his ally? But after weeks of collaboration, Hugo still didn't trust Michelman.

Keep things professional. "I have eyes on the target."

"Good," Michelman answered gratefully. "This would be easier if I saw what your suit's camera sees."

Hugo bristled at the request. "No fucking way. Tracking me and the transport will be good enough."

Brief, taut silence followed. "Suit yourself," Michelman said in wooden tones. "How many vehicles?"

"Five," Hugo said. "Armored truck flanked by two Hummers front and back. Three Khamber-Statham military drones just below me." It seized Hugo how normal this was now. Just another night doing the work.

"Two transports left Paxton-Brandt's Bakersfield facility," Michelman said.

"I know." Hugo dipped under a fluffy cloud blanket. "The one heading to Fresno is a decoy."

"You sure?" Michelman challenged. "Both trucks have soundproof hulls and silencers."

Hugo rolled his eyes, already knowing about the silencers. "When both transport trains left the facility, I listened for differences in weight on the road." Hugo banked a sharp right, staying above the drones. "The transport heading toward Lake Isabella is carrying more mass. Probably several stasis chambers." Superhearing had its benefits as Hugo kept pushing his limits.

"Good catch." The doctor sounded impressed. "And they're not onto you?"

Hugo shook his head. "I'm in stealth mode." Settings in his gauntlets activated a camouflage, rendering him invisible to most forms of detection. "Contact you once I'm done." He tapped on the side of his hood to end the call, tapping again and speaking another name to dial.

"Sheriff Foster?" he greeted in his deep Aegis voice.

"Aegis," the Kern County sheriff replied flatly. By the background noise, he was driving with a passenger. "Sheriff Redmond told me to expect your call."

Allegedly, Foster wasn't fond of superheroes. But since Hugo wasn't in SLO County, he had to work with this sheriff for proper jurisdiction. Whatever. "Are you close?"

"I'm bringing three squad cars," he said. "We're on the 58 East five miles from your location."

"You should've brought *more*. Be ready," Hugo said, tapping his hood to end the call.

He returned his attention far below to the transport roving through dark, rugged landscape.

Just below him, the trio of deadly drones kept pace with the Paxton-Brandt vehicles, oblivious to his presence. A smirk played across Hugo's mouth. "Drones first."

Thrusting out both fists, he dove with a burst of speed. Reinforced metal hulls shredded like paper around Hugo's extra-durable frame as he punched through the lead drone. Swelling heat and fire engulfed him. Then Hugo emerged, costume smoking but unharmed.

The drone, however, plummeted in many blazing pieces.

Pleased, Hugo twisted around mid-flight to the remaining drones. Both unlocked their weapon banks.

Hugo opened his mouth and screamed. Waves of unyielding sound rippled the air, smashing the drones. Bright-yellow eruptions lit up the skies. More overpriced, smoldering wreckage fell to earth.

The transport had to have seen that.

"Let's say hello." Hugo switched off his suit's stealth mode and dove. Seconds later, the five-car transport grew in size and proximity.

Hugo shoulder-tackled the lead Hummer; the blow was a cannon echoing across the terrain. The massive SUV bounced off his durable body, dented and tumbling off-road into the dark.

Hugo U-turned and punched the second Hummer to the right. Another booming strike. Another vehicle flipped over, rolling half a mile off-road onto patchy terrain.

Hugo landed in a crouch on the dusty road, dirt clouds wafting around him—perfect superhero landing. The armored truck screeched to a halt before him. The two Hummers behind it jarringly followed suit.

The armored truck engine revved up to plow into Hugo.

"NOPE." He slammed both fists through the truck's grill, clutching a red-hot engine. He yanked it out sideways in a symphony of shredded metal and gushing car fluids.

The vehicle died instantly, bluish and red fluids gushing from the gaping frontside tear.

"That looked important." Hugo chucked the glowing engine away casually, right as flaming tendrils of drone shrapnel rained down around him.

He marched to the driver's-side door, ripping it off and flinging that like towel paper. "Hello there—"

A lanky soldier in all-black body armor and matching helmet greeted him, futuristic-style rifle pointed in his face. The passenger, in matching body armor, also aiming his rifle at Hugo.

Hugo's shock lasted a millisecond, quelled by rigorous training.

As the soldiers fired, he unleashed a sonic scream.

The sonic shout blasted both out the other side of the car, ripping the door off its hinges.

"Rude!" Hugo focused his hearing on the overturned Hummers several yards off either side of the road. Five of Paxton-Brandt's private security in the closest Hummer, six in another. Groans aside, everyone had survived. Hugo took comfort in that, rounding the truck to face the two Hummers behind it.

Eleven soldiers silhouetted by headlights were waiting, firearms trained on him. Night vision wasn't needed to tell him those outlines were more Paxton-Brandt soldiers. Despite their weaponry and battle-ready formation, their heartbeats all galloped.

Hugo almost laughed. But Aegis had to preserve his mean face for intimidation purposes.

"It's him!" one soldier's voice tremored. "Fire!"

Bursts of searing-red plasma streaked across the night, pounding Hugo's body. The rifle rounds briefly stung even at low settings. But his costume could take the punishment.

"Really?" Hugo rumbled. "That just tickles." Then he moved, reaching his foes in a fraction of a second.

A palm thrust to the closest soldier rocket-launched him off the road. Hugo zipped toward another soldier, hauling him up by the throat to end his blaster fire. Spinning superfast, he javelin-threw his attacker into four other soldiers. All five collapsed in a tangled heap of grunts and breaking bones.

Hugo zigzagged through the last six soldiers with a flurry of punches while they almost seemed frozen in place. Well, until Hugo decelerated just behind them.

Every soldier, returned to normal speed, went flying in several directions.

Hugo fought down laughter. "That never gets old." He moved for the rear door of the armored truck. But the presence of a new threat stepping out of the last Hummer turned Hugo around. For the first time tonight, cold fear jolted through him.

This new foe cut a lanky profile, coal-black in complexion and bald with severe features. At a glance, this man's vibe was creepy at best, hide your children at worst. But the way his pupils glowed a pale, ethereal white in the dark unveiled his true nature.

A siphoner. Hugo had only heard of them but never seen one before. Siphoners were rare among supers—and despised. As they drained other supers' lifeforces and powers with skin-to-skin contact, the communal hatred made sense.

Whatever fear appeared on Hugo's face amused the siphoner, revealing a crooked smile.

"You're not touching that cargo," the siphoner grunted, advancing aggressively.

Hugo snapped out of it, remembering the mission. "You're not touching me." He wrenched an armored truck door off with both hands and shoved it in the siphoner's face.

As his foe gave a baffled squawk, Hugo leaped and dropkicked the door.

A jarring clang was married to the cracking of bone against a windshield. The dented door tumbled out of the Hummer's headlights' radius and the siphoner slumped off the hood.

Hugo quickly slapped his spare power inhibitor cuffs on the unconscious siphoner's wrists.

Three separate sirens grew closer. Hugo smiled. Then he looked inside the truck's rear cabin.

His breath caught. Paxton-Brandt's depravity never ceased to disturb him.

"Better work fast." Hugo hopped into the compartment, pulling a thumb drive from his gauntlet.

"Oh my God," were Foster's first words when he and his officers arrived fifteen minutes later. The stocky sheriff was a tough-as-nails member of law enforcement of two decades. But his jaw dropped as he toured the truck's interior.

Six teenagers, probably supers, were floating in tall cylinders filled with yellow fluids. All kinds of tubes protruded from their bodies, hinting at whatever horrid experiments they'd endured.

Hugo stood at the entrance, watching Foster while listening to the surroundings. Kern County PD was rounding up Paxton-Brandt's operatives. None put up any more fight.

Because they'll get bailed out by morning. Hugo swallowed the anger when Foster faced him, bone-white.

"Oh. My. God!"

Hugo recognized that response. "All this is from Paxton-Brandt."

Foster hopped out of the truck compartment, shaking his head. "I thought you were being overdramatic. But this?" He whistled, glancing at the skies. "I shoulda brought twice as many squad cars."

"Told ya," Hugo remarked, earning a glare from Foster.

The sheriff then called for more backup and a CSI team on his walkie.

Hugo pointed a gloved finger at the touchscreen console rigged to the far-left wall inside the truck. "There should be a computer console for the stasis chambers keeping those kids alive." Luckily, Hugo had entered Dr. Michelman's override code before the police arrived to prevent the console from self-erasing. The whole mission would've been a waste without the data he'd copied. Even worse, the console self-erasing would have killed those subjects in stasis…like in his previous mission for Michelman. The memory still turned his stomach. He clenched his jaw and forced the guilt back down.

Foster now spoke with a chubby female deputy about these soldiers needing medical attention.

Hugo felt no guilt there. "Need anything else?" he asked.

Foster shook his head. "Thanks." Gratitude softened the sheriff.

Hugo replied with a tight smile. "Always." Crouching slightly, he blasted into the starry skies.

"Got the data," Hugo announced to Michelman once he was racing through thick, murky clouds. "Meet at the usual place?"

"I'm at the Whitestone property in Paso," the doctor answered.

That surprised Hugo. Usually they met after their Paxton-Brandt takedowns at Michelman's underground bunker out of town. The last time Hugo had visited Whitestone had been this summer…with Spencer.

The recollection tugged at Hugo's heart. Whatever. He hung a right over the encroaching expanse of lights. San Miguel, the City of Wonder.

He soon arrived over Paso Robles's well-lit sprawl. Michelman owned two wineries in San Miguel's largest suburb, the heart of San Luis Obispo County's wine country.

Hugo landed noiselessly in the backyard of Whitestone Vineyards' ivory-walled Victorian main house. He pushed away memories of enjoying time spent here with Spencer.

Dr. Michelman waited by the back door. He wasn't tall, with neatly trimmed wavy hair and a narrow face. Yet under his blue button-down and khakis, the retired superhero's wiry build was obvious.   .

After exchanging greetings, Hugo handed him one of two thumb drive copies he'd made. "I'll get you footage from my costume's cam tomorrow."

Michelman studied the thumb drive, then Hugo. "Good work. And you can drop the Aegis voice, kid."

His mocking tone warmed Hugo's cheeks. Mom, Simon, and J-Tom had teased him for carelessly using the Aegis voice around them.

Michelman pocketed the thumb drive and moved back inside. "This data will do wonders in building a case against Steve Olin and Paxton-Brandt."

This brought a nagging concern as Hugo followed him. "About that…" he said in his normal voice, entering a spacious, well-lit kitchen with a table island. In the living room, a TV with *National News Network* on showed vicious hurricanes devastating South Carolina. Flooded streets and Charleston's superhero team Future Force cleaning up dominated the screen.

"When is PB going down?" After six weeks and five stealth missions, Hugo wanted results.

"Soon," Michelman stated without looking back.

Hugo scoffed impatiently. "Such precision!"

Michelman stopped and sighed. He turned, massaging his wrinkled forehead. "It's very complex."

The doctor's condescension deserved a backhand. Hugo got in Michelman's face, towering over him. "Then use small words," he snarled.

Michelman immediately stepped back, hands raised. "Not what I meant." His voice softened. "Black Wednesday and the disastrous *SLOCO Daily* buy hurt Paxton-Brandt severely."

"And losing so many government contracts." Hugo loved calling that out.

Michelman nodded, also amused. "But they still have lots of tentacles and capital across the globe.

"Meaning what?"

"To dismantle Paxton-Brandt," the doctor explained, "my case against them has to be a killshot."

In short, no timeframe. Hugo prickled at the non-answer. Michelman's secrety-secret missions were getting riskier, and Hugo was taking all the risks. If not for Hugo exposing the megacorp's unethical projects, he knew Paxton-Brandt would've retaliated by now. And that would derail his mission to protect San Miguel right as it'd begun.

"Fuck that!" It baffled Hugo how Michelman had been Titan's best friend, let alone a superhero.

"I'm done." He whirled around to leave and fly home. "Call me when Paxton-Brandt is cancelled." It was almost eleven p.m., and he had homework.

"She's upstairs."

Hugo froze. "Here?" He hated that Spencer still affected him so viscerally.

Michelman had his daughter under house arrest after learning that she'd been capturing supers for Paxton-Brandt. The Michelmans put the "fun" in dysfunctional. "At the vineyards?"

"I'm spending time with her before she goes to Verdant in three weeks."

Hugo suddenly couldn't find his voice.

Ezra leaned against the kitchen island. Under the lights, he looked haggard. "I won't suppress her powers again. But after what she's done…Steinholt Academy is a no-go. Maybe Verdant can help."

Hugo knew of Verdant Correctional Academy by reputation, and the teen TV series *Northgate High* loosely based on its inner drama. The Cincinnati-based school for adolescent supers from bad circumstances regarding their powers. Spencer was leaving San Miguel for good.

"Do you want to see her?" Michelman asked with a weary smile.

Hugo almost said yes. Then fear of Spencer's anger, her hatred, her rejection, took over. "No," he decided, and strode out of the estate without waiting for a reply. The sooner he left, the faster Hugo could escape the regrets.

And on the flight home, the night grew colder.

Much later, Hugo lay in his bed, wearing only boxer-briefs, staring at the ceiling. He couldn't sleep, still stuck on Spencer. *You should've said goodbye.* Remorse ran deep. Right then, his "conversation" with Titan in Alaska came to mind. His bio-dad said memory walking could be done from afar.

Maybe... Hugo focused his thoughts on Spencer: the good, the bad, the ugly, the beautiful.

His bedroom washed away...and Hugo found himself back at Whitestone, nighttime again. Wearing a white tee and jeans, he found himself being led by the hand up a winding stairwell.

I'm in Spencer's memories. Hugo's long-distance memory walking worked. But which memory?

Then Hugo saw her, giving his heart a horrible lurch.

Spencer's back was facing him while she led Hugo upstairs in a skintight negligee of flowing cream fabric, glossy black bob falling to neck length.

Hugo remembered. *Valentine's Day... What a memorable night.*

He stopped and squeezed Spencer's hand, forcing her to stop.

She turned, youthful and somewhat paler without makeup or spray tan.

Hugo looked up at her fondly. Despite the chaos she'd wrought, his affection for this girl lingered.

Spencer's features hardened. She yanked her hand away.

Hugo measured his words before speaking. "Hey, Marshmallow," he greeted. "You getting shipped off to Verdant isn't what I wanted."

Spencer's face became a beautiful, empty mask as she watched him.

Hope jolted through Hugo. "I'm sorry." Maybe they could part on good terms.

Spencer's eyes flashed wrathfully. "Not yet," she seethed. "But when you, Jenny, and Daddy pay for betraying me?" A cruel smile split her face. "When you pay so *fucking* hard? Then you'll be sorry, Aegis." She shoved him. Hugo stumbled, falling down the stairs—jolted out of Spencer's mindscape.

He sat upright, consumed by panic. After a moment, he recognized his bedroom and relaxed. But the encounter stung, especially the nasty way Spencer uttered his alias. She *hated* him.

"I guess that's it," Hugo murmured sadly. Even when sleep arrived, sorrow still haunted his dreams.

INTERLUDE: STEVE OLIN

Steven Olin would rather stand in front of a firing squad than his current situation.

During his decade as Paxton-Brandt Industries' CEO, he'd stood before his board of directors in the conglomerate's sleek New York offices. Whenever he was explaining his ideas to expand the company's vast portfolio and fattening its coffers, Olin knew that he and the board saw eye to eye.

Until exaggerated abuses about the Elite had been leaked, leading to Black Wednesday and over one hundred employee deaths.

Stupidly pursuing Quinn Bauer had led to a death on government property, killing their lucrative OSA contract. The cherry on top had been purchasing *SLOCO Daily*, originally meant to control a vocal adversary. Then someone posing as Helena Madden had published how that greedy tub of guts Dave Packer overcharged clients for years. That had killed the news site and triggered countless lawsuits.

All those events had led this emergency board meeting at 7:30 in the evening to decide Olin's fate. Now he stood before thirteen of the company's most prominent board members in this glass-walled room that felt increasingly small. Their stares lasered into him. But wearing a pristine suit and crimson tie, Olin showed no fear...despite his bowels nearly liquefying.

Before the votes, he'd requested time to showcase his plans to turn around Paxton-Brandt's cratered revenue. In short, Olin came to beg. A man like Steve Olin didn't beg.

"The last three months were rough," Olin stated after finishing his detailed presentation. "Especially in the stock market. But my strategies take Paxton-Brandt beyond previous revenues."

At the other end of the table, an older man cleared his throat. Johann Mueller, one of Paxton-Brandt's first investors, had a surly look. "Under your watch, over a hundred employees lost their lives."

"And we lost over half our US government contracts," another board member, Hal Preston, added.

Mueller wasn't done. "And it will be years before we settle this avalanche of lawsuits from Black Wednesday and *SLOCO Daily's* former advertisers…"

The indictments landed body blows on Olin. Even longtime friend Jeffrey Brasher turned on him. "Why should this board trust your leadership anymore?" the dark-skinned man decried, several other board members agreeing. A few remained silent, watching Olin carefully.

For a soul-crushing moment, Olin wanted an end. He was almost sixty, and his wife wanted to move to France. *Let them vote you out. Take the golden parachute.* The moment was crushed by fury and drive. This wasn't how Steve Olin left Paxton-Brandt. "You have no one else," he spoke over the noise.

Many were outraged. One board member, a lovely Latina woman in a white pantsuit, smiled at his gall.

Olin straightened, confidence restored. "Anyone you've auditioned for my job, which made you all even richer, worked under me." He smirked at their shock. Like they could've hidden that from him. "You think someone else can do this job as good as me? Never."

Heated murmurs bubbled around the table.

"Steve isn't wrong," the Latina woman said with a noticeable accent, fingers steepled. The youngest board member at forty-three, she owned more Paxton-Brandt stock than many board members in this room—combined. "The Elite project should've succeeded if not for that internal leak."

"Riva…" Johann protested.

"And," Riva de León plowed over him, "a new CEO means an onboarding period, lowering consumer confidence further." She gestured at Olin like a smiling gameshow hostess. "Give him another shot."

Not much opposition proceeded. Riva's words always carried weight.

Brasher snorted, rubbing his hands impatiently. "Shall we vote then?"

Olin's heart was in his throat as the vote began.

After the votes were checked, Olin was a mess. His legs felt leaden on the long walk back to his office.

Once he reached his vast corner office overlooking lower Manhattan, Olin wanted to do nothing but gather his belongings and head home. Today had been exhausting.

However, Bradley Reynolds, his untiring chief of staff, was pacing before the office agitatedly.

Olin paused, eyes widening. "Did the meeting go well?"

Olin almost told the thirty-five-year-old wunderkind to go home. But Bradley would find out before tomorrow. "Yes," he revealed with a weary smile. "I have eighteen months to fix things." The vote had been 7-6, Riva breaking the tie. *Again, I owe her*, he realized while entering his office.

Bradley was elated. "Great! Then Operation Elevate is still on?" he asked, closing the door behind them.

Olin stared at the younger man with reproachful eyes. "Absolutely. We continue experiments and the training sessions with successful subjects."

"About that." Bradley made a wincing face, running fingers through his thick, shaggy mane. "Aegis."

Olin felt clouds of anger gathering overhead. "What about Aegis?"

"He smashed another transport an hour ago, even with our insurance policy," Bradley said. "The subjects being transported are in the custody of Kern County's Department."

This motherfucker again? Olin fought the urge to throw something with some quick mental triaging. "Do we have friends in Kern County government?"

"In contact." Bradley kept stride with his boss. "One of our pharma subsidiaries has labs out there."

Olin's blood pressure nominally dropped. "Find their price and get our property back. With NDAs."

Bradley's brow beetled with discontent. "That's five times, Mr. Olin. Why aren't we retaliating?"

Olin raised a hand, silencing his overeager subordinate. The impulse to crush this "Shield of Justice" made sense and would've been pleasurable if Paxton-Brandt was in a position of dominance.

"We've been able to blunt exposure after his attacks," he remarked calmly. "Plus, the public and media love Aegis. As opposed to Paxton-Brandt." He added another fact as Bradley began to reply. "It doesn't help that Aegis saved Paxton-Brandt's San Miguel headquarters on Black Wednesday."

Olin posed a question for his protégé to contemplate. "How would attacking him openly look?"

Bradley looked ready to protest, then recoiled. "Bad, with all the new leaks these last few weeks."

He understands now. Olin furrowed his brow at another theory he'd been nursing. "Those leaks have to be from whoever is feeding Aegis information. Once we plug that leak, then we deal with Aegis." Olin looked forward to coming after Aegis like a freight train and destroying his life.

"I'm investigating suspects who might be our leaker or leakers," Bradley declared, puffing his chest out.

Olin scratched his chin, satisfied by this direction. "Keep digging and be discreet."

"Done." His chief of staff marched out of the room.

Olin watched Bradley go, sitting heavily on his desk. He'd run the last six months through his mind hundreds of times. Paxton-Brandt had almost broken into the superhero market, with assets and teams ready for municipal usage. Helena Madden had been silenced, along with every traitor in the company leaking to her. And The Vanguard had imploded before the whole world.

Olin glowered, knowing everything had gone south following that inside leak about the whole Elite project. He smoldered over how he'd make that leaker suffer and…

A door knock jarred Olin from his musings of revenge. After he welcomed in the guest, a slim woman with fair skin strutted in carrying an iPad. Lazy waves of brunette spilled down her shoulders, complementing her purple trench dress.

Olin relaxed at the familiar face. "Ms. Pierce. You're back."

"Sir." Gwyneth Pierce nodded dutifully. She'd been his special assistant for two years on many off-book issues. And she never disappointed. "Mr. Greyson returned from Mexico, with a body count in El Paso."

Olin's mood soured again. "I heard. Seems like two weeks down in Mexico didn't slake his bloodlust." As useful as Greyson Hirsch would be to Paxton-Brandt, his talent for murder could become problematic if he drew too much attention too soon.

Pierce watched him with unemotive eyes. "I'll talk to him," she replied, flat and final.

Hearing this, Olin knew the problem was handled and switched topics. "What about his next targets?"

Pierce's slow smile didn't reach her vacant eyes. "I have a list of Seneca International solo heroes and teams by city." She handed over her iPad.

Olin studied the list. Number eleven stood out. "*Shenandoah?* That shithole city has a superhero team?"

"The Natural Born Thrillers activated early summer last year but got overshadowed by Titan's death," Pierce confirmed. "Supers and vigilantes local to the Shenandoah Valley and Northern Virginia."

Olin paced a few moments after clicking on the Natural Born Thrillers data profile link, studying its six members. They were young, photogenic, and wielding combat-ready powers. This looked like a formidable team. Then again, Shenandoah's collective sentiment toward supers and heroes was the polar opposite of San Miguel's. "How solid are they with the locals?"

"Making progress," Pierce admitted cautiously, wrinkling her nose. Shenandoah's anti-superhuman laws were some of the harshest in America. "But the city hasn't forgotten the Chicago Massacre."

Chills ran through Olin recalling the Chicago Massacre. Titan vs Paragon, a dream matchup for the ages, paid for with almost five thousand Chicagoan lives. He shrugged off the grisly memories, seeing an opportunity there. "They'll be Hirsch's target." A smile played across his lips at the possibilities.

Pierce's elation mirrored his own. "I'll get on it."

"Any word on Ultraviolet?" Olin said as his special assistant turned to go.

Pierce shrugged, indicating her lack of progress. "Her father claims he sent her away to a boarding school for supers, but I've found no records of such."

Olin didn't like that. Ultraviolet, aka Spencer Michelman, had been one of Paxton-Brandt's most promising operatives. Plus, she'd secretly bugged Helena Madden's home and helped them learn what the late reporter had almost published. Then Spencer had vanished three months ago. *Right before Black Wednesday.* The situation felt rotten, gnawing at him.

Olin ground his teeth and faced Pierce. "I'll take lead on the Ultraviolet situation." He faced Pierce fully, arms folded. "Ezra Michelman has grown...prickly after the Elite incident."

"You reactivated his daughter's powers without his knowledge or consent," a bold, female voice declared. "Did you expect a fucking block party?"

Olin winced, recognizing the voice. Riva de León in her ivory-white pantsuit, dark hair in a low and tight bun with a side part, stood at the door.

Olin gulped hard. "Gwyneth, excuse us," he dismissed without making eye contact.

His special assistant nodded and glided toward the door.

Riva slammed it behind Pierce, then walked over like a runway model. "Good evening Steven."

Her extra approach coaxed a chuckle out of him. "Riva." Her petiteness forced him to lean down and her to stand on her tiptoes for their usual double-cheek kiss greeting. Riva's firecracker personality more than made up for her size. This billionaire venture capitalist, with ties to global elite, was an uncompromising goddess.

"Thanks for that save," Olin said breathlessly.

"And for keeping Operation Dom Pedro on track." Riva batted her eyelashes. "Now you have to deliver."

"I will." Olin meant that.

"I know." Riva's stare turned cold-blooded. "Or I'll flay you of everything you hold dear."

Olin stood petrified, making the executive question if anyone would miss him at his funeral. The rumors he'd heard about those who let Riva down came to mind. "Understood."

Riva's megawatt smile returned full force. "Great. Oh, and I know who your mole is," she announced with such indifference, one might think she spoke about finding her car keys.

Olin perked up, not doubting Riva's veracity or sources. "Who?"

Riva playfully beckoned him closer with one finger.

He sighed and leaned down as ordered. Riva stood on her tiptoes again and whispered a name in his ear.

Olin jerked away, almost backing into his desk. He heard but couldn't believe. "Oh. My. God."

CHAPTER 5

"Are you kidding?" Connie snapped.

Greyson, as incensed as his wife, rose from his seat. They were currently in Paxton-Brandt's Odessa, TX facilities in the office of Gwyneth Pierce.

Steve Olin's special assistant remained seated and indifferent to their outrage. "This comes from Steve himself," she explained, adjusting her sleeveless red jumpsuit.

"I don't give a shit." Greyson leaned over the desk. "A no-kill order on my targets?"

Gwyneth studied him, unimpressed. "Too much bad press."

Greyson glanced at Connie. "I want to speak to Olin. Now."

Gwyneth's elfin features grew frosty. "I speak for Mr. Olin."

Connie caught Greyson's arm right before he could erupt. "Bad press?" she inquired.

Gwyneth's brow raised. "We invested a lot in you. And cape-killers have very short careers."

The steely threat in her words stiffened Greyson's posture. "What is that supposed to mean?"

"You think other heroes will just turn a blind eye while you keep murdering heroes?" Gwyneth noted. The posh English accent added to her condescension. "Eventually, they'll unite and hunt you down."

"She's right, Hirsch," Connie remarked, wearing a flowery romper. "The good guys will push back."

Greyson wanted to kick himself for being so shortsighted. "Now what?"

Gwyneth's emotionless smile gave Greyson the chills. "We've found your next target."

"That's easy," he scoffed. Another target, another win.

Gwyneth tilted her head in reproach. "Not so much. This is a corporate-sponsored ERAT, a superhero team, unlike what you and Connie have faced in between your trips to Mexico."

Connie palpably soured. "You make it sound like we're weekending in Cabo."

Gwyneth arched an eyebrow. "Are you?"

"Fuck off, Gwyneth."

"And Aegis?" Greyson asked. Now was the time to take him out.

"That mandate hasn't changed," Gwyneth replied flatly.

Greyson was over this. "All these restrictions on who and how I engage." His anger rose with each word.

"Hirsch…" Connie warned.

"No, Connie." Greyson shrugged her off and pointed at Gwyneth's smug face. "Paxton-Brandt recruited me for what I bring to the table," he declared. "Why aren't I choosing my own targets?"

Gwyneth chuckled and shook her head, then tapped her desk phone's speaker. "Send her in."

The office door opened. Connie gasped. Greyson found himself staring at a ghost.

"Excuse me." Lauren Gerard entered wearing a lab coat over her pink blouse and pencil skirt, ash blonde hair in a tight ponytail. "I have the pathogen test results." She handed Gwyneth a flash drive.

Greyson's brain could barely form coherent thoughts. "Oh my god…" He collapsed into his seat. Greyson knew his ex-fiancée was alive. Seeing her alive just ripped his spine out. "Laurie…"

Lauren looked his way for the first time in bemusement. "Yes?"

Her curt response confused Greyson. "Why are you here—?"

"Sorry." Lauren gave him a blank look. "Do I know you?"

Greyson's surprise drowned away deep-rooted heartache. *Why doesn't she know me?* He stood.

Gwyneth cleared her throat. "Dr. Gerard works at Genex Labs, a Paxton-Brandt subsidiary."

Greyson was speechless, his brain grinding to a halt. "I…I…"

"Laurie," Gwyneth's voice startled Lauren, who seemed fearful of Greyson and Connie. "These are two of our field operatives, Mr. and Mrs. Hirsch."

Lauren offered a tight-lipped smile. "Nice meeting you both." She left the room as fast as possible. Greyson watched her, struggling with that bizarre encounter.

He turned slowly around to Gwyneth, who studied him and Connie closely. "Was that some sick joke?" Greyson demanded softly. "An impostor of Laurie?" His voice cracked when saying her name. Energy rippled through his veins, itching for freedom to rip this cruel bitch limb from limb.

"That was no impostor." Gwyneth looked none too pleased as she sat back down. "Your former fiancée, Lauren, has worked at Paxton-Brandt for years."

Greyson had no clue Genex Labs was part of Paxton-Brandt. In fact, he had no clue about anything.

Luckily, Connie asked for him, a hand on his shoulder. "Why didn't she recognize Hirsch?"

"Like I said," Gwyneth answered, "we've invested a lot of resources in our partnership."

Greyson clenched his teeth at the doubletalk. "You didn't answer the question."

Gwyneth sighed. "For three months, our telepathic agents have altered memories of your family, friends, and colleagues." She tapped her desk with each point. "Your medical details were changed. We even fed the local St. Louis news media false stories and hacked in to government databases to change your records."

Connie let out a wordless cry. As shocked as Lauren's appearance had been, this news took Greyson's breath away. "Why?"

"The narrative," Gwyneth spread her hands, looking smug, "is that you, your father, Connie, and Hurricane were killed by your alias, Damocles. Except that your first names were changed."

"What the hell?" Connie remarked.

Greyson opened his mouth, stopped to gather his colliding thoughts, then tried again. "You're saying that I murdered myself." Yep, just as insane out loud.

Gwyneth laughed. "In a way, you did, the night you killed your father and Hurricane." She spoke of his crimes as if discussing a grocery list. "The world thinks Graham Hirsch and Cordelia Ishibashi are dead, while your alter ego gets elevated."

Greyson cradled his aching head. "Whoa…"

Gwyneth went on. "Offing a few heroes shows how dangerous you are. A string of murders makes them martyrs and puts too large a target on your back."

That snapped Greyson out of the data overload. "Martyring them isn't our goal."

"Then what is?"

Greyson felt like he'd stated this hundreds of times. "To expose how poisonous and parasitic superheroes are to society, and stop them from doing further damage."

Gwyneth's eyes glittered. "Then do it publicly. Force them into lose-lose situations."

That statement shook Greyson's confidence in his approach. Gwyneth was right. He looked to Connie, who nodded favorably. "Where do we start?"

"Shenandoah."

Greyson recoiled. "*That* shithole?"

Gwyneth rolled her eyes understandingly. "That shithole has a team, the Natural Born Thrillers."

Greyson had never heard of them, but he'd heard about Shenandoah, Virginia. The once-booming city had an economic collapse over a decade ago, leading to record poverty and crime.

Connie snapped her fingers in recognition. "The team name sounds familiar."

"Superhuman discrimination is sky-high in Shenandoah," Gwyneth remarked. "The Thrillers are trying to change the conversation about supers and superheroes."

Greyson perked up. "Are they making progress?"

Gwyneth pulled a face. "Slowly."

Greyson suddenly found this challenge far more intriguing than Aegis—for now. By Connie's elation, the feeling was mutual. "When do we leave?" he asked.

CHAPTER 6

"I just can't with you, Bogota," Jordana blurted out.

She'd been amused earlier today when Hugo offered to help unbraid her cornrows.

Now Jordana sat mystified as he unbraided every braid himself.

He paused and looked up at the bedroom mirror. "What?" he asked playfully. The reflection showed him on the edge of Jodie's bed with her cross-legged before him on the floor. His kinda-girlfriend's hair was an explosion of wild bushy curls, except for one last cornrow.

"How are you so good at this?" Jodie demanded.

Hugo chuckled while unbraiding. A logical question. "Before dance battles, I'd get my hair cornrowed."

Jordana's jaw hung open. "And now I got follow-up questions!"

Hugo chuckled. "My hair kept flopping in my face. The cornrows were Grace's idea." He took a quick listen outside the house with superhearing. Today's patrol had been boring. But the good boring.

He refocused on Jodie and her persistent bemusement, which now concerned him. "I'm not pulling too tight?"

"It's just right, baby." Jodie's warm brown eyes studied him through the mirror. "Do you miss dancing?"

"Sometimes." Hugo finished the last cornrow, then reclined as Jodie combed out her hair. "The Phenoms are fine without me." That lie helped mask the dull ache in his chest.

"They miss you..." Jodie held his gaze. "Especially Grace."

Hugo stood and turned away to escape the guilt. "I know." Their ongoing rift was his fault. He just needed to speak with Grace when their schedules didn't conflict.

Jodie's bedroom, decorated with all kinds of NYC souvenirs, could've been mistaken for a boy's room. But Jodie's many Extreme Teens posters, which Hugo mocked repeatedly, disputed that belief.

Hugo noticed a stack of large envelopes on Jodie's desk. Curious, he walked over. "What are these?"

"College applications. You started looking yet?"

"Nope," Hugo replied distractedly, scanning over the university names on the envelopes.

Morehouse. Princeton. Vassar. UNC Chapel Hill. Brown. Dartmouth. Columbia. Boston University.

Hugo's chest tightened. "These are all East Coast schools." He turned to see Jordana's guilty face.

"Yeah…" She focused on the mirror while combing out her hair. "I've always wanted to attend college back east. And…" She shrank back. "My family's moving back to NYC when I graduate next year."

Cold shock flooded Hugo's veins. "But…why?"

Jodie placed her comb down, leaning against the drawer for support. "My mom's wanted to move for a while. Hates all the superhero fights. But after Black Wednesday, she finally convinced my dad." Jodie still couldn't meet Hugo's stare.

"Shit…" Hugo knew what this could mean. Time was flying so fast, graduation would arrive before he knew it. *If we're still together.*

"Bogota. Relax." Jodie approached and cupped his jaw. "I'm not bouncing tomorrow." Her sexy smile soothed him somewhat, bushy curls spilling around her face.

"The same shit happens in NYC." Hugo took her hands in his. "Protectorate and the Harlem Knights fight plenty of supervillains."

"I told her," Jodie replied wearily. "My mom's got tunnel vision." She sat on her bed.

This irked Hugo more than expected. "Cable news makes it seem like big cities have superhero battles every damn day."

"Aegis fought some Godzilla monster," Jodie threw back, unwittingly parroting her mother's gestures. "The Elite thrashed downtown. Then there's that teleporting weirdo, Saracen, spray-painting monuments all over the country."

Hugo had no comeback. Everything Jodie said was true. According to Clint, Saracen had leaked about classified OSA and CIA programs to control supers for years. Defacing monuments was new behavior, forcing news media to stop ignoring the cyberterrorist.

And Jodie's mom wasn't the only citizen who felt heroes were the problem.

Hugo kept things light. "Your mom won't escape superheroes unless she moves to Newfoundland. And even they have a few."

Jordana doubled over laughing as her cellphone rang. "Hold up." She popped to her feet and rounded her bed to pull the cellphone from her purse. One look, and her face drained of color.

Hugo frowned, hearing her pulse spike. "Who is it?"

Jordana hastily swiped to voicemail. "Robocall." Tossing her phone in her bag, she forced a smile.

Hugo almost pressed further. But if he wanted her to trust him, then he should do the same.

"Shower time." Jordana took off her Mets tee, sashaying to him. "You joining?"

Hugo stared at her ample chest. "Do birds shit on sidewalks?"

"Boy!" Jodie tossed her shirt in his face. "You watch that gutter mouth!"

Hugo chuckled, flicking the shirt aside. "You love my gutter mouth. C'mere...." He hoisted Jordana up with one arm, silencing her delighted squeal with a kiss. Her arms draped his neck, thick thighs squeezing his waist. Hugo nearly yanked the bedroom door off its hinges and carried Jodie to the bathroom as fast as humanly possible.

He loved their little routine when at her place. Sex. Shower. More sex. A meal with TV or homework on school nights. Even when they didn't have sex, Hugo loved the other ways they'd fool around. The normalcy kept him grounded. He wouldn't lose himself in his alias like Titan.

Later, they took Jodie's car for their date, the Aegis interview, and dinner with his family. The hazy orange sun began setting. Jodie was dolled up, black hair in a sleek topknot, short-shorts and an off-shoulder creamy sweater. Still drunk off her body, Hugo ran feathery fingers along Jodie's neckline. Her eyes rolled back a little.

"Soooo," Hugo prompted. "About what I've asked?" He'd given her space to decide what she wanted from their relationship.

Jodie stiffened as they reached a red light. "I just… I'm not there yet."

Hugo's buzz withered. He withdrew his hand. *I knew it.*

Jodie eyed him anxiously. "Please don't hate me!"

"I wanna be with *you*," Hugo declared, his voice thick with longing.

"Me too…" Jodie turned away guiltily, focused on the road. "Just gimme more time? Please?"

"Okay." The mood got awkward the rest of the trip until they arrived at Hugo's house.

AJ was back from soccer. Mom had on some flowing purple dress.

"Hello!" She scurried toward Jordana for a hug, and the two started chatting.

Hugo greeted AJ, or "Junior" as he called himself now. "Hey, little uso." They pounded fists.

AJ frowned. "I'm not that little."

Hugo waggled his hand. "Kinda."

AJ wasn't wrong, now standing five-foot-eight at thirteen years old and covered in lean muscle. His hair had grown somewhat longer than a buzzcut for the first time in years. AJ was looking more like a man each day…more like Dad.

His dad, Hugo self-corrected, which AJ didn't know—*couldn't* know. He cleared his throat. "We ready?"

Mom and Jodie moseyed over to the couch. "We ready." Mom eyed her youngest son keenly. "Angelo?"

"Let's go." AJ turned on the TV, skimmed to channels, and clicked *Newsworthy.com's* turquois icon.

As the channel loaded, Hugo's nerves grew fraught. This had been his first interview as Aegis. Countless people would be watching. Pressure sat like an anvil on his chest.

Mom watched Hugo, eyes brimming with reassuring love. AJ squeezed his shoulder, causing the younger Malalou to wince. Ha!

Jodie, oblivious to the silent exchange, slipped an arm around Hugo's waist. Soon, rows of video thumbnails appeared. One included an interview of Senator Noah Huntley from West Virginia. The well-dressed Senator, with curly red hair and an oddly flat face, was delivering another anti-superhero rant. Ugh.

Another video discussed a ninth former sponsor suing the defunct *SLOCO Daily*.

Jodie's eyes lit up, and she held Hugo tighter. "The shit my cousin experienced there was crazaay."

Hugo already knew that, exchanging looks with Mom and AJ, both whom he'd told. "Huh."

When the interview started, Quinn Bauer appeared on the TV. Her hair in big kinky curls and wearing a peacoat, she waited between two buildings in early morning downtown.

Hugo smiled, remembering that day. August this past summer. Jodie squealed in anticipation.

A purple figure blurred into the frame. Then Quinn started shrieking as everything blasted into the air.

Hugo choked down laughter at Jodie's, Mom's, and AJ's reactions.

Quinn and the camera vantagepoint were abruptly on a rooftop, stumbling about.

Aegis dwarfed the petite reporter in his purple-hooded costume. *Damn, I look good,* Hugo mused.

"What?" Aegis asked innocently in his deep cadence. "Just making sure everyone knows it's me."

Quinn glared daggers into him on camera. Hugo lost it, as did everyone in the living room.

The interview went better than Hugo remembered, the cameras never focused long on his face.

He and Quinn had discussed Black Wednesday, Titan comparisons, superheroes on social media, and The Vanguard's demise. Hugo had said the standard respectful things about these topics. When Blur and his trash-talking came up, Hugo had been more unfiltered. "Blur is great at what he does. Run fast and run his mouth."

Jodie gasped in scandalized shock. Mom applauded the wisecrack.

Hugo shot his mother a warning look. *Not too much enthusiasm.*

Then Quinn had asked about Tomorrow Man taking credit for Aegis's saves. "Tomorrow Man has four brain cells. None stop fighting long enough to form an original thought. Or the truth." Onscreen, as they walked under a pinkish sun, Aegis went on. "He's a bootleg Titan 0.75 created by focus groups and consultants, since he doesn't have the brains or personality to be Titan 2.0."

Hugo couldn't decide what tickled him more. Quinn turning from the camera to hide her amusement or the collective howl of laughter in his living room.

Saying the interview had been well-received was an understatement. J-Tom, Simon, Quinn, and Therese texted their enjoyment. Annie Sherwood, his PR Goddess, texted an approving thumbs-up.

Reactions across social media were overwhelmingly positive.

Hugo kept that love close to his heart for hours after Jodie headed back home.

Presently, he soared through maroon evening skies in costume, the cityscape a jagged grid of dazzling lights. Hugo loved evening patrols over the city, getting time to think.

Jodie wanting to keep things casual and applying to East Coast colleges left a bad taste in his mouth.

Hugo was glad he'd kept his dating options open. He then mulled over citizens who found heroes dangerous and public perception of a superhero versus the reality. As a government-sanctioned superhero, Hugo followed the rules of engagement. Provide support for disasters, earthquakes, and fires. Non-powered crimes except mass shootings, bomb threats, and large hostage situations were avoided. Incidents like fighting kaijus weren't common. If the crime was supervillain or superhuman-related, San Miguel PD's dispatch center pinged Hugo. Geist had introduced him to some police contacts before departing the City of Wonder.

Brief sadness filled Hugo. He really missed Geist, surliness and all.

Hugo dove and flew low over Grand Blvd drawing honks and cheers below. There was one call Hugo had been impatiently waiting for since last week. Vincent Van Violence. Just his idiotic name pissed Hugo off. V3 had kicked his ass months ago, but Hugo was still green as stadium turf back then.

V3 had skipped town after locking horns with Justice Jones this past summer.

Now the police had informed Hugo that V3 was back in San Miguel after committing a string of murders. "When we draw him out," his police contact, Detective Beale had said, "we'll let you know."

They better, Hugo fumed. He'd worked his own contacts to no avail—

"Aegis."

The cavernous voice sounded right next to him, stopping Hugo in mid-flight. He swiveled his head around, scanning the surrounding skyline. Who? How? Where?

"It's a frequency only you can hear," the voice startled him again. "We're on the Sanwa Building."

The two figures stood on the Sanwa building roof, dressed in dark suits like *Men in Black* agents.

Hugo floated down but remained a few feet in the air, studying them closely.

He knew the blonde female, deep blue eyes but vacant features. Agent Devon Strauss from the Office of Superhuman Affairs, Quinn's friend.

The older bearded man was a mystery, with rigid confidence to his carriage, and sporting a blown-back white shock of kinky hair. This couldn't be good...

"Hello again, Aegis," Strauss greeted. Her blue eyes warmed.

"Agent Williamson." The man's voice was so deep, it must've had its own subwoofer.

Hugo narrowed his eyes. "What do you want?"

A dangerous half-smile pulled at the side of Williamson's mouth. "A partnership."

"Not interested."

Williamson's smile vanished. "That would be a mistake." His voice dropped another octave.

Hugo began floating away from these people. "I have no use for an organization that let Paxton-Brandt kill Helena Madden." Yeah, Quinn had told him all about that.

Agent Strauss's expression spasmed briefly before she regained control.

Williamson's glare never wavered. "You know nothing, Mr. Malalou."

The agent uttered his name so casually, it took a moment for Hugo's brain to process it. *He knows about me?* He forced on a poker face. As a registered superhero, Hugo understood that his identity was known to a handful of high-level state and federal officials. Quinn wouldn't have told Strauss. How did these random OSA field agents know his identity?

Williamson's dangerous half-smile returned. "We could be your best friends. Be smart, for the sake of your mother and brother—"

In half a second, Hugo was on the ground and nose to nose with the smarmy bastard. "If you value your chest space, NEVER mention my family or friends." His skin was crawling underneath his costume. He barely stifled the urge to backhand Williamson across this roof. "Do you fucking understand me?"

To his credit, Williamson never flinched from Hugo's superfast charge. His glare hardened.

"*Enough.*" Strauss wedged her slender self between the two. "Back off, Williamson." She glared at her partner then focused back on Hugo. "Let us help you fight Paxton-Brandt. Quinn Bauer trusts me. You can too. Don't let your pride force a bad decision here."

And Hugo was done. "Buh-bye." He crouched and blasted upward. Staying any longer wasn't safe for either of these agents.

Hugo climbed into the starry heavens, seething. Beneath that anger, fresh fear took root. Would OSA hurt his friends and family for refusing? He shivered, not wanting to find out.

CHAPTER 7

"No way," Greyson stated as soon as he saw the costume sketch.

He sat in a Paxton-Brandt private jet headed for Washington DC, having a face-to-face with his "team."

Not a team of superpowered operatives. Not a team of combat strategists.

A marketing trio.

An hour into their spiel about synergy and other idiotic buzzwords, Greyson contemplated throwing them all from the plane. Asher Barton, Mindy Blunt, and Darrell Cartwright gaped at his rejection.

"But…Mr. Hirsch," Asher said, a living Ken Doll with a plastic smile and aggressive handshake. "This costume *radiates* menace and mystique. It will strike fear in the hearts of heroes everywhere."

The Damocles getup was a silvery monstrosity, with a flowing red cape and helmet studded with horned spikes.

Greyson stared at Asher. "Have you been in a real fight?" he questioned. "This isn't some Battalion movie with cartoonish supervillains monologuing. I won't be able to move in that eyesore."

That drew a wounded gasp from Mindy and scowls from Darrell. Greyson didn't care.

Asher raised his hands to quell the tension. "We remove the cape and half of the helmet spikes—"

"NO," Greyson barked. The cabin went deathly quiet. He'd expected financial backing and intel on his foes, not abysmal 90s-style costumes. "And none of that means shit if I don't know my targets."

Asher's face went blank. He waved his aggrieved cohorts away to the back of the cabin.

Then Asher typed on his tablet, projecting a needle of light out before Greyson.

A group of six costumed heroes appeared in a hologram with the self-serious faces and stoic poses seen in hero photoshoots. Greyson chortled.

"Erika Skye, aka Erika Bossley." Asher pointed at the tall black woman at the center in golden body armor. Her long braids complemented her fierce stare. "Team leader and influential activist lobbying to change Shenandoah's superhuman laws. She's a big threat on the field with her 'hot knives' power."

Asher pointed to the bald man dwarfing everyone else, a mountain of hulking muscle with bronze metal skin and glowing amber eyes. "Bulldozer, aka David Correia, the team's powerhouse. Can shift his skin to metal like a modern-day Ace Steel," Asher marveled. "Stronger than a locomotive."

He switched to a slim blonde in a provocative white-and-red costume. She would've been pretty if not for the Instagram kissy face she made. "Brightburn, aka Esther Katz. Electrokinetic and most popular member with men for obvious reasons." Asher smirked. "Huge social media following."

Oppo research was exactly what Greyson needed against these Natural Born Thrillers. He leaned forward with interest while Asher continued.

"Shattershot, Nero Mendes, is interesting." The marketing exec gestured at a generic Caucasian man, average in height and build. But how his dark-green eyes knifed into one's soul was unsettling. "Empathic and Neuro manipulation. Former villain. But after two years in jail, he got paroled on a Seneca-sponsored rehabilitation program."

Greyson frowned. He'd never encountered any hero with psychic abilities beyond teleportation. Shattershot would need to be the first one he took out or killed. The clinical and heartless way he discussed death was no longer jarring. "Next."

"Reverb, aka Alvin Choi!" Asher sneered at this beefy yet fit young man, whose neon disaster of a costume sported green goggles. Choi was the only one in the photo smiling. "Kinetic field lets him bounce off most surfaces and absorb impact. Also popular on social media."

Greyson's attention was drawn to the final team member, a woman with black wings sprouting from her back. Her regal manner evoked Lady Liberty, but her image was greyed out. He pointed. "Who's that?"

Asher raised an eyebrow. "Former team member. Nighthawk, aka Marianne Studi. Hated Shenandoah. Seneca International relocated and repackaged her in Pierre, South Dakota, as a solo hero. Much better fit." Asher spread his hands expectantly. "Any questions?"

Greyson leaned back. He'd have to plan on how to defeat this young, powerful team without martyring them. "Are there fuller profiles?"

Asher nodded. "They'll be sent to your temporary home base once you reach Shenandoah."

"Thanks…" But something deeper gnawed at Greyson beyond the Natural Born Thrillers. He'd heard various horror stories about Shenandoah's current crime-riddled state. But as a child, he recalled a completely different city, like how San Miguel was now. "What happened to Shenandoah?"

"The Chicago Massacre," Asher answered immediately.

Greyson made a face, lost. "How are those related?"

Asher sighed and sat opposite Greyson. "Titan vs Paragon." Asher's intro came with hand gestures and starry-eyed expressions to emphasize the spectacle. "The Almighty vs the American Original. Destroyed downtown Chicago, ended the Midwest Miracles, and killed thousands."

Asher continued in gentler tones. "Despite being brainwashed, Paragon's reputation was toast."

Greyson snorted. "I know all that." As a St. Louis native, he knew all about the Chicago Massacre.

Asher stiffened at his impatience. "You know who lost more? Paragon's hometown."

The dots connected instantly. "*Paragon's* from Shenandoah?" Greyson gasped.

"Born and raised," Asher said. "Since his debut in 1973, Shenandoah went from a small town to a booming metropolis based off its Paragon connection. It became a mecca for the golden age of superheroes." Nostalgia filled his eyes. "And a prototype for cities like New York and San Miguel."

"Like how Paragon was the prototype for Titan," Greyson added. *And Titan for Aegis.* The similarities between the late superhero and the so-called Shield of Justice were obvious.

Asher nodded eagerly. "After Paragon's disgrace and self-exile, Shenandoah couldn't associate with a mass murderer." He quivered theatrically. "Businesses that used Paragon and other heroes to advertise shut down from lost business, leading to sky-high job losses. City laws got very restrictive for supers. Local superheroes face all kinds of restrictions, including Shenandoah's Public Identity Act."

Greyson blinked a few times. So the adversary wouldn't just be The Natural Born Thrillers. "How will I move around Shenandoah without running into the police?"

Asher's megawatt smile returned. "You'll get a new identity with no mention of your powers." He announced that like Greyson had won a new car. When his enthusiasm met stony silence, Asher deflated. "We'll discuss more tomorrow."

"What the fuck did I sign up for?" Greyson mouthed once Asher went to confer with his team.

Greyson felt more like a new product launch than an operative. He missed Connie intensely, to have someone in his corner. But Gwyneth Pierce needed her for a mission in San Miguel…where he should be instead of fighting these Mickey Mouse Club heroes.

The Natural Born Thrillers are one major step, Greyson retold himself. Aegis would have to wait.

An hour later, the jet landed in a private airfield outside DC.

Greyson exited with his bags under a pitch-black sky and a muggy evening.

Asher directed him to a black Escalade parked several yards away.

The nearest passenger-side window rolled down. "Get in," Steve Olin ordered.

Greyson swallowed his surprise and rounded the SUV, pulling open the passenger door.

The Paxton-Brandt CEO's slim, charcoal-grey suit fit him well. His curly silvery-gold mop looked styled with an egg beater. "You wanted to meet?" he asked as Greyson strapped in.

"Yes." Greyson locked eyes with Olin. "I expected a video call or something."

A half-smile inched up Olin's lined face. "You're an important part of the Paxton-Brandt family." The response sounded very focus-group tested.

Greyson reclined in his seat but couldn't fully relax. "Thanks." Scrubbing his criminal record and an audience with Olin did make him feel valued. But there was something rotten about this partnership that he couldn't shake. "Why is my wife being sent to San Miguel?" *And why am I not with her?*

"A search and rescue operation requiring her set of skills," Olin answered smoothly. "Constance will be with you in Shenandoah before you engage the Natural Born Thrillers." He softened. "You like Italian?"

"Who doesn't?" Greyson said.

Olin's reaction was reproachful while he checked his cellphone. "You'd be surprised."

The two didn't speak for the rest of the car ride. Olin busied himself with business calls and emails. Greyson stared out the windows as America's capital rushed by. These changed circumstances were a lot to digest. And everything would change again once his crusade took flight.

His wandering eyes locked on to a billboard showcasing The Nationals, DC's top ERA team, all smiles and uber patriotic costumes and heroic poses. Greyson's stomach soured, and he turned away.

Their car stopped in front of a fancy Italian restaurant in the heart of Mount Vernon Square. Greyson stepped out of the vehicle to the sight of crosswalks bustling with pedestrian traffic. Gleaming high-rises and swanky bistros lined D.C.'s busy streets.

Olin moved to his side, eyes twinkling. "Nice, isn't it? Not having to look over your shoulder."

Greyson inhaled a steadying breath. It had been months since he'd felt this free. "It is nice."

Olin clapped a hand on Greyson's shoulder. "That's why you'll be wearing a costume and mask," he murmured. "To protect your renewed anonymity." Olin turned to his driver. "I'll call when we're done."

The car merged into evening traffic and drove off. Then Olin guided Greyson into the restaurant.

By the dimmed rouge lighting and chic layout, Greyson felt the miasma of influence and affluence oozing from every table. Hushed dialogs, covert dealings, and shady handshake deals.

The restaurant host, a delectable young black woman, led them to a private booth in the rear.

The spacious booth was away from most tables, definitely VIP. Greyson sat across from Olin, skimming through the menu, feeling off-balance. Which had to be Olin's plan. But why he had the full-throated support of the multinational to defeat superheroes still mystified Greyson.

"Are you ordering or just staring at me?" Olin asked without looking up.

"Why are you doing this?" Greyson demanded.

Olin remained focused on his menu. "Doing what?"

"Targeting heroes." Greyson glanced around, still paranoid, before continuing quietly. "Paxton-Brandt created a team, which failed spectacularly and killed hundreds." His already shaky trust wavered.

Olin placed his menu down and gave Greyson his full attention. "The painful lesson we learned from The Elite was that superheroes in their present format shouldn't exist." His expression conveyed sadness. "Nowadays, most superheroes just want fame and wealth." Olin shook his head. "None truly want to better this world."

Greyson arched an eyebrow in disbelief. "And Paxton-Brandt's mission? Besides making money."

Olin's frown deepened. "Our primary goal is profit. But that doesn't have to come at the expense of healing this planet. Even if sacrifices must be made."

Greyson found no fault in that argument. The world would improve without superheroes.

"And yours?" Olin asked. "What does the world look like after this twilight of the gods?"

Greyson's cheeks warmed. He'd never fully considered the aftermath. "Society becomes self-reliant again. Then…" He did some quick thinking. "Connie and I live our lives in peace."

Olin's response was a fatherly smile. "That's where Paxton-Brandt comes in. To shape the brave new world you're envisioning."

Greyson sagged as his role smacked him across the jaw. "That makes me a corporate-sponsored supervillain." Saying that sounded cartoonish. But there was no other term to describe his role.

Olin threw his head back with a belly laugh. "You're a necessary evil," he corrected. "And Shenandoah is the starting point of this world we'll reshape." He picked up his menu again, scanning with ravenous eyes. "Now let's order before my stomach eats itself."

CHAPTER 8

"I'm watching on the news," Simon lamented over the comm channel. "How bad is it?"

Hugo, floating miles above the scene, didn't have to think hard. "Looks like Hell on Earth."

Right after school, he'd suited up and hurtled toward Colorado's Gunnison National Forest at top speeds. Wildfires were spreading through the woodlands at a frightening pace.

Hours later, Hugo wondered if his efforts had made even a dent.

Everywhere he looked below, bright angry flames belched and roared. Hundreds of miles of lush pine trees had been consumed by the ravenous firestorm.

Heat buffeted Hugo from all sides. But he barely noticed, his own emotions already boiling as he sensed the vast loss of forest life.

Smoke stained the night skies, rising in gloomy charcoal grey columns. Hugo shuddered and swooped closer, carrying a large red container with several hundred gallons of sloshing water. He'd lost count of how many times he dumped and refilled.

Many of Colorado's flying heroes circled around the towering flames like moths, dipping low enough to dump flame retardant over swaths of forest.

After visitors had been evacuated, the priority was containing the fire from spreading to nearby cities.

National Guard firefighting choppers sprayed colorful fire suppressant onto the hungry inferno. The *womp-womp* of their blades got muffled by rumbling fiery tongues. The choppers stayed higher to avoid colliding with other heroes.

Hugo flew a few miles over the hungry flames, emptying his bucket on a section he'd been assigned by Colorado's Grand Circle team. Loud sizzles arose as water met flame. Steamy tendrils entwined with dirty smoke in the skies.

Out-of-state heroes lending support during national emergencies wasn't unusual. Heroes from Arizona, New Mexico, Utah, and Wyoming had arrived to help.

Hugo had heard Tomorrow Man was here somewhere. According to media rumors, he was livid over the Aegis interview. Oh well…

"N3 says seventy-thousand acres got burned," Simon exclaimed. "Jesus."

"It's not even dry season," Hugo added.

The fire had spontaneously sparked two days ago, leading investigators to suspect arson. The same couldn't be said for the floods ravaging the Carolina coastline.

Hugo forced his heart to go dead, a Lady Liberty teaching when handling such crises. He silently thanked his former teacher while hurtling over either lush pine layers or stretches of scorched soil to refill. A crackle caught his ears when he reached the lake.

Hugo looked up. Pillaring storm clouds were churning overhead.

Moments later, sheets of rain bucketed the lake and the fiery stretch of forest he'd targeted. Hugo smiled as rain soaked him. "Took you long enough!"

"There were plenty of hotspots scarring these forests," a solemn voice called back. A tall man with fluid black hair floated toward Hugo. The Colorado superhero called Cumulon dressed like a shaman, his rugged costume covering a rail-thin frame. His somber features aged him past twenty-seven years.

The fires ravaging this part of Colorado woodland began dying out.

"This part seems contained." The weather-controlling hero's blue eyes found Hugo. "You're free to go."

Hugo eyed the sea of roiling flames beyond Cumulon's storm. "I can do more."

Gratitude cracked Cumulon's seriousness. "You've been here for hours. San Miguel needs you, Aegis."

Hugo opened his mouth to protest but checked the time on his eyescreen. After nine at night. Jesus… He still had homework and training with J-Tom. "I'll return tomorrow."

"Your view on Tomorrow Man." Under bucketing rain, Cumulon's smile revealed white teeth. "It's appreciated."

Hugo guffawed. Superheroes were such gossips. "Thanks." Leaving his bucket near the lake, he soared from the glowing forest. Hopefully, there was no fire to return to tomorrow.

"OMG," J-Tom cried loud enough to wake the dead. "That…was Cumulon! Nature's Champion!"

Hugo and Simon burst out laughing at J-Tom's fangirling.

"How we doing, Jenny?" Hugo asked, sensing energy thrumming beside him.

Suddenly, she appeared on his left in cobalt armor with glowing yellow eyes. J-Tom's suit looked both intimidating yet scrapyard-ish. "The cloaking works perfectly."

Hugo was still floored by how smart Jennifer Thomas was. Like genius-level smart. She'd reverse-engineered the cloaking in Hugo's costume, adding it to her armor in two days. That was how J-Tom had hovered above Gunnison National Forrest undetected.

Hugo smiled proudly and rocketed back west. He could've flown faster, but J-Tom's propulsion had speed limits to conserve power. "And your power levels?"

J-Tom followed a few feet behind, her jet boots leaving a burn trail. "Forty-two percent. Stealth mode drained lots of energy."

"And your heatshields?" Simon asked.

"I'm really sweaty," J-Tom admitted in disappointment. "The suit's ventilators need upgrades."

She was silent until they passed over Las Vegas, a dazzling island in the dark desert. "You were amazing tonight! That's the kind of hero I want to be."

Hugo's cheeks warmed from the praise, which J-Tom never skimped on. "Just doing my job."

"Wish I could've helped," she continued. "Once my armor's ready for primetime and I register, I will."

Or not… Guilt shot through Hugo as they crossed California's border. "Simon, how's San Miguel?"

"Quiet," Simon replied. "Mostly human-on-human crimes. You need anything?"

"I'm good," Hugo replied tersely. "Talk tomorrow?"

"Sure," Simon said. "Later."

After signing off, Hugo threw his arms back and dove lower. "Pop quiz."

"Yay!" J-Tom squealed, right on his heels.

Hugo choked on laughter. "Nerd!" J-Tom loved pop quizzes. "Another name for superhero team?"

"ERAT or Emergency Response Action Team."

That question was easy. Hugo chose something harder. "Superhero types with examples."

"Government-sanctioned like you or all UK superheroes," J-Tom recited. "Corporate-sponsored like the Extreme Teens. Street-level heroes like Ballistic. Vigilantes like Blackjack and Domino."

Hugo nodded approvingly. He'd registered officially as government-sanctioned at the end of tenth grade. Lady Liberty had worked out his charter with San Miguel since Hugo was a minor. And the lucrative government salary didn't include merchandise royalties. They raced over the suburban maze of the Inland Empire. "Name five kinetic-type supers besides telekinetic."

"Hydrokinetic, pyrokinetic, terrakinetic, aerokinetic, and chronokinetic."

Hugo shook his head. This girl was a sponge. "Chronokinetic's a made-up word."

"*All* words are made up," she disputed.

Hugo smirked. "Smartass. What ERAT is Cumulon part of?"

"Trick question!" J-Tom's jubilance was infectious. "Cumulon isn't part of any team but occasionally works with the Grand Circle when the threat's big enough."

Hugo chuckled. "*Damn!*"

They reached his lair at the base of Arroyo Grande's Picacho Peak in an hour, regaining time thanks to the Pacific-Mountain time zone difference. Geist had gifted Hugo this safehouse, a former military bunker. The Midnight Son had rarely used it except to meet with Titan and Lady Liberty. Those meetings must've been epic. Initially, Hugo hadn't been impressed. The bunker was barely furnished and musty, with a training space and monitoring consoles patched into San Miguel's traffic system.

Now, Hugo saw a second home. High-tech computers, wide monitors, costume racks, multiple bedrooms, a shower, and a stocked kitchen. All donated by Ramon Dempsey. Hugo called it the Clubhouse.

After showering and changing into a fresh costume, he was in the training center working on J-Tom's agility and footwork.

With his hood pulled back, Hugo tossed several tennis balls in numerous directions. "Blast each one."

J-Tom moved fast and fluid in her DIY armor. She raised her hand, the palm gauntlet flashing bright gold. POOM. One ball ruptured to ash.

She spun, left hand snapping up to fire. POOM! Another ball destroyed.

POOOM. POOM. POOM. She dusted all eleven. The eyes on her helmet gleamed.

Hugo nodded. "Your aim's improved. Now." He moved directly in her line of fire. "Hit me with your repulsor blasts. Full power."

J-Tom backpedaled with hesitation. "Really?"

Hugo narrowed his eyes. Killer instinct—something J-Tom lacked. "Who better to test your limits than someone as durable as me?" Hugo beckoned with both hands.

She raised her gauntlets. Energy glowed like daylight in both palms.

Hugo expected a tickle—

A scorching beam mule-kicked him across the room.

The floor smacked his back, driving the air out.

"Oooh! Omigod!" J-Tom cried. A *clomp, clomp* of metal boots approached. "Are you okay?"

Hugo waved her off, struggling to a knee. "Yeah…good shot." The pain throbbing through his torso subsided. He rose to his feet. In her armor, J-Tom stood eye to eye with him. "You need more power against supers like me."

J-Tom's helmet opened down the center and slid away. Her face was flushed and sweaty, wavy ginger hair untamed. "Got it. Another item to upgrade."

Hugo moved on to a topic he'd been avoiding. "We need to meet Ramon Dempsey."

J-Tom paled. "Why?"

"Your armor belongs to him." Hugo explained. "He deserves to know."

"I'm not trying to steal the Dynamo mantle—"

"Ramon's a friend," Hugo interjected. "We need his blessing." Given how few close friends he had in the superhero community, this wasn't up for debate.

J-Tom looked down and swallowed. "What if he wants it back?"

Is that a bad thing? But Hugo wouldn't discourage her further. "You're crazy smart, Jenny. You'll find another way."

J-Tom met his stare, forcing a smile. "Tell me when."

Hugo smiled in relief. "I'll schedule a meeting."

J-Tom then trudged out of the training room. "I'll clean up before we leave."

"Cool." Hugo watched her go. "I got trigonometry and Biology 2 homework."

He strode down a narrow concrete corridor toward the monitoring center, the nucleus of his lair.

The monitoring center had a pale-blue lighting. Hugo found his cellphone on the island with monitors and consoles connected to San Miguel's traffic grids. He saw missed calls from Mom and AJ, texts from Brie, Brent, Raphael, and Wale. No messages from Jordana, disappointingly. On his work cell, no info about Vincent Van Violence. He swallowed his frustration…again.

Hugo leaned on the half-circle table with its monitors, earlier guilt knotting up his innards.

He'd enjoyed training J-Tom these past six weeks. She was a quick learner and constantly improving. But it wasn't just her using Ramon's property that worried Hugo. This training seemed like a coping mechanism to get over Spencer. And what if J-Tom's armor got destroyed in battle, and her along with it? *Because I didn't stop her…*

Hugo's mind drifted to The Vanguard's implosion. Robbie Rocket paralyzed, Wyldcat dead.

He shook his head angrily. Hugo wouldn't let that happen to J-Tom. She meant too much to him…

A freshly showered scent drew Hugo back to now. Somehow, twenty minutes had flown by.

J-Tom stood a few feet away in a snug sweater dress, cream-colored with an enticing V-neckline. Her wet ginger locks were pulled back tight, pale features freckled and makeup-free.

"Forgot to mention." She glanced away demurely. "Jordana's still not sure you guys can work."

The words landed on Hugo like a ton of bricks. But they weren't surprising.

J-Tom probed his face with curious hazel eyes. "What should I tell her?"

The Clubhouse seemed to shrink. Hugo's gut said to have J-Tom tell Jordana how much he cared and would be a dedicated boyfriend if she gave him the chance. And J-Tom would deliver his message with sunshiny gusto. Except, Hugo didn't see the point. "This didn't convince her before."

Something shifted on J-Tom's face. "Do you love her?"

Hugo's heart gave a lurch. *Do I?*

A sharp claxon broke the tension. Confused, Hugo turned to the monitors. "What the—?" He saw what caused the alert, and surprise seized him.

A six-foot-seven-inch biker paced outside one of the underground exits, with massive arms sleeved in tattoos. His broad-shouldered frame nearly burst out of a leather vest, and a red bandana wreathed his spiky head of hair.

"Aegis!" he barked. "Open the damn door and face me!"

J-Tom peeked over his shoulder, heart pitter-pattering. "That's Justice Jones?"

Justice Jones, a nomad who fought for America's forgotten citizens, now resided mostly in San Miguel since dating Lady Liberty. And that told Hugo exactly why the Outlaw Superhero was here.

He turned to J-Tom. "Go hide and keep quiet."

J-Tom scurried off without protest.

From there, Hugo typed an access code in the main console to open the entrance where Jones stood. Within minutes, he came stomping into the monitor center from the far-left exit.

Sharp dread speared Hugo, but he stood welded to the floor. With someone like Justice Jones, one couldn't back down. "Yes?"

Jones was in his face, standing three inches taller. "Think you're a man now, you obnoxious punk?" He fake-lunged at Hugo, who to his own shock, didn't flinch. "I oughta kick your ass for disrespecting Libby."

"Like you could," Hugo threw back calmly. He didn't fear him.

Jones knew this too. "This beef with Lady Liberty?" he growled. "End it." Not a request.

Hugo experienced a deep disgust—but not for Jones. "Did she send you?"

Justice Jones's lip curled into a snarl. Being anyone's lapdog clearly offended him. "I sent me. Someone needs to knock sense into you. With words or fists." The ex-biker's massive hands balled up.

Hugo sniggered—almost. Justice was one of the most feared hand-to-hand fighters among superheroes. But against Hugo's vast powerset and combat skills, a fight would end one way. "Did she tell you why we're not speaking?"

Justice gave a brusque headshake. "Doesn't matter."

"Of course she didn't," Hugo fumed. Lady Liberty was at fault— again. "Educate yourself before barging in here being Libby's white knight."

Justice Jones's eyes burned. "Geist's lair," he corrected contemptuously.

"You know the way out." Hugo pointed to the exit, eyes never leaving him.

The ex-biker looked ready to clock Hugo. "Still got lots to learn, boy. So here's another free lesson."

Hugo rolled his eyes. "Okay."

"Never turn your back on someone you respect...or fear." Jones turned his back, storming toward the exit.

Once the monitor revealed the biker hopping on his motorcycle and driving off, Hugo let his shoulders sag. He didn't know which gutted him most, losing Jones's respect or the disgust on the ex-biker's face. Hugo sat heavily into one of the seats at the monitoring station and massaged his forehead.

His hypersensitive ears caught soft footsteps emerging across the chambers.

"Wanna talk about it?" J-Tom offered, several feet away.

"No." Hugo's reply was flat and furious. Speaking would only make him angrier.

After five dainty strides, her breaths and steady heartbeat sounded behind his chair. Two slender arms slid around his neck and down his chest. She rested her chin on his crown. "Wanna hug?" she whispered.

Hugo deflated hearing that. J-Tom gave the best hugs. He sat up and turned his chair around, and she pulled back. "Sure." He took her by the hand, drawing her onto his lap.

She curled up against him and slipped both arms around his waist, resting her damp hair on his shoulder. The twosome embraced quietly for several minutes. Her body warmth felt wonderful.

Hugo had actually told J-Tom first about Titan being his real father while Simon had still been in Korea. Between that confession and both of them losing Spencer, Hugo and J-Tom had grown very close.

"You still smell like smoke," J-Tom murmured into his neck.

Hugo laughed briefly. But he kept stewing over Justice Jones, and by proxy, Lady Liberty.

"She's said nothing about Titan for years," he vented. "Even after she started training me. I can forgive my mom, even if what she did still pisses me off."

A crushing grief he thought had passed reared its ugly head. "Maybe," Hugo concluded, his voice rough, "I could've known him before he died." Tears blurred his vision. Now he was embarrassed.

J-Tom held him closer, rubbing circles on his back, soothing his anger with affectionate hands and soft words.

She sat up straight after some time to meet his gaze. "You have every right to be angry at Lady Liberty." J-Tom's eyes looked glazed and heavy-lidded. "But does Zelda deserve to be shut out?"

Hugo recoiled from thinking about his half-sister, who he hadn't seen in almost three months. But that subject was like touching a white-hot stove while swallowing a ghost pepper. In short, avoid.

"Have you ever wanted to meet your birth parents?" Hugo asked, focusing on J-Tom.

She considered this for a moment. "My mom and dad offered to tell me their names."

"And?" Eagerness gripped Hugo.

J-Tom shrugged. "Wasn't interested."

"Why?"

"I already have parents who love me," J-Tom said. Her damp hair shone from the overhead lamps. "And you choose the family who chooses you." She poked his chest, reciting Hugo's own words back at him.

Hugo gave her an amused onceover. "Who told you that garbage?"

J-Tom giggled. "Some loser." Looking up at him from under her eyelashes, she raised her brow naughtily.

Heat crackled up his spine. Hugo tried laughing it off, until J-Tom's starving lips found his mouth.

Bad idea, a small part of his brain protested. But Hugo still responded to the kiss, overcome with need. Then J-Tom threw her leg over his to straddle him, tangling her fingers in his hair. Memories of their long summer nights together saturated Hugo's brain and drowned that dissenting voice out.

They both had tried ending this fling before school started. But Jordana's rejections and J-Tom's heartache over Spencer kept whittling away Hugo's willpower.

As they were making out, he gently slid his hands up J-Tom's sweater dress. Her encouraging moans made the guilt easier to ignore.

Is this the real reason why I keep training Jenny? That was Hugo's last coherent thought for a long and blissful stretch of time.

CHAPTER 9

"What did they want you to wear?"

"It was hideous, Con." Greyson chuckled at his wife's disbelief, clutching his cellphone with earbuds on. "These Paxton-Brandt marketing types are insane." He walked through downtown Shenandoah, drawing his coat closer. The early evening sun cast a cherry-red glow across town while sinking into the mountainous horizon. Greyson marveled at that, and not much else.

"So, still no costume?" Connie asked.

"None that I'd be caught dead wearing." That won more laughter from Connie. But Greyson was ready to change subjects. He weaved around a group of thuggish teens. "Anyway…"

"Anyway…" Connie teased.

"How is San Miguel?"

"Pretty and so sunny," Connie gushed. "Think I might stay."

"Not until I'm done with Aegis." Greyson's words held no mirth.

Connie laughed it off. "Fine. I'll bring back some Paso Robles wine."

"Please do."

"How's Shenandoah?" she asked.

Greyson took another dispassionate look around him. "Some areas are beautiful. Other parts…on life support." He quickened his pace to escape the faint stench following wherever he walked. He'd arrived yesterday at a Paxton-Brandt condo in Shenandoah's Palisades neighborhood. One day of meandering treks, and Greyson had this city figured out.

Shenandoah was actually three cities that never fully integrated. One city was a gateway to Shenandoah National Park and Shenandoah Valley, kitschy tourist centers on every major street, forest-covered peaks dominating every horizon. The second city was a Civil War tourist trap, boasting antebellum bistros, war museums and nineteenth-century styled hotels.

Enfolding the two cities was the neglected metropolis, its suffocating miasma palpable even on a cloudless day. Police cars and SUVs patrolled the more poverty-stricken parts. Unwelcome amounts of drones swarmed overhead like silent bees. Gorgeous antebellum-type structures stood next to buildings marred by graffiti and neglect. Homeless tent cities stretched for blocks around run-down buildings.

Giving Greyson pause was Paragon himself, or his twenty-five-foot statue crouched with arms thrown back. The statue captured him perfectly. The curly hair, Romanesque face, and Herculean physique. But the cape had been snapped off. And the statue itself was graffitied, dented, and covered in trash. Missing were the statues of Ace Steele and Sonya Bullet. Triumvirate, America's first superhero team in the mid-1970s. Apparently, the other two statues had been removed due to excessive vandalism.

Greyson stared up at Paragon's statue, childhood memories of watching Titan vs Paragon spilling through. "Did you know Paragon was from Shenandoah?"

"Yeah." Connie sounded surprised. "I thought that was common knowledge, old man."

Greyson scoffed and kept walking. The skies had darkened to a velvety plum color. "Superheroes weren't welcome in my household, young pup." His past resembled a half-remembered dream, as if belonging to someone else. "What do they have you doing?" He was entering Luray-Boynton, one of Shenandoah's poorest regions with the largest super population.

"Rescue op," Connie answered. "Some Paxton-Brandt scientist is leaking company secrets and has his daughter under house arrest."

Greyson straightened. What a repulsive human. "I bet your costume's more practical." Confusion blossomed as he pondered this further. "Why do they need you to catch a traitor?"

"The scientist is an ex-superhero."

"Of course." Another hypocrite superhero. Greyson pushed down his disgust, staying present for his wife. "Come back to me in one piece."

"Always," Connie remarked softly.

Greyson slowed, feeling strangely heavy. He leaned on a building, scanning around. Lengthy shadows spilled from every corner. Hero vs Villain rap floated out from the windows of gloomier apartments. Buildings showed damage from a past super vs super battle. More improvised tents and grungy sleeping bags were visible in the darkness. Tranquility settled over the streets tonight.

Greyson's dinner talks with Olin and the new world Paxton-Brandt would build came to mind.

I'm the necessary evil for that world. Suddenly, the pressure weighed on Greyson's shoulders. Everything he'd sacrificed had brought him here. To free the minds of Shenandoah's populace…

Greyson squeezed his eyes shut, knowing he had to deliver for himself, for Connie and his crusade to open this world's eyes. "My mission…our mission," he said. "Now it feels real. It feels tangible."

"I have to pinch myself sometimes," Connie admitted, speaking whisper-soft.

Greyson sank to a crouch against the wall. "We can do some real good through Paxton-Brandt."

"Is that why you were so chill about me going on this West Coast mission?"

Greyson didn't hesitate to answer. "I trust you. And you doing well raises our standing."

"Let's not get too comfortable, Hirsch," Connie cautioned. "Paxton-Brandt wiped our slates clean. But we still don't know the full price tag for that."

Greyson furrowed his brow. "I know." He'd learned never to get too comfortable anywhere. Hence why they were speaking on encrypted burner phones he'd purchased in Mexico. "Corporations have agendas, which always change."

"At the end of the day," Connie concluded, "anyone not us is our enemy."

Greyson smiled. Another reason why he loved this woman. "You have to get to Shenandoah soon, love." After some more idle chitchat, the spouses wished each other goodnight.

Greyson ventured farther into the neighborhood, hands in his pockets, hyperaware but nonchalant. The purpose of his walks went beyond learning about Shenandoah. Greyson had been scoping every location where the Natural Born Thrillers had done battle. Plus, this neighborhood had a White Castle.

Greyson stepped forward when the first screams rang out. And then the swish of something huge spinning toward him.

Greyson threw himself onto his belly thanks to battle-honed reflexes. A second later, wind from a Toyota Camry ruffled his fluffy hair.

He rolled onto his back as it passed, heading toward a screaming couple.

No…they're innocents. Greyson reached out a hand, pooling his gravitational energies and focusing on the hurtling vehicle's momentum.

The car slowed right in front of the couple's faces. Greyson unclenched his teeth and his fist, letting the vehicle drop in a jarring cacophony.

That was close… He fought back to his feet, the world snapping into focus around him.

People were yelling and running with a swiftness as if this was a familiar exercise. More explosions and shouts rang out around the corner the vehicle had come from. Chaos reigned.

Greyson shouldered his way in that direction and shoved out of the fleeing throng. "Oh…shit."

In a filled parking lot, half the cars wrecked or burning, was a fast-paced super vs super fight.

Greyson recognized one side of the battle, all five of them.

The Natural Born Thrillers.

INTERLUDE: EZRA MICHELMAN

"You did *what?*" Ezra Michelman exclaimed with fatherly pride.

"Yeah!" his daughter Rowan confirmed eagerly over the car speakers. "I finally flew, Daddy. For three whole minutes!"

Ezra slumped back in his chair and crowed with pride. "That's great, Rowan!" After this chaotic week, he'd needed that news. "I can't wait to see you do this in person."

"You're coming to Steinholt?" Rowan exclaimed.

Ezra's smile couldn't stretch any wider. He made a turn as the highway veered left. "Once I drop your sister off to Southgate tomorrow, I'll plan to see you soon." This visit was supposed to be a surprise, but Ezra just couldn't contain himself.

"Yay!" Rowan's joy leaped out of the speakers. Then her tone sobered. "How is she?"

Ezra's jovial mood evaporated. Of course, this would come up. "Says that she'll never forgive me."

"Oh." Rowan went silent for a few moments. "She won't take my calls."

Heat rushed through Ezra, tightening his grip to where his knuckles turned white. "Spencer won't admit she was wrong," he fumed, shaking his head. "Has too much of your mother in her."

"You were always hard on her." Rowan's words struck with penetrating force.

"Excuse me?"

"Sorry, Daddy," Rowan apologized. "But it's true. And you hid that she had powers."

"That—" Ezra barely checked his tidal wave of anger. Rowan was too young to understand. "Your sister *hurt* people." Reading reports of the retrievals Spencer had done for Paxton-Brandt broke Ezra's heart.

Rowan wasn't stymied. "I know Spencer acts evil. But..." Her voice cracked. "Do you even *love* her?"

The question rendered Ezra momentarily speechless. "Of course I love Spencer, but—" *She killed your brother...my son.* Sweet Rowan knew nothing of her late brother. Ezra and his wound still ached. "Spencer's my firstborn."

Rowan sighed as if far older than thirteen. "Treat her like you do me. Then she'll be less bitchy."

Ezra was too charmed to chastise Rowan's wording. "You would've been a better big sister."

"Yeah, I know."

Ezra laughed, wiping budding tears with the back of his hand. The green sign for his offramp neared. "I'm close to my satellite office. Talk soon."

"Love you, Daddy," Rowan cooed.

The lump in Ezra's throat grew. He turned right toward his freeway exit. "Love *you*, RoRo."

Ten minutes later, Ezra pulled into the lot of the abandoned strip mall he owned miles from San Miguel. The night sky had cleared when he stepped out of his glossy black BMW. The surrounding flatlands were hushed save for faraway jet engines roaring overhead.

Ezra adjusted his long-sleeved polo and walked to the strip mall entrance. After going through the usual security protocols and teleporting to the underground levels, he stood in his high-tech lab.

Ezra pushed all distractions away as he weaved through the devices and stacks of gadgets and papers, focused on his singular goal. Destroy Paxton-Brandt.

He'd seen the corruption, the unethical practices years ago. But telling himself the cutting-edge science and boundary-pushing were more important had made him stay.

Ezra slumped in a seat in front of countless monitors, knowing the shameful truth. He'd been spiritually dead since his son's passing and his wife's jailing. Ignoring Paxton-Brandt's true nature had been easy when they showered him with money, access, resources, and luxuries.

Ezra now felt a self-disgust so deep, it hurt. How ironic that his dead best friend's son had snapped him out of moral apathy.

But Ezra couldn't blame Hugo for abandoning this mission. The boy was too visible in his new role as San Miguel's protector. And the intel he'd provided had been substantial.

The OSA and the FBI still want more. Ezra bucked his teeth. *How much do they need to finally act?*

He shook off the dismay, his fingers dancing across many keyboards to boot up his consoles. He'd heard rumors on this new project around an asset called "Damocles". Security had tightened after Hugo's attacks, so Ezra would have to be discreet in breaching the PB intranet to learn more.

He began typing in a backdoor hack, when a sharp rustle sounded above the various humming servers.

Ezra paused, narrowing his eyes. No one but Hugo, Titan, and Betty Ortiz had been down here. He rose from his seat, unshakably calm thanks to the countless life-and-death battles in his former career. The servers continued humming.

Ezra stepped away from the console, scanning his surroundings. Was he being paranoid? Better to be safe than sorry. Ezra opened his mouth to order a scan for intruders—when a scarlet blast scorched out of the dark.

"Shit…" He threw himself forward, the discharge sizzling just ruffling his wiry hair.

Old instincts ignited as he rolled in the blast's direction. Ezra snapped a hand up, power coalescing within before he unloaded a subzero salvo.

The icy discharge bowled his silhouetted attacker over.

Ezra popped up and jogged over. The attacker lay sprawled out and shivering, jet-black mask and stealth outfit covered in ice crystals.

"Stay down," Ezra barked.

He knew one truth. *Paxton-Brandt knows.* Panic soared within. He turned his head, barely sidestepping the swipe of an electric baton. A slender, feminine figure, also masked and in black, kept swinging with aggressive strikes.

Ezra brought up his forearms, encasing them instinctively in ice. Loud *KR-KEEESH* noises echoed throughout the lab when she smashed her baton into his hulking, icy-covered forearms. She tried a backswing, which Ezra ducked, leaving her wide open and defenseless. Ezra took advantage with two hard jabs to the face, dropping her.

Before he could inspect, an abrupt burning rolled up his left arm.

"Godammit!" He doubled over, clutching his spasming forearm, a reminder from the battle injury that had retired him. Ezra shook his hand out until the spasms stopped.

He inhaled to gain resolve and stared at his unwelcome guests. "Let's find out who you are?"

Ezra made furious moves toward his targets—until abrupt and blinding pain stabbed his spine.

He collapsed, every muscle seizing.

Everything hurt. He blearily looked up into the striking face of a ghost. "You?"

The last time he'd seen this woman alive, her hair had been shorter and her complexion tanner. Now she sported pale skin that complemented her long wavy brown hair. And she hadn't aged a day since 2005.

"Hello, December," she greeted in a surprising British drawl. "I'm Gwyneth."

Ezra couldn't sit up, let alone move. She must've used a shock dart on him. "How?" was all Ezra could get out. *How are you alive and working for Paxton-Brandt?*

Pierce shrugged with arrogance. Understandable, given her skillset. "Paxton-Brandt's intranet experienced a data breach months ago from Eastern San Miguel," Pierce explained. "The port closed before we could identify the source. Until someone pointed us toward you."

Ezra finally struggled with any remaining strength to a seated position.

Four well-armed figures slipped out of the shadows. "What now?" one man asked.

"Download anything essential," Pierce ordered calmly. "Burn the rest. Then we find his daughter."

Ezra's terror skyrocketed for Spencer. "Please…" he cried out. The helplessness for someone of his former stature was humiliating—*angering*. "Don't do this, Severine—"

"Gwyneth" frowned in fleeting confusion. "Who's Severine?" Lifting a boot, she kicked Ezra in the face.

And that was that.

CHAPTER 10

As panicked citizens fled the fiery disaster scene, Greyson guffawed at his luck.

Erika Skye. Bulldozer. Brightburn. Shattershot. Reverb. The Natural Born Thrillers were several feet away, ripe to be taken down.

Then Greyson realized how exposed he was. No costume or mask. Just flannel, jeans, and boots. "Oh well." He first spotted who the Thrillers was fighting in the parking lot—a brawny humanoid in a red-and-blue suit and a thimble-style helmet. The individual was holding his own against the Thrillers.

Greyson noticed a handful of heavily armed characters at the parking lot's farthest end, running from the fight. *The cyborg's accomplices?*

He felt no interest in pursuing to find out. In fact, he found himself turning around and almost running away. He forced himself to stop, struggling to push away this bizarre terror.

Greyson then realized what was happening. "Shattershot…" He glared at the lean empath standing at the edge of the fight, one hand on the side of his head with a glazed expression.

No wonder everyone was fleeing so uniformly. His psychic defense training from Paxton-Brandt helped him break Shattershot's empathic control.

Greyson scrambled on hands and knees behind an SUV, peeking over to watch the fight. Better to let the heroes contain the threat first.

Bulldozer resembled a giant bronze statue up close, punching spiders made of cobbled-together junk to pieces. Reverb, curled into a ball, bounced and bashed through more skittering spiders.

Erika Skye hovered above the cyborg controlling these metal spiders, barking orders. She had such a regal presence in that gold suit and those braids whipping about. She made a chopping motion with her hand, hurling energy knives through the cyborg's armored torso.

Brightburn, her costume flattering her lean legs, issued forks of lightning from curled fingers. The cyborg got rocked back, chewing up concrete and smashing into more cars.

Erika Skye landed in a crouch. "You're surrounded, Cybrid!" she yelled. "Surrender before this gets ugly."

The cyborg called Cybrid sat up. His helmeted face revealed no emotion, but he radiated fury. "NEVER!" He raised a fist and fired a thick red energy blast, slicing cars in half. Quite a few citizens got thrown to the ground. Greyson clutched his badly ringing ears.

Erika glared at Shattershot. "Speed up the evacuation. We're trying to avoid collateral damage."

Shattershot winced at the rebuke but kept empathically commanding lingering bystanders. "On it!"

Bulldozer stomped on one junkyard spider creature with a size seventeen boot, then punched another's legs off. "Don't get too familiar with those people, Shattershot," he snarled.

Greyson peeked from behind a car to watch Shattershot stiffen but say nothing. *Some disharmony?*

"Bulldozer." Reverb dropkicked Cybrid from behind. "Focus on the enemy."

Bulldozer flitted an indifferent gaze between Shattershot and Cybrid. "Which one?"

"Brightburn! Bulldozer!" Erika Sky commanded, hurling more energy knives. "Focus on Cybrid."

Greyson watched Cybrid fire off more energy blasts. But the Thrillers tag-teamed him with a flurry of gleaming fists from Bulldozer, hot knives from Erika Skye's and Brightburn's energy bolts.

Cybrid soon dropped to his knees, battered and charred. As the Natural Born Thrillers swarmed their downed foe, Brightburn whipped out her cell for a smiling "superhero selfie."

Erika approached calmly. "Your crew fled. Again. The cops are coming. Surrender."

The Thrillers were distracted. The main threat had been averted. Now was Greyson's chance. He rose slowly, gravitational power boiling within.

Then Greyson spotted him from the corner of his eye. A punk kid also hiding behind another car a few yards away, recording the fight on his iPhone. And one of Cybrid's spider creatures, large and rusty, skittered up behind him.

Greyson already saw the scenario play out in his mind's eye. Cybrid took the kid hostage, possibly killing him to regain leverage or escape.

Greyson was moving without thinking. But letting innocents die pointlessly with a dangerous supervillain on the loose wasn't the point of his crusade. He tackled the kid down and tossed him aside. Greyson rolled onto his back to see the spider beast rearing up in front of him. And four of its eight legs rushed down to spear him through.

His fright was brief before determination burned through. Greyson let pure nuclear energy pool into his fists and issued a dazzling burst upward.

A blinding flash coincided with the jarring eruption of shredded metal.

When the smoke cleared, Greyson rolled onto all fours. The majority of the cars were totaled beyond recognition, flattened or devoured by angry yellow flames. The teen boy he'd rescued, with buzzcut hair and dark skin, sat wide-eyed on his behind with no visible injuries.

"Run. Now," Greyson hissed, waving him off.

The boy sprang up and dashed away.

At least the kid's safe. Greyson was relieved until he turned around.

All five Natural Born Thrillers stared at him. Cybrid lay motionless behind them, out of commission.

"Goddammit." Greyson had been made—by his own mercy.

Erika Skye marveled at him. Then she glared at Shattershot, who she stood a bit taller than. "You were supposed to disperse the crowd."

The lean, sandy-haired man cupped a hand over his mouth. "I'm sorry." His contrition sounded ragged and genuine. "I didn't see them."

Now Bulldozer was in his face, dwarfing his teammate in sheer size. "Didn't or refused to?"

Shattershot turned brick-red. "Get off my back, Dozer!"

Brightburn and Reverb shuffled their feet uncomfortably. But Erika Skye wedged herself between her feuding teammates. "Bulldozer! Those bystanders are safe thanks to—"

Greyson popped up and ran out of that parking lot.

"Hey!" Erika cried out. "Wait!"

Greyson didn't stop. To stay and fight meant defeat. And the Natural Born Thrillers had seen his face.

Angry at himself for screwing up a simple victory, he ran faster into the night.

CHAPTER 11

Hugo knew more about the Extreme Teens than he cared to.

Not just because they were ubiquitous on social media, TV, film, and his friends being mega-fans.

Definitely not from them being fellow superheroes. His idiot brother, AJ, was obsessed, watching every 3D *Combat Experience* movie and their unscripted show *Extreme Dreams*.

The Malalou brothers sat at the dining table wolfing down Cheerios. AJ was glued to a Blur interview on N3 about the expansion of Olympian Theme Park's Extreme Teens section.

"His new costume looks stupid," Hugo remarked while chewing.

"Shaddup," AJ threw back.

Hugo sniggered. Blur looked ridiculous in his skintight blue racetrack unisuit, collar unzipped to show off his chest—what little there was. The speedster reclined in his seat, manspreading, goggles resting atop his disheveled dark hair. Blur's "Come At Me Bruh" face was aimed to evoke toughness. Hugo laughed harder, much to AJ's ire.

Equally interesting was the attractive reporter interviewing Blur. The smart red pantsuit highlighted her trim figure, sleek brown hair spilling over one shoulder. *Rebecca Reyes*, Hugo mused. The news veteran had escaped *SLOCO Daily's* implosion unscathed, returning to her *National News Network* gig.

She threw softball questions at Blur the whole interview, laughing at all his lame jokes, constantly pawing at him. And Reyes making bedroomy eyes at someone young enough to be her son was gross to watch. But AJ was oblivious to the onscreen tension.

Hugo itched to change the channel until Reyes asked Blur about rumors of Aegis dating Starchylde and joining his team.

Blur prickled. "Both untrue." He sat up and ranted, "And why are people having orgasms over that Titan cosplayer breaking the sound barrier?" he demanded. "I break the sound barrier like a hundred times a day." The speedster shrugged cockily. "I broke it eight times this morning, before breakfast."

Now Hugo turned the TV off, despite AJ's protests.

"You gonna let him shit-talk you, uso?" AJ remarked, finishing his cereal.

Hugo shook his head. "That overcaffeinated midget is using my name to stay relevant." Blur's taunts, while tiresome, were from obvious jealousy. The speedster couldn't go one day without somehow mentioning Hugo. "I'll focus on saving lives." The Samoan grabbed his brother's bowl, something else nagging him. "Rebecca Reyes goes with Blur everywhere." He tossed the bowls and spoons in the sink.

"She's his communications advisor," AJ said. "But as an interviewer, she sucks."

Hugo snort-laughed. "I bet Blur likes the sucking part."

AJ was aghast. "Ewww! Whatchu mean?"

Hugo eyed his naïve brother. "Rebecca friggin' Reyes is the ultimate cape chaser." He turned on the faucet over the dinnerware. "That whole interview, she looked like she wanted to eat Blur!"

Horror filled AJ's blocky features. "You're right. God, she's older than Mom."

"Hope that's a compliment, Junior."

Both boys turned, high-heels *click-clacking* from upstairs. When Mom emerged at the bottom of the staircase, Hugo gawked. "Wow."

His mother approached her sons in a white blouse and dark maroon skirt. Her hair fell in glossy curls down her back. Minimalistic makeup highlighted her prettiness. "Is this too formal?" she asked anxiously.

"Nope," AJ denied.

Hugo shook his head, heart brimming. "When's the job interview?"

Mom relaxed hearing their approval. "Before lunch. I'm really nervous."

Hugo approached, waving off her fretting. "You'll do great."

Mom loved treating patients and was good at it. An OR nurse's salary allowed her to raise two children. But seventeen years of ten-plus hour shifts had worn Mom down. The breakup with bland-as-broccoli Larry spurred her applying to be a nurse manager.

"This is a management position," Mom pushed back. "Some people applying have MBAs and way more experience."

AJ rubbed her arm reassuringly. "They aren't you."

Hugo had no doubt what she could do. "You keep telling us how you know more than the nurse managers you work with." He smiled at her. "You got this."

Mom's eyes sparkled as she drew both her sons close. "My wonderful boys."

"I am, at least," Hugo quipped, earning a jab from AJ.

"Shush!" Mom squeezed them tighter.

When they pulled apart, she turned to Hugo. "Be careful on morning patrol." Despite him being a powerful superhuman, his mother still worried.

Hugo rolled his eyes. "Always am—" The sentence caught in his throat. Dainty footsteps approached from outside, along with a familiar heartbeat. Ignoring Mom's and AJ's stares, Hugo reached the foyer in half a second and opened the door.

The thirteen-year-old girl at the door was leaner than Hugo remembered. Her bouncy coppery ringlets had also grown longer. But Zelda's sorrowful expression, much like her mother's, left Hugo paralyzed and tongue-tied.

Thankfully, Mom weaved around him. "*Taeao,* sweetie!" she greeted and guided Zelda inside.

AJ brightened and scurried forward. "Hi, ZiZi!"

Hugo snapped out of his deer-in-headlights stupor and closed the door.

"What brings you here so early?" Mom inquired after a long hug.

Zelda gestured at Hugo.

Mom gaped and quickly faced AJ, who was still clueless about Hugo's true father. "Go brush your teeth."

Hugo breathed deep and nodded at the guestroom. Zelda hugged herself and trudged past him.

"Why does she only want to see Bogie?" AJ complained.

"Teeth. Brush," Mom ordered.

Hugo closed the door and sat on one side of the bed. Zelda took the other side. A weird, ugly tension flooded the room. "Hi." Hugo sounded wooden and awkward.

Zelda waved limply. "Sorry to bother you."

"It's fine, Z."

"Do you hate me too?" The whisper held so much hurt.

Hugo suddenly wanted to sprint across the country. "No. NO. You did *nothing* wrong."

Zelda's eyes flashed. "Then why are you avoiding me, you asshole?" She didn't raise her voice. But her anger was unmistakable.

Hugo felt so self-centered and cowardly. The truth had a bitter taste. "I didn't know how to face you."

Zelda looked at her knees. "I'm still me. It's just…that…"

"You're my sister." Hugo saying those words shifted the entire mood. Dizzying feelings crackled up his chest. He watched Zelda's face tighten. "See the difference?"

"Yeah…" Her whisper sounded like a pained sigh.

The tension broke. Buttery warmth encircled Hugo's heart when he stared at Zelda Ortiz, his half-sister. "When did you know?"

Zelda opened her eyes, which were identical to Titan's. "Three years ago. My mom told me not to say anything until you knew. When we saw you last summer at Morro Bay, you looked so much like my…our dad, it freaked us out."

Hugo smiled, remembering their hysterical reactions. "Makes sense." The mirth was brief. "Did your mom send Justice Jones to guilt me into forgiving her?"

Zelda's face shifted in understanding. "No. But she and Uncle Manny were arguing about you last night." She glanced away. "They've been arguing *a lot* lately."

Just as Hugo suspected. Justice Jones was a good man kept in the dark. But it was time for Hugo to be a good man too. "I'm sorry for ghosting you. That was stupid."

Zelda pouted. "Yeah, it was." She threw herself at Hugo and embraced him.

Hugo melted at her exuberance, returning the hug. "Come over anytime." As they pulled apart, he added a caveat. "Alone."

A cloud descended over Zelda's face. "Could you ever forgive her?"

"I…" A month ago, Hugo would've answered no. But Zelda back in his life clouded everything up. "Dunno yet." He wasn't interested in discussing Lady Liberty. "Your mom isn't technically a super. But since…*our* dad is, did you inherit anything?"

Zelda beamed and nodded.

I knew it! "Show me," Hugo encouraged.

Zelda spread her arms and floated inches off the floor. Within moments, her whole body was glowing so bright that Hugo had to shield his hypersensitive eyes.

"Still learning to control the light energy." She floated down to her feet as her radiance dimmed.

Hugo lowered his arm, feeling light and joyful. "We'll figure it out together, ZiZi."

Several minutes later, Hugo had suited up for a quick patrol before school until Detective Beale called.

Hugo's heart sang. Finally, the cops had found Vincent Van Violence.

They hadn't.

Currently, Hugo stood inside someone's Oldtown San Miguel apartment.

A *dead* someone…

All that remained were charred walls, scorched furniture, and a woman's shriveled body burnt to a crisp. Normally, San Miguel PD's Homicide Division handled murders. But if superhuman involvement was suspected, then San Miguel PD's Superhuman Task Force got involved. A superhuman officer and one normie officer were paired off. Occasionally, superheroes were called to consult—like Hugo right now.

He was used to seeing bodies, but they still left him queasy.

Detectives Beale and Dawson, the latter a super, stood back as Hugo scanned the room with his senses.

"Any thoughts?" the taller detective inquired after several minutes.

Hugo sniffed again, turning slowly to absorb his environment. The Samoan silently thanked Lady Liberty and Geist for showing him how to case a crime scene and recognize specific smells. The pungent burnt odor didn't match with a gas explosion. "There's gas everywhere except the body." Hugo was careful not to step on the chalk surrounding the corpse. "No gas or flame accelerant were used to kill her."

Dawson slapped Beale on the chest, annoyed. "That's what I said." He turned back to Hugo. "The gas leak from the stove seemed perfunctory to obfuscate the truth."

Hugo swallowed a smile. Dawson always served up the ten-dollar words. "Perfunctory. Great word. My guess? A pyrokinetic burned the victim alive." Beyond the gas and burnt flesh, the lingering stench smelled oddly familiar. Like the fires in Colorado. Hugo shook off the coincidence, equating it to the déjà vu of putting out forest fires two nights in a row. "The murderer must've burned some of the walls then let some gas fill the apartment."

Detective Beale nodded and approached. "We were thinking that too."

Hugo's pride soared. He felt more and more confident each time doing these crime scenes, trusting his senses. He turned a dispassionate eye to the body. "Who was she?"

"Nina Smarts. Senior geneticist at Salto Research Institute's South Carolina branch," Dawson said. His indifference was no doubt from seeing countless corpses. "Travels between there and San Miguel often."

Hugo turned away, stomach knotting from staring too long at the body. And the smell. "Any word on V3's whereabouts?"

Dawson and Beale exchanged dark looks. "We nearly trapped him last night," Beale explained. "But he got skittish and no-showed."

Hugo bristled. "Why didn't you tell me?" He forced his voice to a more neutral volume. "I could've tracked him down."

Dawson stepped in, alarmed by whatever he saw on Hugo's masked face. "V3 is a piece of shit but desperate. We'll draw him out." He gave a reassuring smile.

"Then you can take him out." Beale's attitude was unflappable. "It's just taking longer than expected."

Hugo forced his expression into blankness. Getting mad over something that couldn't be controlled helped no one. "Okay." From there, a subtle alert went off in the corner of Hugo's eyescreen.

Fifteen minutes until class started. Shiite! He said his farewells and flew off.

Minutes later, he was hurtling over lofty architectural corridors in downtown San Miguel at over ninety miles an hour. This was a usual flight route he took so that San Miguel citizens could see him. Several buildings remained sleeved in drape-covered scaffolding as repairs from Black

Wednesday continued. The worst damage had been cleaned up and fixed around the accursed Paxton-Brant business center. Hugo would get home with enough time to change and superspeed over to school. Still, taking a crime scene this early was risky. Superheroics wouldn't compromise his grades.

He turned a corner, his shadow soaring over the major veins of morning traffic. There was another shadow to his right, similar but much smaller.

"What…the hell?" Hugo realized that shadow had tailed him since leaving Oldtown. Irked at himself for just noticing, he turned in mid-flight to see his pursuer.

And a dazzling violet blast drilled him.

"AAHH!!" The energy attack struck like a mule kick. Excruciating pain seared through Hugo, exactly like when Spencer Michelman had blasted him. *But Spencer's under house arrest.*

He had little time to process, now in rapid freefall. A traffic-packed street rushed up, various pedestrians pointing and shouting in alarm.

Hugo pushed through the pain and pulled up at the last instant.

"Sorry!" he shouted while climbing back into the air. The sting was already fading. A quick check revealed his costume intact and mask in place. Small blessings.

Relief quickly became fury. *Some motherfucker shot me.* Making first period English was the last thing on his mind.

Hugo zoomed to where he'd been struck, scanning the sleek buildings and rooftops in every direction. No trace of any shooter as far as his telescopic vision could see.

And the shadow following Hugo was long gone. He clenched his fists in impotent anger. But that blast, matching Spencer's energy signature?

A new awareness left Hugo cold all over.

Had his attacker been employed by Paxton-Brandt…or the OSA?

CHAPTER 12

Connie's arrival that evening was a godsend.

Parked on their couch in this spacious condo, Greyson listened proudly as his wife discussed her mission. Meanwhile, his secret festered. He'd told no one yet, never leaving the condo except for food.

Once Connie finished, he confessed his run-in with the Natural Born Thrillers. That made his stupidity much more real.

But Connie didn't waver in her supportiveness, sitting while he paced back and forth in escalating panic.

"It's okay, Hirsch," she assured, watching him with fond eyes.

Greyson shook his head, unable to accept the assurances. "I don't think so." He pointed at his head. "They saw my face."

Connie stood and advanced. "It's a setback." She cradled his bearded cheeks in soft, gentle fingers. "And you only used your nuclear powers?"

"Yes." Greyson couldn't see how exposing himself was an advantage. "I should've let that dumbass die," he grumbled. "No one would miss one less cape-chasing paparazzo."

Connie cuffed him upside the head, stunning him out of his self-pity. "You had a lapse in judgment," she stated tersely. "But you saw them in action as a team."

Greyson let his shoulders slump as her words sank in. "You have a point."

"I know." Connie shrugged. "Now what?"

Greyson couldn't think on an empty stomach. "I'm getting us some food before Asher arrives." He gave her a big sloppy kiss then grabbed his coat. "Glad you're back."

The crisp afternoon air was just what he needed on the walk to Alley's Bakery in Valley Square. This part of Shenandoah was fresh and livable, bustling with regular professionals on lunch breaks.

Greyson had grabbed two bagel sandwiches and some salads, pleased with the short wait.

"Levi?" a woman called from his right.

Greyson kept walking.

"Levi Katz," she called again, tapping his shoulder.

Greyson winced. Right, Levi Katz, the new public identity Paxton-Brandt had provided. He turned to see a slim woman slightly taller than him, chocolate-brown-skinned with thick glasses. She somehow knew his new identity, bundled up in a tan peacoat with a beanie hiding a pile of hair underneath. The young lady seemed quite eager to meet him.

Greyson frowned in dismay. "Hello?"

"Remember me?" The woman lowered her glasses. "From the car lot?"

Greyson gaped. Erika Skye. *They found me.* He backpedaled, nearly having a heart attack. "You—"

Erika grabbed his forearm. "Relax," she muttered. "I'm just here to talk."

Greyson froze. Making a scene would exacerbate a bad situation. This mission was over before it began. He quickly scanned the café. Everyone was either on their phones, ordering food, or conversing. Everyone except one man near the door in a cap and hoodie, average height and slim, watching them intensely.

The fucking empath? Greyson jerked his arm free. "Yet you brought your boy," he whispered harshly. Gravitational energy flowed like fire through his veins, about to erupt.

Erika looked impressed. "He's backup." Her eyes narrowed. "Should he be worried?"

She had the element of surprise yet didn't attack. Greyson considered this briefly and relaxed. "No."

Erika's relief was obvious. Subtly waving Shattershot off, she guided Greyson to a table. "Shall we?"

"How did you find me?" Greyson asked once they sat in a corner booth far from prying eyes. He'd been careful about not getting tailed. *What did I miss?*

Erika smiled. "Had the police do a discreet search of your face. You've come here twice a day this week."

Greyson squeezed his eyes shut. "Shit." The closest restaurants weren't great, except this place. And now the police were onto him.

Erika laughed. "It's a Shenandoah original. The cheesesteak sandwiches?" Her eyelids fluttered in ecstasy. "To die for."

Greyson had no interest in small talk. Her team was his enemy. "What do you want?"

Erik sobered. "To discuss what happened three nights ago."

Greyson clenched his teeth. "Just helping out."

Nearby, four young girls whispered among themselves.

"I know," Erika assured, resembling an undergrad with the glasses and regular clothes. "That's why I didn't tell the police who you were. This city has laws against using powers without registration."

Greyson's cheeks flushed. "Are you threatening me?"

Erika waved her hands in a truce. "I'm letting you know the reality here."

Before she could continue, the four girls shuffled up to their table, all smiles and nerves.

Greyson leaned away. But he might as well have been invisible.

"Excuse me," an olive-skinned girl said, shaking like a leaf. "Are you—?"

Erika took it in stride. "Yes, I am," she replied gently.

The girl turned to her friends, and they whisper-yelled at each other. Greyson snorted.

"Can we get a picture?" another girl asked with utmost reverence.

Erika waved the girls forward. "Of course." She eyed Greyson expectantly. "You mind?"

He sighed, taking that girl's cellphone to snap pictures of Erika with her adoring fans. After thanking her, the quartet scurried away, quietly squealing amongst themselves.

Erika watched them go as she and Greyson sat back down. "That rarely happened when the Thrillers first started." She turned to him and slumped back in her seat heavily. "God, Shenandoah used to be a city of gods and angels."

Greyson wasn't sure where this conversation was heading. But he'd play along. "Can it reach those heights again?"

"Definitely." Erika's mouth became a taut line. "We need more time to earn the city's trust."

"Plowing through a full car lot won't help," Greyson snarked.

Erika looked down like a scolded child. "Not our finest moment. Which is why we're speaking. You have great situational awareness and combat-ready powers." Her eyes sparked. "My team has an opening."

Greyson blinked, unsure he'd heard correctly. "You're recruiting me?"

Erika's enthusiastic nod was adorable. "This is just a tryout. What do you say?"

"No, no, NO!" That was Asher Martin's barking answer an hour later when Greyson had told him, his team, and Connie what transpired. The Paxton-Brandt folks were in a panic over this meeting, Asher was about to tear chunks of hair out, and Connie just laughed.

Greyson sat on his couch beside Connie, not reacting to Asher's tantrum. "I already agreed. Tryout is tomorrow evening at their headquarters."

A collective gasp rippled through the pearl-clutching Paxton-Brandt team.

Asher stared a hole into Greyson. "And? The Natural Born Thrillers work for Paxton-Brandt's sworn enemy!" He was like a different person from the suck-up showing off costume designs.

"This could be a trap," Darnell, one of Asher's flunkies, suggested.

"Or an opportunity," Connie refuted, hands spread. "Greyson's records are scrubbed. And the fact that she doesn't know his real name is an advantage."

Asher stared down at Connie like she was an insect. "No one asked your opinion."

Connie reddened. "Excuse you?"

Greyson caught her arm before she did something rash. *That's one.* "Asher." His mind was made up. "I try out for the Natural Born Thrillers. Even if I get cut, I've been inside their headquarters. We can find out when and where to strike." There was no downside to this approach.

Asher purpled. "Are you deaf, Hirsch? NO!" He spoke with such contempt, jabbing a finger in his face. "You're just another attack dog. Do as you're told and leave the thinking to me."

The living room hushed, the tension thick enough to grab.

It was the final insult. *That's two.* Greyson rose, eyes locked with Asher. "Give us the room." He didn't raise his voice. The steel in his words prompted everyone else, even Connie, toward the kitchen.

Asher whipped around, increasingly irked. "No one leaves until I say so."

Everyone immediately cleared out.

Greyson grabbed Asher by the chin and turned his head back to face him. "Let's talk."

With that one request, Asher went bone-white. He tried moving his arms but noticed how heavy they'd grown. Confusion soon became terror.

Greyson forced Asher backward and down on the couch while clutching his jaw.

Asher trembled, sweat beading down his brow. "Do you know how much money we've invested in you and your wife?" he demanded pathetically.

Greyson cocked his head sideways, amused at what this man considered power. "And that's supposed to make me your mindless slave?"

Asher swallowed hard, realizing he had no tether on Greyson. "I...I..."

"No more talking," Greyson decided and palmed the top of Asher's head as if petting a dog. He gradually increased the gravity on his shoulders and head. "I will infiltrate the Natural Born Thrillers to learn their strengths and weaknesses. And then, I will crush them like eggs." He searched the executive's face. "Nod if you understand, boy."

Asher nodded feverishly.

Greyson increased the gravity a tad more. "You owe Connie an apology. Nod."

Asher grunted but nodded briskly.

Only then did Greyson push Asher back and release him.

The Paxton-Brandt executive sagged onto the couch, gasping ragged breaths.

"Tell Olin the plan," Greyson concluded. "You can even take credit." He glanced toward the kitchen. "All finished."

Connie and the Paxton-Brandt team stepped out from the kitchen with curious looks.

"I'm sorry, Mrs. Hirsch," Asher said robotically to Connie, hollowed out.

Connie glanced over him in pure disgust. "Sure." She pulled Greyson aside to the kitchen before any further discussions started. "What happened?" she demanded.

"I happened." Greyson grinned. "Our plan's a go."

CHAPTER 13

"I combed over that whole block, Hugo," Clint said, dropping his hands in frustration. "Any street camera footage was conveniently corrupted." The skinny, tattooed hacker leaned back in his chair at the circular command center of Geist's former lair. Pale lights spilled throughout the chambers.

Hugo, in costume with the hood and mask pulled back, fought down frustration. "Great." That random attack two days ago had him insanely paranoid. "That's some CIA-OSA-level coverup there."

Simon, sitting at the control center, jockeyed for Hugo's attention. His BFF had been learning how Clint quarterbacked Blackjack's and Domino's missions so he could do that for Hugo. He was a better friend than Hugo deserved. "Isn't Spencer under house arrest?"

Hugo shook his head. "The blast felt like the other times she attacked me." Spencer Michelman had attacked him. He knew it in his bones.

"Ask Dr. Michelman." Simon stood. Even after his growth spurt, he still only reached Hugo's chest.

"I've called a few times," Hugo said. "Haven't heard back." That was unlike him. Usually, Dr. Michelman got back to him within a day. He'd gotten radio silence for over two days.

Sounds of grunts and smacking flesh floated out of the lair's training section, where J-Tom had sparred with Domino and Blackjack for almost an hour. Those noises reminded Hugo.

"Don't mention this to J-Tom. Spencer's still a sore point."

Clint snorted, unconcerned by teen angst.

"You and your girl drama," Simon taunted, shaking his head. "I'm your lockbox."

Hugo felt lighter. Those first few weeks after Black Wednesday had been rough, with J-Tom bursting into tears whenever discussing Spencer. Hugo had showered her with affection—probably too much. But supporting his career and then training to be a superhero herself had truly healed J-Tom. *Now that could be taken from her.*

"If I'd known about you and Spencer last year," Simon chided, "this shit wouldn't have happened."

Hugo scratched the back of his neck. "Probably." Remembering the inescapable pull between him and Spencer, Hugo doubted anything could've stopped him. "I'll check Michelman's houses on my afternoon patrol before the Morro Bay Carnival."

Simon frowned. "We're still getting some Beach Bum Burger first?"

Hugo winced, recalling yesterday's plans. "Ramon could only meet Jenny and me this afternoon."

"The moment of truth." Simon nodded with a closed expression.

"Something like that," Hugo remarked remorsefully. "See ya at the Carnival."

"Later." Simon gave an unenthusiastic wave before thanking Clint, then leaving.

Hugo watched him go. That wasn't the first time he'd seen such disappointment from Simon.

Clint was watching Hugo, fingers steepled over his Def Leppard shirt. "Don't take your real-world friends for granted."

Hugo's regret deepened. "Yeah." He'd make this up to Simon somehow. "Can you find someone for me? Vincent Van Violence."

Clint went rigid in his seat. "Definitely," he agreed. "I hate that slice of dog shit."

Hugo smirked and patted his shoulder. "Thanks, Clint." He glanced at other monitors Clint worked on. One featured the domed roof of the Jefferson Memorial, defaced by the terrorist Saracen. *That asshole.* Another screen listed members in Geist's vigilante network in the Bay Area and San Luis Obispo County.

Not my business. Hugo strode from the command center into the training room, where two women traded strikes and blocks. Blackjack watched in the corner, a towering presence, even out of costume.

The tall blonde in crazy shape, wearing yoga pants and a trainer bra, was Carmit Bendavid, aka Domino. She laid in strikes on a slightly taller J-Tom, who had on training shorts and a cutoff tee. The black headband and bun kept J-Tom's hair from her tight, focused face. Domino seemed almost bored.

Hugo listened to J-Tom's heart race with exertion. Domino's pulse remained normal when she moved with viper-like speed, dragging a shocked J-Tom by the arm over her shoulders. One crisp toss later, and she was wincing up at the lights.

Domino stared down at her imperiously. "Your opponent's eyes and body language will always inform their next move," she chided in her Israeli accent, offering her hand.

J-Tom ruefully accepted and got pulled upright.

Hugo didn't hide a wincing face, as he'd seen many variations of this scene play out.

He fixed his face and approached with arms behind his back. "How's she doing?"

Blackjack jabbed fingers at his wife and trainee. "I swear, Thomas is improving."

Hugo eyed his gasping friend and forced a half-smirk. "I'll take your word for it."

J-Tom gasped. "I'm right here."

Blackjack and Domino burst out laughing, making her laugh also.

"Time for our date with Dynamo, huglord," Hugo announced.

J-Tom's smile vanished like clouds over the sun. "Don't remind me." She trudged to the changing room.

While waiting, Hugo gathered the two vigilantes closer. He'd gotten to know them well these last several weeks, hence why he'd trusted them to train J-Tom. "Any word from Geist?"

Blackjack shook his head. "He's off the grid, doesn't want to be found."

Hugo didn't care for that. No one had heard from Geist since he'd left San Miguel to regain his edge, not even his protégés. "Therese said the same." He scratched his chin, surprised to find slight stubble.

"Geist will return." Domino's voice held a mix of sternness and pain. "When he's found whatever he's searching for."

The profound words shook through Hugo. Geist's presence loomed large, even in absence. "I miss him."

Domino's expression warmed.

"Us too." Blackjack's deep voice hitched. "Every damn day."

Hugo gathered his composure. "I guess—Jesus!" He gaped again. "Your forearm."

The exclamation startled Blackjack, whose right arm was bandaged from elbow to wrist. "It's nothing."

Hugo had seen "nothing" injuries. "Your bandage says otherwise."

"Cooking accident." Domino stepped in front of Blackjack. Her face had no give. "Jeff's very clumsy."

Domino's and Blackjack's elevated heartrates gave away their lie. Hugo decided not to push, be it a kitchen accident or kinky sex.

J-Tom reentering the room cut the tension. She wore a long-sleeved striped tee and jeans, ginger hair wild and bouncy. "Ready."

"Gear up, Jenny." Hugo pulled on his hood and half-mask. "Thanks, guys."

Blackjack waved off the compliment with his uninjured hand. "Good luck."

Several minutes later, Hugo flew at modest speed down San Miguel's sandy coastline of beaches and cliffsides. The afternoon sun was a golden disk starting its slow march into the sea.

J-Tom kept pace. Her form had improved, arms thrown back like wings, her turns much more graceful like Hugo had taught her. In daylight, her bootstrapped armor's dents and DIY quality became more glaring. Shame spasmed down Hugo's chest. Vincent Van Violence or The Accelerator would obliterate this armor, regardless of how long she'd worked on it.

"Breathe," Hugo called over the winds, hearing J-Tom's shallow breaths above the whirs of her armor.

J-Tom's round helmet jerked about to meet his gaze, eyes gleaming red. "You heard that saying about never meeting your heroes? Dynamo was my favorite." She turned to focus ahead, no deviation in flight path. Another improvement. "Blew my mind when I found out he's human *and* younger than us."

Hugo nodded as they approached the Santa Maria/San Miguel border. "I almost twisted his head off," he remarked, recalling their first violent encounter. "Now we're bros."

J-Tom gave a nervous laugh, stopping her from almost hyperventilating.

Soon after, they had reached Ramon Dempsey's Santa Maria compound on a private beach. The home, where he lived with his parents, had a boxy shape surrounded by stretches of wilderness. Hugo had called ahead so Ramon knew to lower any security protocols.

"Hang back while I make intros," Hugo advised before plunging down to one of the courtyards. He did a flawless superhero landing in a garden teeming with local plant life and intoxicating scents.

Ramon rolled along a cobblestone walkway in his wheelchair, hair freshly trimmed and wearing a San Miguel Outlaws jersey.

Hugo smiled as he stood, pulling his mask and hood back. "Ray-Ray!"

Ramon smiled back. "Bogie!" They exchanged high-fives and side hugs. "Your call sounded urgent."

Here we go. Hugo tingled with nerves. "We should discuss something." He looked up and waved at the sunlit heavens. "C'mon down, Jenny."

Ramon followed Hugo's stare, increasingly confused.

J-Tom descended in her dark metal armor, her boots' repulsor thrusts blazing bright on the way. As soon as she touched down, the armored helmet popped open, as did the rest of her armor's front chassis. J-Tom stepped out of her armor and approached, giving Hugo a questioning look.

He nodded encouragement, heartened by her regard.

"Mr. Dempsey?" J-Tom stood before a stunned Ramon. "Jennifer Thomas." She waved back at her armor. "I built this from two of your practice drones." J-Tom then explained being a huge Dynamo fan, these drones crashing in her backyard, and crafting this armor with her dad's help.

After she finished, Ramon studied the armor wordlessly.

The silence stretched so long, J-Tom started fidgeting. Hugo waited, growing self-conscious.

Ramon placed both hands on his lap, his expression neutral. "No." That one word detonated like a bomb in this peaceful garden.

Hugo took no joy in J-Tom's wounded reaction, but this was necessary.

"Why?" she demanded.

Ramon's eyes flashed. "That armor is my property." He didn't raise his voice, but his sharp tone conveyed that anger. "And I won't have another pretender ruin the Dynamo name."

J-Tom's freckles vanished under a deep flush. "I'd never try replacing you."

Ramon turned his tight glare on Hugo. "How long have you known about this?"

"Seven weeks," he admitted, bracing himself as Ramon opened his mouth heatedly.

"Don't blame Hugo, please!" J-Tom stepped in front of Hugo as if Ramon was a firing squad. "I didn't tell him until seven weeks ago."

Ramon tensed up and then relaxed. But his eyes burned with emotions he seemed unable to process. "Wearing the suit or armor like Hugo and me is a job. Not some science fair hobby."

J-Tom nodded with terse respect. "I know, sir. I just want to be a hero."

"You say that now…" Ramon rolled closer. "How will you fix that armor after taking damage? Where will you get ammunition? What if someone hacks into your armor?" His voice caught on that last part.

Hugo saw where this was heading, a lump forming in his throat. The horrible day that ended Ramon's superhero career; an ex-teammate hijacked his armor and made it slaughter Pressley Lau's crew with him inside. That horrible day had almost turned Hugo into a cold-blooded murderer after finding those lifeless bodies. The fiery ache forced him to blink back tears.

J-Tom already knew the story. But seeing the lingering scars on him and Ramon left her agape. "I…I…"

Ramon stared up at J-Tom but no longer saw her, reliving that nightmarish day. "You're trapped in your own creation, which you thought was safe, forced to watch while someone destroys your legacy. And there's nothing you can do."

J-Tom stood her ground, scared but unyielding. "I want to help people like you and Bogie—"

"You're nothing like me, Jennifer," Ramon cut her off with chilling finality. "And that's a good thing."

J-Tom deflated, so broken and drained of joy. Witnessing this lanced Hugo through the heart.

Ramon turned back to him. "Why didn't you tell me sooner?"

"I should have," Hugo admitted. "And I'm sorry." He should've ended it there. Then this nonsense of J-Tom becoming a hero would be over. But watching her struggle for composure, Hugo thought of how she'd looked forward to inspiring citizens who'd lost hope after The Vanguard's demise. She wanted to stand up for those who couldn't do that for themselves. She wanted to help Hugo if he ever needed backup.

What if I'm wrong to say nothing? A queer resolve seized Hugo in that moment.

He walked over, gripping J-Tom's shoulders from behind. "Jenny reverse-engineered two of your drones with only her dad's help and crafted her own armor. She's been fight training regularly with Blackjack and Domino." Hugo rounded J-Tom and stood before Ramon. "I'm working with Jenny on her blast coordination and reflexes, which keep improving." No bullshit there. "If Jenny took the certification test, she'd ace the damn thing."

Those words poured from Hugo without thought. "The world needs more heroes as smart, brave, and caring as Jennifer Thomas."

J-Tom blushed and looked down, but her affection was tangible.

Satisfied, Hugo turned to Ramon again. "Aren't you curious to see what she did with your technology?"

Another stretch of time passed as Ramon flitted his eyes from J-Tom to her inactive armor standing nearby. Then he rotated his wheelchair around. "Bring it inside," he grumbled.

Hugo and J-Tom exchanged silent victorious fist pumps.

A little later, the three were inside of one of Ramon's labs with J-Tom's armor lying on a slab of metal. Surrounding them were various consoles, flatscreens, and stray cybernetic components on table islands. Many of Dynamo's previous and unworn suits stood in containment units at the far-right end of the chambers. Hugo felt giddy standing inside Ramon's inner sanctum.

J-Tom was explaining what she and her dad had done to get the basic functions of the armor to work. Ramon appeared almost bored. Clearly, he knew all this. Hugo's nerves rose again. But he knew that his words held no sway. J-Tom had to sink or swim in the technology realm.

"What's this?" Ramon inquired while running diagnostics on the programs J-Tom had installed in her armor. He sounded genuinely intrigued for the first time.

J-Tom brightened. "Stealth-mode program."

Ramon's expression said "Yeah right."

Hugo nodded. "It works, Ray-Ray."

"I studied the stealth mode in Hugo's suit," J-Tom explained, "and reverse-engineered it."

"Huh." Ramon rubbed his throat, then pointed to another program appearing onscreen. "And this?"

"Heat shields." J-Tom's confidence began growing. "Still need tweaking, but they work too."

The threat of a smile pulled at Ramon's lips. "About the stealth mode. Walk me through your approach."

J-Tom rubbed her hands together. "Sure…" The two went into a deep technical discussion back and forth about how she'd built the armor. Kindred souls.

Hugo smiled to himself. Hopefully, it led somewhere for J-Tom's future.

After almost twenty minutes, they were oblivious to anything but each other and J-Tom's armor.

Hugo felt completely invisible. "So I'm heading out. Should I come back in an hour?"

Ramon brushed off the need. "I got it covered."

J-Tom replied with a glowing look, mouthing, "Thank you."

"Cool," Hugo replied, feeling dismissed and okay with it.

"Ice cream helps me work," Ramon suggested. "How about some cookies and cream?"

J-Tom's eyes got big, like a fish on dry land. "YES! Ice cream plus technobabble are my favorites!"

Hugo's heart soared before he turned to leave, pulling his mask and hood back on.

CHAPTER 14

Greyson arrived at the Natural Born Thrillers' headquarters as dawn cracked through the darkness. The location was an old repurposed rubber factory at the edge of Shenandoah.

Greyson took in the boxy and rusted iron exterior, silhouetted against a scarlet dawn. He adjusted his workout attire, inhaling deeply for steadfastness. "Let's do this."

Upon gaining entry, he walked through a vast and empty foyer.

Erika Skye was waiting in full gold costume, all smiles, braids tumbling freely. "Levi! I hope finding us wasn't too hard."

All too easy. Greyson shook her hand, forcing a smile. "Wasn't too bad, Erika."

She guided him down a long hallway before they stepped through another door.

Greyson looked again to make sure he was in the same place. The room they'd stepped into was sleek and futuristic, with all kinds of training equipment. He closed his dropped jaw to focus on the other people in the room.

Erika gestured fondly at her team. "Here's the crew."

The other four Natural Born Thrillers introduced themselves. Reverb was spry and friendly, very young in appearance. Brightburn had doe-eyed beauty and amusing spunk to match, when not working every angle of her toned body to snap selfies. Shattershot, strikingly handsome, came across as reserved. Only Bulldozer was rude, a head taller than everyone, even in human form, with tree-trunk arms and honey-brown skin. He glared at Greyson's outstretched hand.

"Hey, everyone." Greyson turned his rejected handshake into an awkward wave. He then noticed an athletically built stranger standing apart from the team. "Hello."

The man strode forward, dressed in a unitard with a physique seen on fitness magazine covers. He stood noticeably taller with a dazzlingly toothy smile and perfectly cropped brown locks. Greyson felt self-conscious about his unchiseled body and thick beard. This fitness model's aggressive handshake rattled Greyson's arm. "Arthur Strong. Call me Art."

Greyson frowned, still unsure why this person was here. "Hi, Art." He turned to Erika Skye for answers.

Reverb spoke first, boyish face alight. "We've done the background checks and know what you could do. We need to see more of what you can do."

The kid chuckled at his own pun. Greyson stared at him.

"It's a tryout," Bulldozer grunted. "To see if you can cut the mustard."

Greyson understood what was happening. Two contenders for one spot, which Erika never mentioned.

She noticed his irritation. "It would've been just you," Erika began contritely.

Bulldozer steamrolled over her. "But we're exploring all options for our next member."

Erika eyed him with such disdain, Greyson almost pitied Bulldozer. "Thank you, Dozer," she stated curtly.

Greyson caught the palpable tension between them. Shattershot and Reverb looked away in clear discomfort. Brightburn was oblivious, puckering her lips for another selfie. *There's more beneath this.* Definitely a flaw to exploit once he made the cut.

Erika schooled away her displeasure when facing Greyson and Art. "This will go a few hours," she announced. "So bring your best."

Bulldozer guided Art and Greyson farther into the center. "We start with sprint drills. No powers."

"Good luck," Art remarked. His expression oozed with arrogance. "You'll need it against me."

Greyson said nothing. Wasting breath served no one. The sprint drills were forty yards wall to wall for an hour. Ten minutes in, Greyson's leg muscles screamed. He was fit but no athlete.

Art dashed around like a gazelle. The sweaty sheen on his forehead glistened like his insolent smile.

Greyson didn't get angry. He got even while huffing forward.

By Greyson subtly increasing Art's gravity, his rival was slowing and panting within minutes.

"You okay, Art?" he asked in mock concern after passing him.

Art nodded, struggling for breath. "Yeah. Just...need to..." He slowed and bent over, hands on knees, stunned by his own failing stamina. "Catch a second wind."

Greyson shrugged and kept going, catching that important second wind as he struggled to not smile.

The end couldn't have come soon enough. Both Greyson and Art sagged against the wall, drenched.

"Next!" Brightburn announced. "Target practice."

Bulldozer brought out a machine that belched out clays. Art went first, his green optic blasts smashing almost every clay spat out. His aim was sublime, head turns cat-quick, once destroying three clays in one sweeping blast.

"Fantastic, Art!" Bulldozer bellowed, drawing loud condemnation from his teammates.

"What?" he remarked innocently. "I'm encouraging a candidate."

Greyson went next to zero fanfare. Over the last few months, he'd been honing his nuclear blasts to where the energy flowed through him like fire. Shooting clays was easier, his reflexes and targeting honed to near perfection. Then three clays were belched out at once in different directions.

Greyson dropped to a knee, blasting a clay with each hand, then the third with a two-handed burst.

Art seethed, confidence slipping. But only the Thrillers' opinions mattered to Greyson, all of whom were impressed—even Bulldozer.

After a second fifteen-minute break, they'd reached another section of the training center.

What Greyson walked into was a disaster area. Overturned cars, debris, and shattered street pavement.

"A replica of a crisis," Erika explained. "Navigate to the other end looking for any survivors."

"Aaaaaand. GO," Reverb barked.

Greyson ran into the chaos, scanning for any survivors amid the rubble. Digging through chunks of concrete wasn't easy without his gravity-based powers, so he struggled.

Art found his first survivor as if he were a bloodhound, behind an overturned four-by-four truck, a female dummy and a teenage boy dummy. Tossing the female over one shoulder, Art reached for the boy.

Greyson saw the flash of steel in the boy "mannequin's" hand. He snapped up his fist and fired. The dazzling blast smacked the boy's face, tumbling him away from Art.

The other super dropped the female mannequin, bone-white. "Whoa!"

Art got in his face barking obscenities. The tryouts screeched to a halt.

Greyson remained calm until the Natural Born Thrillers approached with varied reactions.

"Why did you shoot that innocent?" Reverb asked.

Greyson gave a knowing smile and punted the mannequin onto its back. There was charred metallic skull where the face once was...and a pistol. "The teenager was armed."

Art's eyes went wide.

Erika beamed. "Huh."

"Very observant," Reverb marveled.

Bulldozer scowled. "Hmmph."

An hour later, Greyson found his sweaty self in the rusted-out foyer with Art. Neither spoke while the Thrillers remained inside the training center, deliberating.

Greyson sat cross-legged, catching his wind, confident. "May the best man win," he told his pacing rival.

Art stared through unfriendly eyes. "The better man will win." He resumed pacing.

Greyson chuckled and waited.

The Thrillers finally emerged, solemn and unreadable. Greyson rose, suddenly uncertain.

"Gentlemen." Erika stepped forward, arms spread benevolently. "Thank you both for your time today."

Greyson stood beside Art, who stared ahead with smirking arrogance.

"Art." Erika beckoned him with her hand. "Step forward."

Greyson deflated. He forced himself to stay pokerfaced, already mulling a Plan B.

Art swaggered forward, full of confidence.

Erika's smile was plastic as she continued. "You performed very well." Her gaze shifted to Greyson. "But we're going with Levi."

Greyson swiveled his head. *I won?* His thoughts ground to a halt, euphoria spreading through his body. "I won," he murmured.

Art looked from Greyson to Erika and back, the reality of not being selected not registering full. "Him?" His tone and demeanor went from dumbfounded to boiling in a flash. "*Him?*" He flushed angrily at Bulldozer. "You told me this was locked!"

Greyson blinked. That motherfucker.

Bulldozer's team whirled on him.

"You *what?*" Erika's voice was a sharp slap bouncing off the walls.

Art glared at the Natural Born Thrillers in disgust. "To think I wasted my time trying out for this pathetic team instead of the one in San Miguel." He stormed off in a huff, pushing the door open and vanishing around the corner.

"Congratulations, Levi." Erika shook Greyson's hand with a smile that didn't reach her eyes.

"Thanks," he said, happier than he expected.

Erika walked toward the training room, and her smile dropped. "Dozer. We need to talk. Now."

The larger man rolled his eyes and trailed her. As soon as the door closed, muted bellowing erupted.

"That's normal," Brightburn dismissed lazily. "Welcome!"

Greyson smirked, filing that factoid away. "I appreciate this opportunity to join the Thrillers."

His three "teammates" swarmed around him.

"You'll start as an apprentice for three months," Reverb declared with a toothy smile.

"Depending on your performance," Shattershot went on. "Then we'll decide whether we bring you on with Seneca International's sign-off or not."

Greyson nodded. So he had three months to destroy the Thrillers from within. "Sounds good."

More muted shouting behind the training center walls. Brightburn maintained her smiles. "We'll be in touch with more details, moving into the compound, all the blah blah blah."

After farewells and more congrats, Greyson headed back to his condo in the Palisades.

Once at home, he plopped onto the couch, laughing hysterically. His crazy scheme had worked.

He was about to exclaim, until a shift in the air near the kitchen caught his eye. Someone wearing a cloaked outfit—inside his condo.

Greyson smiled. "Hey."

The air shivered as the cloak dropped, revealing Connie in a figure-hugging catsuit. "Hi." She sashayed over and crashed beside him. "Well?"

Greyson grabbed his wife's face, planted a huge kiss, then pulled away. "I'm in."

Connie pumped both fists. "Yay!"

"Just waiting for details and my start date." He smiled even wider and drew Connie into another kiss. Besides Art Strong's unexpected arrival, Paxton-Brandt had provided full intel on the tryout thanks to their Seneca moles. He leaned back as a question popped up to Connie's audible dismay. "What about you?"

Connie's mischievous grin set his heart racing. "The command center was too secure. So I placed hidden cameras in the bedrooms and common room." Infiltrating the Thrillers' base had been Connie's mission, which she'd completed.

Greyson looked her up and down in pure delight. "You're swell, Constance."

Connie burst out laughing. "You cornball."

Greyson chortled. "Now the real game begins." He dragged Connie on top of him to start celebrating.

CHAPTER 15

Hugo braked behind a smeared expanse of colors and fast-moving rides. Morro Bay's annual Fall Carnival by the Sea was in full swing. Twelve minutes past seven was later than he'd told his friends. That couldn't have been helped. Afternoon patrol ran long due to stopping a turf fight between the superpowered Wonder Boyz and Mala Tierra Gang.

Plus, stopping by Michelman's penthouse and winery had come up empty. The doctor and Spencer were gone. That wouldn't have worried Hugo if Michelman were answering his calls.

But those worries, like many others, had to wait.

"It's carnival time," Hugo muttered.

At the end of September, the fall carnival took over Morro Bay for three weeks of music concerts, carnival rides, and cheesy local activities.

Dressed in jeans, a black V-neck t-shirt, and red sneakers, Hugo adjusted his white beanie and strode out from his hiding place. Squeals, chatter, the whines of ride motors and EDM performances flooded Hugo's ears. Garish neon lights from lofty carousel-like rides, Ferris wheels, and rows of vendor stands spread before Hugo's eyes. Countless Paso High students were milling about. Competing aromas of deep-fried foods like hotdogs, burgers, and pretzels collided with the stink of too many human odors. But Hugo managed the sensory onslaught with a smile.

Tonight was about enjoying Jordana, his friends, and cheesy carnival fun. Hugo slipped into a back entrance and weaved through the crowds wandering the carnival grounds. He focused his superhearing, quickly locking on to Jordana's and Simon's voices. They'd just gotten off Coronado's Revenge, a freefall ride. After a few minutes of searching, Hugo spied Raphael's head above the swirls of humanity.

The usual suspects had gathered. Jordana was in the center, laughing at someone's joke. Her curves were on full display in a cropped suspenders top with matching black jeans, long curly hair in a J.Lo-style half ponytail. Briseis was gabbing with her, happy and healthy. Her auburn hair was up in a lazy half-knot, the rest of it framing her bewitching face perfectly. Brie's attire, a long cardigan over a t-shirt and hip-hugging capris, fit her slender frame well.

Hugo gazed at her and Jodie, happy to see these BFFs reunited. Simon shared his cotton candy with Grace. Groban, Wale, and JT were arguing over something dance-related. Raphael was a big boulder, eyes only for his girlfriend, Karlee. The strawberry-blonde Stanleys were sniping at each other while glaring at Brent Longwell. The buzzcut blond had deigned to join the group, but with one of his lumbering basketball bros.

My real-world people, Hugo mused. This group and his family kept him grounded.

Hugo almost advanced, only to freeze. His friends didn't seem to miss him, carrying on with relish.

Hugo stood paralyzed, the potential abandonment almost too painful to bear. Eventually, the constant lateness and absences would make them lose patience.

Brie shifted her stare a fraction, and her pale-green eyes brightened. She eagerly poked Jodie and pointed. The shorter girl went from annoyed to happily squealing.

Now the whole group saw Hugo, breaking out into a chorus of animated greetings.

Confidence restored, Hugo strode to them. "Hey, crew!"

He didn't have to walk far as his friends cut the distance between them. Jordana skipped over, long curls bouncing and gold hoop earrings jangling.

"Sorry," Hugo murmured, cheeks burning after kissing Jordana. "Things ran late."

Brie strutted over, smiling her face off, and wrapped her arms around his neck. Hugo embraced her with his free arm. Her pleased sigh quashed his stubborn worries. When Jodie and Brie drew away, the rest of his friends greeted him with side-hugs and high-fives. Even Grace seemed friendlier, thanks to Simon and cotton candy, no doubt.

"Broseephus!" Brent embraced Hugo fiercely. The lanky ballplayer was in great shape.

"Hey, Brent." Hugo pulled back, admiring Brent's attire. The blue t-shirt showed Aegis, hands on hips staring ahead, standing on the words "Beast Slayer." Annie and Johnny made that shirt after the Tiamat battle. This one, and the "Half-Man, Half-Amazing, All Hero" shirt should sell as well as the prior three.

"New Aegis shirt?" Hugo remarked with practiced innocence.

Brent's eyes crinkled from a huge grin. He remained Aegis's biggest fan. "I bought five."

Hugo chuckled. "I believe you." He enjoyed this Brent; loyal, nerdy in his obsessions, kind, and humble. But that version rarely appeared after basketball success last year had gotten to his head. Now Brent usually hung with other popular jocks, bragging about himself to pretty girls. Hugo prayed this was just a phase. "Which ride do we wanna hit up?" he asked.

He held Jodie's hand while wandering through the carnival with his friends, hopping on popular rides where the wait lines weren't long. The rollercoaster, Twist and Shout, whirled up and down like a snake on speed. While Jodie, Brie, Grace, Simon, and others screamed their lungs out, Hugo was bored. Flying had ruined this ride for him, so he took pleasure in his friends' over-the-top terror.

Hugo needed this real-world time, during which he tried speaking with Grace. But each time, she kept getting pulled into other discussions. Or was she avoiding him? Weird.

"Aren't you cold, Bogie?" Brie asked later, gesturing at his t-shirt. The skies had darkened, and the temperature dropped. Everyone else, Jodie included, had some jacket or extra layering.

Hugo scoffed. "I don't get *cold*, Brie." His durability protected him against temperature extremes.

Simon guffawed. Grace almost smiled. His other friends reacted in amusement to his brashness.

Brie flinched melodramatically. "I don't get cold, Brie," she mimicked, strutting about like someone with brawny arms. "I'm Hugo Fricking Malalou with muscles on top of muscles."

Grace outright laughed, as did everyone else. Jodie was doubled over, clutching her sides.

Hugo smiled, taking no offense. "You've been sitting on that one awhile, huh? Try this." He raised a finger to quell the laughter. "OMGeezies!" he pronounced, copycatting Briseis's cadence just short of full imitation. "I will NOT eat at this bargain basement restaurant! All their food looks like *throw-up*."

There was a shocked hush, followed by a crescendo of laughter, drawing stares.

Hugo smirked, openly pleased. But he watched Brie with caution, knowing how she hated ridicule.

"Okay, okay." Brie raised both hands, surprisingly amused. "That was accurate."

Jordana collapsed against Hugo, almost in tears.

"Why are you laughing?" He then mimicked her Bronx drawl. "Ya acting corny as fuck."

That wiped the smile off Jodie's face. Everyone else laughed harder.

"I don't talk like that!" she protested.

"You do actually!" Grace added between laughs.

"Jennifuh would agree," Hugo continued with his Jodie cadence, bobbing his head sassily like her. "Don't mess with me. I'm from the Bronx."

That last part killed his friends, already barely breathing.

"I'm dead!" Raphael gasped, "and that impression is my murderer!"

Brie hugged herself, howling. "I'm shooketh!"

Jordana looked ready to stab Hugo with her eyes.

"I love you, girl!" Hugo exclaimed in his normal voice, going for a hug. "Come gimme that brown sugar."

Jordana wasn't having it, backpedaling. "You're an ass." But she quickly caved, her mouth finding Hugo's, to their friends' loud distaste.

"Another twelve-second kiss," Groban announced.

Hugo's lust withered. Jodie scowled. "You *counted?*"

"Yes, I counted," Groban admitted, beaming. "Which makes me a perv."

Everyone's mockery was just ball-busting. Brie's disgusted eyeroll wasn't.

That surprised Hugo. *Do Jodie and me still bother her?* He almost said something but decided against it as the group roved through the park. Not scanning for trouble with his hypersenses was harder than expected. Hugo focused on the present and Jordana's oddly stiff carriage.

Then he felt someone watching. He looked up, spotting a bald and mahogany-skinned boy, lanky like a scarecrow. He stood at a burger stand on the other side of the vendor strip, eyes glittering with hate.

Hugo didn't know this boy from Adam or what his problem was. Meanwhile, Jordana clung to him, cowering almost as if he were a shield.

From this boy? The realization was a gut punch to Hugo. Oh. He then caught the tail end of an argument. "Why are you asking me where she is?" Simon protested.

"You, Hugo, and J-Tom are the three amigos," Raphael added, popping a potato chip in his mouth.

Hugo welcomed the distraction. "I think she's meeting a friend tonight."

Raphael jabbed a finger. "Told ya he knew."

"Here's a question?" Groban ruffled his fluffy hair. "Where's Spencer Michelman?"

All smiles momentarily died. Jordana and Brie prickled.

Hugo nearly stumbled. Groban hadn't been the first to ask about Spencer. Awkward tension settled over the group, since her betrayal of Brie was common knowledge.

"Boy," Jodie scolded Groban, frightening him again. "Why'd you kill the mood?"

"She's been MIA since junior year started," Brent chimed in, apprehensive.

"I heard she's at some private school in Switzerland," Karin Stanley offered.

"I'm not missing that toxic bitch," Brie snarled, her face dark with loathing.

Many theories raged among the group. Hugo didn't engage, nor did he care to, but a glaring question remained. "Why do you care about Spencer, Groban?"

"He likes her!" Wale's announcement earned him a smack from Groban.

Hugo's eyes bulged. "On purpose?"

"I'm sorry," Brie apologized. That drew bundles of laughter.

Groban absorbed everyone's confused reaction in stride. "If I had the chance," he remarked, "I'd give Spencer the most mediocre three minutes of her life."

Hugo's stomach roiled. Jordana gagged. Many others laughed.

"One hundred eighty seconds? Of the sex?" Raphael gasped in mock amazement. "You stud!"

Groban shrugged. "What can I say? I'm a machine."

"Spencer's a soulless pit viper, Groban," Simon scolded.

"Aww." Brie made a pouting face. "Still butthurt she tricked you into dating Lia, Simon?"

"Still drooling over Hugo, Easy Breezy?" he flung back.

Brie paled and turned away.

Hugo flinched in shock. "Dude..." Before he could fully respond, everyone else dogpiled Simon. Using "Easy Breezy" had crossed the line, even for Grace.

Hugo whistled, silencing everyone. "Simon," he snapped. "Dick move."

"She started it!" Simon pointed at Brie like she was diseased. To him, she probably was.

"And I'm ending it." Hugo glowered at a shell-shocked Brie. "Stop provoking him." He gestured them forward. "You two? Apologize. Not a request."

The duo barely made eye contact but issued grudging apologies. Brie said little afterward, even as Jordana consoled her. The group continued wandering the park with less gusto. And Groban seemed to have misplaced another piece of food, this time a freshly purchased hotdog.

After another half an hour, the constant sensory overload was giving Hugo a headache. Then they reached the Tipsy Turvy merry-go-round, which Hugo was curious to try.

"We did that ride twice," Wale remarked.

"That's what happens when you're late," Grace taunted.

Hugo gave her a look, opening his mouth to reply.

"I'll go with you," Brie offered, almost pleading to escape.

"Sure," Hugo decided. Everyone else agreed that they'd head out after he and Brie rode Tipsy Turvy.

"Thank you," Jodie gushed as the group parted always, kissing Hugo's lips. "We need to talk tonight."

Her odd expression needled Hugo's heart. "We need to talk" was never good when coming from a girl. *Is she dumping me?* "Sounds cryptic," he quipped.

Jordana didn't respond, turning to Brie. "Drop you off at my place first, okay?" She stroked Brie's cheek.

"Sleepover?" Hugo asked once he and Brie went off alone.

She looked up, her eyes soul-meltingly gorgeous. The pain from Simon's remark lingered there. "I'm staying with Jodie until my dad returns from his business trip."

Hugo perked up, adjusting his beanie. "You two are talking?" After Brie's dad's hostile reaction to her brother coming out, their relationship had been nonexistent. "That's great, right?"

Brie hugged herself tighter. "Mumu went after my weight two days ago. Then her face ran into my fist."

"Holy shit," Hugo exclaimed, shocked yet elated.

Brie's sad little smile was heartbreaking. "Ramses is pissed that I'm living with Dad. But I can't live with Mumu...for her own safety." Her laugh was harsh and humorless. "My life's a crazy-ass mess."

"Or a Taylor Swift album," Hugo snarked.

Brie's mood improved when they got on Tipsy Turvy, whipping around in jagged circles at crazy speeds. Hugo soaked in the flood of sounds and sights like a dog peeking out a car window. Brie shrieked in delight, hands up in the air, auburn locks rippling back in waves.

Hugo and Brie stepped off the ride leaning on each other and giggling, high off adrenaline.

Then they nearly ran into Baz Martinez.

The varsity basketballer looked dapper and wiry in jeans with a long-sleeved tee, dark hair combed back. His handsome face emptied as he saw Hugo and Brie together.

Fresh odium boiled inside Hugo, followed by surprise at his rival holding hands with one of Brie's former friends. Natalie Rodriguez, curvy and gorgeous with flowing caramel locks, offered an awkward smile.

Brie nodded stiffly at her ex-boyfriend and ex-friend before scurrying past them.

Hugo's eyes locked with Baz until the latter passed, then he caught up with Brie in three strides.

"When did *that* happen?" Hugo murmured once they were farther away, roaming through mazes of unsavory-smelling food vendors. He felt Baz's and Natalie's eyes on his back.

Brie stared off, blank-faced. "Mid-summer." The strength went out of her voice. "Nat asked for my blessing before things got serious."

Hugo cringed. Neither Jodie nor Spencer had asked permission to date him. "You okay with that?"

Brie raised her shoulders, then let them drop. "Why be the bitter bitch keeping happy couples apart?"

Hugo wasn't expecting such maturity. "Speaking of..." That brought him to another topic as they emerged from the main rows of vendor stands. "What was that bitter beer face back there?"

Brie reddened. "C'mon..." Her laughter sounded forced and shaky. "You and Jordana put on a show. I've never seen her this hooked."

Hearing that, Hugo felt like floating. He shrugged with a cocky smirk. "Well..."

Brie smacked his arm, disgusted. "Oh. My. God!"

"Your compliment." Hugo deflected her deflection. "And you're avoiding."

Brie's eyes tightened. "It's just hard sometimes seeing you with Jodie, knowing that *should've* been me."

Surprise shook Hugo to his core. "OH." The tension grew thick and awkward real quick.

Brie hastily brushed off his worry. "I'm a big girl and I'm processing." Her voice gained strength. "Most days are easier. Others aren't...like today."

"Jodie means the world to me," Hugo stated. But the feeling might not be mutual anymore...

Brie's eyes flashed. "Then *why* did you fuck Spencer?" She blocked his path. "Was it hate sex?"

Hugo fought every instinct to superspeed away from this conversation. They'd discussed many issues at length since rekindling their friendship. Except Spencer Michelman.

"When did you find out?" he asked quietly.

Brie glared a hole into him. "Last November, Spence was bragging about her latest boytoy." She stepped aside and resumed walking. "Never revealed his name, which isn't like her." She shook her head. "A few weeks later, I see you and Spence pass each other at school. She's gazing at you and *blushing*."

The memory visibly curdled Brie's soul. "Couldn't believe it, but clearly something had changed."

Hugo gulped, recalling many times he and Spencer had done that. "Not even Simon knew then."

That rocked Brie back on her heels. "Wow."

Tension reached up to Hugo's neck. He looked her over, not sure where this discussion would lead beside hurt for them both. "You really wanna discuss this?"

Pain spasmed across Brie's face. "I thought Spence would be a friend for life. So yeah."

Hugo closed his eyes and steeled his resolve. "At Fall Fling, seeing me dance aroused her, I guess."

Brie snorted. "Totally understandable."

The light moment was fleeting. Hugo gave a summary of the Spencer relationship, the November to mid-December timeline, then the February to summer stretch. "She'd be so giving sometimes," Hugo murmured. "The day before my birthday in December, we skipped class and did breakfast. Then we went to San Simeon and watched the elephant seals." The ghost of a smile traced his lips. "Then she took me to El Marquez for lunch and shopping. Paid for everything." Hugo discussed Mr. Butterworth, the assistant basketball coach who'd been convinced that he'd attacked Baz, DeDamien, and TJ. Without Hugo's knowledge, Spencer had paid Kendall Caruso to honeytrap Butterworth. When the coach had exchanged texts with Kendall, despite knowing her age, Spencer had informed Principal Walker. "I never told her about Fall Fling," he finished as Brie's eyes widened. "One day she said what she'd done and that Butterworth wasn't my problem anymore."

Meanwhile, Hugo searched the carnival with his senses for their friends to escape this conversation.

"I thought there was good in her," Hugo admitted frankly. Some part of him still did. "But she kept trying to prove me wrong. And I'd keep trying to prove her wrong." That secret tug of war had continued for months. Like Spencer pushing Lia Kim into dating Simon while having then-junior Evan Parker court Grace. But Hugo had always found ways to undo her schemes. "It was foreplay for us in plain sight."

Brie's face was a cocktail of emotions, amazement and rage being most prominent. "I didn't know."

Hugo blinked back tears, old wounds reopening. "Dating her wasn't revenge on you."

"You told me." Brie looked dazed. They passed the long line of another neon-colored rollercoaster. "Just felt like my friends were just…sexual Pokémon to you. You gotta catch 'em all."

Hugo choked back bile. "Not even. But…thinking back, my relationship with Spencer was fucked up."

"Do Jodie or Jenny know?"

Hugo glanced down at Brie, nodding. "Yes." Correction, J-Tom knew everything. Jodie didn't know about him and Spencer being supers. If Brie started hating Hugo again after this, he didn't blame her.

Instead, she blew out a sigh, like a huge weight had lifted. "We do get into the dark and twisty a lot."

Both chuckled, but neither could meet the other's gaze for long.

Fortunately, Hugo's hearing picked up Brent and Raphael a quarter mile ahead arguing over who'd win a Titan vs Aegis fight. "Where did the others say to meet them?" he asked, playing dumb.

Brie pulled out her cell. "Let me text Jodie—"

Hugo froze, hearing something flying at them from behind. *Incoming attack,* he deduced.

On instinct, he shoved Brie as gently as possible. She yelped while stumbling sideways.

Everything that followed went too fast to process.

A full-speed freight train slammed into Hugo's kidneys. Agony scorched up his spine.

A pair of arms seized Hugo's neck and waist from behind, then rocketed upward.

Briseis cried out in wordless terror. Distance and winds swiftly swallowed the sound. The carnival shrank swiftly beneath Hugo's dangling feet.

And he was helpless to break free.

CHAPTER 16

Hugo gagged, oxygen becoming an issue. Vise-like arms around his ribcage and throat tightened the more he struggled. As he and his captor burst through upper cloud layers, a forest of stars twinkled before Hugo. Forcing himself to calm down, he assessed his situation.

They were far above San Miguel, heading farther inland. Hugo prayed that Brie hadn't been injured by whoever grabbed him. This motherfucker was strong, maybe stronger than Hugo.

And they know who I am. The thought chilled him more than the winds buffeting his face.

This was Paxton-Brandt. They were probably tailing Hugo the other day.

Now he had to figure out an escape. *As soon as I'm free, they'll fly away.*

"Enough of this." Clutching the arm around his waist, Hugo accelerated at a downward angle.

His captor, briefly caught off-guard, tried yanking back in the opposite direction. Hugo choked but kept barreling ahead. The city lights spread out more the further east they headed, shadowy ground rushing up quickly. Hugo somersaulted forward so his captor took the brunt. *This is gonna hurt.*

The bone-shivering force of their crash-landing rippled out for miles in all directions.

Hugo lay gasping for air, free from his kidnapper. He scrambled away to get distance. From what his night vision revealed, they'd landed in the rugged edges of Eastern San Luis Obispo County. Not heavily populated, thankfully. San Miguel's city lights formed a bright line on the distant horizon.

Hugo sprang up, fists cocked to fight. "Okay…" He stopped, stared, and pointed. "The HELL?"

His attacker stood yards away, wide-legged stance, fists on hips, same height and size, same purple-and-black Aegis costume. Hugo's mouth fell open.

The attacker was Aegis. Except, Hugo was Aegis. His brain nearly broke. "Who are you?" he demanded.

Fake Aegis said nothing, eyes glowing in silent menace. A quick listen found heartbeat and breaths.

A clone? Pissed off, Hugo charged headlong. Fake Aegis crouched to brace himself.

The collision cracked across the landscape. Soon they were rolling around, hitting each other with bone-shaking blows.

Hugo drilled the impostor with a flurry of superspeed punches. But Fake Aegis retaliated brutally, giving back as good as he got, deftly countering many of Hugo's attacks. The two fought back and forth for a while, smashing surrounding rock formations to dust.

This impostor knows my moves, Hugo fumed before Fake Aegis dropkicked his chest.

Painful weird flashes crackled down his sternum as he tumbled across the ground. Hugo lay still, head ringing, ribs aching, and nose bloodied. Fake Aegis hovered a few feet above but did not press his advantage. This fight could go on forever if Hugo didn't find an opening.

"Bye bye!" He stood, inhaled, and screamed.

The air quivered, potent soundwaves bashing Fake Aegis out of the air.

Hugo marched forward, upping the intensity to pin Fake Aegis against a nearby rocky wall. Cracks spidered along the impostor's costume.

Hugo cut off his scream, then backpedaled in alarm.

The imposter struggled upright with robotic jerks. Large chunks of his face, torso, and legs were stripped off, revealing sparking bronzed cybernetics.

"Holy shit!" Hugo couldn't decide between being flattered or frightened that someone had built an Aegis robot.

The robot, clenching broken fake teeth, advanced furiously.

Before Hugo could consider his next move, the sound of approaching jet thrusters caught his ear. He looked up.

Twin yellow energy beams floodlit the night, slicing down through Fake Aegis's chest and legs. The android collapsed in smoking pieces before Hugo's eyes. Still it tried crawling for him—until half a dozen tiny missiles needled his body, then detonated.

Hugo shielded his eyes from the fiery plume. When the flash subsided, another android in smooth, silvery armor with angular blue lines landed on the smoldering debris. Its smooth face had a line for a mouth, narrow and slanted eyes pulsing deep blue.

Goddammit, Hugo seethed. Another potential foe. "And you are?!"

"Relax, Bogie!" the android assured in a digitized yet feminine tenor. "It's me!" The android's head split open and slid into its shoulders like liquid metal.

It took a few seconds of Hugo staring for his brain to recognize the cute and freckled face grinning at him. "J-Tom? Your new suit…it's amazing!"

This wasn't the armor that J-Tom had worn to Ramon's house. The finish and design were gorgeous, like Dynamo's suits.

J-Tom smiled broadly. "Right?" She gave a nimble twirl as if merely wearing another layer of clothing. "Ramon and I worked in his lab for hours, vibing like we shared a brain. It was in-SANE!" She couldn't stop smiling. "This suit had so much cool shit, and it's just a prototype, so I'm going back tomorrow to Ramon's to upgrade. And now I'm rambling!"

Her enthusiasm coaxed a laugh out of Hugo. *Ray-Ray's still a sucker for pretty girls.* He then realized they both were unmasked. "Put your helmet on!" he hissed.

J-Tom blushed. Her helmet quickly slid back over her head. "Sorry!" she apologized, eyes burning blue.

Hugo scanned his surroundings, sensing nobody else for miles. Good. "Wait. How'd you find me?"

"Simon texted me. Then I tracked your cell." J-Tom stepped away from Fake Aegis's smoking remains. "What happened?"

Hugo recapped the ambush, starting with the Morro Bay Carnival attack.

J-Tom gasped in surprise. "Did anyone see the robot grab you?"

Hugo gulped. "God, I hope not." That would cause problems for his alter ego. "Was busy getting air-tackled." Hugo then considered his friends at the carnival, who must've been freaking out. "Does that armor have telescopic zoom?"

J-Tom scoffed. "Does Jodie have big boobs?"

"So yes?" Hugo replied. "I need you to scan the carnival from above." He looked at the Fake Aegis debris. Half of the head appeared intact. "Make sure Brie, Jodie, and the others are okay. I don't know if there are more Aegis-bots. Stay high and out of sight."

J-Tom nodded her smooth, silvery head. "Got it. What else?"

"Call and tell Simon I'm okay." Hugo squatted over the android, his mind spinning. "But have him tell you what happened to me out loud so it seems like you're just finding out." Meanwhile, Hugo needed a cover story.

"Oooh, smart," J-Tom marveled. "What about you?"

Hugo pulled out his cellphone, somehow undamaged. "I'm finding out where it came from."

After wishing each other luck, J-Tom launched into the skies. The burn of her jet boots left trails in her wake.

Hugo texted Ramon, then gathered up as much of Fake Aegis as he could carry.

The former hero waited in his wheelchair at his compound's courtyard when Hugo arrived.

"Sorry to bother you twice today."

Ramon waved off the concern. "You saved me from a boring family dinner. By the way, J-Tom is awesome! She's got potential." Ramon paused, staring at Hugo and his cargo. "What happened?!"

Hugo smiled grimly. "This attacked me." He motioned with the charred cybernetics in his arms. "In public. I need to know what this is and who sent it."

Ramon hastily gestured him forward. Once inside Ramon's lab, Hugo placed the android parts on a table slab. Under the lab's potent lights, he gave himself a thorough onceover. His shirt was in tatters, jeans torn, and a shoe was missing. Plus, his beanie had gone missing. The other guy looked worse.

He then noticed Ramon staring at the android parts in clear recognition. "This is Vulcan's handiwork."

Hugo staggered backward. "Your Vanguard teammate Vulcan?" From what he'd heard, the Greek hero had semi-retired after Vanguard's demise, focusing his talents on medical and green energy tech. *And android versions of me.* "Why?"

Ramon eyed him as if the question was idiotic. "You kicked Vulcan's ass on live TV." He typed a string of code into a workstation keyboard. "He wanted a practice android in case you two locked horns again. He asked for my help, but I declined."

Then Paxton-Brandt wasn't the culprit. Hugo felt immense relief. "When?"

"A few months ago."

"Months…" Hugo choked back anger. "Now who's keeping secrets?"

"I told Lady Liberty," Ramon threw back. "She ordered Vulcan to mothball this project."

"Vulcan disobeyed her?"

Ramon shook his head. "He followed her orders. But this android was stolen a few days ago."

Hugo's breath caught. So Paxton-Brandt could still be the culprit? "That must have been the person following me. Do you know who stole this?" He gestured at the remains.

"No clue," Ramon said. "Security footage in Vulcan's lab revealed it there one moment, then gone the next. No fingerprints or DNA traces."

Hugo swore under his breath as his cellphone buzzed from incoming texts.

Simon: DOOD!! Spoke with J-Tom.

ME: I'm okay. Getting some answers. How's Brie?

Simon: Worried out of her mind about you. Jodie called the police.

ME: Where are you guys?

Simon: Heading to your place. J-Tom told your mom too.

ME: Thanks, uso. I'll be home soon.

Hugo stashed his phone in his pocket and found Ramon watching him. "Can you do your analyzing ninjutsu to find the thief?" he requested. "Whoever they are knows my secret."

Ramon nodded. "On it."

"Thanks." Hugo shook hands with Ramon. "Gotta calm the masses at home."

Once in the courtyard, Hugo took off toward Paso Robles. And without a cover story.

CHAPTER 17

"The cops?" Hugo exclaimed, floating miles over his neighborhood. The homes resembled small dark squares delineated by glowing yellow. A police car sat outside his home, which brimmed with chatter. Most of his friends from the carnival were inside.

The most recognizable voices were Briseis and Jordana, both barely holding back tears. Hearing their sorrow struck Hugo harder than he'd expected.

Better get down there. He landed in a crouch five houses away. Making sure no one saw, he pulled off his remaining shoe and supersped through shrubbery and shadows behind the row of houses. Pale lights spilled from the kitchen windows onto the backyard. Hugo hopped his own fence and peered inside.

Simon leaned against the refrigerator while AJ sat on the kitchen counter in dog-covered pajamas. The mood was dour. The door to the living room was closed.

"You're sure he's okay?" AJ whispered.

Simon nodded. "J-Tom saw him half an hour ago, and he texted me."

Hugo whipped out his cellphone, speed-texting Simon.

ME: Backyard.

Simon started at his cellphone buzzing. He checked it, gaped, and shoved the device in AJ's face. Both scrambled for the backdoor. AJ slowly opened it, wincing at the squeaky hinges, then dashed outside with Simon. "UCE!" He hugged Hugo.

"I know, I know," Hugo sighed after side-hugging Simon. "I'll explain later." Tonight's adrenaline was wearing off. But thorny fears began jutting through. He still had no clue who'd stolen the Aegis-bot and knew his secret. Hugo gestured at the closed kitchen door. "I heard lots of people in there."

Simon snorted as the three boys headed back indoors. "The regular group, a cop, and your mom. We headed back here after the drama. Things got crazy after you were nabbed."

Hugo gulped. There had to be like fourteen-plus people in the living room. Jesus. "I better go say hi."

AJ slid open the kitchen door, revealing a jam-packed living room. Brent, Raphael, Wale, Groban, Marin, and Karin gathered around the TV watching news of some building collapse in Shenandoah.

To Hugo's surprise, J-Tom sat in regular clothes at the bottom of the stairwell with an arm around a dumbfounded Grace. How had J-Tom shed her armor and gotten here so fast?

But he zoned in on the couch where Mom and Jordana sat consoling Briseis.

Her dark-auburn hair was disheveled. She sobbed while answering the uniformed officer standing before her. Brie was clutching something with a death grip. Everyone but the cop seemed shellshocked.

Heads turned at the kitchen door opened, followed by gasps.

AJ and Simon popped out from behind Hugo.

"Look who we found," his brother said, pointing.

"Hello!" Hugo spread his arms. "Why so serious?"

The living room erupted in relief, joy, and other emotions.

"Bogota!" Mom beelined for him, with Jodie right behind her.

Brent and Raphael followed eagerly. "What happened?" the larger boy demanded.

"Are you okay?" the Stanleys asked in unison.

"Lord!" Grace caressed Hugo's face after she and J-Tom approached. "Your *clothes!*"

Jordana embraced Hugo, showering him with kisses. "You're okay! Thank God!"

Hugo and J-Tom exchanged a charged glance. There was plenty to discuss later.

Everyone's affections and questions crashed together, making it hard for Hugo to answer anyone. An overwhelming experience. The cop, leanly built with combed back brown hair, smiled at the scene.

Amid the chaos, Hugo locked eyes with Brie across the room. She slowly rose off the couch, joy on her tear-stained face. She almost approached and then froze, clutching his beanie even tighter.

133

In that moment, Hugo's concern centered on her. "HEY," he barked, silencing everyone. "You alright?"

Brie sniffled and nodded.

Hugo wasn't convinced. "You sure?"

"Yeah." Brie's voice trembled. Her eyes sparkled with tears.

"I examined her," Mom reassured. "No injuries."

"Glad you're not dead," Brie said, smiling through her sorrow.

The tension in his shoulders dissolved. "Same here, kid." That drew nervous laughter around the room.

He beckoned everyone onward. "Continue." His friends resumed bombarding him with affection.

"Good evening, Hugo," the police officer greeted cordially after Hugo reached the couch. "Officer Simmons. If you can provide a statement on what happened, we can get to the bottom of this."

Hugo inhaled deeply for show, starting the cover story he'd crafted on the way home. Meanwhile, Brie quietly shouldered her way into the kitchen. Hugo caught J-Tom's eye and nodded in that direction.

She nodded back and strode after Brie.

Jodie held Hugo's hand while he told a version of what happened. Only Brie's sobs from the kitchen could be heard after Mom muted the TV, which showed news of tornadoes ravaging southern Montana.

Hugo told Simmons that his attacker had been a robot—true. He also stated they'd landed near San Raphael Wilderness—false. His fight against the Aegis-bot had been near Machesna Mountain. But his slightly quivering voice drew unanimous sympathy. Jordana sidled up closer. The lies and calculated façade felt gross. But Hugo needed this to protect his family, his friends, and himself.

"Not sure why it attacked." Hugo gave a limp shrug. "Maybe it malfunctioned?"

Simmons narrowed his blue eyes. "How did you know it was a robot? And how did you escape?"

Hugo put on an innocent smile. "Aegis was patrolling nearby. He saved my ass."

His friends approved loudly. Simon, AJ, and Mom looked confused. Hugo ignored them.

"Aegis saved you too?" Brent gushed, raising a fist. "Ring that bell, broheim!"

Hugo cough-laughed and obliged as another worry surfaced. *Did Briseis see the Aegis-bot?* That could create huge problems. "Did anyone see what grabbed me?" he asked the room.

Simon shook his head, arm around Grace. "Brie said she only saw a blur."

The cop nodded. "That's what other bystanders told officers canvassing the carnival."

Simmons then wrapped things up, seemingly buying his story.

"We'll call if any more questions arise." He clapped Hugo's shoulder. "Be careful out there, son." Once Simmons left, most of Hugo's friends departed since it was past eleven at night.

Simon had to kick his girlfriend out. "We'll talk tomorrow. I'm crashing here to protect Bogie."

A smirk pulled at Hugo's mouth. "I feel safer already."

Grace marched up, no anger or bitterness in her almond-shaped eyes. "Stop trying to get killed."

Hugo laughed. "At least I wasn't trying to be a hero."

Grace shook her head in commiserating fashion. "Dork." Receiving her fierce embraces again felt wonderful. When she left, only Jordana, Brie, Simon, and J-Tom remained.

"I'm gonna check on Briseis," Hugo announced, untangling from Jodie. This sudden clinginess kind of irked him after what had happened tonight. But Hugo wouldn't address this now.

He found J-Tom cradling Brie's anguish on the other end of the kitchen island, murmuring comfort. They'd been friends since fifth grade, longer than Brie and Jordana. As soon as J-Tom saw Hugo, she rounded the island toward him. Brie turned away, mortified.

J-Tom caressed Hugo's cheek before leaving, closing the door behind her.

"Hey, Breezy," Hugo greeted gently.

Brie couldn't face him, brushing away tears. "Hi…" Her face crumpled beautifully when she broke down. This girl couldn't ugly cry even if she tried.

"Hey, hey." Hugo advanced and drew her into his arms. "I'm okay, despite how I look." His shirt and jeans were ruined. His white beanie lay on the kitchen island.

Brie stepped back to inspect him, still in his arms. Fat shiny tears rolled down her high cheekbones. "How are you so chill right now?" she demanded, her voice rough.

Hugo pursed his lips, doing some quick thinking. "We live in times where Godzilla monsters exist."

The passion in Brie's green eyes drilled straight through his brain. "If you'd died." Her voice got all low and husky and intense. "That would literally *kill* me."

The kitchen temperature seemed to skyrocket, staggering Hugo. *Whoooa.*

Brie, grasping the import of her words, looked ready to die from embarrassment.

Hugo recovered first, placing a finger on her lips before she could recant. "I'm not going anywhere," he assured quietly. "I promise." He pulled Brie into another embrace. Her ragged breaths settled as she sank on into his arms. He relished the proximity and her warmth—until the kitchen door slid open.

He froze, recognizing Jordana's scent and a surprised catch in her breath.

Hugo's kneejerk reaction was to leap away like Brie was on fire.

But I did nothing wrong. Hugo stayed calm and grounded, partially turning to beckon Jodie. She shuffled forward to hug both him and Brie.

"I know what you're both thinking," he murmured, grin stretching wide. "Threesome?"

Brie slapped his chest, which only succeeded in hurting her hand by the ensuing yelp.

Jordana just snorted. "Boy, you need to hush."

Afterward, Brie was in better spirits. As was Jordana, who wanted to spend the night.

So now she wants to spend the night? Annoyed, Hugo found a legit reason to decline.

"Brie needs you more tonight," Hugo explained, to Jodie's clear disappointment. He glanced at Brie chatting with Mom and AJ. "And you're her ride."

Simon walked up, hand raised. "I'll watch over him."

"Me too," J-Tom seconded from the couch.

Jordana gave her friend a weird stare but reluctantly accepted this.

As she and Brie prepared to leave, Hugo had to ask, "What did you want to tell me earlier?"

Jodie had a brief, bewildered face. "That I love you." Standing on her tiptoes, she kissed him.

"Same," Hugo murmured, meaning it. Yet her lie rang hollow. She probably felt guilty for wanting to end things beforehand. But Hugo didn't need that drama tonight.

"Jesus," Simon sighed, peeking through the blinds once they drove off. "I thought they'd *never* leave."

Mom plopped down beside Hugo, running gentle fingers through his spiky hair. He didn't realize how tired she looked until he closely inspected the bags under her eyes. "Now…What really happened?"

J-Tom, Simon, and AJ gathered on the floor around him.

Hugo reclined in his seat, surprisingly wiped. Then he revealed everything, including his visit to Ramon.

Simon clutched his skull after Hugo finished. "Sweet merciful crap!"

AJ shivered angrily when hearing of someone attacking his brother. "Then who stole the Aegis robot?"

"Ramon's investigating that," Hugo replied. "Hopefully, he'll get answers."

J-Tom placed a hand on his knee, searching his face with worried eyes. "Are you okay?"

"Besides a robot clone of my alias attacking me in public?" Hugo snarked. "I'm great."

Nobody laughed. Mom's expression was stony, which meant she'd decided on something. "Go talk to Lady Liberty—"

Hugo's heart seemed to leap into his throat. "No."

His mother rose heatedly. "You were attacked in public, Bogota. Someone knows who you are."

The room hushed. Hugo rose, dwarfing his mother. He couldn't back down over this one setback. "Ramon Dempsey is helping. I got this under control."

Mom finally backed down. "Fine."

Now Hugo had to find his attacker. Not just for his own safety, but the people in this room.

"Speaking of Ramon." He turned around to J-Tom. "How did you ditch your armor and get here so fast?" That drew Mom and Simon's attention.

"Yeah, you arrived before everyone," AJ noted.

J-Tom sprang up so excitedly, Hugo thought she might hit the ceiling. "Watch this!" She reached behind the couch, grabbing a gym bag. J-Tom then pulled out a silvery briefcase and placed it down. Kicking the latch flipped open the case, revealing two tube-shaped protrusions.

J-Tom bent over, sticking her forearms inside, then stood and drew the briefcase onto her chest.

Hugo couldn't really process the next thirty or so seconds. The briefcase shifted and unfurled across J-Tom's torso, then wrapped around her limbs. Thin lines fashioned angular patterns along the metal, glowing bright blue. Before long, J-Tom was sheathed in menacing dark-silver armor.

The helmet formed last, engulfing J-Tom's head in an armored mask with glowing blue eyes.

Mom slapped a hand over her mouth. Simon stood, then fell back down.

Hugo picked up his jaw, recognizing the suit from earlier. "Good...LORD! Portable armor?"

"Right?!" J-Tom's digitized voice answered.

"How's that shit even possible?" AJ demanded.

J-Tom's helmet slid away, revealing her grinning and freckled face. "Technology, young Angelo."

Hugo's heart was full from this welcome surprise. "You ready, Jenny!"

After J-Tom collapsed her armor back into a briefcase, she, Hugo, and Simon retreated upstairs. Then the Samoan confessed his suspicions of who'd orchestrated this attack.

"It's gotta be Paxton-Brandt." J-Tom leaned forward in Hugo's chair, shamelessly watching him change.

"Maybe..." He pulled on a fresh tank top with black boardshorts.

"Or the OSA," Simon rebutted, lying on the bed.

J-Tom shook her head, ponytail swinging. "Why would they attack a possible recruit?"

Hugo frowned at her naiveté, plopping down beside Simon. "The OSA does shady shit. That Aegis-bot could've been a warning shot."

J-Tom sank back in the chair with familiarized comfort. "Well, I'm staying to guard you."

Simon looked at her sharply. "Me too."

Hugo rolled his eyes over this jockeying for BFF position. "Simon. What happened at the Carnival probably hit the local news, which your parents watch. Go home before they freak."

Simon looked deflated. "But—"

Hugo mussed his BFF's Bruce Lee bowl-cut hair. "We'll talk tomorrow. And call G-Mama tonight."

The Korean boy grumbled a sullen goodbye and trudged off as if being sent to a gulag.

"Thanks for protecting me," Hugo muttered to J-Tom.

Her smile was magical. "Always." J-Tom raised both arms in a catlike stretch, her long-sleeved shirt inching up to reveal a flat and firm belly.

Hugo's eyes lingered there a moment. "I wasn't sure you could be a superhero." His chest tightened as J-Tom's smile vanished. But he continued. "I worried that you might get hurt."

"I know."

Hugo choked on her nonchalance. "You what?"

Her lips pulled into a grin. "Your poker face needs work." She tapped her foot against his shin. "But you believed in me when it counted." J-Tom grew serious, hunching her shoulders. "Why Paxton-Brandt?"

"They have enough reason."

"Cuz you trashed The Elite and their Titan-cloning project," J-Tom recited.

Hugo felt a sudden, sick fatigue. "That…" Only Simon knew what he was about to say, and even he hadn't been happy. Hugo braced himself for J-Tom's reaction. "And I've been lowkey working with Dr. Michelman to take Paxton-Brandt down since summer."

J-Tom flinched as if she'd been stung. "What?" The single whispered word carried such revulsion.

He hastily pressed forward. "I don't trust Dr. Michelman. But he's got reasons to hate them—"

J-Tom shot out of the chair like a spring. "You *can't*."

Hugo leaned away from the terse demand. "Excuse me?"

"The Michelmans are *monsters*." Anguish contorted J-Tom's face. "Spencer's scheming *destroyed* Briseis, ripped my heart out. She literally almost killed you." Her voice rose. "Her Dr. Frankenstein dad created the Elite and tried cloning his best friend!"

Hugo absorbed her tantrum. "*Keep* your voice down." Admitting this was a mistake. He forgot sometimes how deep Spencer had sunk her claws into J-Tom, and how much healing she still needed.

J-Tom breathed heavily, lowering her hands as if settling her emotions. "Promise that you'll stop."

"Jen—"

"*Promise* me." Her ragged voice almost cracked Hugo's resolve—almost.

But a threat like Paxton-Brandt cared nothing for feelings. Hugo pushed upright, standing six inches taller than J-Tom. "Can't. We need Michelman's help against Paxton-Brandt."

J-Tom's eyes narrowed and turned hard. "Fine. Get yourself killed." She whirled around to leave.

Good lord... Hugo caught her elbow. "Stop. I need you in this fight." He wouldn't bend on this mission, even for her. "Especially now."

J-Tom glared up at him but relaxed in his grip.

She's listening. Hugo released her arm. "Once PB's toast, no more Michelmans. I promise."

J-Tom nodded hesitantly, still not facing him. God, she looked so wounded.

Hugo couldn't leave things so frayed and held out his arms.

J-Tom walked up and hugged him like a teddy bear she couldn't part with.

Electricity coursed through Hugo as they embraced in blissful silence.

Since the summer, he'd pulled J-Tom from the black hole of heartache. And tonight, Hugo was desperate for an escape. He walked his fingers along J-Tom's flat midriff.

A soft little gasp escaped her lips. Hugo slid his hands under J-Tom's shirt, murmuring sweet nothings in her ear, distracting her further. She gasped again and sagged in his arms...

Much later, Hugo stood in his bedroom fastening on his Aegis costume. He looked in the mirror and shivered. That robot had been identical.

AJ and Mom slept soundly in their rooms. The neighborhood was tranquil aside from a few households watching late-night TV. Outside, a pale crescent hung in the sky.

He studied the leggy outline draped across his bed, facedown and passed out.

Hugo traced a thumb along J-Tom's freckled shoulder blades, then down the soft and supple length of her left arm. He smiled, remembering her eager mouth, how his touch made her melt into a puddle, causing him to melt away with her. The familiar guilt was absent tonight. Jodie probably would've dumped Hugo until the Aegis-bot nabbed him.

He drew a bedsheet over J-Tom, placing a folded paper sheet beside her pillow. She'd enjoy his gift. Then Hugo pulled on his hood and half-mask.

There was another location he hadn't looked for Dr. Michelman.

He left home in a rush, flying to the abandoned strip mall outside of San Miguel.

Touching down minutes later, he entered the complex's maze of hallways. After going through body scans and security checks, he stepped within the elevator to Michelman's lab.

The expected blinding flash washed everything away, fading seconds later.

Hugo then choked on putrid, smothering smoke.

The high-tech laboratory with its futuristic workstations had been reduced to smoldering wreckage. No sign of Michelman or anything salvageable.

Paxton-Brandt did this. Frightened, Hugo crouched and ran his fingers along the burnt flooring. His psychometry activated instantly. Ghost-like images floated up around him. What happened here had been a fierce battle between the wiry form of Dr. Michelman and a pair of masked operatives.

By the way the spectral images viciously danced and collided, Michelman had held his own for a few minutes. Then old injuries and numbers took the ex-superhero down.

Hugo yanked his hand off the floor. The ghostly images vanished. Scorched tech encircled him again.

"They got Michelman." His best ally against Paxton-Brandt had been neutralized. "Fuck."

CHAPTER 18

The day after getting chosen, Greyson moved into the Natural Born Thrillers' compound. He only brought a few suitcases of clothing and some personal belongings, but not much else.

But Greyson quickly learned that trying out had been the easy part.

Day one was pure torture, starting with an onslaught of sprint drills at the crack of dawn. After that and some breakfast, he'd sparred with each Thriller in one-on-one combat.

"You'll enter the circle," Erika had stated on the first day. "So we can see how you square up against us and keeping a battle contained." The circle occupied another part of the training center, a gymnasium space with a blue outlined circle in its center for sparring.

Greyson got his ass kicked—on purpose—to see what each superhero could do.

Basically, the Natural Born Thrillers were showing him how to defeat them.

He first squared off against Brightburn, who'd traded her provocative costume for a figure-hugging sports bra and yoga pants. Greyson thanked the lord he was happily married. Social media narcissism aside, Brightburn could fight. She shaped weapons out of her electricity to deflect Greyson's radiation bursts, then electrocuted him with relish. Their matchups would've gone shorter if she wasn't such a showoff.

He faced with Erika Skye next, who proved why she was in charge. She could fling those hot knives from any direction or wield them like claws. Greyson made more effort with her, dodging and weaving around her swipes and throws. In three battles, each won a match and fought to a draw in the final.

"Nice, Levi," she commended breathlessly while helping him up. "Your combat instincts are solid."

Bulldozer harrumphed, massive arms folded. "Yeah, solid."

Erika ignored him.

Shattershot entered the circle eagerly. "Let's see how you do with me." He didn't take a fighting stance.

Greyson cracked his neck, fists glowing. But something in him couldn't attack. It would be like kicking a puppy. Greyson dropped his fists, powering down.

"You don't want to fight, do you?" Shattershot inquired, smiling warmly.

Greyson really didn't. "No..."

"Where are you really from, Levi?" Shattershot asked.

"St. Louis..." Greyson answered readily. Why wouldn't he admit that? Luckily, the Paxton-Brandt folks made sure his new identity hailed from the same city.

He glanced at Bulldozer then, who was watching with intense, gleaming eyes.

That poked a hole in the fuzzy haze surrounding Greyson's brain. *Why so curious?*

He looked back at Shattershot advancing. "What's the extent of your power—AWWW!" The empath's face scrunched up—after Greyson field-goal-punted him between his legs, and felt horrible doing so.

When Shattershot crumpled, a fog lifted. Greyson felt like himself again.

"Nice try, Shattershot." Cold fingers of dread crawled up his spine. That could've gone badly if Shattershot had asked the right questions. Greyson had to watch himself around that kid.

Bulldozer snarled in disgust at Shattershot. "Useless."

In a burst of scary speed, he charged.

He struck, full-body tackle, launching Greyson out of the circle.

Coming to, Greyson found Bulldozer loomed over him, blotting out the lights.

"Lesson one, newbie." He poked his chest, which felt like a piston to the ribs. "Never drop your guard."

"Noted," Greyson managed to groan.

Bulldozer stomped off without offering to help him up. Asshole.

During a break, Greyson limped off for some water outside the training center. Instead, he found Bulldozer and Shattershot in a quiet yet terse argument. Correction, Bulldozer was chewing Shattershot out.

Greyson tried finding a place to hide and listen.

But Bulldozer caught him. Grumbling under his breath, he stomped back inside the training center.

Shattershot leaned against a wall, visibly shaken by whatever Bulldozer had said.

Greyson approached and placed a hand on his shoulder. "You okay?"

Shattershot pushed him off. "I'm fine."

Greyson backpedaled, not taking it personally. "Sure." He repeated his question. "You okay?"

"I'm *sick* of him!" Shattershot erupted. Tears streamed down his cheeks. "That asshole's still like this, even when I'm a full member!"

The candor shocked Greyson. Seeing an opening, he dug deeper. "How long have you been full-time?"

Shattershot wiped his tears with a trembling hand. "Six months. He's just waiting for me to break bad." He suddenly glanced around in pure panic. "I shouldn't have said that—"

"No worries," Greyson interrupted softly. "I won't tell anyone."

Shattershot walked off, red-faced.

Greyson watched him go. *I might have an unknowing ally*, he mused.

By day's end, Greyson couldn't move. Every muscle ached, but in the good way. Steaming hot showers and seasoned chicken eased the soreness.

His room was simple in its trappings: large bed, workstation, nightstand, closet, drawers, and a wall-mounted TV.

Currently in a t-shirt and pajama pants, he texted with Connie on his encrypted phone. The nightstand lamp provided enough illumination as the couple talked business.

CIH: How goes it so far?

ME: Team training. Learning their strengths and weaknesses.

Greyson texted over flaws in each Thriller's fighting style, useful for when he moved on the team.

A knock startled Greyson. He glared at his steel-grey door. Who was visiting this late?

"Levi?" Erika announced from outside. "You awake?"

Greyson fired off a quick text.

ME: Got company. Goodnight.

He hastily aborted his VPN and encrypted chat app before hiding the cell beneath his bed. "Come in."

The door opened. Erika entered wearing an "I Love Shenandoah" t-shirt and slacks, her braids piled on top of her head. She waved with both hands. "Hey there."

"Hi, Erika," Greyson greeted.

The Thrillers' leader took a seat on the side of the bed. "How's the first few days been treating you?"

Greyson made a wincing face and shook his left arm. "Sore all over."

Erika's smile revealed crinkly laugh lines around the eyes. "Bulldozer can be rough. But he's just making sure you're cut out for what we do."

Greyson nodded. "Understood." Bulldozer could definitely become a problem. But Greyson deflected to another Bulldozer victim. "He bullies Shattershot."

Erika looked wounded hearing that. "Dozer doesn't feel villains can change, which is cynical as hell."

Oh, the irony. "Completely agree," Greyson replied, fighting the smirks off his face.

"If we don't believe in the best of people," Erika gestured as she grew more passionate, "we might as well become like Geist and murderize them."

Greyson jerked back a little. "Murderize?"

Erika side-eyed him. "It's been a long day, and I'm tired." Both of them laughed.

"Is Bulldozer why Nighthawk left?" The question killed the jovial mood, but Greyson wanted insider dirt.

Erika shook her head. "They were close friends. Us three grew up here." Sadness passed over her face. "She was burned out on Shenandoah. And Blackbird's so much happier." Her pain ran deep.

"So then," Greyson went on, tickled at this woman's frankness, "are you and Bulldozer together?"

"*Were,*" Erika corrected frostily.

Greyson shifted uncomfortably in his seat, knowing he'd crossed a line. "Sorry." He raised his hands to emphasize the apology.

Erika softened. "We broke up a few months ago." She let out a heavy sigh. "Dating a teammate, seeing them every hour of the day is hard." She shook her head, visibly tired. "The arguments were worse when we were together."

Greyson scrunched his face in mock discomfort. "Eeesh." *Another flaw to exploit.*

Erika shrugged indifferently. "It's for the best."

Sensing the finality in her tone, Greyson switched topics. "You told me there was a plan to regain Shenandoah's trust."

Erika predictably brightened. "We're working to improve our relations with the police, the fire department, and other emergency services. Then hospitals and charitable events appearances."

Erika went on for a while about her plans to help revitalize Shenandoah while Greyson listened. The scope of her vision was quite impressive.

"Paragon and the Chicago Massacre left so many scars," Erika admitted, gesturing with her hands. "I'm focused on pushing this city toward a renaissance, top to bottom. And whatever I can do to shepherd that forward, I'm game."

Greyson blinked, almost feeling…guilty. "Your passion is inspiring."

With hands on hips, Erika nodded with such pride that Greyson had to smile. "That's what leaders do…I guess." She turned and smiled at some unbidden thought. "I used to work at a community center for troubled kids, many of them supers." She met his gaze with hopeful eyes. "I can effect more change using this platform."

"I'm sold," Greyson proclaimed, arms wide. "Find me a synagogue to spread the good word." Erika burst out laughing again. "I'll keep that in mind. Anyway…" She stood and winked. "Get some sleep. More training torture awaits tomorrow."

"Goodnight," Greyson said. Once the door closed behind Erika, his smile grew pained. This was unfortunate. Striking Erika down would now be harder than expected once he eventually fought her team.

CHAPTER 19

"No fingerprints," Ramon said over the phone. "Tracking got disabled, which was why Vulcan couldn't find the Aegis-bot. There's plenty of footage shadowing you on patrols."

"Damn it." Hugo scowled, crouched in the dilapidated storage room that was his gear stash on Paso High's campus. Dark-blue jeans and a blood-red tee were today's attire. Snack period had started a few minutes ago, allowing him time to speak with Ramon. "Were you able to track the video feed to the person controlling it?"

"My attempts kept bouncing off high-level encryptions I've never seen before." His voice brightened. "On a positive note, checking the data logs, that attack on you was user error."

Hugo stood in bafflement. "The thief is effective, incompetent, and a stalker?" So, they had no leads.

"Seems like it," Ramon replied blandly. "I'll keep looking. How are you?"

Hugo rubbed at his face in frustration. "I'm insta-famous at school." The Aegis rescue had made the local news two days ago. When school started this Monday, Paso High students had badgered him for details about Aegis.

At least Taylor von Stratton, Songs cheerleading captain, had asked how he was and gave him a big hug. Then she'd hassled Hugo about the size of Aegis's arms.

"We didn't go on a romantic beach walk," Hugo had quipped, drawing laughs. He'd then complimented his alter ego, which felt bizarre.

Ramon giggled listening to this. "You swept yourself off your feet." He stopped laughing when Hugo growled at him. "This should blow over by afternoon with how ADD kids are."

Hugo sighed. "Here's hoping."

"Ooh. One more thing," Ramon added. "Are you cool with Jen coming to my place twice a week? I want to teach her more about building and maintaining her own the Arclight armor."

That brought a smile to Hugo's face. "Absolutely. Thanks for believing in her."

"I believe in her because of you."

After the call ended, Hugo shouldered his backpack and dialed up his hearing. The coast was clear. He slipped out of the storage unit, locking the door. No student visited this part of campus, but he remained vigilant.

When Hugo reached the Quad, countless stares turned his way. Ugh. He ignored them and headed toward his friends.

"There he is!" Harlan Mills swaggered by, slapping Hugo on the back. His fellow basketball teammates, Brent and Cody Banks, approached, snickering.

Cody, husky in frame and rotten in spirit, still sported his shaggy "midlife crisis mom" hair. *Why are he and Brent hanging out again?* Hugo wondered.

"How was it?" Harlan asked. "Being the dude in distress?"

Hugo shrugged. "I'll tell ya once Paso High wins a basketball championship."

Harlan stopped smiling. The team's failure to reach last year's playoffs still stung.

Brent and Danny guffawed before ushering their salty teammate along.

Hugo watched them cross the Quad as Brent resumed a story. "I kissed Chloe first. I used my being upset over Hugo getting nabbed. I win the bet!" Brent smugly held out a hand. His grumbling teammates reached for their wallets.

Hugo's stomach turned. "What the hell?" Either Brent's basketball bros were rubbing off on him or they were showing his true self. Either way, Hugo and Brent needed to talk soon.

His gaze landed on Brie and Jodie seated on a table flanked by their friends. Jodie's silky curls cascaded down her shoulders, complementing her jean jacket and little black dress. Brie looked gorgeous with her high ponytail, white blouse, leather pants, and white-rimmed glasses. She and Brie were chatting up Grace about vintage clothing. Hugo had texted with Jodie yesterday, but Brie never returned his messages. That bothered him pointedly.

Hugo approached, greeting his friends. Their lingering concern was appreciated. Simon was working on another school-commissioned website. J-Tom was at a student council meeting.

Jodie bounced from her seat and gave him a big kiss, much to his friends' ridicule. "Hi!" She enfolded his waist.

Hugo smiled plastically, recalling how Jodie almost dumped him on Saturday. He turned to Brie. "Hey."

She saw him and frosted over. "Hi, Hugo." Brie sounded annoyed with the interaction.

"You doing better?" Hugo continued. "I didn't hear back from you this weekend."

Brie slid off the table, reaching for her bag. "Me and Ramses moved my stuff into my dad's place."

"Oh. I could've helped—"

"*Hugo*," Brie cut him off curtly. "Just stop."

Hugo exchanged uneasy glances with Grace and Jordana. "Stop…having a conversation?"

Briseis's pale-green eyes held such raw emotions. But she quickly put on a blank, beautiful mask. "Forget it," she murmured. "I can't do this right now." She spun, almost smacking Groban with her school bag, and marched off.

Hugo stood there, dumbstruck. "What just happened?"

"Breezy isn't sleeping well." Jodie leaned close. "What happened at the carnival gave her nightmares."

Hugo's stomach knotted up. "Oh." Writing this off as Brie being dramatic would've been easy. But her rejection left him feeling small, unworthy—a flashback to their relationship before tenth grade. Hugo refused to revisit that toxic mindset. Then again, who knew what ran through Brie's mind after the carnival incident?

"I'll talk to her," Jodie assured as the bell ending Snack rang. Students swarmed toward third period.

"See you at lunch?" she suggested with a sexy smile.

"I guess," Hugo replied blandly. He really needed to hit something.

Jordana looked put off. "Are *you* okay?"

The buzz in Hugo's pocket from his work cellphone was a godsend. *Yes!* "Peachy." He leaned down and kissed her. "Later, babe."

Hugo checked his phone while walking to class, ignoring more comments about Aegis rescuing him.

BLOCKED: *Update on V3.*

Hugo's excitement soared as he called Clint. "Got your message."

"Found ya boy," Clint boasted. "Vincent Van Violence is definitely in San Miguel."

Hugo smiled from ear to ear. Exactly the face he needed to punch. "Where and when?"

By the time Hugo stood outside his third period class, Clint had delivered V3's whereabouts the last few days and his current location.

Hugo could handle this himself, using the tried and true "family emergency" excuse to get out of class. Then Hugo considered how V3's capture could need backup. He moved into an isolated hallway nook and dialed another number on his encrypted cell.

Dawson answered after two rings. "Hello, Aegis."

"Detective," Hugo stated quietly in his Aegis voice. "I have a lead on V3."

By fourth period's end, Beale had amassed the resources to move on Vincent Van Violence. Also, many students no longer cared about Aegis rescuing Hugo. The big news across campus was that nutjob Saracen's latest data dump revealed the OSA's black sites for holding criminal supers.

As soon as the lunch bell rang, Hugo jogged toward his gear stash, suited up, then sprinted downtown. Time to kick some ass.

Within minutes, he reached Dawson's location between downtown and The Junction.

The makeshift staging ground occupied a gutted warehouse. The interior was filled with San Miguel PD's Superhuman Task Force slipping on vests, cleaning firearms, prepping for war.

Hugo exchanged greetings with San Miguel's finest, finding Beale and Dawson at the monitors watching the tavern across the street.

"Did a quick casing," he told Beale. "The surrounding block is clear aside from drones."

Dawson nodded. "We got one of our own in the meeting."

Onscreen showcased a small gathering in black-and-white between members of the criminal underworld. Half a dozen heavies in tracksuits were packing firepower, hard-bitten and solemn. A pair of slender, attractive twins occupied the bar, scanning the scene. Were they eye candy or muscle? In one corner booth sat a man with a pockmarked face and an impeccable suit. Yuri Broytman, a captain in the Ukrainian Brotherhood.

Hugo cared more about the man sitting across from him.

"There," Dawson murmured, pointing.

Hugo tensed. Vince Van Violence, baby-blue-skinned and bald, taking up the whole chair with his massive physique. At six-feet-nine inches, insanely strong and burly, he was a walking mac truck. Hugo flashed on their first conflict and nearly getting decapitated by V3's punches.

Now Hugo was stronger and more experienced. *I still need to be careful.*

"V3's done business with the Brotherhood before," Detective concluded. "He's probably asking for protection in exchange for his services." His brow furrowed in confusion. "How did you find V3?"

Hugo offered the threat of a smile. "My eyes and ears around town."

New footsteps entered the staging ground. Hugo turned and squinted. "Is that—?"

Detective followed his stare. "Ballistic," he confirmed. "Another local hero we coordinate with."

The man codenamed Ballistic approached the monitors, sporting a spare and wiry gymnast's body. His gold-and-blue costume resembled a speedskater suit, a translucent green visor covering his eyes.

Hugo knew Ballistic by reputation, a superhuman vigilante operating in Nipomo as part of Geist's vigilante network.

"Hey," Hugo greeted.

Ballistic nodded, several inches shorter. "Nice to meet the new kid on the block. Hope you got it."

Hugo didn't enjoy his mocking tone. "Got what?"

Ballistic grinned cheekily. "The right stuff."

Hugo stared at him.

Beale and Dawson took to the center of the small staging ground. "We do this quick and clean. Aegis takes down V3." He gestured at Hugo behind him.

"Ballistic can handle any other supers present," Dawson pointed to Ballistic. "We handle the others." The room rippled with various agreements.

Hugo watched the Superhuman Taskforce move into position. God, he felt giddy. And scared. He extended a fist to Ballistic. "Ready?"

The vigilante fist-bumped him. "Hangin' tough."

Dawson handed Hugo a set of dampener restraints, which he hooked to his belt.

"Ready. Set. MOVE!" Beale hissed.

Hugo grabbed Ballistic under the armpits and hurtled forward. They'd have mere seconds before the Ukrainian Brotherhood's drones spotted them. He flew low, straight for the tavern's entrance.

He let Ballistic go and barreled ahead.

The door burst into splinters against his fists. Everyone and everything moved in slow-mo. Yuri Broytman slowly shielded his face. Rage gradually contorted Vincent Van Violence's hideous mug. Yuri's men were pulling out firearms.

Hugo sailed straight for V3. One swing to the stomach folded him up like cheap paper. Another uppercut knocked him head over heels. V3 dropped flat on his face with a hard thud.

Hugo landed astride his dazed foe, triumphant.

Broytman and his thugs then aimed their weapons at him. And the sexy twins abruptly...*multiplied*.

Hugo now saw eight identical women. "A duplicator?"

Ballistic somersaulted through the wrecked entrance then, landing in a crouch. The vigilante tossed three small silver marbles at frightening speeds. One marble struck the ground in front of a group of Broytman's heavies. A heatless discharge sent shockwaves outward, blasting those flunkies into unconsciousness. That was Ballistic's power, charging objects with kinetic energy to erupt on impact.

Another metallic marble snapped the lead duplicator's head back with sickening force, then smacked off the other women's temples. All eight crumpled.

A deafening thunderclap went off right in Hugo's ear. Yuri Broytman shot him in the head. Annoying.

Hugo reached left without looking and flicked Broytman's jaw. A grunt followed by a body hitting the floor confirmed he was unconscious.

SMPD stormed the bar, Dawson and Beale leading the charge with guns drawn. "Everyone on the ground! NOW."

V3 tried fighting upright. Hugo drove a knee to the back of his neck, bringing him back down.

The big man flailed. "Get off me!"

Hugo grabbed one of V3's thrashing arms. He itched to just wrench back and break it. But why? Hugo had him pinned. "Don't make this harder," he whispered in the criminal's ear.

V3, realizing he'd lost, slumped in defeat. Hugo kept hold of his arm while reaching for his handcuffs.

Dawson and Beale surveyed the scene as their team cuffed the many unconscious foot soldiers.

Dawson knelt beside the unconscious women lying in a heap. "Wasn't expecting Myriad."

Hugo looked up. He'd heard of Myriad, a one-woman army for hire to criminal orgs. She'd never been caught until today. "A two-for-one special," Hugo quipped, reaching for V3's arm with his cuffs. He'd wanted more of a fight. "That was easy—"

The wall beside him exploded apart, concrete debris flying everywhere.

Dust rolled over everything as an imposing man in orange and black emerged, cape flapping.

"Nobody fear! Tomorrow Man's here." The timing was catastrophic.

"Fuck this!" V3 threw Hugo off violently and bolted for the door, bowling over several STF officers.

Hugo swore and scrambled to his feet.

Beale coughed and waved away smoke. "Idiot!" he barked at Tomorrow Man. "You ruined it!"

"I'm on it!" Hugo zoomed outside the bar in seconds.

Vincent Van Violence dashed toward a more populated area.

Hugo wouldn't allow that. He sped up, closing the distance—until someone grabbed his ankle.

"V3's mine!" Suddenly, Hugo got swung like a pendulum. Concrete shattered against his face.

Stunned, Hugo flipped onto his back and gaped. "Are you shitting me?"

Tomorrow Man loomed over him. "You're not stealing this win." He sailed in with a haymaker right.

Hugo easily moved, and the blow shattered more concrete.

But Tomorrow Man kept on him with a barrage of furious punches. And V3 had disappeared. Fuck!

Hugo shoved Tomorrow Man off. "What are you doing? V3 is getting away!" He turned to chase V3 and got suckerpunched in the jaw. That stung like a motherfucker. Hugo went tumbling down the road.

"This victory is mine!" Tomorrow Man cried, charging forward. His bulging blue eyes made him look unhinged. "Now I prove who's better!"

As Tomorrow Man dove in for another attack, several anguished shrieks rang out.

Hugo sprang to his feet, catching Tomorrow Man's fist.

He swung with his right. Hugo caught that too.

"Fuck your quarter-life crisis!" Hugo headbutted Tomorrow Man in the nose, staggering him backward. A punt to the crotch buckled Tomorrow Man's knees, his face scrunched in agony.

Hugo then bearhugged Tomorrow Man and bridged back, tossing him overhead into a car. The impact folded the vehicle in two. Tomorrow Man slumped to all fours. More screams sounded nearby.

The more Hugo glared at this selfish moron with his stupid cape, the angrier he got.

Leaping several feet up, he stomped his foot down hard on the back of Tomorrow Man's stupid head.

A loud crunch married with a shockwave quaked the concrete in all directions.

Tomorrow Man lay facedown in a small crater, breathing but not moving. Good.

Hugo dashed toward the fading screams in Grant Square blocks away.

He found civilians panicking and teeming around something.

Hugo flew closer for a better look, and the warmth left his soul. "Oh no…"

Four bodies lay across the sidewalk, a young couple flattened by massive footprints. Two teen boys were contorted in sickening angles. Several bystanders pointed where V3 had gone.

But Hugo could smell V3's stench and raced off in pursuit.

Hugo spotted him at the other end of Grant Square escaping into an alley.

He's not escaping this… Hatred running through his veins, he spear-tackled V3 from behind.

"Murdering shitbag!" Hugo drove V3 up into the air, away from civilians. Finding a vacant rooftop, he flung his opponent down.

Hugo landed and advanced angrily. "There's no escape!"

Vincent Van Violence stumbled to his full height and just stared. "Am I supposed to care who you are?"

Hugo flinched. Of course V3 didn't recognize him. When they'd last fought, Hugo had a totally different costume. "You will." He launched himself forward. But V3 was ready, catching Hugo by the throat. A meaty fist to the chest drove the wind out of him.

"Like I thought." V3 body-slammed him down. Pain roiled up Hugo's spine.

"All bark, no bite." V3 rained down fast and furious punches on his face. He struck like an *avalanche*!

Hugo's jaw screamed under the barrage. He cursed himself for losing his cool, embarrassed that this fucker got the upper hand again. Even worse, a news chopper high above was recording the humiliating beatdown.

V3 wrapped both hands around Hugo's throat and squeezed. His cruel grin revealed yellow teeth. "Thanks for the tune-up…whoever you are."

The ridicule crackled through Hugo's battered body, becoming fuel. Re-energized, he grabbed V3's wrists and pried his hands off.

The criminal's smile slowly turned to confusion. He struggled to regain the advantage. But Hugo was stronger, climbing back up, shaking off the cobwebs.

Now I bring the pain. A cat-quick throat jab drove Vincent Van Violence back, clutching his neck.

Hugo stood tall and composed, power flowing through him. "My name…is Aegis," he declared.

"Don't care." V3 shrugged off the pain, coming in swinging.

"Not yet." Hugo blocked with a forearm then backhanded V3's jaw, followed by a sharp sternum jab.

V3 staggered and coughed. Glowering through cautious eyes, he charged again.

Hugo sidestepped behind him, unloading twenty piston-like punches to the kidneys in three seconds. Swift, brutal, and contained offense, using someone's momentum against them. One of Geist's lessons.

V3 staggered forward, grimacing from unmistakable pain. His sloppy backhand met thin air.

Hugo was already in front of V3, seizing his throat. Jackhammering his jaw with three right hooks, the teen doubled V3 over with a hard knee to the stomach. Then another, and another.

A knee to V3's face stood him straight up, eyes crossed.

Hugo reveled in his supremacy, savored it. A hard uppercut sent V3 skidding to the roof's edge.

"Fine." V3 wiped his bloody nose and raised both hands. "I give up."

Hugo's mouth and sternum were on fire, thanks to V3's earlier assault. "Don't care." He moved, everything slowing to a crawl.

His first charge cracked V3 across the face. Hugo boomeranged back around, images of V3's victims filling his thoughts. Hugo rocketed ahead, cocking his fist back, driving it into V3's spine.

The *snap* sounded like a breaking bough, echoing across the roof.

The strength went out of Vincent Van Violence with an inhuman scream. His legs turned to spaghetti beneath him.

Hugo caught him by the scruff of the neck and floated over San Miguel's veins of traffic.

Looking down with telescopic vision, Hugo found the right spot.

"Aegis," he whispered in a hyperventilating V3's ear. "Remember it." Then Hugo let go.

V3's massive blue frame fell several stories, pancaking a vacant SUV parked beside this building.

Hugo floated down to see V3 motionless atop a flattened vehicle. Bystanders murmured and pointed. Many applauded. More looked afraid.

Fingers of dread seized Hugo's chest as he stared at his handiwork. A moment of unchecked anger had caused this.

Not knowing what to do, Hugo waited in mid-air over V3's motionless body as several SMPD officers approached. More sirens neared Grant Square.

Once V3 was cuffed, Hugo soared back to the tavern.

He found Beale, Dawson, and their team escorting The Ukrainian Brotherhood out in handcuffs. Nearby, Tomorrow Man struggled to stand on wobbly legs.

This is ALL his fault. Hugo had a visceral reaction, anger taking over again. He marched straight toward Tomorrow Man.

"*Hey*, motherfucker!" Hugo backhanded him as hard as possible, launching him into the stratosphere.

Hugo rocketed up at top speeds.

Now several miles above San Miguel, he stopped and waited.

Tomorrow Man's somersaulting frame almost came sailing past seconds later.

Hugo caught his cape just in time and dangled him in front so they were face-to-face.

"Four civilians died because of you," Hugo snarled. "Sandbag me again, and I will beat your ass so hard, your grandkids will feel it."

He started spinning Tomorrow Man round and round by the cape, becoming a cyclone of motion.

Then Hugo flung him across the city. The caped hero shrank over the horizon, losing momentum before dropping into the sea.

Now Hugo felt better, despite the sore jaw.

CHAPTER 20

"Wow!" Greyson remarked, sitting at a long oval table with Reverb, Brightburn, and Shattershot. They were in the Natural Born Thrillers' Situation Room where the team held meetings and briefings.

But his bemusement and his teammates' wonder came from the large flatscreen broadcasting N3 with breaking news out of San Miguel.

SHIELD OF VIOLENCE? The news chyron displayed in big bold letters.

Reverb was wide-eyed and breathless. "Aegis kicked Vincent Van Violence's ass like it was his job."

Shattershot side-eyed him and chuckled. "Kinda is his job."

Those two kept gushing over Aegis like fanboys. Meanwhile, Brightburn snapped a "surprised" selfie.

Greyson sat hunched and stewing at the hooded superhero in purple floating in the sky ominously.

In the news replay of the fight, Vincent Van Violence had the early upper hand, pummeling Aegis down. Then Aegis's flurry of brutal, surgical strikes dropped the larger V3 to his knees. The fight should've ended there. But Aegis had bookmarked the beatdown with a spine-shattering punch.

Greyson's concerns had come true. The so-called Shield of Justice had shown his true colors.

Like when Aegis had sliced off Athena's forearms months ago. *What was next? Judge, Jury, and Executioner?*

Greyson spun in his seat to face Aegis's new fan club. "Aegis broke a man's back." His declaration silenced the room. "Are we supposed to be okay with that?"

Brightburn finally stopped preening for selfies to answer. "No. But V3's a murderer who's had it coming for years."

"Then," Shattershot chimed in, grinning like an idiot, "Aegis chucked Tomorrow Man into the ocean, while the guy was livestreaming." The empath howled with laughter.

Greyson shook his head. They were too enamored with Aegis's badassery to see straight.

Reverb drummed his hands on the table. "Polls on the San Miguel Tribune say most people felt he went too far. And San Miguel's police is distancing themselves from his actions."

This was the perfect time to attack Aegis physically, and force San Miguel's populace to take a hard look at their chosen one. But since he'd been ordered to stay away from Aegis, Greyson would do that for these Natural Born Thrillers.

"What's your problem with Aegis, Levi?" The question drew all eyes to the entrance.

Bulldozer took up the entire doorframe, his bronze-metal skin gleaming under the overhead lights.

Greyson met his glare unflinchingly. "I don't agree with his use of ultraviolence."

Bulldozer stepped into the room, eyes never shifting from his prey. "Then how would you have stopped V3 if he'd escaped prison yet again?"

Greyson knew many ways to stop degenerates like Vincent Van Violence. *All which would make me a big hypocrite.* He kept his mouth shut.

Bulldozer gave a smug nod. "The world isn't black and white, newbie. You'll learn that if you make the cut." Those last words had an ominous edge. The room hushed, tension mounting.

"Everyone, sit." Erika Skye's entrance broke the tension. She scanned the room. "First, it was great seeing V3 finally get what he deserved. But that isn't how we'll regain public trust in Shenandoah."

"Good to know," Greyson said. It was a shame he couldn't let that happen. But his task wasn't personal. "Second." Erika Skye paced slowly. Her gaze landed on Greyson. "Levi survived his first full week as a trainee. Now it's time to christen him."

Greyson's cheeks burned as he grasped her gist. A codename. "In my case, don't you mean ablution?"

"Your codename," Erika announced over the room's laughter, "is Hazard."

Reverb and Shattershot stood and clapped. Brightburn, Erika, and even Bulldozer offered their congratulations. Greyson rose from his seat. "Thank you for this opportunity." *To destroy your team.*

A claxon broke up the adulation, startling the shit out of Greyson. The mood in the situation room immediately shifted. The Natural Born Thrillers put their game faces on.

Greyson stared at them, lost. "What's that?"

Reverb offered a grim smile. "Code black. A superhuman attack in progress."

Erika Skye walked with purpose to a black console near the TV. "I'll contact our Shenandoah Police dispatch." After speed-dialing a number, Erika got in a low and terse dialog Greyson couldn't make out.

"Situation in Crayton Heights," Erika announced after finishing. "Protests between supers and Pax Humana over new city anti-super laws. All hands on deck."

Greyson made no attempt to mask his glee. "Am I coming too?"

Erika nodded as the team marched out of the conference room. "You'll ride along but watch only."

That cooled much of Greyson's enthusiasm. "Whatever you need." He scurried after her.

The team had no fliers (that they knew of), so everyone hopped into a repurposed SUV. Reaching Crayton Heights took ten minutes, Greyson holding on for dear life thanks to Brightburn's wild driving.

They parked in an alleyway within walking distance of the gathering. One side had all normal-looking people, many wielding guns. Some brandished the Pax Humana logo. The other side had more normies, some with claws or glowing fists. A few levitated off the ground. Both sides were snarling at each other. No blows were exchanged yet, thanks to the police presence.

"We'll wait." Erika adjusted her costume. "Getting involved right now might make it worse."

Greyson watched, salivating for things to worsen. He focused on one human protester's handgun, invisible fingers feeling its weight and body.

Greyson lowered his hand and flicked his fingers. The gun got ripped from that man's hand, smacking a super's face. His comrades took umbrage. In seconds, both sides charged before the police could react.

Erika Skye swore and threw the car door open. "We'll have drones and bodycams connected to the car's monitors," she called out over her shoulder. "Keep an eye out!"

"Okeydokey," Greyson replied.

"Okeydokey?" Bulldozer mocked.

"Stop," Reverb chided.

Shattershot hung back, looking guilty. "I'm sorry for how far I went the first day of training," he confessed. "Dozer wanted me to make you admit any embarrassing secrets."

Greyson felt cold from head to heel. "Thanks for owning up." Clearly Bulldozer was a problem that needed solving before Greyson moved against the team.

"Shattershot!" Erika called, prompting the empath to slam the door, leaving Greyson alone.

The Natural Born Thrillers converged on the large-scale brawl. Bulldozer clapped, the shockwave from his metallic hands walloping the crowd. Many of them stopped and stared. From the bodycams, Greyson saw humans and supers alike already bloodied and injured.

"Stop or get stopped," Bulldozer boomed. Yet hostilities restarted in a violent clash of humanity.

"I love when they don't stand down," Reverb admitted, rubbing his hands.

On Reverb's bodycam, Erika wielded hot knives on each finger. "Y'all know what to do."

Greyson marveled at how quick and efficient the Natural Born Thrillers were. Within minutes, Shattershot pacified portions of the crowd. Reverb bounced and pounded the more aggressive supers. Erika Skye's hot knives streaked through the crowd, impaling several humans and stunning them. Bulldozer was a wall of iron, Pax Humana protesters emptying their guns on him. He smiled while tossing them like lawn darts.

Brightburn contained the nastiest superhuman protesters in a crackling cage of bluish electricity. She lifted both hands, elevating them off the ground. "Got these suckers." Besides a few stragglers, the situation was safely defused.

"Crowds are contained," Shattershot declared, one hand on the side of his head as many protesters walked away indifferently.

Only then did Erika Skye allow herself a big smile. "All too easy."

Bulldozer was in a brawl with the last defiant protester, a mammoth of a man almost as tall as he was. But Bulldozer had peppered him with vicious body shots, leaving the other man on spaghetti legs.

Greyson flashed on a fateful night during his Heroes Anonymous tenure and saw his opening.

"Say goodnight, punk." Bulldozer cocked his sledgehammer-like fist back and swung.

A sneer played across Greyson's lips. "Goodnight, punk." With a thought, he tethered the gravity of Bulldozer's fist to his opponent's face.

In the distance, the blow struck like a sonic boom. The mammoth man sailed into Brightburn's floating electricity cage.

Jolts of lightning sizzled the big man and shattered the cage before he and the four prisoners got flung through a glass building.

Glittering shards blew outward, showering bystanders.

Screams erupted. Formerly docile crowds dashed for cover. Confusion swept the square.

Uniformed police officers present scrambled toward the injured, barking into their radio devices.

Greyson watched the car monitors greedily to see Reverb's bodycam. Erika looked on in horror. Bulldozer staggered away, seeing but not believing.

Brightburn covered her frightened mouth. "OHMIGOD!"

But Erika snapped out of it and took charge. "Bulldozer. Reverb. Help survivors." She whirled to Shattershot. "Calm and evacuate."

"Already trying," the empath shouted over the chaos, teeth clenched. "It's a lot."

Greyson switched to Shattershot's bodycam as Erika turned, braids tossed over one shoulder. "Brightburn—"

"I'll call emergency responders," her teammate finished, already on her cell.

Erika nodded in approval and then turned toward the accident. "I'll get to the sixth floor where…Jesus, this looks bad." She ran out of the frame.

Greyson leaned back in his seat with satisfaction. "And the chaos begins."

CHAPTER 21

"I'm not sorry."

That had been Hugo's response to his publicist two days after the news showed him bashing V3's face in. There was the predictable social media backlash and rebukes from superhero pundits. Hugo had received a stern email from the State Superhero Commission but no official punishment.

Blur had also weighed in when asked by reporters at a signing event. "Stop clutching your pearls. Someone had to take Vincent Van Violence out." The speedster then smirked. "But Aegis still sucks."

Despite all this and Mom's scolding, Hugo wasn't budging.

"Hugo," Annie Sherwood replied wearily on the phone. "This looked *bad!*"

Hugo shook his head, pacing in the rear parking lot of the Beach Bum Burger near school. "Don't care," he spat, defiant. Well, he cared somewhat. J-Tom and Simon supported him after he'd told the full story.

"You broke Vincent Van Violence's spine in two places," his publicist exclaimed to emphasize the gravity of Hugo's actions. "Then tossed Tomorrow Man into the ocean. This gives people the impression that you're one bad day from becoming like The Elite."

That stopped Hugo in his tracks. "That's not true."

"How would the public know that?"

Hugo massaged the bridge of his nose. The lingering ache from Vincent Van Violence's blows throbbed. "V3 killed six people, Annie! Myriad escaped because Tomorrow Man interfered." Hugo grew heated all over again. What pissed him off more was the corporate-owned news media's slanted take on his actions, using headlines like 'Shield of Justice? Or Shield of Violence?' Fuck them.

"I get your point…" Hugo let his hand drop, watching the line of cars crawl through Beach Bum Burger's drive-thru. "But how many times has V3 escaped prison, killing more people? Now he can't escape."

Annie sighed in exasperation. "Personally, I agree with you. But as your PR Goddess, I care that the people you're protecting can trust you. Then there's Tomorrow Man."

Hugo bristled. "That asshole's stupidity caused this. Now the world knows it too."

Tomorrow Man had been livestreaming yesterday to show himself as a man of action.

Annie giggled, cracking the tension. "That video cooked him for breakfast."

Tomorrow Man's livestream had showed an unnamed officer tipping him off to the police operation before his arrival, causing V3's escape. And that had been after. But his attack on Hugo had been labelled by many as a nervous breakdown. The cherry on top was the livestream capturing Hugo curb-stomping Tomorrow Man's face into the concrete, then tossing him into the sea. Millions had watched the video before Tomorrow Man's team eventually deleted it. This had shifted public opinion in Aegis's favor. Even Tomorrow Man's corporate sponsor, Aethon Management, had to issue a public apology.

But detractors remained. Anti-superhero firebrand Senator Huntley had called him another Black Wednesday waiting to happen. *Fuck* him too.

Annie's voice drew him back to the present. "I can spin yesterday thanks to V3's rap sheet and Tomorrow Man's dumbfuckery," she stated. "But a pattern of ultraviolence can turn the public on you."

Hugo exhaled. Annie was right. A few bad days could ruin a hero's reputation.

"Fine," Hugo agreed. "I'll watch my temper." After the call, an exchange at the back of Beach Bum Burger grabbed his attention.

Brent, in basketball warmups, cornering a slim and raven-haired girl. Scanning the lot, Hugo spotted an Escalade with other Paso High basketballers hollering. Hugo's heart sank. Now the scene made sense.

"I wanna get to know you," Brent pressed. "Don't you wanna know me?"

"No," the girl remarked uncomfortably, sidestepping him. "I have to go."

He blocked her path, still encroaching on her space. "Can I get your name? You're so pretty—HEY!"

Hugo yanked Brent backward by the collar.

The girl ran, practically leaving cartoon dust in her wake.

Hugo ignored protests from the parked SUV and focused on Brent.

"What the hell, Bogie?" he complained. "I had that one locked."

Hugo stared down at his delusional friend. "That girl wasn't interested. What's wrong with you?"

Brent's bland good looks registered shock. "Chill, brosef!" He gave a shaky laugh and scratched his neck. "I'm just perfecting my pick-up game."

Hugo couldn't believe his own ears. Who was this kid? "Seems like you're becoming the same flavor of douchebag you claimed to hate."

A cloud descended over Brent's face. "You're lecturing me?" he shouted, veins bulging from his neck. "You go through girls like socks then wonder why Jodie doesn't wanna be your girlfriend?" He jabbed a finger in Hugo's face. "I don't need judgement from someone who's barely around, even when he bothers showing up. So get outta my face!"

Hugo's thoughts ground to a halt. He'd been clueless about how his tardiness was upsetting his friends.

Brent shook his head in disgust and turned to leave.

Hugo could think of one chance to reach his friend. "Are you still that brave kid who saved me two summers ago? Or is this who you really are?"

Brent stopped. Hugo couldn't see his expression, but hearing the hike in the basketballer's breaths confirmed that his words had struck home.

Hugo departed before Brent could reply.

Instead of racing home, Hugo walked aimlessly around downtown Paso Robles. The afternoon sun kissed his skin. People chatter and car traffic overlapped with aromas of wine bodegas and fusion bistros typical of San Miguel's largest suburb. Hugo eavesdropped on conversations, eager to hear people's random opinions on Aegis. While quite a few sided with him, most had other concerns. *Get over yourself, Hugo.* During this walk, he mulled over Brent's harsh but correct words. Hugo had been an absentee friend, even when he did show up.

This sacrifice was what he'd signed up for. Still, the reality was hard to digest. How could he blame Jordana for wanting more with someone else?

Hugo reached his neighborhood before he knew it. The golden sun began to sink, splashing fire across the skies.

As he neared home, there was a visitor sitting on the doorsteps. For a moment, Hugo thought he was seeing things.

Baz Martinez stood, wearing a clingy hoodie and jeans. His handsome face paled when he approached.

Hugo paused, pulse rising, fists clenched instinctively. Of all the motherfuckers to bother him…

"Hugo?" Baz Martinez stated cautiously, hands raised in surrender. "I'm not here to fight."

"Why the hell are you here?" Hugo snarled, unable to contain his venom. Glancing around the block, he scanned for an ambush. Only Baz's black BMW was present. He'd actually come alone.

Baz stopped a few feet away. No anger or smirking arrogance dominated his handsome face. "Hugo…" His very carriage conveyed supplication and fear. "I just want to talk."

"I don't," Hugo snapped. "Goodbye." He sidestepped Baz toward his door.

Baz blocked his path. "I'm not leaving until we talk." He set his jaw, trembling all over.

Hugo had to laugh. This guy had balls. "Are you begging for another ass-kicking?" He stopped smiling. "Leave." His growled warning sounded animalistic. He moved around Baz again.

Baz grabbed Hugo's arm, seething. "We're not done—"

Hugo just reacted, triggered by years of Baz's bullying. He whirled quicker than normal but not superfast, slamming a gentle enough palm thrust to his enemy's chest. Baz went flying, the wind knocked out of him in a pained whoosh. He landed hard on the front lawn.

Hugo loomed over him, a familiar hatred searing through every pore.

Baz stayed down, coughing for air. There was no fight in him.

That reached Hugo. *I could kill him without a thought.* He unclenched his fists and backpedaled. "Don't ever come back." Hugo turned to hide his self-disgust.

"She was *pregnant.*"

The breathless declaration snared Hugo by the waist, spinning him around. "What?" He didn't need to guess who "she" was.

Baz pushed up to his elbows. "I got Brie pregnant last year—"

Anger flooded Hugo's veins. "*Bullshit!*"

"I'm not lying!" Baz protested.

Desperation dulled his rival's eyes. It was the same look Baz had on at Fall Fling after Hugo had almost crushed his ribcage. He sank down on his front steps, not trusting his legs for support. "When?"

Baz sat up and pulled those long legs into his chest. "The basketball party," he admitted. "Brie told me in late spring. She was seven weeks along. I freaked out, needed time to process. But after a few days, I knew I wanted to raise the baby with her." Tears were budding in Baz's eyes.

Neither Brie nor her friends had mentioned this. Hugo shuddered at what might've occurred. "What happened?"

Baz bowed his head as tears flowed. "Miscarriage…"

"Jesus…" Horror knifed Hugo in the chest. He looked away. That explained why Brie nearly vanished into this ugly darkness late sophomore year. "Why are you telling me this?"

"My parents found out." Baz lifted his head. His eyes were red from crying, which Hugo hadn't seen since they were little kids. "They're sending me to military academy."

Hugo stared back, hearing but not believing. "Holy shit." A year ago, he'd have been throwing a block party. But since Baz was so irrelevant to his life, Hugo just felt hollow.

"I know I have no right." Baz stared at him. "But I need you to watch over Briseis after I'm gone."

Hugo's brain nearly imploded. "Of all people you could ask at Paso High…"

A snarl curled Baz's lip. "I don't trust my friends, especially after that basketball party." He was obviously still in love with Brie. "You've taken care of her since the summer. Just keep doing that. Please."

Hugo struggled to find his voice when a woman swearing loudly in the Samoan dialect caught his ear. He stared down the street at an approaching car and shot up. "You gotta go."

Baz straightened. "Wh…why?" Following Hugo's frown, he also rose. "Oh shit."

Mom's Forerunner pulled into the driveway. Right after killing the ignition, she was out of the car marching toward Baz.

"What the HELL are you doing here?" she shouted loud enough for the whole block to hear. "After you vandalize my house, you have the nerve to show your face, you waste of sperm!"

"Mom!" Hugo strode across the lawn to intercept her. "Please calm down!"

"I will NOT calm down, Bogota!" Mom struggled uselessly in Hugo's unyielding grip.

Hugo turned his head, catching Baz's terror. "Go home."

The basketballer jogged away to his BMW down the street.

Once Baz drove off, Mom focused her rage on Hugo. "Explain."

He repeated the story Baz had shared once they were inside. Mom wasn't surprised. "Briseis's parents told me last summer but didn't know who the father was."

Hugo flinched. One more secret she'd kept. But this one wasn't about him. "After her suicide attempt?"

Mom nodded idly. Her eyes sparked again. "Before I pick AJ up, we're discussing what happened with this Vick Van Violent person."

Hugo rolled his eyes. Mom had already given her thoughts, meaning she had more. How wonderful. Luckily, Hugo's phone buzzed.

"Hold that thought…" Hugo pulled it from his pocket and laughed when he saw the caller ID. *Speaking of Brie…* "Hey, Ramses," he greeted.

"Hi…" Briseis's brother sounded anxious. "Are you with Briseis right now?"

Hugo scowled. "No." Brie was still avoiding him. "Why?"

Ramses let out a worried sigh. "We're supposed to grab dinner. Now I can't reach her, and she's not at either of my parents' places."

"You try Jodie or J-Tom?"

"Both of them," Ramses replied. "Jenny said Briseis and Jodie are hanging out. But Jodie's not replying."

Hugo stiffened. That was odd but didn't set off alarm bells. "I'll keep an eye out."

After that, Hugo called Jordana's house, raising a pausing finger to Mom's mouthed questions.

"Jodie went to grab Brie," Jordana's dad explained. Her brothers were setting the table in the background. "She's running late. Is something wrong?"

"No, sir," Hugo replied immediately. He fought down rising panic. "I just want to talk with her." Unless Jordana had plans with friends or a softball game, missing a family dinner wasn't like her.

"What's wrong?" Mom asked after Hugo hung up.

"Hopefully nothing. Could be something," he answered an octave higher than normal. That worry grew as he skimmed through mobile apps. "Just making sure that something is definitely nothing." He found the phone-tracking app Clint had whipped up in case any friends went missing.

"Aha!" Hugo exclaimed. The location of Jordana's and Brie's phones pulsed red waves on the app's Google-style map. At Cisman Ridge near the riverbed.

"Be right back, Mom." Hugo kissed her cheek, then raced out the back door.

He reached Cisman Bridge in under two minutes. This dry riverbed looked abandoned save for some vagrant tent cities.

Jordana's blue sedan was parked next to the riverbed.

Hugo almost crowed, until he heard no heartbeats or breathing sounds.

He marched up, driven by dread, and looked inside.

Two cellphones rested on the driver's seat. The car was otherwise empty.

Every alarm bell in Hugo's brain went off.

CHAPTER 22

The last few days had been brutal. Local news lambasted the Natural Born Thrillers, detailing eight casualties and fifty-five injured. Pax Humana and other local anti-super groups demanded that the team disband.

Large protests had formed around the compound, picket signs, posters and everything, led by Senator Huntley. The anti-superhero politician was all over the news nowadays. He'd started chants like "Natural Born KILLERS! Natural Born KILLERS!"

After issuing a public apology for their actions, the Thrillers holed up in their compound for the next three days to let things cool off. But Reverb admitted that their corporate overlords had benched them.

Greyson had sat in meetings that became heated arguments. Brightburn blamed Bulldozer, while Bulldozer blamed Shattershot. Erika was barely holding things together. Any meetings with Seneca International management, Greyson was shut out. The situation was glorious. But more damage had to be done.

Thankfully, Erika allowed him a day of leisure. Greyson snuck out the compound's rear exit with no civilian access, heading back to the Palisades and to Connie.

His first act of freedom was filming a vignette under his masked alias. Greyson initially felt hokey spewing his sermon against the Thrillers using his mask and voice modulator. This corporate-sponsored supervillain schtick wasn't a snug fit. But Asher Martin's marketing team compiled footage of the damage caused by recent Natural Born Thrillers battles. The ninety-second promo Greyson and Connie watched had been superb.

Visuals of Shenandoah and the Thrillers in action filled the screen as Greyson's modulated and menacing voiceover began. "Citizens of Shenandoah. You gave these Natural Born Thrillers permission to be your protectors, which exacted a heavy toll. Did that permission include causing more damage than the villains?" the voice scoffed. "I doubt San Miguel gave their Shield of Justice permission to paralyze a man who surrendered. Your consent makes these heroes arrogant enough to hire a former villain in Shattershot. It's time that Shenandoah's residents take their city back." The visuals faded to reveal Greyson's masked face with alternating imagery of the Thrillers behind him. "These Natural Born Thrillers must answer for their crimes," he said onscreen, glowing red eyes opening. "Or Damocles will answer first." The promo ended.

Greyson was mesmerized. He glanced at Connie. "I love it."

She was bouncing in her seat. "I know, right?"

"The reveal at the end…"

Asher cleared his throat obnoxiously for their attention. "We're happy with this?"

Greyson looked over his shoulder and nodded his approval. "When's it launching?"

"Already launched an hour ago through anonymous social media accounts," Asher said with a respectful nod. "That codename was a pure genius."

Greyson offered a proud smirk. Damocles. The name had come from a Biblical parable, and the significance to his crusade was unmissable. "If these heroes feel a sword hanging over their neck, then they'll be afraid. Fear causes mistakes. And mistakes can break reputations."

Connie's proud gaze seared through his loins. "Where does that lead these broken heroes?"

"To their end. By my hand." Greyson then faced Asher. "Nice work."

Asher's expression grew excited. "Ooh, the Natural Born Thrillers' news conference is on."

Connie grabbed their TV remote and switched to a local channel. The team stood in costume and somber-faced behind some podium in downtown Shenandoah. Seneca publicists stood behind them. Greyson hadn't been invited to attend as a trainee. That was a relief, since his plans weren't complete.

Erika Skye was concluding her drawn-out apology. "Our sincerest apologies for this tragedy." She looked and sounded genuine, and Greyson pitied her. "And we'll work hard to regain Shenandoah's trust."

Their publicist started fielding questions.

"Many of your fights cause significant collateral damage," a female reporter challenged. "Can you promise this won't happen again?"

Bulldozer and Reverb shifted awkwardly behind Erika.

"I cannot," she confessed. "But…our goal is to lower and prevent these occurrences."

Brightburn stepped forward, photogenic and charming. "The NBT will pay the hospital and funeral bills for all victims of this recent tragedy."

That drew gasps and murmurs of approval from the gathered reporters.

Erika Skye nodded, jostling her braids somewhat. "This won't bring back their loved ones or heal the injured, but we hope it can help."

This annoyed Greyson. The last thing he wanted was the Thrillers navigating out of this mess. *I'll have to step up my game—*

"Erika Skye," a male reporter asked after being chosen. He had a thick Irish accent. "Is it true that Shattershot is an ex-criminal?"

More murmurs from the gathered reporters.

Their publicist went rigid. Shattershot turned bone-white. His teammates all appeared blindsided.

"Where did you hear this?" Erika pressed.

"A claim by the activist, Damocles," the reporter continued. "Is it true?"

Greyson stood riveted. Connie guffawed.

The Thrillers' publicist dove before the microphone to answer, only for Shattershot to grab the mic from her.

"It's true," he blurted out. "I worked for the Conglomerate criminal organization in DC."

More gasps from the gaggle of press with some angrier reactions bubbling to the forefront. This was getting juicy.

"But that's not who I am anymore—" he got out before the publicist wrestled the mic away.

Bulldozer then yanked Shattershot behind him like a rag doll.

"Why wasn't this publicly disclosed?" another reporter demanded. "How can the public trust your word when this was hidden?" The entire press corps piled on the team, which stood helpless.

Greyson clicked the TV off. "That was a spectacular shitshow," he exclaimed, beyond pleased.

Asher grinned. "A reporter we kept from *SLOCO Daily*. He'll sell whatever story we feed him."

Connie hugged Greyson's waist, hunger in her eyes. "You in the mood to celebrate?"

There was nothing Greyson wanted more. But a glance at the clock revealed how long he'd been away. "Yes, but I should get back." He leaned in for a long, loving kiss. "Next time."

After departing his condo, Greyson took a rideshare back through Shenandoah's derelict streets. God, what a wretched city. From alerts on his phone, news about Shattershot's past was gaining traction. Even more news outlets were digging into who Damocles was. Let them wonder.

Greyson reached his destination, half a mile behind the compound away from the protests.

As he stepped out of rideshare, his burner phone rang.

"There's an unwelcome guest in your room," Connie warned.

Greyson's brow beetled. Back at the condo, Connie could see footage from the hidden cameras she'd installed. Greyson hung up and ran to the entrance as fast as his legs would carry him.

Once inside, he beelined for his room to find Bulldozer's massive frame rummaging through his closet.

"What the fuck?" Greyson came this close to gravitationally tossing this clod across the room. Swallowing the urge, he marched forward. "Get out of my closet, asshole!"

Bulldozer spun around in metallic form and advanced. "Who did you tell?"

Greyson was forced to backpedal, too pissed to grasp his meaning. "What?"

"Who did you tell about Shattershot?" Bulldozer jabbed his finger on Greyson's chest.

Greyson recovered quickly, clinging to his outrage. "Seriously? I don't know anyone in Shenandoah!"

Bulldozer took another menacing step forward. "You're lying."

Greyson almost got knocked over by Bulldozer. "I don't care what you believe. I'm innocent." Outward anger aside, he felt icy fear within. This could all end if he didn't play it properly.

Bulldozer continued forward, fixated on him. "First, you didn't help when our mission went to shit."

"I stopped one of the protesters from escaping," Greyson countered.

"Then you vanish for hours."

"Erika gave me time off today." Greyson was pressed against the wall of his own room. "I walked around the city to clear my head."

Bulldozer narrowed his suspicious, gleaming eyes. "I doubt that."

Greyson didn't enjoy how close Bulldozer was with those sledgehammer-like fists. So he went on offense. "No wonder Nighthawk left if this is how you treat your teammates."

Bulldozer reared up to his full seven-foot-three height. "What did you say?" The words were like thunder across a plain.

Now I got him angry. Greyson leaned forward, fists clenched for a fight. "Was that a nerve?"

"Hey!" Erika's arrival into the bedroom forced Bulldozer several steps back. She wedged between her teammates dressed in a t-shirt and jeans, eyes darting between them. "What is going on?"

Bulldozer jabbed a massive, accusing finger at Greyson. "Your new boy vanished when Damocles spilled the beans about Shattershot." He sneered. "Real convenient."

Greyson remained calm, locked onto his enemy. "Bulldozer went through my stuff without permission."

Erika whipped around. "What?"

Bulldozer's righteous anger wavered. "Only this team and Seneca international knew about Shattershot! He must have told someone." His accusation sounded petulant now.

Erika was disgusted. "Conspiracy theories, Dozer? You pulled shit like this with Shattershot."

Bulldozer was looking surly again. "So you're trusting him without question?"

"He's being more of a team player than you right now."

Bulldozer appeared more hurt than incensed. "How *dare* you?"

Erika steamrolled over him. "How *dare* you continue to bully new team members. Back off of Levi!" The order was firm and furious, just like Erika.

Greyson said nothing during the exchange, pretending to be aggrieved.

"Erika—" Bulldozer tried.

"Understand?" Erika demanded.

The giant man shot a venomous glare at Greyson before stomping off.

Only then did Greyson exhale the breath he'd been holding. Bulldozer's paranoia had become a blessing.

Erika was visibly ill when turning to Greyson. "You okay?"

Best to not gloat. He raised both hands in contrition. "Sorry for causing any conflict."

Erika immediately waved the accusation off. "This isn't on you, okay?" She offered a commiserating smile, like they were in this together.

You have no idea. "Thanks, Erika," Greyson said with a grateful smile. "You're a great leader, by the way."

Erika stopped smiling. "Tell that to the eight dead and fifty-five injured."

Greyson flinched. That might have sounded too ass-kissy. "Right."

Erika turned to leave, then stopped. "Levi?"

"Yeah."

"Did you leak about Shattershot?"

"Absolutely not," Greyson lied, meeting her stare unwaveringly.

Erika relaxed. "I just needed to hear that."

"I understand." After she left, Greyson closed his door wearing a Cheshire grin. Time to escalate the plan.

CHAPTER 23

The skies had darkened after almost three hours of searching.

And Hugo was losing his shit.

He'd flown in costume over downtown, Paso Robles, Atascadero, and the City of Wonder's other suburbs listening for two distinct heartbeats.

Hugo had zoomed past Brie and Jordana's favorite hangouts, his telescopic vision combing over anyone who looked familiar. Simon was tracking Briseis and Jordana by way of their school laptops and tablets. It was like they'd vanished off the face of the earth.

Now he floated miles over the city, stiff winds buffeting his durable frame. San Miguel and its suburbs was illuminated beneath him from the silhouetted mountaintops to the dark churning sea. The two girls he treasured weren't in any part of it.

What made this harder to digest was that Hugo couldn't find them.

The crackle of his comm channels startled him out of self-pity. "Hey, Bogie—" Hugo scowled. "Aegis on comms," he snapped.

Simon drew a flinching breath. "Sorry…Aegis. Any luck?"

Hugo listened again, parsing through thousands of voices. None were Brie or Jodie. "I've searched Paso High, their favorite hangouts, everywhere." He forced back tears. "What about you?"

"I found footage from a faraway traffic camera of Brie and Jodie parking at the riverbed," Simon replied, employing Clint's training to help. "No one followed, and they never left the car."

Hugo fumed. "What the hell?"

"I'm cross-checking with Clint to be sure," Simon hastily reassured.

That made this disappearance even more bizarre. His hypersensitive smell hadn't picked up any scents in the car besides Brie's and Jordana's.

"Got off the phone with Ramon," J-Tom declared on the comm channel.

Hugo's heart leaped in eagerness. "What do you got?"

"That Aegis-bot wasn't following just you." Worry and fatigue encroached on J-Tom's usual perkiness. "Ramon also found video footage and GPS stats of it following Jodie and Brie separately."

Pure ice slithered down Hugo's spine. *Shit...* The disclosure left him more violated. Whoever knew his identity had targeted his friends too. "Are more Aegis-bots flying around San Miguel?"

"Ramon checked with Vulcan," J-Tom said. "He only built one."

"Vulcan could be lying."

"Ramon says Vulcan is truthful to a fault," J-Tom pushed back.

"Then we keep looking," Hugo countered.

"It's been three hours," J-Tom said. "If this keeps up—"

"Don't say it," Hugo barked.

"*Aegis,*" J-Tom spoke over him. "If Briseis and Jordana aren't found tonight, we *have* to tell their families...and the authorities."

Hugo squeezed his eyes shut. The failure sat like a pile of bricks in his stomach. Somewhere in this city, Brie and Jordana were scared or hurt...

Or dead.

And Hugo couldn't save them. That reality was too agonizing to imagine. "Another hour," he begged. "Please."

J-Tom said nothing for several seconds. "I'll buy you as much time as I can." Empathy laced her voice.

Hugo opened his eyes, grateful for the reprieve. "Thanks, Jenny."

She exited the comm channel.

"Simon, you still there?"

"Yeah."

"Is this my fault?" Hugo tried to sound strong, but his voice cracked at the end from holding back tears.

"No!" Simon denied immediately.

A sad half-smile pulled at Hugo's lips. Of course Simon would say that. That didn't erase the contradicting evidence. "Dr. Michelman is missing. Some android attacks me in public. Now Brie and Jodie get kidnapped..." The tears flowed, and Hugo didn't stop them. "How is this not on me?"

Simon remained silent while Hugo regained his composure. "Working with Dr. Michelman probably wasn't smart. But you were fighting a greater threat," he decided, firm yet tender. "And I see how careful you are with your secret identity. You never intentionally put them in danger."

"They still got kidnapped," Hugo pressed, his voice quivering, "because they know me."

"We'll find them, uso," Simon encouraged. "Don't lose hope."

Again, Simon Han revealed his quality. If Brie and Jody were found unharmed, Hugo promised to be a better friend to him and everyone else. "Thanks," he whispered. The call ended shortly after.

Hugo was about to resume flying around San Miguel, looking and listening.

He turned his attention on downtown San Miguel's dazzling skyline miles away and the one skyscraper rivaling the OWE Tower. That ugly Paxton-Brandt spire stabbed into the sky like a bloody spike. Extensive scaffolding still enclosed the foundation as its smaller business centers underwent reconstruction.

Hatred clung to Hugo's skin while he glared at Paxton-Brandt's HQ. That hatred was urging him to punch a real hole into the building and demand answers.

Then you're the bad guy, a voice said, sounding like Annie. And what if they didn't have Brie and Jodie?

Hugo slowed his ragged breaths to just think. There was a path he hadn't tried. One that his mother would've suggested.

Steeling away any ego, he tapped the right side of his hood. A list of contacts appeared on his eyescreen. After scouring the list, Hugo made the call.

"Hi," he greeted, thankful that she answered. "I need your help."

"I was just calling you," Lady Liberty replied. "It's about your two missing friends?"

Hugo's shock quickly became dark fury. "How do you know that?"

"The person who has them reached out," his former mentor said, calm and collected as usual. "Both girls are unharmed."

Hugo couldn't describe the monumental relief he felt contrasted to his cold hatred for the kidnapper. "Who has them and where are they?" he demanded.

"Meet me at Ragged Point," Lady Liberty requested. "We'll get your friends back."

CHAPTER 24

Hugo found her floating over the craggy coastline of Ragged Point, a picturesque town at northernmost San Luis Obispo County. Moonlight peeked through the clouds, illuminating Lady Liberty's iconic red costume and her long legs in knee-high gold boots.

Accepting her help made Hugo sick, but he had no choice. She turned when he drifted a few feet away. Lady Liberty smiled. "Your flight form keeps improving."

Hugo had been watching footage of other fliers—even Lady Liberty—continuously applying their techniques with his own. He didn't know how to respond kindly, so he just nodded.

Disappointment dimmed Lady Liberty's smile. She turned and flew down over Ragged Point's stretch of inns, homes, and gardens. They landed in front of a small lighthouse, white-walled and unlit. Totally ordinary—which was the point.

Hugo's eyes narrowed. No matter how much he focused his hypersensitivity on this lighthouse, it might as well have been part of the rocky outcrop.

A cloaking array, he realized. "A Vanguard safehouse." It wasn't a question.

Lady Liberty nodded. "Follow me."

Hugo followed her down to the grassy terrain around the lighthouse and entered. When the door slid closed behind them, a red laser scanned Lady Liberty head to toe.

Like Dr. Michelman's hideout, Hugo noted as the floor beneath them zipped down two levels.

This narrow passage had gunmetal walls all around, ending at a round vault-like door.

Hugo pointed. "Behind there?"

When Lady Liberty nodded, he marched forward off the elevator. His thirst for vengeance grew with each stride. "I'm ripping this asshole's head off."

Lady Liberty caught up and spun him around. "No, you're really not." His strength and four-inch height advantage aside, her presence loomed large.

Hugo was in no mood for lectures. "I don't take orders from you."

Lady Liberty stood unmoved. "And your fists are better solutions? My way won't get anyone paralyzed."

Anger boiled beneath Hugo's skin. But right now, he needed Lady Liberty. He gestured for her to pass.

"Travis?" Lady Liberty called out once they reached the rounded entrance. "I'm here with Aegis."

Hugo perked up. "Travis who?"

When the rounded door slid open, he understood why.

At the door was a lanky young man, pale-skinned, his costume a shoddy army-green color.

Travis Carter, aka Polymer, a metamorph from the Warguard, The Vanguard's training squad.

Him? Hugo fumed.

Polymer's lean face shifted upon seeing Lady Liberty. "Thank God. You're here." He turned to Hugo. "Aegis, I—"

"Shut up," Hugo snarled in his Aegis voice, bowling Polymer over to get inside. The compact room had rocky ceilings and spare décor save the high-tech consoles. In a conference room across the chambers, Hugo spotted a V-shaped table, smaller than the one at The Vanguard's main HQ. Under normal circumstances, this might've been awesome. But not tonight.

Hugo turned to Polymer. "Where are they?"

The metamorph jabbed a finger at an opaque windowed room to their left. "In there."

Hugo dashed forward and wrenched the door off the hinges. Inside a small medical bay, he found them.

But something was wrong.

"Jordana? Briseis?" Hugo called out in normal tones, not caring if they recognized him. Both girls lay unconscious on parallel slabs side by side, Jodie in a Mets jersey and jeans and Brie in crimson Paso High tennis warmups. They looked so young.

Hugo circled the slabs, listening for heartbeats and breaths, sniffing for traces of poison. Their scents were off, squeezing his heart with worry.

He saw Polymer at the door. "What did you do to them?"

The ex-Warguard member entered, hands raised in surrender. "I kept them sedated." Contrition dominated his face. "They're unharmed and don't know about you—AGGGH!"

Hugo reached him in half a heartbeat, holding Polymer by the throat against the wall. He squeezed Polymer's neck, which felt like rubber. "Why did you kidnap them and steal that Aegis android?"

Lady Liberty watched from the door with steely eyes, making no move to stop this.

Polymer gagged and flailed his limbs. "I didn't kidnap anyone or steal that robot!"

"I'll beat answers outta you." Hugo drew his fist back, eager to make Polymer beg for mercy and offer none.

When Polymer gave Lady Liberty a desperate look, she just shrugged. "Start talking."

"I didn't kidnap your friends," Polymer repeated. "I used this safehouse for their protection."

Hugo squeezed tighter in spasming rage. Polymer's eyes bulged. "From *who?*"

Polymer was purpling from Hugo's grip. "I don't…know. I only agreed to watch them."

"And the android attack?" Lady Liberty asked.

Polymer's visible shame convicted him before his words. "I was controlling the Aegis android remotely to watch and study your movements. I mistakenly activated the attack protocols and couldn't figure out how to stop it. Sorry…"

Hugo loosened his grip but still viewed Polymer as an enemy.

Polymer breathed deep and continued. "Briseis's and Jordana's lives were in danger. The android was supposed to rescue them in your stead, if needed. But after it was destroyed, we had to improvise."

Hugo glanced at Lady Liberty, who also seemed confused.

"We?" she inquired.

"The person who stole the Aegis android, then kidnapped your friends," Polymer threw back. "They warned me about the threat on their lives and tasked me to guard them."

Hugo needed more. He jerked Polymer closer. "WHO?"

"Saracen."

The room temperature plummeted to sub-zero. Lady Liberty gasped.

Hugo dropped Polymer like a sack of dirt. Part of him didn't want to buy this. The enemy behind Brie and Jodie's kidnapping was a known terrorist who wanted to burn the government down—and knew his secret identity. "Yeahbuthuh?" This world got much scarier.

Lady Liberty loomed over Polymer. "You're working with Saracen?"

Polymer fought up to a crouch. "Saracen knew things about me. About you." He focused on Hugo. "He knew what losing Brie and Jordana would do—ERRGH."

Hugo stepped on Polymer's chest. "What does Saracen have on you?"

Polymer was in tears. But he didn't defend himself. "I didn't get blackmailed. Saracen wanted to protect your friend, and I was recruited to help."

A hand on Hugo's shoulder jarred through his anger. "Get your friends home," Lady Liberty offered. "I'll handle Polymer."

Hugo struggled with this suffocating terror. *Saracen knows who I am.* He eyed Brie and Jodie, two sleeping beauties. "How do I wake them?"

"Hethapren 12 is in there." Lady Liberty waved to the cabinets at the other end of the room. "It's like coffee injected into the bloodstream."

Hugo dashed across the room, finding plenty of Hethapren syringes. He snatched two, stashing them in a suit pocket. From there, he slung Jodie and Brie over either shoulder.

Lady Liberty typed the elevator access code so Hugo could leave.

He soared back to Jordana's car near the riverbed. Sliding Jodie into the driver's seat and Brie into the passenger's seat, Hugo strapped both in so neither would slump forward. There were several calming breaths to still his hands before he injected each girl with Hethapren.

Within seconds, the two stirred.

Hugo's relief was so profound, his eyes watered. He closed both car doors, then flew a mile up.

"Guys," Hugo stated, smiling fiercely when he called Simon and J-Tom. "They're safe."

"Thank god!" J-Tom exclaimed.

"What—?" Simon began asking.

"Later," Hugo cut in, hearing Jodie's breaths shift. "When they're home safe."

Jordana woke up as soon as he ended the call. "Mmmmmm." Her breathing shifted and quickened, like her heartrate. "Brie? Brie, wake up." Clothing rustled as Jordana was shaking Briseis awake.

Briseis's yawn sounded musical to Hugo. "Whoooa." Her pulse jumped. "When did it get dark?"

"Guess we passed out." Jodie sounded fuzzy.

"Seems like," Brie murmured. "Wow! My cellphone's blown up."

"Mine too," Jordana remarked. "Let's reply to everyone before driving back."

Hugo heard relentless tapping and clicking from inside the car as the girls texted family and friends. Whatever Polymer had injected them with them had no apparent side effects.

Minutes later, a text scrolled across Hugo's eyescreen. He'd linked his regular phone to his suit in case either Jodie or Brie contacted him.

Jordana: Hey, papi. Just woke up from a nap. Driving home now.

Hugo chuckled when speaking his reply. "Good. Text me when you're home." Once his suit converted the audio to text, the response went to Jordana.

Jordana: Of course, baby.

Twenty minutes later, Jordana's car hummed to life and left the riverbed.

Hugo followed from several miles above. He wasn't letting these two out of his sight until both were home safely. The car soon reached Rancho Huerhuero, the ritzy neighborhood where Brie's dad lived.

"About the thing earlier." Brie sounded like she was in pain. "Why did you force me to admit that?"

"I wasn't trying to hurt you, Breezy," Jordana replied in equal distress.

"I'd never risk our friendship again," Brie half-sobbed, "no matter how I feel about him."

Hugo's eyes bulged. *Brie admitted her feelings for me...to Jodie?* He kept listening.

"I know *you* wouldn't." Jordan's voice trembled. "I...I just needed you to admit it."

"But *why?*" Brie demanded.

"For me. And you." Jodie's voice gained strength. "You bottle things up until it erupts. After what you've been through, I won't let that happen again."

Old guilt weighed on Hugo's neck. His and Jodie's romance nearly ended her friendship with Brie.

"Love ya, boobs," Brie professed.

"Love ya, bitch." The smile in Jodie's voice had Hugo smiling.

Jordana pulled up to Brie's condo. "So," the latter girl said, "when are you telling Bogie about...ya know?"

Hugo hovered above, heart accelerating.

"I almost told him at the carnival," Jodie replied. "Then he got grabbed." Her voice grew emotional. "Saying anything felt asshole-ish that night."

"Bogie's insanely observant," Brie warned. "He's gonna know something's up."

Hugo reminded himself to breathe. Was she seeing someone? Or was the secret worse?

Jodie groaned. "I think he already knows. Things are weird now."

"Whatever you decide, I'm here," Brie assured. After a hug, the twosome gabbed a few minutes more about L.U.N.A.'s new rumored beau. Then Brie exited the car and headed inside her condo complex.

Jodie drove to her more modest Paso Robles neighborhood through dwindling traffic. She had a habit of reciting items on her to-do list. Or cursing at reckless drivers, which brought out her Bronx accent more.

Hugo's heart warmed at these little Jordana moments. She deserved someone she could trust. *Is that me?* Hugo flinched from considering that answer as he followed Jodie's car from above. Only when she'd parked outside her house and scurried inside to her berating parents did he know peace.

He never wanted to experience that level of worry again.

A new call pinged in his ear, the caller ID scrolling across his eyescreen. Irritation flared but not as strongly as before. "Yes?" he replied after answering.

"Above the cloud layer over Arroyo Grande." Lady Liberty then hung up.

Hugo just wanted to sleep. But she might have more details on that idiot Polymer. He reached Arroyo Grande quickly, bursting through the blanketing clouds above the suburb. A pale crescent dominated the skies, splashing soft light across a sea of grey clouds and billowy pillars reaching for the stars.

Lady Liberty was partially silhouetted by moonlight, a goddess of the skies. Harsh winds tousled her long bob of brunette, silvery diadem gleaming bright. She smiled like Betty Ortiz, not Lady Liberty. "Hey."

"Thank you." Hugo floated closer and forced away his gratitude. "This doesn't mean I fully forgive you." He pointed to emphasize his stance.

Lady Liberty glanced away as if stung. "But it's a start."

Hugo got to the point. "About Polymer." There had to be punishment for working with Saracen. "What's happening to him?"

"Nothing."

Hugo momentarily thought she was joking. "What?" Her stony expression said otherwise.

"Hugo." Lady Liberty raised both hands in peace. "Polymer…Travis deserves another chance. He's a good kid."

Hugo opened his mouth heatedly. Lady Liberty interrupted. "The Warguard was a casualty of The Vanguard's demise. Polymer and his peers have been rudderless ever since." Her gaze fell. "My former teammates and I failed them."

Hugo balled up a fist to stop from trembling with anger. He wasn't interested in forgiving an attack this personally. "My friends could've died."

Lady Liberty looked up sharply. "Then we'd be having a different conversation. Worry more about why Saracen is interested in you."

That reminder felt colder than the frigid winds whipping around them. "Right. That."

"Polymer's willing to tell you everything he knows about Saracen."

Distaste coiled tightly in Hugo's chest. "I'd rather not see him again."

Lady Liberty glowered. "You're passing up a valuable source of information because of pride? I taught you better than that."

The two superheroes glowered at each other from across the moonlit sky. Hugo itched to tell Lady Liberty to fuck off. But there was no escaping the logic in her advice. Goddammit. "Fine," he grumbled.

Lady Liberty gave an irritatingly smug nod. "I'll send his contact info." She then performed an Olympic-level dive into the clouds and vanished.

Hugo floated alone, puzzled how his life had become so batshit bonkers.

CHAPTER 25

"My arms wanna fall off," Greyson grumbled, eyeing a juicy cheeseburger in his hands. "But I gotta eat!"

That won laughter out of Shattershot in their small corner booth at the supers' bar Mega Pantry. The empath used a hat and glasses as a disguise, enjoying a taco salad while skimming his phone.

Erika Skye had worked everyone hard on minimizing collateral damage in the field. It was the team's only option after being temporarily benched by Seneca International.

As a reward for three straight days of grueling combat drills, Erika gave the team a night off. Greyson was happy to be out, but for different reasons.

The bar was crammed with patrons drinking and eating and carrying on. Most were supers mixed with some humans, a place in Shenandoah where racial divisions were forgotten. On the wide TV behind the bar, Lady Liberty looked gorgeous while battling the Dangerous Divas, a villainous trio in San Miguel. Havoc, Fatale, and Trauma always provided an edge-of-your-seat battle against their longtime enemy. But as expected, the Glorious Glamazon eked out a win before restraining the defeated villains.

The victory drew cheers across the bar. But Greyson pretended to ignore the mountainous man at the bar in a laughable disguise glancing in their direction for the past two hours.

Shattershot hadn't seen Bulldozer spying on them, but Greyson didn't have the heart to share. The empath was enjoying their night out. Plus, Greyson wanted to keep gaining his trust.

Shattershot's grinning face was illuminated by his phone. "I think I like this Saracen dude." He handed over his phone unprompted. "He dropped the motherload of data dumps."

Greyson stared back, stunned by the unexpected gift. He quickly brought out his own phone, placing the two devices side by side and opened a tracking app when Shattershot focused on his own salad. The tracker wirelessly uploaded onto Shattershot's cell to run invisibly in the background.

Then Greyson read the news app on display. The media portrayed Saracen as a rogue hacktivist akin to Snowden after he'd dropped countless classified documents. This latest release specifying American interference in Amarantha struck at Greyson's core.

He shifted in his seat, memories of his time on the island littering his mind like a bad dream.

Shattershot shook his head and laughed. "I always knew something was screwy about what happened in Amarantha despite what N3 kept peddling."

Greyson handed back the phone, a risky idea surfacing. Providing some real backstory might build more trust with his unwilling pawn. "Everything the news media reports on Amarantha is bullshit."

He then told Shattershot the truth, from the OSA's tech fueling the oppression of Amarantha's supers to the botched AmeriForce invasion.

By the time Greyson finished, Shattershot's jaw was hanging open. "You're *fucking* kidding me…"

Greyson shook his bushy-haired head. "America, Canada, and Mexico left their own heroes to die. And the current Amaranthine government is completely legitimate."

"That's crazy!" Shattershot whisper-yelled, leaning over the table. "How do you know all this?"

I have Amarantha's leader on speed dial. "A bounty hunter friend does work there," Greyson lied. "Keeps me updated."

They discussed the matter several more minutes before Shattershot switched topics. "You think Seneca will dump me?" He looked shaken.

"Because you're an ex-criminal?" Greyson challenged, arms folded. "Or do you have any dirtier secrets?" He hoped there were dirtier secrets.

Shattershot walled off. "I just…I can't screw this up."

Greyson's heart softened. "You won't." He reached over to slap his teammate's shoulder. "We need to watch each other's backs."

Shattershot beamed. "I'm cool with that." Shoveling down the rest of his meal, he then stood, lean and well-dressed. "Anyway. I'm off to get sloshed. I got this," he stated as Greyson reached for his wallet.

"Have fun, brother." Greyson watched him head to the bar and pay for their meal. Shattershot then disappeared through the crowd toward the back.

That left Greyson with his stalker, still nursing on the same beer bought almost three hours ago.

Greyson shot off a quick text to Connie.

ME: SS's on the move. Tracker's on his phone.

Greyson slipped on his coat and shouldered his way toward the same exit as Shattershot.

From the corner of his eye, the hulking figure at the bar rose.

He stepped into the frosty evening at a brisk pace. Several yards back, the large shadow trailed him at a slower yet persistent pace.

"Alright, big man," Greyson whispered. "Let's play." Spying the nearest alley, he powerwalked forward and made a quick left. His pursuer's heavy footfall became a sprint.

Greyson negated his tether to the ground, flying straight up. The anti-gravity leap was a risk with all the monitoring drones soaring about. But it was worth embarrassing Bulldozer.

Moments later, Bulldozer, in his hoodie, rushed inside the alleyway to one end and peeked out. He then ran back to the entrance. "Where the *hell* did he go?" Bulldozer demanded.

After a few more minutes of searching, Bulldozer gave up. "Shoulda tailed Shattershot," he grumbled.

Once he was a significant distance away, Greyson stood from his perch and laughed. What an invasive asshole. A buzzing text disrupted his gloating.

CIH: You close? I'm in Valley Heights.

ME: Gimme the address babe.

Greyson leaped back down to the alleyway and called a rideshare.

Fifteen minutes later, he reached his destination. Connie was waiting atop one of Shenandoah's many empty buildings. She wore a catsuit, hair in a ponytail. Her infectious smile greeted him as they kissed.

"Hey, you." Greyson just enjoyed looking at Connie, holding his wife.

"Hi!" She pecked his lips, wrinkling her nose. "Everything kosher?"

Greyson rolled his eyes, not wanting to think about his stalker. "Yeah. Had to lose a tail. Bulldozer."

Connie's smile vanished. "Say the word and he's dead." The request held no hesitation.

Greyson gave her an alarmed onceover. "Love the enthusiasm," he remarked, higher than normal. "But I got plans for him." He switched from his wife's murderous impulses. "Do you have something on Shattershot?" In his sparse free time, he'd tasked Connie and Paxton-Brandt with deeper investigations into his teammates for more dirt. And by Connie's excited text, she had something big.

Connie stepped back from him and nodded at the building across the street. "Last location before he shut off his phone. A hostel for those coming in and out of town."

One building over, a couple was kissing and groping in one of the fourth-floor windows. Greyson almost turned away on instinct, until recognizing Shattershot. "Nice."

The woman all over Shattershot was stunning, slim, and with spiky blue hair. "Who's the booty call?"

"Bam-Bam," Connie answered.

Greyson frowned, that name inducing hazy memories. "Sounds familiar."

"Works for The Conglomerate…like Shattershot before."

"Oh shit!" Greyson turned back to the building across the street. Paxton-Brandt had given them a rundown of known East Coast rogues. Shattershot and his lady had retired into the bedroom, shutting off the lights. "I doubt the other Thrillers know."

Connie had that mischievous look that he loved. "We can spill the beans."

Greyson brushed off the notion. "Let's get more intel on his girlfriend. We can use this against Shattershot."

Connie pouted but recovered quickly. "Done. I got something else you're going to love."

Greyson pecked her forehead. "I love your surprises."

Connie pulled out her phone and clicked on something. "Thanks to the tracker you put on this teammate's phone, I've tailed them for a week whenever they sneak out." She showed him the image of a pale older gentleman who would've been handsome except for his beer-bloated stomach and bad combover. "Robin MacKay. Successful restaurant owner. Crappy boss."

Connie swiped the phone screen to another image of Robin MacKay lying prone. "Hospital-bound as of thirty-five minutes ago."

Greyson recoiled. MacKay was covered in gruesome, smoking burns. "What happened?"

"Brightburn happened."

Greyson's stomach dropped out. "What?"

Connie nodded, solidifying his bewilderment. "Robin has a sexual assault charge against him. But he copped a plea deal two years ago and barely got a month in jail." She gazed at the image of MacKay's burnt body. "Brightburn took justice into her own hands."

Brightburn, vapid selfie queen, had a dark side. "The public will love that," Greyson gushed.

"MacKay isn't her first." Connie drew closer, eyes glittering in the darkness. "Or worst."

Greyson beamed at the possibilities. Damn, he loved Connie. "Show me every victim."

CHAPTER 26

Hugo waited three days before contacting Polymer. First off, he wanted to make sure Jodie and Brie were okay.

Jordana was being more lovey-dovey than usual, which he always welcomed. Yet she still wouldn't reveal her secret.

Brie finally stopped avoiding Hugo, but the lingering tension between them led to brief and stilted conversations. Not welcome. She'd get this weird look on her face whenever she saw him. Definitely uncomfortable. Startled, almost.

In short, both girls showed no side effects or memories from their kidnapping.

Secondly, J-Tom was going for her psych evaluation to become his trainee. She'd been panicking, but Hugo had been coaching her through what to expect.

And thirdly, Hugo had kept a lower profile as Aegis, sticking to rescue missions. Lower profile made him, his friends, and family less of a target. In fact, Hugo wasn't planning to contact Polymer.

Until Saracen's latest data dump, revealing America's role in Amarantha becoming an apartheid state. The OSA's involvement was extensive, along with its Canadian and Mexican counterparts.

Saracen could out me too. Fear had forced Hugo to grudgingly reach out yesterday.

Polymer had been thrilled. "Let's meet at Danger Room," he'd suggested. "Neutral territory."

Hugo wasn't crazy about such a visible meeting place, especially a popular superhero-themed nightclub. At least he would get this meeting over with.

AJ sat cross-legged on Hugo's bed. "You sure about this?"

"Absolutely not." Hugo stood before a mirror, adjusting his costume but hadn't pulled his mask and hood on. "I gotta see what he knows." He glanced at his brother in soccer gear. But AJ didn't have practice or a game tonight. Hugo had been paying closer attention. "Where are you going?"

AJ immediately perked up. "Homeless shelter with Dallas and the rest of the soccer team."

Hugo wasn't expecting that. "Interesting hangout spot."

"My idea," AJ insisted. "Playing soccer with homeless kids."

A smile slashed Hugo's face. "Mom raised you right." He walked over, tousling his brother's hair.

AJ's cheeks reddened. "You inspired me to help people." He looked away.

"Oh." Dizzying warmth enfolded Hugo's heart. "Thanks, uso."

Cellphone vibrations interrupted the brotherly moment. Hugo reached for his work cell on the desk.

Knox: Polymer's here.

ME: On my way.

Hugo sighed. Developing contacts independent of Lady Liberty was paying off. "I'm out."

AJ hopped off his brother's bed. "I wanna know how it all goes."

"Absolutely." Hugo pulled his mask and hood on. "If you need anything before going to the shelter—"

AJ scoffed. "I'm thirteen, uso. And Mom will call every half-hour." Hugo chuckled. "Later." He raced from the house and then his neighborhood before taking to the skies.

Minutes later, Hugo floated high above downtown San Miguel's vast sea of lights and traffic.

Most big metropolises had diverse collections of superheroes, but San Miguel was the epicenter of the superhero world. Danger Room embodied that supremacy, a club where superheroes, admirers, and cape chasers converged.

From what Hugo recalled, ex-hero Leviathan had opened several clubs in the mid-1990s to be like Planet Hollywood for superhero fans. Chicago's Watchtower, HQ in Manhattan and London's Elseworld were hotspots in their respective cities. Regardless, Danger Room remained the crown jewel.

Danger Room stood out among Grand Street Row's nightclubs. Its large half-dome reached three stories, sporting an Art Deco façade with reflective sea-blue windows covering the front. Bright spotlights ringed the nightclub, reaching to the heavens.

From what Hugo saw, the line to enter Danger Room wrapped around the block, taxis and rideshares pulling up constantly. Mobs of paparazzi gathered near the front entrance to snap major arrivals.

Hugo gulped. He'd defeated a six-person team singlehandedly. But a popular nightclub creeped him out?

He slapped himself. "We're doing this."

He plunged to earth feet-first. Air whistled past him, tiny buildings and narrow streets ballooning quickly. Hugo slowed his descent right before touchdown, landing on one knee with both arms thrown back. Picture-perfect superhero landing.

A shockwave billowed around Hugo followed by a woman's squeal. The world briefly held its breath.

Moments later, the line and paparazzi erupted as Hugo rose. Cameras flashed like crazy.

He strode for the entrance, passing Tsunami in her little black dress, long caramel-brown hair combed back. God, she looked hot…and windblown. Tsunami pressed her skirt down, glaring.

Hugo winked at her. The reaction from those in line was even crazier.

"Aegis! Aegis!"

"I'll be your shieldmaiden, Aegis!"

"We love you, Shield of Justice!"

"Aegis," a reporter caught his ear. "How do you respond to rumors that Tomorrow Man might retire?"

That turned Hugo around. The reporter, a slim black man with glasses and long dreads, held out a recording device. He should've kept quiet, but the urge was too great. "How can someone retire when they barely had a career?"

The crowd *ooohed* and roared like school kids at lunch. The reporter choked on a laugh.

Annie's gonna kill me. Hugo shrugged, then nodded at the waiting line. That drove them into a frenzy. Fucking wild. The door person unfastened the rope to let him in.

A shapely female waited beside the entrance, superstrong like many of Danger Room's bouncers. The short-sleeved leather romper put her cleavage and killer legs on display. She was tall, but Hugo had several inches on her. The right side of her frizzy purple hair was styled in Viking braids, complementing smooth coffee-brown skin.

The bouncer smirked at him, arms folded. "Shield of Justice."

"Rebekah Knox," Hugo replied in his Aegis voice, equally cheeky. "You texted?"

Becky Knox's almond-shaped eyes crinkled. "This way, young man." Hugo followed her inside. Their first meeting months ago had been a violent misunderstanding. Thanks to Justice Jones's peacemaking, Knox was now Hugo's informer. Bouncing at superhero clubs and villain bars got her close to valued secrets.

As they stepped inside, Hugo saw more superhero mecca than nightclub. Framed costumes and signed posters decorated the walls, along with photos and videos of superheroes in action. Wax replicas of Titan, Lady Liberty, Sentinel, and Geist filled several display cases. It dismayed Hugo that only one of them remained active.

"The fliers' roof entrance avoids the plebs and photogs," Becky called over her shoulder.

Hugo stared at her. "There's a fliers' entrance?"

Becky spun around. "Aww. A Danger Room virgin." She gave Hugo sultry eyes, fussing at his collar. "Don't worry, baby. I'll pop your cherry right." She gave him a love pat on the face and moved on.

Hugo's cheeks burned. "Cute." He followed, reminding himself that Becky was twelve years his senior.

Mom had taken Hugo and AJ to Danger Room's café many times for lunch, when the club was closed.

A night visit as a superhero was something Hugo had never imagined. Following Becky through the café to the second level, he basically entered an alternate universe.

The best way Hugo could describe this was a costume party on steroids and psychedelic drugs. The song moving the dancefloor was "Marvelo vs Evil Genius," a hero vs villain hip-hop duo. The rap subgenre featured two rappers battling back and forth in a song, the "villain" rhyming his schemes while the "hero" rapped on stopping them. Simple but catchy.

Shouldering through the dancefloor, Hugo spotted Sunrider and Starchylde writhing to the music. Tonight, the pair wore sexy versions of their costumes. Blur sat at a VIP table with XT on the surface, in costume minus the goggles. He was sucking face with some striking Latina woman who happened to be spilling out of her body-hugging tube dress.

Hugo did a double take. The woman was Rebecca Reyes.

Is that business or pleasure? He snorted and let his eyes wander. Hugo spotted C-listers like Tatanka, muscle-bound with curved metal horns, his tight pants leaving little to be imagined. He flirted with Strobe, whose brilliant glow allowed her to get away with minimal covering. Woodstock, with a green shrub afro and skin like pale beechwood, chatted up Megaplex, a megamorph in a red unisuit accentuating his muscles.

Hugo knew Danger Room was packed with out-of-town heroes trying out for San Miguel's new superhero team, desperate to be seen. But he was more interested in the cosplayers and costumed fans. Some cosplayers looked like clones of famous heroes. Hugo gawked at two Aegis cosplayers whose costumes and physiques were identical to his. Other cosplayers dressing as gender-reversed heroes were a real mindfuck. Two leggy girls wore risqué versions of Titan's iconic green-and-yellow costume, with silver-dyed buzzcuts. But with the good came the bad, like a flabby gentleman in a Missy Magnificent crop-top and microskirt.

Hugo didn't know where to fit that visual in his brain...or how to erase it. "Wow."

Becky Knox followed his disgusted stare. "Danger Room can give first-timers' performance anxiety."

Hugo glowered at her. "Enjoying yourself, Bex?"

"Little bit." Becky stopped and pointed at the top floor where certain rooms had opaque windows. "Vanguard's third-floor VIP suite."

"That's still open?" Hugo remarked.

"Still funded by the government," Becky said over the booming music and directed him up the staircase. "Vulcan, Wyldcat, and Robbie Rocket were regulars." She paused and laughed at something. "Titan swung by semiregularly. He had a thing for cosplayers. Especially when they dressed like—"

Hugo cut her off with a hand chop. "Not interested." He knew enough about Titan's promiscuity.

Becky said no more until they reached the VIP lounge door. "Find me when you're done. I got news."

"Will do." Hugo snuck a peek at the sway in her hips as she headed back downstairs.

Opening the door, he found a spacious lounge with plush couches, and gold Vs engraved on each table and chair. Hugo couldn't see The Vanguard in here partying it up. *I felt the same about Titan being a slut.* Polymer was in costume on the middle couch fretfully sipping his drink. He shot up when Hugo entered.

"Thanks for coming." Polymer extended a hand, which Hugo shook. "I figured neutral ground made sense."

"And protected you from me." Hugo plopped down where Polymer had been sitting.

Polymer looked like he'd choked on a chicken bone. "Want a drink? The lounge gets concierge service."

Hugo waved that off. Not just because he was a minor, but drinking on the job was a no-no for him.

"You know Becky Knox?" Polymer sat, visibly leery. "Tread carefully."

Hugo turned, noticing how the window was clear inside the lounge. Any outside sound was muted with the door closed. Nice. "Because she occasionally bounces at so-called villain bars?" Justice Jones had spoken about Becky's history before she became one of Hugo's sources.

"Cape chasing is a sport to her." Polymer viewed Hugo's reaction smugly. "She loves the popular ones. Justice Jones, Hyperion, Wyldcat. Even Titan from what I heard. Then there's the villains she—"

Hugo's low opinion of Polymer dropped further. "We here to gossip or discuss Saracen?"

Polymer jolted at his snappish tone. "Right." He cleared his throat. "Saracen approached me a month ago. Said he needed my help in protecting the future of humanity."

Hugo arched an eyebrow beneath his mask. Polymer couldn't be *that* gullible. "You believed him?"

Polymer shook his head adamantly. "No. But he said if I refused, he'd wipe my memory of the meeting."

"He's a telepath too?"

"I guess," Polymer supposed. Up close, he had dark circles around his eyes. "I played along to get close and eventually take him down. It's why I never told anyone."

Now they were getting somewhere. "What changed?"

"Everything he said would happen did, exactly as described." Terror filled Polymer's long face. His breaths grew faster. "He knew things about me that aren't even on my file. It was insane."

Hugo's heartrate quickened. He understood why Polymer was afraid. "What does he want with me?"

"Saracen never said." Polymer reclined on the couch, staring at the ceiling. "Only that you were important to his plans. It was after grabbing your two friends that he gave the okay to contact you."

The memory of Brie and Jodie missing rekindled Hugo's anger. "Has he contacted you since then?"

Polymer shook his head again, in his own world. "And I'm fine with that."

"Thank you." With that, Hugo moved to rise.

Polymer raised a hand. "One more thing." Annoyed, Hugo sat.

"Would you be interested in reviving The Vanguard?"

Hugo thought Polymer was joking. The other hero's face showed no mirth.

"Think about it, Hu—" Whatever reaction he saw from Hugo made him go pale. "Sorry, Aegis. You're the new "It" hero now. Someone like you could convince the government to reup The Vanguard."

Hugo's reply was an instant, massive NOPE. "Why don't you ask yourself?"

Polymer's smile didn't reach his eyes. "An untested Warguard reservist? They laughed in my face."

The rejection in his voice reached Hugo unexpectedly. "And your teammates?"

"Some quit." Polymer's stare grew unfocused as he recounted. "Others are trying at solo careers or joining the new ERATs being set up across America." His eyes focused on Hugo. "I wasn't blessed with a Herculean body or a combat-ready powerset." He raised his right hand, which shifted and swelled into a large mallet. "I'm a kid from Topeka with stretchy powers who wants to protect people."

With that, Hugo's dislike faded. "Powers don't make heroes. Actions do." He stood, heading for the exit.

"So that's a maybe?" Polymer called out.

"Goodnight, Polymer." Hugo closed the door. The discussion had helped but didn't reveal why Saracen had targeted him.

The balcony gave him a full view of the dancefloor. Heroes and cosplayers grooved to the music, their faces fluctuating between pleasure and pain. If not for being in costume, Hugo would've joined. He missed dancing desperately.

He spotted Sunrider at a VIP table perched on some Asian pretty boy's lap. He looked barely twenty with wild, shaggy hair. The pretty boy had to be a popstar or out-of-town superhero, especially with a ridiculous fur coat splayed open to reveal his chiseled torso. Four other Asian men similarly dressed sat nearby, all schmoozing with gaggles of ladies thirsty for their attention. Their entourage included several burly bodyguards. Hugo squinted, recognizing the superhuman K-Pop group Beasts from the Far East. They'd performed at Paso Robles's Parthenon Stadium last night.

Their latest hit, *Beast Mode*, came on the speakers. The club response was volcanic.

The quintet smirked knowingly at each other. The lead singer, Stylo, cuddling with Sunrider, locked eyes with Hugo. He raised his glass, his human flesh transforming into sparkling crystal. The other band members raised their glasses as well. Several turned and stared, but they quickly returned to their own business. Fanboying on superheroes and superhuman celebs was taboo at Danger Room.

Hugo stared back in a daze, reminding himself to nod. How was this his life?

Desperate to escape the attention, Hugo scanned the dancefloor for Becky. She stood like a statue in the writhing crowd, watching him in amusement. "Rooftop," she mouthed, then exited the dance floor.

Hugo passed a few more third-floor VIP lounges before finding the elevator to the roof.

The night winds howled across the roof. Hugo took in his surroundings, perfect for a flier's landing. Below, downtown was alive and electric. Becky was waiting, silhouetted against the light pollution behind her.

"Hey." Hugo advanced, eager for her scoop. Becky's prior intel helped him squash a gang war last week.

"Your boy Polymer's cute." She pursed her lips as if ashamed by her confession. "From certain angles."

Hugo's mood soured. "He's *not* my boy." Yet for some reason, Polymer's plea took root. Not to revive The Vanguard. But with J-Tom being his apprentice along with what happened to Brie and Jordana, having allies made sense. "Before you tell me your thing, I need to ask something."

Becky frosted over. "No." Her response was terse and stiff.

Hugo bristled. "You didn't hear my question."

"It's written on your face," Becky countered. "You want me to join your quest for truth, justice, and all that other horseshit."

Hugo had no rebuttal. "Maybe…"

"I don't pick sides or get involved," Becky stated vehemently. "And I'm happier for it." She only cared about whoever paid most as a bouncer or bounty hunter. Superhuman strength and being able to track any super by energy signature made her highly desired at the latter profession.

That answered that question. "Then why pass me free intel?" Hugo asked.

Becky softened. "Our first meeting."

Hugo remembered. She was bouncing at Paragon's. "Because I kicked your ass?"

"No, idiot!" Becky looked down, shuffling her feet with unusual bashfulness. "Missy Magnificent was hammered. And you protected her from assholes trying to take advantage, even though I was too boneheaded to realize then. Most heroes are disappointments away from cameras or fanfare." She looked up at him, brimming with vulnerability. "Don't become like them."

Hugo was astonished. "I'll do my best." Someone else inspired by him. The responsibility was frightening. "You have something?"

Becky smiled again, her armor back on. "Since the non-cynic in me respects your mission, I have someone searching for a new cause."

Hugo leaned back. Between training J-Tom, Polymer's desire to team up, and now Becky bringing potential allies, the universe was sending a message. "What's their story?"

"Teenager from outta town," Becky explained. "She started at Danger Room in the loading docks three weeks ago. Strong as me in her werewolf form. Interested?"

Hugo wouldn't commit to anything yet. He trusted Becky enough but not entirely. "I'll meet her."

That pleased Becky. "I'll bring her up to meet you." She pulled out a cellphone and texted.

Then Hugo reconsidered her description. "Wait, werewolf?"

Before Becky could answer, the door behind them opened. A solitary figure stepped onto the roof. She was petite yet compact and curvy, with olive skin and dark coppery hair styled in long twin French braids. "Hi, Becky, what do…" The girl's voice died.

The moment Hugo saw her, smelled her, he felt jarred out of his body.

And the feeling appeared mutual. "H…" She caught herself from blurting out Hugo's name, glancing nervously at Becky. "You?"

"Max?" Hugo replied, not believing his eyes.

Mercedes "Max" Ochoa knew all about Hugo after their team-up at Halloween last year. He'd visited her twice in New Mexico since then. But they'd lost touch these last few months.

Seeing Max at Danger Room threw Hugo's whole world off balance.

"You know each other! Amazing!" Becky gushed, turning to Hugo. "You're welcome." She sashayed to the exit.

Hugo and Max stood on the roof, facing each other.

"So…" The werewolf wrung her hands. "We got some catching up to do…"

INTERLUDE: CONNIE

Currently, Connie was gagging from unbridled cheesiness.

When she'd snuck into this apartment by walking through the walls, the owner and her guest had been busy in the bedroom.

Now she hid in the bathroom listening to the lovebirds suck face and coo sweet nothings by the door. Jesus, they were worse than horny teenagers.

"I don't want you to go," Bam-Bam whimpered.

"I wanna live inside your pants," Shattershot admitted.

Bam-Bam's laugh filled the apartment.

Connie made a vomiting face. Were those the pickup lines that reeled her in? Really?

"When can you come back?" Bam-Bam asked.

"Not sure," Shattershot admitted, sounding sad. "The team's been doing some non-active PR appearances to repair our images. I'll see if I can sneak again."

"Don't stay away too long, babe."

"Wouldn't dream of it, Joanie."

By the wet smacking noises, Connie suspected more kissing. She rolled her eyes and waited.

"What are we going to do about my situation?" Bam-Bam's words exposed her need.

Shattershot sighed. "Soon. Erika took a chance on me. Why won't she do the same for you?"

"I hope so," Bam-Bam murmured. "The life I'm leading. Not sure how long I can continue."

"I won't let you down, love," Shattershot crooned. More smacking noises ensued, to Connie's disgust.

"Okay!" He sounded winded, as if coming up for air. "Now I have to go."

Once Bam-Bam closed the door, soft sobs floated throughout the apartment.

Connie adjusted her jacket. Greyson had insisted on a Plan B in case his primary plan fell through, which included Shattershot's lover Bam-Bam.

Connie inhaled and advanced. A tingle ran through her as she walked through darkened walls and into the sparsely decorated living room.

Bam-Bam sat slumped against the front door, shivering with sobs under that flowery robe.

Connie snickered. "You guys are cute," she remarked, winking. "When's the wedding?"

Bam-Bam rose like a viper. "Who the—?"

Connie raised her hands peacefully. "Relax, I'm just—"

Bam-Bam pitched a crackling green energy orb like a fastball.

Connie made a gagging face. "Jesus. Really?" She reacted quickly. The orb shot through her intangible chest, bursting in a harmless flash against the wall behind her.

Bam-Bam gaped, then flung more shimmering orbs. By their low blast potency, Bam-Bam clearly was holding back to avoid outside attention.

It's the hard way. Connie advanced aggressively, more orbs passing through her. Rapid-fire green flareups lit up the apartment. "This isn't helping," she critiqued.

Bam-Bam backed away, still lobbing explosive orbs. "Did the Conglomerate send you?" Her fierceness became worry, seeing her powers have no effect. "I'm not taking any jobs again—AAKK!"

Connie snaked out a solid hand, clutching Bam-Bam's throat. "Calm. Down." She never raised her voice, but the message was received. Bam-Bam powered down and lowered her hands.

Connie relaxed her grip. "Now if you—"

Bam-Bam sank a knee deep into Connie's mid-section. Pain exploded into Connie's stomach, doubling her over. She held a glowing hand to Connie's face. "Leave. Or I'll burn the heart out of you, bitch!"

"Ugh," Connie wheezed. "Soooo dramatic." She plunged a phased hand through Bam-Bam's chest, turning partially solid for a split-second. Bam-Bam wailed in anguish.

Connie yanked her hand out, and Bam-Bam collapsed like a puppet cut from its strings.

As her opponent lay gasping on the floor, Connie placed a rock-solid foot on Bam-Bam's throat and pressed down. "Are you finished?"

Bam-Bam kicked and thrashed, turning a worrying maroon. Then she finally relaxed.

Connie waited a few seconds before removing her foot. "Good." She crouched beside Bam-Bam and smiled. "Let's talk."

The criminal rubbed at her throat and blinked rapidly. "You're...not with The Conglomerate."

Connie snorted. "Hell no. But I do represent people capable of solving your dilemma."

Bam-Bam's brow furrowed. "You know nothing about me."

Connie swallowed a laugh. "Contract killer falls for someone who escaped the criminal life. You want out, but your employers won't let you go without their pound of flesh." She cocked her head sideways smugly. "Am I close?"

By Bam-Bam's wide-eyed shock, the portrayal had struck true. "I'm listening."

CHAPTER 27

"You did *what* for the government?" Max exclaimed with wide eyes.

Hugo nodded, reclining in his chair. They sat in the shielded safety of the Clubhouse lair. But still Hugo instinctively glanced around like they weren't alone, having just detailed a hush-hush mission he'd been recruited to several weeks ago. He still got goosebumps wondering what could've happened if he and his fellow recruits had failed. Would the world as they knew it would've ended? "I've only told like two people about that," Hugo murmured tersely. "So tell no one."

Max nodded, her twin French braids jostling. They'd been up most of the morning catching up. Correction, they'd been mainly discussing Hugo's crazy life these last few months after breakfast at his house.

Hugo donned a San Miguel Titans NFL jersey and baggy jeans, Max in a crop top tee and leather jacket with sweatpants. "Enough about me," the Samoan groused.

A smile split Max's cute features. "Bogie, you've been everywhere since Black Wednesday. I especially loved you curbstomping Tomorrow Man." She laughed.

Hugo rolled his eyes. Not just from the media overexaggerating his feud with Tomorrow Man, but Blur still trashing him to the press. Ignoring the speedster was growing difficult.

Hugo focused on Max pointedly. "I'm interested why you've been here nearly a month and never called?"

She looked down ruefully. "Sorry about that."

"Speak, muchacha." Hugo gestured for her to continue.

After a laborious sigh, Max finally met his gaze again. "There's been lots of pack drama in New Mexico. My dad's brother pulled a hostile takeover." Her hand motions were as languid as her tone. "He and my dad fought, but my uncle got help from one of Father's betas and won. Then he captured my mom to keep my father away."

Hugo's stomach knotted up. "Oh my god. Is your dad—?"

Max waved off his worry almost nonchalantly. "Papa's in hiding, regaining his strength and gathering allies." The ghost of a smile appeared when discussing her father. "Since my siblings and I are a threat to his rule, Papa sent us away." Her eyes burned. "But I snuck in our former territory and rescued Mom."

Hugo clenched his fists, ready to kick some werewolf ass. "I could've helped."

"I know." Max rested a hand on his knee. "But you've seen how wolves don't like outsiders involved."

Hugo snorted. Visiting Max on New Year's months ago had been a crash course in wolfpack intrigue. "If you change your mind, tell me." He rested his hand on hers and squeezed. "So how'd you meet Becky?" Hugo had to hear this story.

Max rose from her chair. "I came to San Miguel via train and wanted to call you. But Becky literally walked up and introduced herself." Her brow furrowed in bewilderment. "Almost like she'd been waiting. I was cautious, but she bought me dinner, and we talked." The werewolf grinned. "Then Becky got me a job at Danger Room and is letting me crash at her condo."

The serendipity bothered Hugo. "That's unusually generous." How Becky Knox had found Max at the train station seemed like she'd tracked down a bounty.

"I wanted to settle in more before calling such a big damn superhero." Max looked unsure while studying his reaction. "Should I not trust Becky?"

Hugo brushed away her doubt and rose. "Becky claims to only care about money." He recalled again how she'd helped his mission. "But she's alright. Has a soft spot for lost girls."

Max slapped his arm, her superstrength making him yelp. "I'm not lost, jackass." She shook her hand in discomfort. Max's rolled up jacket sleeves revealed the *vegvísir* mark on her right inner forearm, which still weirded Hugo out. The blurry runic tattoo resembled a compass in constant motion, giving Max total control over her werewolf shifts.

"How do you know Becky?" she asked.

Hugo opened his mouth to reply but caught someone entering the Clubhouse. Max's ears perked up, meaning she'd heard too.

"Hold up." Hugo turned and reached the entrance into main operations before the door even opened.

J-Tom breezed in, a loose white tee and tight black jeans her choice of attire, hair up in a bun and black headband.

Her unbridled joy was contagious. "I'm certified as your trainee, Bogie." She shimmied her shoulders like a dork.

Hugo was beaming. "Your psych eval came back. You aren't in danger of melting down during a bomb evacuation." In short, Hugo had a sane, trustworthy ally.

"Yay!" J-Tom leaped into his arms. "We did it!"

Hugo returned her hug, her feet briefly dangling. "You did it, babe," he murmured, placing her back down.

"Not without you, Bogie." She did that flirty eyebrow raise. "Wanna see how much I appreciate you?" She stood on her tiptoes, their lips almost touching.

"Jen…" Hugo reluctantly pried her off. "We got company." He awkwardly pointed behind him.

J-Tom followed his gesture and jerked back. "Oooh."

Max stood near the command hub looking from J-Tom to Hugo. She shook her head and chuckled. A flush crept up Hugo's neck.

J-Tom adjusted her shirt and scowled. "Didn't know we were giving Clubhouse tours…hold on." She squinted. "I know your face."

"Max." The teen werewolf approached and extended a hand. "We met last Halloween."

"Oh, hi!" J-Tom's eyes brimmed with recognition as she accepted the handshake. "You're the werewolf who saved Hugo from certain…supernatural threats?"

"I saved her more times that night," Hugo snapped.

Max gulped hard and glared at Hugo. "You told your girlfriend about the supernatural community?"

J-Tom's freckles vanished under a deep blush.

Hugo's heart lurched. "J-Tom's not my girlfriend." Viewing J-Tom like that screwed with his head for some reason. "And I trust her."

J-Tom's smile returned. "I'm a hero-in-training." She pointed at herself adorably.

Max calmed. "You have powers?"

J-Tom shook her head. "Only power armor."

"You're like Lady Dynamo."

J-Tom wrinkled her nose. "Yeah…sorta."

A loud alert interrupted thankfully. Hugo had the Clubhouse's monitoring systems send alerts in case of nearby large-scale accidents or disasters.

Max's head swiveled. "What was that?"

Hugo and J-Tom exchanged a serious look before striding for the monitoring hub.

He leaned forward to scan three flatscreens displaying the news. Sections of a massive freighter train had derailed in a city's downtown, several regular cars flipped over or burning.

Hugo hissed. J-Tom made concerned noises.

"Freight train accident between Fresno and Stockton Counties," he summarized. The reports said no sabotage or supervillainy were involved. Death toll was unclear.

That gave Hugo an idea. "Ready for your debut?" he asked J-Tom.

She gawked momentarily. "Hell yes!"

Hugo turned to a baffled Max. "We'll be back in a few hours. The fridge is stocked, and we got all the streaming services."

"Good luck!" the werewolf encouraged.

Hugo faced his trainee, who was bouncing on her heels. "Gear up." He'd always wanted to say that.

Several minutes later, Hugo was suited and soaring over golden pastures north of Bakersfield.

J-Tom easily kept pace in her latest silver-and-blue armor, calling it the Solomon Build.

"By the way, Wolfgirl's hot," she remarked.

"Focus, rookie," Hugo scolded, not knowing how he felt about that pairing.

Dark smoke tendrils in the horizon beyond Kern County grew closer.

He was nervous, heart thudding. But not for himself. In her official debut, J-Tom *had* to deliver.

When they reached the crash site, Hugo heard J-Tom gasp inside her helmet. And he totally understood. Below looked like a bomb had exploded. The freight train had collided with several cars, its many derailed segments striking nearby buildings in this city. Injured survivors cried out around the wreckage site, hard even for Hugo to stomach. Emergency services converged and set up triage zones.

By the white-and-gold flash of motion zipping around the crash site, Hugo knew Blur from the Extreme Teens had arrived. Half a dozen other fliers from LA's Battalion team and Bakersfield's Rockabilly team swooped around to rescue trapped victims.

The rest of the train remained on the tracks. Automobile traffic sat at a standstill for over a mile. Local police were redirecting traffic below.

"Oh my God," J-Tom exclaimed, her digitally altered voice not sounding female. "The destruction…"

"Jenny," Hugo said quietly, drawing her helmet's glowing blue eyes to him. "Remember your emergency services training. We take cues from rescue workers. So follow my lead, yeah?"

"Okay."

"Got an alias?"

J-Tom nodded.

Hugo prayed that she'd chosen well. "Tell me."

She told him.

He was impressed. "That's good." Hugo began descending to the circle of white tents making up the makeshift command center. "Let's go."

When Hugo and J-Tom touched down, he took scope of the cops, firefighters, and other emergency workers. While several appeared elated at his arrival, they watched J-Tom with curiosity or distrust.

"Ladies and gents," Hugo announced in his Aegis voice. "Where can we help?"

One officer, an older black woman with greying hair, approached. By her uniform, she appeared to be a firefighter. "Lieutenant Sykes." She nodded at J-Tom. "Can your friend match your strength?"

"She can hold her own," Hugo replied.

Sykes looked relived. "Good. Folks like Hyperion and Lady Liberty are helping with the fires. We need to move the derailed cars first.

"Just tell us where you want them moved."

Sykes and her team gave instructions. Hugo and J-Tom moved quickly to move derailed train cars away from downtown, holding opposite ends of cars weighing several tons with ease. The duo positioned nine severed train cars outside of downtown, connecting them to waiting railroad tow trucks. The whole time, Hugo observed his friend, assessing her performance. Beneath her armor, he detected that she was scared shitless. But no one with normal senses would know by how smoothly she reacted and worked with Hugo.

As J-Tom helped him free those trapped in cars with a veteran's poise, Hugo's heart burst with pride.

Before he knew it, three hours had passed. The yellow sun was the unhurried midday descent. But downtown didn't completely resemble a disaster film. Even better was news of no casualties.

With the train cars cleared, the news media swarmed.

Hugo stood beside a ruined Suburban and looked to J-Tom, who stood eye to eye with him in her armor. "We can ignore them."

"No," she said. "I'm ready."

Hugo nodded and faced the media.

"Aegis!" A female reporter with a teased perm motioned at J-Tom. "Is your new partner Dynamo 2.0?"

"There's only one Dynamo," Hugo answered. "This is someone else. Something else." He nodded at J-Tom to speak.

But she froze. And the media waited. The silence lasted so long that Hugo almost stepped in.

"Call me...Arclight," J-Tom declared. The gathered reporters jabbered in approval. More questions were barked along with flashing cameras.

"Thank you, Arclight," the original reporter stated.

Now Hugo intervened. "The rescue work is just beginning. Excuse us." Looking up, he lifted off.

J-Tom rose with him until they were a few miles above the destruction.

"Great job," Hugo marveled. J-Tom did better than he could've imagined. But by her quick breaths, she sounded close to hyperventilating. "You alright?"

"Yeah." J-Tom placed her gauntlet over his gloved hand and squeezed. "Everything's a lot. Just soaking in the moment."

Hugo smiled, knowing that overwhelmed feeling. "No, I get it…" He glanced at the train cars still on the railroad, spotting a singular figure far to the right.

Thanks to his telescopic vision, Hugo saw him clearly.

The man was stocky in build, average height. By his features, he was of Asian descent for sure.

What caught Hugo's attention was his explosion of white hair and travel-worn military gear, like a cyberpunk soldier of fortune.

Hugo had only seen grainy photos of him on the news. Saracen, in the flesh.

He stared at Hugo and smirked.

The Samoan's heart stuttered. *Did Saracen cause the train derailment?* Hugo rocketed forward, closing the distance between them in seconds. Saracen just stood there unconcerned, still smirking.

Inches away and counting, Hugo slowed enough to not smash Saracen apart and reached out—grabbing at air.

"What the hell?" Hugo braked hard in mid-air. Saracen was gone. No fanfare or energy emission.

Baffled, Hugo scanned the surrounding fields and train cars. Not even a trace of his scent or body warmth lingered in the air.

"Aegis!" J-Tom flew to his side. "What's wrong?"

Hugo knew he hadn't imagined seeing that. And his senses never lied.

"Saracen…" Hugo paused, still in disbelief. "I just saw Saracen."

CHAPTER 28

"You saw Saracen?" Clint sprang from his chair. "In real life?"

Hugo ran shaky fingers through his tousled black hair. "Staring right at me. When I got close, he was gone."

The encounter still rattled Hugo. He'd flown directly to Geist's lair after leaving Fresno County. J-Tom had gone to the Clubhouse and escorted Max to Hugo's house. "Saracen's gotta be a teleporter."

"Sweet Jeezus." Clint brightened as if he'd seen a complex encryption to crack. "He's my hero."

"Not helping," Hugo growled.

Clint chuckled. "Sorry."

Hugo cut to the chase, wringing his gloved hands. "I want to see if he's been around San Miguel recently. Then I'll hand over what I know to the authorities."

Clint nodded in acceptance. "I'll take a look."

Hugo owed Clint for all these favors. "Thanks—"

A detonation shuddered through the walls, followed by a gut-wrenching wail from one of the dojos.

Hugo whirled in alarm. "Who?"

Clint flattened against his seat. "Ruh-roh." He pointed to where the sound came from.

Hugo raced forward. In a heartbeat, he stood at the entrance of the sparring dojo. "Guys—" Hugo stopped and stared.

Blackjack and Domino lay sprawled on opposite sides of the dojo. Weapons, boxing bags, and other equipment were strewn everywhere.

In the center was a slender slip of an Asian girl, longish pink hair and blunt bangs, screeching her lungs out. Her body was a living sun, growing increasingly brighter. Like a bomb about to blow.

Blackjack struggled onto an elbow. "Stay back," he wheezed.

Hugo couldn't believe Blackjack's logic. "You stay back, meathead." He bellowed out a short sonic scream, knocking this girl on her back.

Immediately, her glow and temperature dimmed.

Hugo advanced aggressively, only for her to scramble on all fours toward Domino. The vigilante gathered the frightened child into her arms.

Hugo stopped, utterly lost. "What—*who* is that?"

Blackjack pushed to his feet, wincing. "Cherry Blossom."

Hugo guffawed. "For serious?"

Domino nodded, Cherry Blossom sobbing in her arms. "Wish he was kidding."

Bad fruit jokes flooded Hugo's brain. But he stayed serious. "Your forearm injury. That was her?"

Blackjack let his head drop. "We're helping Cherry control her powers, which are…explosive." He looked exhausted. "It's been a long couple of weeks."

Hugo was brimming with questions. "Where's she come from?"

Domino helped Cherry Blossom up. "She's one of the Rockland Supermax escapees."

"Really?" Hugo watched this frightened girl with bubblegum pink hair burying her face in Domino's shoulder. "I remember the escapees list," Hugo stated, recalling when he and Lady Liberty helped recapture Rockland's convicts. "This girl wasn't on it."

Blackjack advanced. "She wasn't listed. The prison was experimenting on Cherry to make her a weapon."

The admission gripped Hugo's throat. "Paxton-Brandt?"

Domino shook her head. "Rockland Supermax has been doing this for years. Cherry was dropped onto our doorstep with instructions in her jacket."

"Like a LEGO set?" Hugo quipped despite himself.

"Pretty much," Domino replied. "We can't patrol as much because one of us needs to watch her. But Ballistic's been helping."

Ballistic again. Hugo had enjoyed working with him, despite the mess that Tomorrow Man made.

Cherry Blossom murmured in what sounded like Japanese. Domino kissed the girl's brow.

Clint leaned on the doorway with smirking insolence. "Should've told him earlier."

Blackjack ignored him. "We tried finding her real family." He stood beside his wife. "But can't even find records of her real name. So we're keeping her."

Cherry Blossom darted over and embraced Blackjack's waist, barely reaching his chest. The vigilante gazed at her and *melted*. "Our priority is managing her outbursts, which are tied to her powers."

The girl seemed harmless now to Hugo. "If you need help, I'm sturdy enough to take the punishment."

Blackjack and Domino glanced at each other uneasily.

"You don't have to," the latter dismissed.

Hugo raised a hand. "You guys trained J-Tom and gave me access to Clint."

Clint made an amused face. "Ooooph, I feel so dirty."

"Let me help." Hugo would rather help a super in need before they possibly went bad. The vigilantes said more with their eyes than an entire speech. "We'll take you up on that," Domino said.

Hugo felt accomplished when returning to the Clubhouse, changing into regular clothes.

On the walk home, he was surprised by a call from Detective Dawson. Hugo switched on an app to mask his voice in the Aegis cadence, courtesy of Ramon. That way, he could speak to contacts in broad daylight.

"Lieutenant. Been a while."

"Sorry. The department needed some distance after the V3 debacle."

"Okay." Hugo understood San Miguel PD's radio silence. "What do you need?"

"That burnt scientist, Nina Smarts," Dawson said. "Her work ID got used twice since her death," Dawson continued. "One at Salto Institute's facility in Powderhorn, Colorado."

Hugo stiffened, recalling the recent forest fire. "Is that near Gunnison National Forest?"

"Yep." Dawson popped the "p" in his answer. "The second facility was in Kingstree, South Carolina."

"During the floods." Hugo glanced both ways before crossing a street. "Those can't be coincidences." And that dead scientist's stench matched that of the Gunnison forest fires. "What was stolen?"

Dawson sighed. "Lots of genetic materials that I can't pronounce…plus blood samples and preserved remains of dead kaijus. Like the Tiamat you killed a few weeks ago."

Hugo gaped. This case had just taken a turn toward interesting. "Someone wants to build their own Godzilla."

"Seems like." Dawson sounded irritated. "Salto Institute is ramping up their security. I'm trying to account for their other sites that could have anything worth stealing. They aren't making it easy."

"Let me know if you need me." The call ended as Hugo neared his neighborhood.

The aroma of baking bread filled his home. AJ and Mom were in the kitchen. Max and Zelda sat across from each other. They were more interested in a staring contest than the TV showing *Alpha Academy*, a teen drama loosely based on Steinholt Academy.

"Ready?" Max asked.

Zelda adjusted her position confidently. "Ready." For several moments, neither moved.

Hugo locked the door, watching this silent face-off—until Max shifted.

A shaggy wolf's head abruptly appeared on her body, gnashing sharp teeth.

Zelda jumped, covering her mouth to muffle a squeal. "Omigod, omigod!"

Max's face returned to normal within seconds. Her grin remained wolfish. "Guess you weren't ready."

Zelda smacked her arm, then popped off the couch and dashed at Hugo.

"Hey, you." He embraced his sister, relishing the contact.

"Bogie," Zelda murmured, a smile in her voice.

Hugo felt like an asshole hiding the truth about Zelda from AJ, but what good would telling him do?

"What was that?" he asked when embracing Max.

"Trying partial shifting," she said as they drew apart. "Becky is getting me a gig at Danger Room. Can't go full howl at the moon for that."

Hugo chewed on that decision. "Makes sense."

Max eyed him critically. "And when did you and Jen become a thing? I thought you're with Jodie and she was screwing that bratty *puta* with the nice tits."

A flush crept up Hugo's neck. He could practically feel Mom's ears bleeding from the kitchen.

"It's hard for us to keep track," AJ added, amused.

"Quiet, Junior," Hugo snapped. "I'll explain later." He headed into the kitchen, seeing Mom and AJ preparing Samoan Chicken and Coconut Rice, one of his favorites.

Mom frowned over her shoulder. "You should've told me about your guest, Bogota."

Hugo rolled his eyes and kissed her cheek. "It was last minute. I wanted Max to have something besides bar food." He fist-bumped AJ, who was chopping garlic. "Any word on the job?"

"You'll know when I do." Mom placed the chicken in a soufflé dish. Her impatience was palpable. "Thanks for asking."

After Hugo set the table, AJ pulled him aside. "Can we talk?" He glanced back at Mom. "Upstairs?"

The gravity on his brother's blocky face gave Hugo pause. "Sure." They headed upstairs without a word.

AJ's bedroom differed considerably from Hugo's, featuring basketball and soccer merchandise. Also gracing his room were posters of hero rock bands like Leap of Faith and Silver Age.

Hugo sat on his brother's bed. "What's up?"

AJ sat beside him after closing the door. "I talked to Mom."

Hugo arched an eyebrow at the admission. "Talking is healthy for mother-son relations."

AJ didn't laugh. "We talked about you, Dad…and Titan."

Hugo's heart dropped. *Godammit, Mom.*

AJ continued in the same calm voice. "Your weird fight with Mom before Black Wednesday. Zelda not coming over anymore. I knew something was up." AJ took a breath. "Were you guys seriously never gonna tell me?"

The crack in AJ's voice gutted Hugo like a knife. "I…maybe?" God, he did not want to have this conversation. *But here we are.* His brother started

215

looking blurry. Hugo wiped away tears with the back of his hand. "I'd just found out Dad wasn't my biological father," Hugo countered to regain control over this situation. "That's a lot to process."

AJ dialed back his indignation. "Oh…"

"And you were in a good place," Hugo continued. Unpleasant memories of AJ's past defiance resurfaced. "I didn't…couldn't ruin that."

Surprisingly, AJ laughed. "Bogie, we're usos!" He was tearing up. "Daddy drama and all."

Hugo momentarily thought he'd imagined this response. "You're not mad?"

AJ shook his head emphatically. "Only that you guys said nothing. I mean…" His expression turned questioning. "Should I be pissed at Mom?"

"NO," Hugo answered immediately.

AJ relaxed. "I know there's superhero stuff you can't share. Otherwise, no more secrets. Deal?"

Hugo's heart felt so much lighter. "Deal." He drew AJ into a long embrace.

Dinner was over two hours of laughter, animated discussions, and amazing food.

The one thing missing was Simon. But Hugo's BFF was at the Fab Phenoms' latest dance battle. *Which I wasn't told about.* The omission stung. Then again, he'd attended maybe one of their last five dance battles due to superhero stuff. The gulf between his normal and Aegis identities kept growing.

Brie's texts were a welcome surprise after days of radio silence.

Brie: Sorry for being such a nutjob lately.

Brie: I had to step back from our friendship and get my head straight. Talk soon?

ME: Sure.

Hugo dropped Max off near Danger Room for her work shift before suiting up for tonight's patrol. San Miguel was fairly quiet, but he knew the value in citizens seeing their heroes watching over them.

Late next morning, he woke up with a girl's arm draped over his abdomen.

Hugo grinned drowsily. *Yeah…that happened.*

After returning home last night, Hugo had realized he hadn't heard from Jordana since Friday at school. Any calls went straight to voicemail.

That only fueled his doubt…and hurt. Was she with Carnival Boy or just done with Hugo?

J-Tom would come over to comfort him, but Hugo decided against that. Their relationship had been so emotionally nourishing. But growing too attached to a protégé was risky.

Jordana would never forgive me or Jen, Hugo had understood, texting someone else.

ME: Busy?

TVS: Just got home from the football game. You?

ME: Bored.

TVS: LOL. I'm not hooking up with you.

ME: Who said anything about sex?

TVS: Dude, you're texting me after 10 PM on Saturday.

TVS: I know exactly what u want.

The biting reply burned Hugo's cheeks. Sitting in the sudden tension, he could either get offended and give up or own his desire and move forward.

ME: And I know exactly what u like. Now come over and get it.

She replied a minute later.

TVS: Be there soon.

Hugo had beamed and reclined on the couch, feeling triumphant.

Taylor von Stratton had arrived half an hour later, wearing her red-and-white cheerleading outfit. She'd smirked, casually pulling out the ribbon holding up her high ponytail as she glided into his bedroom.

That whole night, Hugo explored the wonders of her tight and tanned body. Taylor had replied with equal hunger, whispering every way she wanted to please him—and doing each one. Even little things, like the rhythmic rock of her body when she'd arch into him felt amazing, making his toes curl and her groan.

Maybe this is for the best, Hugo wondered, admiring Taylor beside him in her birthday suit, prone and slumbering. Her face was hidden under messy curtains of blonde.

Jordana deserved an *honest* boyfriend. Meanwhile, Hugo could casually hook up with Taylor, who was down for whatever situationship he wanted.

No lying. No drama. No baggage like with Jordana, Spencer, and J-Tom. *Gotta catch 'em all. Jesus…*

Such a carefree reality felt euphoric—and empty.

Can I kill my feelings for Jodie in one blow? Instead of dwelling on the bad, Hugo preferred leaning down to gently blow on the nape of Taylor's neck.

Goosebumps prickled down her spine to the slope of that perfectly formed butt. Taylor shivered and made a contented sort of sigh, still asleep.

His buzzing work phone interrupted before he could kiss on her neck.

Annoyed, Hugo delicately removed Taylor's arm off and slid out of bed. He pulled on some pants and fished the phone from his backpack.

Cautiously checking on Taylor, who remained asleep, he tiptoed out into the hallway.

Downstairs, AJ wasted more brain cells watching *Extreme Dreams*.

Hugo crouched outside his door and unlocked his phone.

BLOCKED: Found Saracen in the city. Drone images are a week old.

Hugo gaped at the image timestamps. *The day after Saracen kidnapped Jodie and Brie.*

Texting Clint his gratitude, Hugo scrolled through five zoomed-in images, showing Saracen on a rooftop. Same explosive white hair. Same travel-worn gear. Saracen was in a heated discussion with someone hidden behind a partition.

It had to be Polymer. Hugo fumed and kept scrolling. The last picture captured Saracen's cohort entirely: a dark-skinned woman, one side of her frizzy purple hair styled in Viking braids.

Hugo felt cold all over. "Becky Knox."

INTERLUDE: J-TOM

Watching her armored alter ego lifting a train car on YouTube was so bizarre. But J-Tom still squealed with a "sugar rush meets carnival ride" euphoria.

Viewing the clip with the adorable parentals cheering behind her was a gift that never stopped giving.

"Our baby girl is a superhero!" Her mom grasped J-Tom's shoulders from behind. "Can you believe it?"

"Arclight." J-Tom's father stroked his beard as he considered the name with a smile. "Love that name."

J-Tom's cheeks warmed from their praise. "Yeah. Pretty crazy." She picked lint from her green ribbed V-neck sweater and white plaid skirt. Even after weeks of training and anticipating, yesterday still felt dreamlike. And J-Tom didn't want to wake up.

"Arclight" was all over the national news and trending on social media, thanks to the Aegis connection and Hugo's awesome publicist.

But a knot of guilt formed in J-Tom's stomach over not involving her dad in future development of her armor. She'd started this project with him. All that had changed after she'd met Ramon Dempsey.

"That's why I've been away so much." J-Tom spun in her chair to face her father. "Training with Aegis and building the new armor with Ramon Dempsey."

Mr. Thomas waved off any extra explanation. "Learning from Dynamo himself will take you further than I ever could." So many emotions filled his twinkling eyes. Love, eagerness, and some sadness.

J-Tom placed a hand over her heart. Her father's sympathy was endless. "Thanks so much, Daddio." She rose and embraced him fiercely.

Mom stroked J-Tom's face, standing a head shorter than her daughter. She was plump, petite and pretty, with sleek black hair and light-brown skin courtesy of her Filipino descent. "Are you sure about working with Aegis?" Mom's round face scrunched in worry. "I mean, I like him. But he seems rather…" She paused and lowered her voice as if someone was listening. "He's *violent*." Mom was usually less pearl-clutching than Dad. That had changed since J-Tom began her superhero's journey.

J-Tom adjusted her ponytail and kissed Mom's forehead. "That Vincent Van Violence situation went sideways thanks to Tomorrow Man." She understood Mom's worries. But her parents didn't know Hugo like she did. "Aegis is the best mentor anyone could have."

That endorsement was enough for Dad. He puffed out his chest. "Now my daughter is his sidekick."

"Apprentice," J-Tom corrected. Nothing against sidekicks, but she planned to be Aegis's partner.

"Isn't that the same thing?" Dad asked obtusely.

"My book club is obsessed with you," Mom gushed.

J-Tom made a face. No way did she already have fans. "I debuted yesterday, Mom."

"You made a huge impression." Her mother's eyes sparkled with pride. "Their heads will explode if they knew Arclight's my daughter—"

"*Mom*," J-Tom snapped in knee-jerk terror. "You can't tell anyone. Ever."

Blood drained from Mom's face. J-Tom instantly regretted her outburst.

"Jennifer," Dad began in that calm lecturing tone whenever she was in trouble. "That was very rude."

She closed her eyes, choosing her next words carefully. "I'm sorry. It's just to protect you." She opened her eyes. "Criminals finding out my secret puts you in danger." That had haunted J-Tom since starting her training. But Hugo had calmed these fears as usual, with advice on identity protection.

Dad looked lost. "But you'll just do search and rescue. So supervillains aren't a worry."

J-Tom fought back a cringe. "Right." She wouldn't half-ass being a superhero. *All in or not at all.* But the parentals didn't need to know…yet. J-Tom pulled them close, overcome by emotion. "But please don't tell anyone."

Mom rubbed her back. "Understood, Jennifer. But will you have time between school, and friends, and volleyball?"

Great question. "I'll make it work," J-Tom said as they drew apart. Her schedule had been nuts since school started. She expected that to be worse now that she was an active hero.

"By the way," J-Tom said as her parents were leaving as a nagging worry came to mind. "Haven't heard from Aunt Steph in months." Aunt Steph was an old college friend of Dad's and a legend in her industry. J-Tom had known her since she was in diapers. "Where is she?"

Her parents suddenly grew somber.

"Your auntie's still on sabbatical," Dad said. "I think in Botswana currently." The finality behind the answer was palpable.

"Okay," J-Tom remarked in a small voice. The answer wasn't satisfying, but she didn't push further.

Aunt Steph had taken her to different parts of the USA on every spring break since J-Tom was eleven. She'd gone to her aunt first with her confusing feelings for Spencer two summers ago and her desire to be a hero. Hopefully her favorite auntie was well after getting screwed by *SLOCO Daily*.

At least she got her revenge in the end, J-Tom mused happily.

After breezing through her homework, she spent the next few hours on her laptop, tweaking a 3D diagram of the Arclight armor's next build. After the train crash rescue, J-Tom noticed several functions needing improvements.

She typed in notes and linked them to points on the armor diagram before sending to Ramon via an encrypted cloud server. He'd become a fantastic partner, usually finding solutions that J-Tom wouldn't have thought of based on her suggestions. She dusted off her hands, satisfied with herself.

Right then, a text buzzed her phone.

S-Han: AWESOME debut. U good?

J-Tom: Very. Thx for checking in.

Simon's approval warmed J-Tom from head to toe. He'd been slow to accept her presence in Hugo's life. J-Tom hoped that she and Simon could bond over more than just a mutual friend and a shared love of Japanese pop.

She spotted another new text, and her heart sang.

H-Mala: You're kinda famous now, Jenny.

J-Tom: Yep. Craziness.

H-Mala: How are you handling it?

J-Tom: Denial.

H-Mala: LOL!

J-Tom: Whatcha doing right now?

H-Mala: Got company.

J-Tom: Jodie?

H-Mala: Nope.

J-Tom: SLUT!

H-Mala: Yeah you know me. Clubhouse around 7:30. Patrol then training.

J-Tom: Can't wait.

J-Tom put away her cellphone, grinning like an idiot, as usual with Hugo. 7:30 PM couldn't come soon enough. She could never repay Hugo for expanding her world, saving her from imploding this summer. He made her feel safe, seen, and desired. She'd known this about him even before learning about his powers, giving her courage during her relationship with Spencer.

Even his small gestures were topnotch, like his flawless speed sketch of her Arclight armor the night of the carnival. His note stated *So glad I was wrong.*

J-Tom felt herself blushing and covered her face. She knew this tryst couldn't last, but *god,* was it so fun.

Another text drew her attention.

Briezilla: Dinner at 7? Higuera Street Grill?

Jordana: I'm down.

J-Tom: Can't. Got plans.

Briezilla: BOO! You're always busy J.

Jordana: You're as bad as Bogota.

The jab stung. J-Tom grimaced, racking her brain for a compromise.

J-Tom: Let's meet Monday night.

Briezilla: Can I invite G-Mama? She's my new favorite human.

J-Tom: Obvs! Grace is magic.

J-Tom placed the phone down to avoid the coiling grossness filling her stomach. Hiding her secret life from the girls weighed on her each day. But betraying Jodie, a long-time friend, had been unbearable.

Just like Spencer betrayed her.

J-Tom shook her head, pulse quickening. "I'm not like Spencer." She'd remind herself until it stuck. Pushing Spencer from her thoughts made her long for Hugo's company. But his last text irked her. Why was he with some random girl unless…? J-Tom instantly texted Jordana.

J-Tom: Did something happen with Bogie?

Jordana: Ugh. I'm avoiding his calls.

J-Tom: You tell him about the other situation?

Jordana: No. I'm such a chickenshit.

J-Tom: You so are.

Jordana: Ouch! I thought Brie was the bitch.

J-Tom:

J-Tom: Talk in ten minutes?

Jordana: Deal.

J-Tom sagged in her chair and zoned out on the ceiling, easily forgiving herself. Why should she feel guilty if Jodie wasn't telling Hugo the truth?

Mom knocked before entering with a decent-sized cardboard package. "Hey, baby." She placed the package on the floor beside J-Tom's bed with a huff. "This just arrived."

J-Tom rose, scanning the box for a return address. "Thanks. No sender?"

Mom shrugged. "Dinner's in half an hour." She left and closed the door.

Curious, J-Tom used scissors to open the package, finding something round and hefty wrapped in newspaper. Pulling all that off, J-Tom found a cobalt Dynamo helmet.

"Huh?" J-Tom gawked. Based on time spent in Ramon's labs, she knew this helmet was legit, probably one of his earlier versions. Ramon could've given this to her himself. As she turned the helmet over, a letter slid out.

J-Tom placed it back in the box, kneeling to grab the paper.

I prefer the old you to a Dynamo cosplayer.

XOXO

Spence

J-Tom flung the letter like it was diseased, her legs buckling. "Ohmigod."

Spencer's poisoned gifts left her so weak. As J-Tom stared at the box, that black hole of despair was drawing her back in.

CHAPTER 29

"Stand back," Greyson warned, pointing a glowing finger like a pistol.

The crowd did as requested, shuffling across the gym with bated breaths.

Once Greyson had his target, he fired a thin golden beam once, twice, then three more times.

He lowered his hand. The bull's-eye set up several yards away had smoke rising from five holes—all through the center circular target.

The crowd around him erupted.

Greyson took an exaggerated bow, drawing laughter. The team currently occupied a drab room large enough for a sizable crowd. A dozen security guards with nightsticks and guns lined the blue steel walls.

The audience was thirty inmates from Stanton Correctional Facility for Young Men, in the heart of Shenandoah Valley. These were the worst juvenile criminals that society had forsaken.

Before him, Erika and Brightburn had demonstrated their powers to raucous applause.

The Natural Born Thrillers were paying the better-behaved inmates a visit on day four of their apology tour. To his chagrin, Greyson had to participate today since these kids had no cellphone access. At other events, the press only snapped photos of official team members, which Greyson wasn't yet. The timing had given Connie and Asher's team a few hours to find more dirt on Brightburn's colorful past.

As for the Stanton juveniles, Erika and the other Thrillers spoke to them in groups, offering motivation.

Greyson marveled at how well Erika connected with these boys. As she spoke about Shenandoah's opportunities, her audience sat riveted. And not just because they probably found her hot.

Regret squeezed on Greyson's heart as he watched her spread hope. *Sorry in advance, kid.*

Most surprising was Reverb's speech. "I was in a juvenile delinquent hall just like this at your age," he'd begun, gesturing with his hands. The large spots on his costume still looked silly, but the hero stood rooted onto that stage. "Did really dumb stuff as a kid I'm not proud of. Titan came and spoke to our group with that British team The Champions." A wistful smile inched up his boyish face. "That inspired me to be a hero. So I'll repeat what Titan told my group. This isn't the end."

Mostly applause, and some boos sounded from the hardened cynics.

Reverb didn't seem bothered. "Sounds easy. But I kept improving every goddamn day." He waved disarmingly at his crowd. "Yeah, yeah. Language."

That won genuine laughs.

"Once you leave these halls, you can own your story. Be your best you." Now everyone applauded.

One strapping sixteen-year-old approached Greyson, tall and prickly. He gave him an unimpressed onceover. "Who are you supposed to be?"

"Hazard," Greyson answered. Nearby, Bulldozer juggled three small kids like tennis balls.

The boy scoffed. "Never heard of you."

Greyson arched an eyebrow. "Maybe that's the point."

The ride back to the compound was awash with overlapping chatter about today's success. Shattershot and Greyson had become buddies since their dinner the other night, slinging jokes back and forth.

As their vehicle entered the compound's garage, he secretly fretted if Paxton-Brandt had come through.

His faith was restored once everyone entered the common room.

Erika gaped. Brightburn looked like she'd swallowed a whole lemon.

The common room and kitchen walls were covered in full-sized photos of Brightburn's victims. All forty-six. Battered mugshots of men from Shenandoah and Washington DC, in full color for all the other Natural Born Thrillers to see.

Brightburn's knees gave out. She would've collapsed if Bulldozer hadn't caught her.

Greyson strolled to one end of the living room, admiring Paxton-Brandt's fine art. "What are all these?" he remarked.

Brightburn rose and glowered at Reverb. "You motherfucker!"

No one expected that, especially Reverb himself. "What?" he replied.

"You turn my secret into a joke?" Brightburn wailed.

The accusation left Reverb wounded. "I didn't do this. I wouldn't."

Greyson hung back, fighting off satisfaction from his face. *Here we go...*

"Like you wouldn't put water balloons in my bed?" Brightburn reddened. "I TRUSTED YOU!" Her hand was a blur, cracking Reverb across the face.

He stumbled back clutching his cheek, much to Bulldozer's, Erika's and Shattershot's open dismay.

Greyson's heart soared, but he approached with his best mock confusion. "What's going on?"

Brightburn spun about on him. "Stay outta this!"

Greyson did an exaggerated backpedal as his teammate turned back to a cowering Reverb.

"Brightburn." Erika stepped between her and Reverb, making a sweeping gesture at photos plastered all over their common area. "Who are these men?"

"Back off, Erika!" Brightburn moved to sidestep her leader.

Erika moved in concert, blocking her path. "Not until you tell me why these photos are upsetting you."

"And why are they beaten up?" Bulldozer skimmed from the images to his teammate. "Did you do this?"

And the common room hushed. No longer was Brightburn the confident, social-media-savvy superhero. She'd become a scared little girl crumbling under her dark secrets.

Greyson scanned his phone then. *Time for another bombshell.* "Shit..."

The five Natural Born Thrillers turned. "What?" Erika demanded, annoyed.

Greyson schooled his features into shock. "I think I know who did this." He lifted his phone for them to view. "Damocles posted another video."

At Erika's encouragement, Greyson played the video he'd filmed two nights ago.

The images of the battered men cluttering the team's lair now flashed across the screen as Damocles spoke. "The Natural Born Thrillers hid their recruitment of an ex-villain. But are the rest of their team white hats?" The question hung in the air for a long, dramatic moment. The mysterious figure appeared again with his mask and glowing eyes. "What if one of them brutalized those they felt escaped justice?" The way Damocles cocked his head sideways with such reproach tingled down Greyson's spine. *Damn, I look great.*

"Would you still want a superhero selfie with hypocrites to up your cool factor on social media?" Damocles went on, to Brightburn's silent horror. "These heroes have abused your permission again. Take it back." The video ended, leaving another tomb-like silence in the common room.

Erika looked gutted. Bulldozer staggered, seemingly punch-drunk.

Greyson's main focus was on Brightburn, who was in a stupor.

"Oh God," she whispered.

Erika held her teammate by the shoulders with a stern motherly carriage. "Brightburn. Talk. Now."

"Yeah, I did this." Brightburn nodded. Her eyes locked on her like a lifeline as she spoke. "To all these men."

Erika backed up, utterly heartbroken.

Reverb, Bulldozer, and Shattershot jointly groaned. Greyson massaged his temples to feign dismay. Internally, he was rejoicing. A few more prods would push them to the point of no return. "Why?"

"They're disgusting pigs who got away with horrible things!" Brightburn howled. "The law failed their victims. I didn't!" She spewed the wrath of a true believer, showing zero remorse.

"This is bad," Reverb murmured to Erika.

"Worse." Bulldozer studied the room. "Damocles was here. Someone in this room betrayed us."

Greyson almost leaped with joy, wondering who'd accuse whom first.

CHAPTER 30

"She's still out of town?" Hugo exclaimed. It was after 7:30 in the morning, sunrays burning through the fog draping his cul-de-sac heaven neighborhood.

Max shrugged. "Yeah." She kept pace with Hugo's strides as they headed for the SMAT Subway Stop blocks away. "Becky's coming back in two days."

Hugo shouldered his backpack impatiently. He had to learn what Becky knew about Saracen. "Do you know where she went?"

Max gave her patented "You're an idiot" look. "Yeah, cuz me and Becky are tighter than a pair of balls."

"Right…" A flush crept up Hugo's neck. He'd never revealed his identity to Becky, unless she already knew and had told Saracen… "Her working with Saracen is dangerous. For everyone."

Max softened. "What do you need?"

"When Becky returns, please tell me," Hugo necessitated.

"Okay."

Hugo realized he hadn't checked in on her. "Hear anything from home?"

Emotion spasmed across Max's face. "I talked to my parents last night." Her admission was thick with longing. "Still not safe back home."

Hugo hated seeing her distressed. "Let me talk to my mom." He reached out, caressing Max's cheek. Her eyelids fluttered a little. "We'll make your stay in San Miguel more comfortable."

Max blushed. "Thank you." She turned away. "Good luck on your thing."

Hugo gulped. "Arrgh." Today, he was ending things with Jodie. This scared the crap out of him, but she deserved someone better.

Hugo parted ways with Max and slipped into an empty alleyway, then supersped to school. On the way, he made a to-do list. Class. Quick lunchtime patrol. Breakup with Jodie (ouch), patrol, follow up with Dawson and Beale about stolen kaiju remains, dinner, homework, train with J-Tom. Hugo couldn't let some hacktivist fuck up his life. He coasted through his first two periods and Snack, half-focused on class and half-listening beyond school. So far, today was running well. Anxiety was building around Jodie, but he could manage that.

At fourth period, Mr. Raines returned everyone's tests from last week.

Hugo accepted his, glancing at the grade, and did a double take.

"C minus?" Hugo stared up at his teacher, shock becoming rage.

Mr. Raines stood over him, normally youthful in energy. "I'm just as surprised, Hugo. Study harder next time," he remarked gravely and moved to another student.

Hugo scanned the test up and down, puzzled and fuming. Math was his strongest subject. Halfway through class, the reason he'd tanked struck him upside the head. He'd forgotten to study the night before—when Brie and Jordana got kidnapped. Hugo would ask for extra credit so this didn't screw up his overall grade. Mr. Raines was always fair like that.

When the lunch bell rang, Hugo strode outside to overcast skies. Smelling the air hinted at possible rain.

The chatter he'd been ignoring amplified while approaching his usual burrito stand, still surly over his test. Mouths were gossiping his name. Eyes were watching from all around the Quad.

Hugo spied a nearby group of ill-fashioned students' unwelcome interest.

"Can I help you?" Hugo growled, scattering them. The gossip and stares increased.

"Scumbag."

"That's why the Sensational Six aren't friends anymore."

"How many do you think he nailed besides Spencer and Jordana?"

Hugo coughed. How the fuck did people know about him and Spencer?

"Definitely Brie at some point," Kendall Caruso said. "No wonder her and Jordana had that falling out."

"Not Jen Thomas. She's into girls."

"I heard J-Tom's bisexual. So maybe…"

"How—" Swallowing mortification, Hugo fled from the Quad as fast as possible without running.

That shock soon became a sea of rage. Who sold him out? It couldn't have been Abby Dunleavy. This summer, AJ had threatened to unfriend her brother if she said anything about her and Hugo's fling.

"Who haven't you slept with, Malalou?" some random called out.

"Your sister," he threw back without breaking stride, drawing a chorus of "OOOOHS."

J-Tom and Simon wouldn't do this. Brie six months ago would've, but not anymore. That left one Benedict Arnold. Hugo marched for the gymnasium, anger quickening his pace.

He found Grace at the indoor basketball court chattering with Songs cheerleaders in sports bras and yoga shorts. She wore absurd polka-dot jean suspenders with her hair tied up in several Bantu knots.

The two adult coaches were already leaving the gym. Taylor, gathering her bags near the bleachers, waved at Hugo less eagerly than usual.

Whatever... Hugo nodded back, waiting until Grace was alone.

"Can we talk?" he asked once they were face to face.

"Yeah." Grace looked concerned. "How are you—?"

Hugo cut to the point. "Did you tell anyone that I slept with Spencer?"

Grace's eyes tightened. "You're serious?"

Hugo stood firm. She'd been angry at him for weeks now. "Did you tell anyone or not?"

A bloodless expression he'd never seen before. "First off, no. So fuck you very much," she declared, her contempt very clear. "Two, Spencer posted about you on IG."

That knocked the indignation out of him. "Huh?"

Grace grabbed her cellphone, did some impatient scrolling, then shoved it in his face. "Here."

Hugo stared and kept staring at a carousel of images showcasing himself and Spencer—together. Cellphone snapshots that were never supposed to see the light of day. In each photo, they were mugging for the camera, or cuddling, very coupled-up. More revealing was Spencer's photo caption.

Find yourself someone who looks at you the way Bogie Malalou does.

"Errgh." Hugo's brain short-circuited. Of course Spencer was behind this. Why? To screw with him, J-Tom, and Jordana.

Jordana... Jesus. She must have already seen these photos.

Grace looked so hurt. Hugo and his big mouth. "Grace, I'm sorry—"

"Leave me alone!" She stormed off, leaving him in an empty gymnasium.

The situation worsened back in the Quad. Simon was waiting for him near their tables with a sullen face. "G-Mama texted me. She's really upset."

Hugo stomach's roiled. "I thought she'd told everyone about Spencer," he said wearily. More students passed by, chattering and pointing. "Didn't know Spencer was behind this."

Despite their height difference, Simon's anger soared over him. "Grace is ride-or-die. You *know* this."

"I know and I'm sorry." If Hugo could kick himself, then he would've. Grace had always been in his corner. "I'll apologize once I see her."

"I'll handle Grace." Simon's tone left no room for negotiation. "Deal with that." He nodded past him before marching away.

Hugo turned, and his blood froze.

Jordana approached with Briseis and J-Tom. She looked stunning, hair in a donut bun with a flowery spaghetti-strapped dress. But her expression was closed off.

Hugo reached her in three strides, wanting to hold her so badly. "I saw Spence's post."

"Yeah…" Jordana replied flatly. Their bond felt…withered and frayed.

Hugo didn't like that. Brie watched him blankly. J-Tom was miserably hiding her face beneath her baseball cap. Hugo inhaled deeply, defense already prepared. "Everything in that post, you know about." He and Jodie had discussed Spencer extensively before dating again, except for her being a super.

Jordana's eyes flashed, but not with affection. "Hearing is different from seeing photos. I need space." She backpedaled from him.

The rejection sent a hard slap to Hugo. He should've seen this coming.

Jordana whirled on J-Tom angrily. "And you knew about them since spring." She marched off.

Brie called after her BFF to no avail.

"Shit." J-Tom looked closed to hyperventilating. "Bogie…"

Hugo pointed after Jordana. "She needs you."

J-Tom jogged after her hastily.

Before Hugo could wallow in self-pity, the rest of his friends arrived to pile on.

"Really, Hugo?" Groban scolded. "Spencer and Jodie at the same time?"

Raphael shook his head in displeasure. "That's messed up. J-Tom was dating her, and Jodie was her close friend." Wale and JT both loudly approved.

The strawberry-blonde Stanley twins chimed in.

"How could you do that to Jordana?" Marin demanded.

"That was one of her best friends," Karin added.

"Both relationships weren't exclusive," Hugo defended, then realized how weak that sounded.

Many of his friends seemed appalled. Brent, like Brie, said nothing.

"Doesn't make it right," both Stanleys retorted simultaneously.

Hugo was sick of their lectures, sick of their judgment, sick of the gossiping about his life from people who didn't know him. "It was a mistake," he spoke over them. "And it's no one's business!"

His friends' uproar was expected and obnoxious. Hugo let them verbally pummel him. Why not?

"Guys!" All eyes turned.

Briseis was visibly irritated, dressed in an oversized white shirt that almost covered her green miniskirt. Her hair was in a low and sleek ponytail, putting that absurdly stunning face on display. "Hugo made a mistake. Spencer Michelman fooled a lot of people. Hugo and J-Tom thought she was someone special. Jodie and I thought she'd be a ride-or-die." Her gaze fell. "She ended up hurting everyone because she could."

Marin Stanley wasn't pleased. "But—"

Surprisingly, Brent stepped in. "Everyone relax and have a strawberry cupcake. Nobody died."

With that, the group dispersed, grumbling their disdain or shooting him salty looks. The verbal beatdown left Hugo feeling hollow. Even Simon was angry with him. But he'd deserved it for being a crappy friend and an even worse not-boyfriend. *Wait till they hear from Grace.*

Surprisingly, Brie and Brent stayed.

"I knew something changed with you and Spencer," Brent pressed as they stood in line grabbing burritos. He seemed fascinated and boyish, like the Brent who Hugo had befriended last year. "Anytime I saw you two snarling at each other, there was...sexual tension."

Hugo shrugged. "Kinda was." Discussing his relationship with Spencer openly felt odd yet liberating. He turned to Brie, baffled by how chill she had been. "Surprised you're not leading the pitchforks against me."

Brie pointed at herself in mock surprise. "Who am I to judge? Easy Breezy, recovering mean girl? Slept with two basketball players on the same team?" Self-deprecating Brie was a huge departure from Queen Brie, the self-obsessed tyrant. "Let's not forget my viral sextape. Need I go on?"

"Please do," Brent requested, leaning in.

"Pervball!" Briseis aimed a kick at him, which he sidestepped. She then draped her arm around Hugo's shoulders with a teasing smile. "We sluts should stick together."

Hugo found himself laughing gratefully. "But Jordana needs you."

"I'll be there for her after school." Brie's gaze penetrated through his doubts. "I'm here for you *now*."

The trio sat together in the highest bleachers the rest of lunch, talking about anything else. Hugo tried not to think about Jordana and the old wounds that Spencer's post must've ripped open. On a side note, watching Brie devour her burrito guilt-free was heartwarming.

"I have a question, Brosef," Brent announced, blue eyes sparkling.

Hugo braced himself. "Shoot."

"I like two girls." Brent sounded frustrated. "And they both like me."

Hugo waited for the problem. "How's that an issue?"

"*Terrible* problem to have, Lefty," Brie scoffed, wiping guacamole from her lips.

"Shush!" Brent focused on Hugo. "They gave me an ultimatum to choose between them. Not sure if I can. It's why I've been...avoiding a choice." His handsome face tightened. "What would you do?"

Hugo was the last person anyone should ask for dating advice. But he answered. "Don't date close friends. Or in your case, twin sisters."

Brie's eyes widened. Brent's jaw dropped. "How...you—"

Hugo smiled. He'd seen sparks between Marin and Brent, then him and Karin last summer. "Am I right?"

"Short answer? Yes," Brent replied blushingly.

"Long answer?" Brie quipped. "Yeeeeeessssss."

"First rule." Hugo raised a pointer finger. "Know your value."

Brent frowned, as if trying to solve a hard math problem. He wasn't getting it. "But what about—?"

"Rule two. Be honest about your feelings," Hugo went on, two fingers held up briefly. Just like he should've been honest with Jordana about Spencer. "They'll at least respect you for knowing what you want."

By Brent's "eureka" face, he was digesting this. Brie listened attentively.

"Last thing." Hugo had learned this the hard way. "Thinking any girl has more value than you leads to bad decisions and her not respecting you." The energy around him grew thick and heady. Hugo dared a look at Brie sitting bolt-upright, staring at the ground. The guilt on that face told so many stories. She sighed and finally met Hugo's stare with a remorseful smile, almost in tears.

Uncomfortable, Hugo hastily turned back to Brent.

If Brent saw the exchange, there was no sign. "Sounds scary," he admitted.

Hugo poked his ribs. "Which means you should do it." A twisted thought forced the smile off his face. "Just don't ask Marin and Karin for a threesome."

"Ewww," Brie said with a disgusted snort-laugh, swatting at Hugo's head.

Brent shuddered. "I'm not into that Lannister shit!" His laugh sounded like a car that hadn't started up in twenty years, coaxing enjoyment out of Hugo for the first time today.

Speaking of shudders... Hugo tensed up. At a glance, the football field appeared normal. But Hugo felt very subtle tremors running up the bleachers where he, Brent, and Briseis sat.

The micro tremors reached across campus, stopping after several seconds.

Hugo turned to Brie and Brent. "You guys...feel that?"

Brie watched him in alarm, shaking her head. "What's wrong?"

This was more than the Spencer problem putting Hugo on edge. "I think I felt aftershocks."

Brent took a look at his cellphone, almost toppling from his seat. "Are you half-canine, Bogie?" Hugo and Brie stared back, lost.

Brent held his phone up, displaying the N3 news app.

The color drained from Brie's face. "Oh my God!"

Hugo's bones liquified when he saw the headline. "Oh no..."

EARTHQUAKE LEVELS SEATTLE-TACOMA.

CHAPTER 31

"*You're* behind this!" Brightburn cried, pointing a manicured finger at Shattershot.

Greyson stepped back, eyes darting from accused to accuser. *This is getting good.*

Shattershot looked like he'd been slugged in the jaw. "Me?"

Brightburn's fingers crackled with energy. "I used to think Bulldozer was too hard on you." Her stare turned venomous. "But now it makes sense. You're working with this Damocles asshole."

"I am not!" Shattershot sounded genuinely hurt. "And *fuck* you!"

Erika spun Brightburn around. "You're in no position to criticize him." Her anger soared with each word. "Do you realize how much trouble your freelancing could get us in?"

"Guys…" Reverb spoke up.

Greyson spied him in the hall leading to the bedrooms. *Ah, my other surprise…* But he pretended to ignore his teammate, focused on the present conflict.

Brightburn's eyes watered as she ranted on. "I never got the justice I deserved," she wailed. "The least I can do is get that for some women victimized by these predators."

"GUYS!" Reverb shouted.

Everyone turned. "What, Reverb?" the team shouted back.

Reverb walked slowly out of the hall, visibly dumbstruck. He held up a picture. "These pictures were all over the hallway." The blurry images featured Shattershot and his lover, Villanelle.

The empath's face drained.

Greyson feigned confusion. "Who's that, Shattershot?" he asked.

"Bam-Bam, from the Conglomerate in DC," Erika answered when facing the empath. "You two are lovers?"

The awkward tension grew more delicious. Shattershot looked away. "Yes."

The uproar was as angry as Greyson had hoped.

Reverb, for once, grew livid. "Are you *kidding* me?"

"She wants out of the criminal life," Shattershot assured, waving his hands with a desperation that matched his voice. "I'm helping her!"

Bulldozer snorted in derision. "More like helping yourself to her."

Something changed on Shattershot's face as if some limit had finally been reached. "Go fuck yourself, Bulldozer! "You probably followed me and took these pictures."

Yes! Greyson mused, barely keeping his joy under the hood.

Bulldozer's eyes widened. However, he deflected with a dismissive laugh. "Don't flatter yourself."

Brightburn studied Bulldozer in disbelief. "Dozer?"

"I didn't tail that sawed-off midget!" he lied again.

Greyson saw his opening and walked right in. "Actually, you followed us four nights ago." He pointed at Bulldozer to clear up any misconception.

Erika, Reverb, and Brightburn flinched from this new accusation.

A vein pulsed on Bulldozer's forehead. "Of course *you'd* lie for him."

Greyson ignored his mockery and continued. "You followed Shattershot and me to the bar. Then you tried following me after we left."

Shattershot eyed him in disbelief.

"Bullshit!" Bulldozer lied again.

"I *knew* that was you!" Shattershot exploded. He looked repulsed. "And I thought I was being paranoid!"

Erika facepalmed, at her wits' end. "Seriously, Dozer?"

Bulldozer closed his eyes, realizing he'd been made. "I don't trust them. And for good reason."

Greyson twisted the knife deeper. "I want to prove myself," he admitted, a wounded edge to his voice. "But let's be honest. You're a bully who likes throwing your weight around to make yourself feel tall."

Bulldozer reddened. "Watch your mouth, boy," he warned.

Erika pushed Greyson back. "Levi," she cautioned.

He rounded her with ease, locked on his target. "Or what? You'll beat me up? Give me your best shot, big man." He stuck his chin out. "If that's what it will take for you to finally accept me." The last line just popped into his head, drawing the desired sympathy from Brightburn and Reverb.

Erika threw herself between the two snarling men. "Both of you back off!" she barked fruitlessly.

Bulldozer ignored her, jabbing Greyson in the chest, trembling. "You think you want this? They'd have to mop you off the floor." He was close to the edge.

Greyson pushed harder. "I'm seeing why Blackbird left with a teammate like Bulldozer."

The room hushed.

Bulldozer purpled. "This team's problems started when you showed up!"

Greyson spread his arms in challenge. "This team's problem is looking right at me."

Bulldozer's skin shifted from flesh to metal, and he launched himself at Greyson.

"Bulldozer, NO!" Erika shrieked.

Before Greyson knew it, Bulldozer hoisted him up by the throat with frightening ease.

Suddenly, he was airborne to the chorus of two women's screams. His back struck the common room table, oxygen dashed from his lungs. Greyson's ribcage screamed. He slid to the floor with a grunt.

On his back, Greyson witnessed a metallic behemoth stampeding toward him. Bulldozer's metal face contorted when he swooped down to grab him.

Greyson fought every instinct to defend himself and raised both hands in mock fear.

Then lightning forked across the room with white-hot knives, daggering Bulldozer in the back.

He arched his spine and roared, collapsing.

Greyson lowered his hands to behold a fearsome sight.

Brightburn was in combat stance, her fingers sizzling with yellowish electricity. Her pretty face was a merciless mask. "Touch him again, and I'll blind you!"

Their defiance snapped Bulldozer out of his rage. He stared at Brightburn and Erika with such hurt.

Erika helped Greyson up to a seated posture. She stared at Bulldozer with pure loathing. "Get out of my sight!" Reverb and Shattershot formed a wall around Greyson.

The unified rejection gutted Bulldozer. He switched to his normal skin and walked away. No one spoke until he'd left the room.

Reverb answered a cellphone call and moved away.

Everyone else fussed over Greyson. "Are you okay?" Shattershot asked.

Greyson didn't need to fake his wincing expression. "He's out of control."

Erika had an odd expression on her face. "I know…I'm so sorry." Her face crumpled with such disappointment. "What Bulldozer did to you and Shattershot is unacceptable."

This was exactly where Greyson wanted the Natural Born Thrillers. Divided and at each other's throats. *Now I can publicly take each of you out one by one*, he mulled while Brightburn guided him onto the couch. Then Shenandoah would be free.

Before anyone else could chime in, Reverb approached. "Boss lady. Our Seneca overlords called."

Erika's features tightened. "Oh God."

"It's not about Brightburn," Reverb countered solemnly, "or anything else team-related."

Greyson watched him carefully. Why did he feel such worry gnawing at his belly?

Reverb massaged his temples. "Something happened in Seattle. Something bad."

CHAPTER 32

Most Americans' fear of the Big One always centered around California. Few knew or cared that Washington sat on three fault lines, the Cascadia Subduction Zone.

Not until today.

The "Cascadia Quake" at the end of lunch was the only topic discussed during fifth and sixth period. Hugo's first impulse was to leave immediately. Instead, he devoured every news source, gaining as much info as possible. J-Tom, Simon, and Hugo were texting back and forth, plotting their next move before Aegis and Arclight leaped into action.

Many kids were in shock. Teachers and school staff struggled to stay calm in front of their students.

Of course they're freaked out, Hugo realized. The adults were old enough to recall the 1987 quake that caused San Luis Obispo to become San Miguel.

Hugo's stomach sank with each phone alert, every damage and casualty report more dire.

By mid-fifth period, President Khan addressed the nation and declared a national emergency. California, Oregon, and Nevada's governors had deployed their National Guard and ERAT teams.

As a government-sanctioned hero, Hugo regretted not having a liaison for detailed instructions.

Hugo and J-Tom met in the storage unit five minutes before sixth period ended, both convincing their teachers to let them out earlier. Neither spoke while changing into their gear. Then Hugo picked up J-Tom and raced off. Once clear of campus, they blasted into the air.

Hugo could've reached Seattle in under an hour, now able to surpass Mach 2. But as J-Tom's armor could only push past Mach 1, he went slower to keep pace. Plus, her armor's GPS systems were better.

The whole flight, Hugo and J-Tom were patched in to data channels providing more details.

This earthquake had been a 9.1, beyond anything to hit the Pacific Northwest in decades. Damage reports came in from Bellingham near the Canadian border to as far inland as Yakima. Tsunamis were pounding coastal towns between Neah Bay to Ilwaco.

What Hugo knew of Seattle came from photos. An urban peninsula dressed in clumps of green flanked by Puget Sound and various forest-covered islands—a nature lover's dream.

When Seattle came into view thousands of feet below, Hugo looked upon a post-apocalyptic hellscape.

"Jesus Christ," he murmured as he and J-Tom dipped lower.

Downtown Seattle's tight skyline cluster overlooking the waterfront had been reduced to wreckage. The high-rises' foundations lined the streets like rows of broken teeth. The Space Needle was still standing but looked very wobbly. Dark clouds rose from the fires ravaging Seattle, shrouding the sun. As Hugo and J-Tom weaved around the pillars of filthy smoke; noxious fumes stung his eyes beneath his half-mask.

The floating bridges linking Seattle to Mercer Island and Bellevue had sunk beneath Lake Washington. The I-5 and I-405 freeways running through Washington State resembled concrete jigsaw puzzles.

Puget Sound and Lake Washington flooded Seattle and its nearby islands in frothing waves.

Hugo drank everything in: the shattered structures, the thousands screaming for help, the stench of fire and death. Unbridled desolation overwhelmed his brain.

J-Tom floated at his side, her horror clear despite the inexpressive helmet. "Where do we even start?"

Hugo had no answer. For all his bluster at going solo, he now felt like a teen cosplayer. "I don't know—"

A ping in his hood's earpiece tore Hugo's attention away. He answered. "This is Aegis."

"Have you reached Seattle?"

"Lady Liberty," he exclaimed, openly relieved. "Yes. Where do we go?"

She directed them to FEMA's makeshift headquarters north of Seattle. Suburbs like Boeing Creek and Shoreview Park overflowed with tents, emergency trucks. Flying superheroes were landing or taking off from the base.

In the largest tent, hundreds of emergency workers prepared a makeshift hospital for incoming patients.

Battalion and San Francisco's Golden Guardians were among many heroes gathered near the center.

Lady Liberty stood alongside Gambrel of Seattle's Green Squadron, and Sentinel, of all people, providing directions. No one had seen Sentinel in months. The supersoldier appeared hale and in control, unlike the burnt-out man Hugo had dressed down.

"Holy crap," J-Tom hissed. "It's the Valhalla of heroes. Except no one's a dead Viking."

Her joy brought a smile to Hugo's face. "Don't fangirl too much, huglord," he murmured.

J-Tom nodded her silvery helmet. "On it."

Once the meeting ended, the heroes gathered into assigned groups. Lady Liberty spotted Hugo and reached him in a few long strides. "Aegis." She gave J-Tom's armor a stern onceover. "Arclight."

Hugo nodded. "Lady Liberty..." He paused when catching another approach. "Dynamo," he blurted out.

Ramon towered over Hugo in his cobalt-blue-and-black-armored Dynamo suit.

"Hello." He waved a hand down his own torso self-deprecatingly. "I know, I'm retired. But natural disasters don't care about your feelings."

"Good to see you." Hugo glanced at the departing groups. "Where can we start?"

"The focus is search and rescue," Lady Liberty said. "Emergency Services will assign zones to each team."

"Team up?" Dynamo asked Hugo.

Despite Ramon being younger, he had three years of field experience on The Vanguard.

"Tell us where we're needed," Hugo agreed readily.

He and J-Tom followed Ramon into the heart of Seattle's decimated downtown. Pike Market was under rubble, firefighters and hydrokinetic responders fighting the boiling fires.

Hugo served as a bloodhound, his hypersensitivity ferreting out trapped survivors. From there, he, J-Tom, and Dynamo burrowed through to reach these poor civilians.

After EMTs extracted the wounded and the deceased, Hugo tracked down the next pocket to repeat the process. Finding survivors were moments to enjoy. The shock of another corpse didn't get easier.

These searches continued until dark settled over the ruined cityscape.

Green Squadron's members were directing their own teams around downtown to search other pockets. In one group, Hugo spotted Polymer stretching his elastic limbs to clear large chunks of demolished buildings. The two exchanged weary nods and continued onward.

After nightfall, Hugo, J-Tom, and Ramon returned to the park encampment where the rescued had been delivered. The living had maxed out the beds and makeshift cots. The dead received their own tent, hundreds laid out in rows covered by blankets.

Lady Liberty, covered in grime, stared blankly at the fallen. Hugo watched them as well, taking a few minutes to mourn. Then he made his heart go cold and left. More lives to save, more dead to bury.

Many out-of-town heroes were staying at makeshift motels. Ramon directed Hugo and J-Tom to a Vanguard waystation. Hugo welcomed the refuge, bone-tired. J-Tom could barely keep her eyes open.

The waystation, while spare in furniture, held abundant food and water. From there, Hugo disrobed, and J-Tom shed her armor in privacy.

After two hot showers and dinner, Hugo called home to say he'd be staying in Seattle longer and miss school tomorrow. Mom almost protested but soon understood. What he didn't reveal to Mom were the horrors he'd seen or his despair. Hugo would spare her that. J-Tom told her parents she was staying, getting no resistance. Their joint cover story would be working at donation centers to collect goods for Seattle.

Hugo came to his room in Vanguard-logoed black sweats, eager to crash.

J-Tom sat on his bedside, damp ginger hair up in a knot. Her face was empty, body swaying from the weight of today's many tragedies.

Hugo's heart cracked, knowing that look. He approached without a second thought.

They lay in bed a long while holding each other. But J-Tom couldn't stop shaking. Hugo wiped away her tears, then kissed her mouth. Slow, sweet kisses.

She reacted like a switch had been flipped, climbing onto him with lust-glazed eyes. Before long, the teens were devouring each other.

"You're my happy place…" J-Tom murmured after they finished, drifting off with a smile.

Then Hugo let sleep pull him under.

The next morning, part of him wished yesterday had been a bad dream.

Then he clicked on the news. Ugh. In one day, the casualty count had reached nine thousand.

Ramon had already left in his Dynamo armor to continue cleanup efforts. J-Tom joined Hugo in the waystation dining room as he spoke with Simon via cellphone. His BFF was still miffed over the Grace situation but kept focus on the Seattle crisis.

"What else can I do?" Simon asked, yawning.

J-Tom leaned closer to the phone. "A school donation website? Like the one you did for a new library."

"That's good," Simon agreed.

J-Tom was watching Hugo. "What else can Aegis do?"

He wasn't sure what that meant. "Besides what I'm already doing?"

J-Tom rolled her eyes. "Obviously. But charity can be the work that brings awareness."

Hugo rose from his seat. Using his fame to bring exposure struck like lightning. "You're a genius, Jen."

J-Tom did her flirty eyebrow raise. "Maybe I just inspired your genius."

After his call with Simon, Hugo called Annie straightaway. "I have an idea for charitable outreach." He winked at J-Tom, who blushed. He and Annie devised a plan that included bodycam footage from his and J-Tom's suits. The finalized plan sounded amazing.

When Hugo and J-Tom returned to action later, Lady Liberty was still leading her rescue team. Apparently, she'd been working through the night.

"The laws prevent teen heroes from doing that," Ramon explained when Hugo and J-Tom met up with him.

Today, Hugo got assigned to clearing roads and overpasses. J-Tom went with Dynamo for more search and rescue. Hugo welcomed the ease of removing debris. Still, he found bodies. Steeling away grief wasn't easy, but he persisted.

He worked with Chicago's Second City Saints to replace ruined overpasses with moldable foam connectors.

While in action, he watched other heroes using their powers to clean up. One lone super, bearded and fluffy-haired, levitated away rubble by telekinesis in Little Saigon. Firecracker, from Freedom's Ring, used her explosive plasma to destroy debris blocking FEMA trucks. Late afternoon, Hugo stopped by a newly erected camp. Despite being exhausted, he stayed for hours taking pictures and talking to victims. Seeing Aegis lifted these kids' spirits as well as his own.

On day three, he had stopped tracking the death toll. With extensive debris cleared and more survivors being found, new camps had sprouted around Seattle and Tacoma.

Hugo and J-Tom reunited to carry supplies from nearby military bases to Mercer and Bainbridge Islands. His only issue was with one of the suppliers, Paxton-Brandt. But now wasn't the time for animus.

"Maybe they're evolving," J-Tom suggested, always finding the good in everything, even evil megacorps. Hugo loved her for that.

The first several flights went smoothly. While he returned to the base, Hugo's superhearing caught trouble on Mercer Island. The natives were getting restless from hunger.

"This food line ain't moving fast enough."

"We're moving as fast as we can, sir."

"My kids haven't eaten in almost two days."

"Fuck this!"

Hugo and J-Tom decelerated above the south end of Mercer Island where food container lines had devolved into a full-on brawl. Some threw haymakers while others shot energy blasts. The poor volunteer workers were overwhelmed. No other heroes were on site. Shit.

Hugo tapped the side of his hood. "Ops. This is Aegis. We got rioting in Pioneer Park."

"Remove the food container and stop the fight," a voice replied. "Backup is coming."

"Understood." Hugo turned to J-Tom beside him. "Get the container back to the Army Reserve base."

"On it." She dove for the food container. "Go easy on them."

Hugo plunged toward the crowd. "Not sure they feel the same." He touched down amid the chaos in a crouch, textbook superhero landing.

"ENOUGH," he barked. That stopped most of the group, until someone jumped on his back. They swarmed him. "Seriously?" Then someone peppered his backside with energy blasts.

"Aegis—" J-Tom cried in the comm channel.

"I'm okay," he growled. "Get the container and go." He flung his arms back, throwing several attackers off, and shouted. The sonic scream mowed down the crowds but didn't harm them. A loud creak drew his attention to the right. J-Tom hoisted the container overhead. Her boot jets erupted as she took off. Many rioters cried out in anger. Soon she'd risen high enough to be out of danger.

Thank God. Hugo was turning away when a violet energy jet shot from the ground, punching J-Tom in the back. The container she was carrying got sliced in half.

J-Tom dropped like a stone, sparks and thick smoke trailing her descent.

Hugo's heart stopped. "Arclight? ARCLIGHT!" No response. Was she unconscious? Or dead?

He exploded upward, flinging protesters in all directions. He didn't care, racing for his falling friend.

Panicking, he scanned below. No sign of the shooter. Hugo pushed himself faster. "Fuckfuckfuck!" The illuminated sections of J-Tom's armor were dead, including her eyes. Not good.

Hugo reached out to catch her limp body, when the second energy blast caught him in the stomach.

"Aaaah!" He folded up like a paper bag, pain overwhelming his nervous system.

Hugo was falling fast, unable to stop. Agony had scorched away his strength. The landing cratered a service street. He rolled onto his side, writhing and groaning. Someone approached. The shooter? His pain-blurred vision couldn't make them out.

Hugo barely struggled to a knee before another dazzling jet sent him skidding across a sidewalk.

He slid to a stop on grass, swallowing a scream.

The shooter loomed over him, silhouetted by sun and smog.

The shooter crouched beside him. "Miss me?" Definitely a girl by the hourglass figure, donning an athletic dark-red jumpsuit. Her raven-black hair was longer with shaggy bangs, up in a ponytail. But Hugo couldn't forget this girl's beauty, with dark-blue eyes oozing venom.

He stared up in disbelief. "S-Spence?" Spencer Michelman, in Seattle. She'd shot them down.

She straddled him leisurely. "Ultraviolet." Her voice was soft and gripping. "Told ya this would happen."

Spencer being free confirmed that Dr. Michelman was either captured or dead. The truth pierced through Hugo's torment. He struggled to sit up. "Where...is your dad?"

Spencer's face contorted in hatred. "Worry about yourself." She wrapped both hands around Hugo's throat. "I could end you right now." Her fingers glowed neon purple, igniting Hugo's bones.

The snowballing agony was too much to even move. He screamed.

Suddenly, the pain lessened to where he wasn't about to faint.

Spencer shook her head, jostling her ponytail, smiling a demented smile. "Could, but won't."

Hugo struggled to lift his hand and push her off.

Spencer tightened her chokehold. Fire ripped up Hugo's spine. She leaned closer. "I'll make you wait until you go insane." Her whisper caressed his ear, akin to a lover's kiss. "Then make you and Jenny suffer until you beg for mercy. And I'll say no."

Spencer hauled his ragdoll body into seated posture by the throat. "Your identities are safe. For now." She kissed his mouth forcefully, grinding her hips onto his waist.

Hugo tried resisting. Spencer squeezed tighter; excruciating jolts of radiation kept him immobilized.

What shamed Hugo most was the part of himself enjoying her tongue in his mouth again.

Jenny... Fear for J-Tom kept him conscious. *Have to...save her...*

Spencer finally pulled back with a pleased sneer. "This is just an appetizer." She shoved Hugo down and stood. "Cuz every superhero needs a supervillain."

That was the last thing Hugo remembered.

CHAPTER 33

Greyson sat hunched and stewing in this stupid yellow-and-green costume.

The Natural Born Thrillers had been divided and at each other's throats, exactly where he wanted them. All he needed was to push a little more before extinguishing them.

Then Seattle-Tacoma happened.

A 9.1 earthquake had flattened Washington's two largest cities.

With thousands dead and millions displaced, President Myriam Khan declared a national emergency.

Several heroes and ERAT teams were already converging on Seattle to start the gigantic relief effort.

The team currently sat on a Seneca private jet, an hour away from SEA-TAC. No one spoke for most of the flight. Tensions remained high after this morning's blowup.

For that, Greyson was thankful. He wasn't done fracturing the team. But would these cracks remain after Seattle? The worry gnawed at him throughout the flight.

Greyson sat beside Shattershot, in a yellow-and-green suit like the rest of the team.

With them was Piper Parsons, a Seneca executive serving as the Thrillers' corporate liaison. She was best described as pert, pretty, and blonde with a smile imprinted on her face. "Alright, team!" She stood at the front of the passenger cabin. "We're almost at Seattle and Tacoma." She pumped a fist like some cheerleader. "Let's all bring our A-game effort."

Greyson wanted to toss her overeager ass out of the plane. He settled for a death glare.

Erika's face was solemn when she stood. "We need this win. Doing good here helps our image at home."

The speech drew murmured agreement and a terse nod from Bulldozer.

"Understood, boss," Greyson mumbled.

Shattershot poked his shoulder. "Look…" He nodded at the window beside his seat.

Greyson leaned forward, and his world cracked open. He'd never visited Seattle before but had seen images of the famous skyline.

That version of Seattle no longer existed. As their jet pierced through blankets of mucky clouds, Greyson saw a warzone surrounding Puget Sound. Distorted and crushed buildings, fractured freeways, residential areas that looked trampled by bulls.

The sight wrenched Greyson's heart in ways he'd no longer thought possible. This looked worse than the 1987 San Luis Obispo quake, endless devastation stretching in all directions.

Seattle's Capitol Hill neighborhood burned. Dense clumps of trees smoldered. Ruined buildings were engulfed in flames, like funeral pyres…

Greyson flattened against his seat. "Jesus." He flashed on a half-forgotten nightmare from over a year ago, the night of Titan's death. An almost identical apocalyptic scene.

Greyson clutched his chest, thankful to find a fluttering heartbeat. *A dream or a premonition?*

He remembered where he was and Shattershot sitting beside him.

"You alright, Levi?"

"I'm fine," Greyson lied hastily. "It's just…horrible."

Their jet landed on a repaired runway at McCord Air Force Base 30 miles south of SeaTac Airport. From there, the team drove over to the disaster response command center at Camp Murray near Tacoma.

Greyson felt awfully exposed among Seneca's portfolio of corporate-owned heroes.

Los Angeles's Battalion was present, gorgeous movie stars turned heroes. Gross. Seeing the Second City Saints, Chicago's new team, rankled Greyson considerably. The Midwest was rebuilding its superhero community around them. Aces & Eights, the Vegas-based team with their card-themed costumes, chatted up everyone.

The team drawing the most attention was Freedom's Ring from Philadelphia, led by Sentinel rip-off Commando-in-Chief.

His teammates included American Dream, John Plymouth, Firecracker, Cheyenne Blackbird, and Rushmore. All were slathered in patriotic gear. Up close, Greyson understood their allure to a naïve populace. Freedom's Ring was a throwback to 1980s flag-humping patriotism but modernized to avoid cheesiness.

The Natural Born Thrillers stayed in their corner watching the proceedings.

Reverb was the only one showing any bit of joy. "Under happier circumstances, I'd be geeking out now."

A smile inched up Erika's face. "You kinda are, Verb."

"Don't judge me," Reverb scolded, then pointed. "Holy crap. That's Sentinel!"

Greyson and the other Thrillers turned and gaped.

Sentinel himself was huddled with Seattle's Green Squadron. He remained a blond-haired, blue-eyed model of masculine perfection, despite looking like a lion with his shaggy mane and beard.

But his glorious fall from grace stayed fresh in Greyson's mind.

"I thought he retired after Black Wednesday," Brightburn remarked awkwardly, "and…ya know."

"Beating up the teenager that fucked his ex-fiancée?" Bulldozer added. "And getting owned by Aegis."

"Yeah. That."

Erika pushed off the wall, all business. "Let's not judge someone else's mistakes." She had a quick discussion with Seneca's organizers before returning to her team. "Hazard, Shattershot, and Reverb. You'll go to Columbia City with the Golden Guardians to help search and rescue efforts. Bulldozer, myself, and Brightburn are going to West Seattle with Freedom's Ring to build more temporary bases."

Greyson spotted her strategy. Reverb, everyone's friend, would babysit him and Shattershot. Meanwhile, Bulldozer got watched by Erika and Brightburn. Those three could possibly talk things out, undoing Greyson's hard work. He opened his mouth to protest.

"Done!" Reverb eyed Greyson and Shattershot. "Follow my lead, boys."

Erika and her group headed into the cluster of heroes.

Greyson clenched his teeth and marched alongside Reverb.

"Is Aegis coming?" Shattershot asked once they stepped out into smoke-clogged air.

Greyson went rigid. He'd forgotten the proximity from here to San Miguel. "I don't see why not. Seattle's on the same coast," he replied with forced nonchalance, silently praying for Aegis's arrival.

"Don't tell Sentinel," Reverb concluded, drawing laughs from Shattershot.

Greyson fake-laughed to not appear out of place as his cell buzzed. Excusing himself, he wandered off to a private corner.

CIH: I'm here with other Paxton-Brandt assets.

He smiled. These separations weren't easy. Greyson texted back.

ME: I'm in Columbia City.

CIH: Asher has an idea to decimate the Thrillers here in Seattle.

Greyson snorted.

ME: You lost me at Asher having an idea.

CIH: LOLOLOL!!

Greyson glanced up from his phone at this who's who gathering.

ME: Kinda risky with so many heroes present.

CIH: Don't worry. Once the trap is set, you humiliate them here and destroy them back in Shenandoah.

ME: Works for me.

From there, Greyson and his teammates went to the heart of downtown Seattle, hazy with dust and smoke, rubble lying in various towering piles.

Battalion cleared paths for emergency service vehicles while feigning sadness for the cameras. Greyson ignored their vapidity, disintegrating rubble with nuclear bursts to remove obstacles. Reverb bounced atop various concrete debris, breaking them apart. Meanwhile, Shattershot sensed for buried survivors with his empathic talents. Greyson saw how the flashes of pain, fear, or grief affected Shattershot. But he gritted his teeth and soldiered on toward more survivors.

This was a good man. *Far better than myself.* But Greyson had accepted being a necessary evil.

Their shift didn't end until close to midnight. Greyson was wiped. Some part of him felt good at the lives they'd saved, but that didn't make the countless dead bodies any easier to swallow.

"I've never seen anything like this before," Shattershot wheezed after they'd retired into their shared motel room miles outside of Seattle.

Bulldozer and Reverb shared a room, as did Brightburn and Erika.

Shattershot had a faraway gaze after taking a shower.

Greyson nodded, also showered and in PJs provided by Seneca International. "There was the San Luis Obispo Quake. Leveled the whole city."

Shattershot wrinkled his nose. "Giving birth to a parody of a city."

Greyson laughed, glad more people saw San Miguel this way. "Not a fan?"

Shattershot shook his head. "Too manufactured and commercialized." He made a face. "The City of Wonder? C'mon!" The pair laughed heartily. When the dust settled, Greyson had to get Shattershot out of this mess.

The following morning, Greyson attended a team breakfast. Everyone was exhausted and haunted by yesterday. Per the Seneca brass, Greyson would continue nuking debris in midtown Seattle while the Thrillers built homes on Maury Island.

"Sorry you're not included, Levi," Erika apologized. "But a trainee appearing will confuse the media."

Greyson played the gracious teammate. "As long as I can do my part." Inside, he was bursting with excitement. *This must be the sign*, he pondered as the Thrillers were driven away toward Maury Island.

A call from Connie confirmed it. "Everything's ready, babe. The Natural Born Thrillers will be on Maury Island working on temporary housing. No other heroes but them."

Greyson stared up at the barely penetrable sky. No heroes and no civilians put this in his favor. The last thing they wanted was the Thrillers becoming martyrs. "What is Asher's plan?"

"Scavengers with powers trying to steal supplies," Connie laid out. "The Thrillers engage, but the battle gets out of hand and destroys the new housing, with your help." Her animated voice was so sexy. "We'll give you the signal. Then you fly over and cause the required chaos."

Greyson stared at the phone. His wife's lack of hesitation was a thing of beauty. With the plan set, he returned to midtown. Today, downtown Seattle's boulevards were mostly clear, the damaged buildings lining them like hedges. Apparently, several fliers like Lady Liberty had worked through the night removing rubble.

He regrettably got paired with the Second City Saints and hated them in short order. Being a young team making waves came at the cost of maturity.

Disgusted, Greyson ambled to an abandoned boulevard. Other than the echoes of the Saints' sophomoric jokes, this area was hushed besides the whistling wind cutting through the alleys.

Seeing a big city reduced to a ghost town, its buildings hollow and cracked open, sent shivers down Greyson's spine. Sunlight needled through the dirty clouds, walling off the heavens.

He moved toward a large pile of debris to start disintegrating. Then a whoosh signaled the arrival of a flier, goosebumps prickling Greyson's skin for some reason. He looked up.

A lone silhouette hovered high above like some god surveying his realm, tall and well-built and hooded.

Him. Greyson knew it in his bones. Aegis, in Seattle. Just like his dystopian dream.

The hero tilted forward and hurtled across the heavens, soiled billows rippling in his wake.

All Greyson could do was stare. He ignored his buzzing cell, tracking where Aegis landed.

"Hey," the deep, modulated voice came from one street over.

Greyson scurried through a cluttered alley, peeking out the end for a better view. "Oh my god," he mouthed.

The Second City Saints resembled children clamoring for a selfie next to Aegis, who was built like a Michelangelo sculpture. That royal-purple costume accentuated his musculature even more.

One of them, Freestyle, stuck her gloved hand out, batting her eyelashes. "Pleasure meeting you."

Aegis shook all their hands and greeted them with kind words.

Greyson watched the exchange from his hiding place, fixated on the "Shield of Justice." The cellphone buzzed again, and he ignored it. Being in the same place as Aegis was a coincidence—no, an opportunity Greyson could not ignore. But how? In his mind, he'd already mapped out his attack plan.

Aegis was the biggest threat. Kill him first. Then slaughter the Second City Saints, keeping the Midwest free of major superheroes. Quick and clean.

The risk was ridiculous. No plan. No backup.

Greyson scanned the alleyway for a weapon. Most of the garbage in this alley was useless junk.

He then spotted a long, metal rod lying a few yards away. Over six feet, sharpened. Normally, a piece of metal like that would flatten against Aegis's impenetrable skin.

If I superheat the metal with nuclear energy and tether its gravity to him, Greyson mused, *at seventy times above normal?* The idea brought a smile to his bearded face.

Greyson waggled his fingers. The metal rod's gravity was negated as it floated up. He grabbed the middle of the rod, heart pounding so hard, his chest ached. Greyson's fist burned with nuclear energy. Before long, so did the metal rod. He let go. The rod floated beside him. This was actually happening.

He began tethering the searing metal rod's pull to Aegis, with gravity strong enough to impale his durable body through the shoulder blades. *Say goodnight, Aegis…*

The cellphone rang.

Godammit! Greyson dropped the glowing rod and sprinted back down the alleyway before he was seen.

Anger roiled as he whipped out his phone. Connie was calling and had left several messages.

"*Where* are you?" she demanded when he answered. "The Thrillers are engaging the scavengers!"

That cut through his rage. He smacked his forehead. The Natural Born Thrillers on Maury Island. "Be right there." He'd have to fly there at top speeds and risk exposing his gravity powers.

"Don't bother," Connie interjected dejectedly. "They won. No property damage."

Greyson checked his phone, catching a *Seattle Tribune* notification. In the video he saw the five Thrillers basking in snapshots and cheers from the gathered press. At a glance, he noticed a change. The Thrillers looked and felt like a team.

Greyson watched Lady Liberty touch down beside Erika and Brightburn, as did Seattle's top local team, Green Squadron. In the video, Erika seemed winded but content. Even Bulldozer, monstrous in size, was slapping Shattershot on the back.

And Greyson had only himself to blame.

CHAPTER 34

Someone was calling Hugo's alias in the cloudy darkness. Everything hurt too much to even move.

"Aegis?" The voice was clearer. Darkness was replaced by putrid smog hanging low and heavy.

"Hugo!"

A shoulder shake jolted him awake. "Whuah!" He sat up, and a hot flash roiled down his spine. His vision cleared to find Lady Liberty beside him. Her red costume was stained from digging through debris. By the luxury homes lining either side of the street, Hugo momentarily thought this was El Marquez. Then his brain caught up. *Mercer Island, Washington.*

"Lady Liberty, I…" He hesitated, seeing she wasn't alone. "Polymer?"

The ex-Warguard member stood behind her, wide-eyed. "I saw you go down over this neighborhood."

"He called me." Lady Liberty helped Hugo up. "Who attacked you?"

Brief vertigo buckled Hugo's knees. He sagged against his former mentor, almost collapsing. Once it passed, he straightened and met her worried stare. "Spencer."

Lady Liberty's brow rose. "What?" The word was a sharp slap.

Hugo scanned his surroundings methodically. "Spencer Michelman attacked me." Anger refueled his strength. But all these houses were empty. How long had he been out?

Lady Liberty stayed close as Polymer trailed them. "But your mom said Ezra had her confined," she muttered.

Hugo stopped, shaking his head. Spencer was long gone. "Paxton-Brandt freed her and I think captured Dr. Michelman. Now Spence shot me and…" Naked horror swallowed him. "Arclight."

Polymer looked confused. "Who—?"

Hugo blasted into the air. "ARCLIGHT!" His mind was reeling. If J-Tom was hurt or worse…no force on Earth would save Spencer. Hugo floated above the expanse of mansions filling Mercer Island. Panic along with headaches from Spencer's attack made telescopic vision strenuous.

He tapped his hood, activating his comms channel to J-Tom. "Jen, where are you?"

Static answered.

Hugo's terror spiked. "J-Tom!" He turned right and left, listening with superhearing for J-Tom's heartbeat.

"Bogie!" she gasped from some tiny space flooding rapidly with water. "Help…Please."

Hugo whirled in the direction of her voice. A sprawling estate with a pool larger than most apartments. The Arclight armor had sunk to the bottom.

Hugo zoomed down, punching through the pool, water erupting in every direction.

Grabbing J-Tom, he exploded through the surface, splashing more water.

Hugo burst through the screen door of the empty house and laid J-Tom down.

"Jenny? Jennifer," Hugo called out. No movement or humming or lit-up sections. Just water sloshing around the insides. The armor was dead. He prayed J-Tom wasn't the same. Knowing what to do, he pressed a hand on a circular dial of the left hip, then a circular symbol sitting on the Arclight armor's chest. Hugo twisted them in opposite directions three times. Immediately, the armor slithered off J-Tom like liquid metal, collapsing into a suitcase. Water splashed across the marble floor, right as Lady Liberty landed beside the pool carrying Polymer.

J-Tom lay on the floor in a black tee and yoga pants, soaked and coughing up a lung.

Hugo's joy was overwhelming. "I gotcha." He cradled her shivering body. "You're safe."

J-Tom clung to him. "Didn't…koff…activate my…koff…shields," she wheezed, teeth chattering. "Sorry."

If Hugo had found her a minute later…that prospect would've been unbearable. He turned to see Lady Liberty and Polymer approach. "She needs a medic. A discreet one."

"I'm a medic." Polymer stood over Hugo like an overeager puppy. "Trained EMT."

Hugo still didn't trust Polymer, but Lady Liberty's approving nod decided for him.

Polymer pulled out basic medical tools attached to his belt and checked J-Tom over. Other than red splotches on her back that looked like bad sunburn, she was okay.

"If that pool hadn't broken her fall," Polymer caveated, "this could've been worse."

"Spencer was here?" Lady Liberty inquired.

"On Mercer Island," Hugo stated, vitriol searing away his aches. He held J-Tom closer. "Check the Paxton-Brandt camps."

"On it." Lady Liberty marched out of the house and flew skyward in a ripple of wind.

"How can I help?" Polymer asked, putting his tools away.

"Here." Hugo pressed a thumb on Polymer's forehead, memory-walking Spencer's appearance into his mind. Skintight jumpsuit, venomous sneer, and those eyes, dark-blue like bruises.

Polymer jerked backward, blinking. "How the fuck?"

Hugo had no time to explain. "Search for that girl near any Paxton-Brandt encampments."

Polymer nodded, limbs melting into a ball around his body. Then he bounced outside and over the fence.

J-Tom's armor, however, was damaged by Spencer's blast. At least it could expand over her body. Not willing to risk her safety, Hugo flew J-Tom in her armor back to San Miguel.

He speed-changed them both into normal clothes at the Clubhouse, then supersped her to Paso. Thankfully, Mom was home.

"What did you two get into?" Mom fussed over her in the guestroom. Again, no signs of injury. But J-Tom could barely hold her head up, taking the Spencer news way better than expected.

"Guess we should stop her," she murmured drowsily.

Once Mom left, Hugo cradled J-Tom like a baby until she snapped out of her stupor somewhat. Hugo caressed the nape of her neck, memory-walking into her and her family building sandcastles at Grover Beach. J-Tom must've been eleven by her height with an adorable babyface. Hugo guided her into a deep dream state around that cherished memory.

J-Tom wilted in his arms, eyelids fluttering in total bliss. Only then did Hugo know peace. He kissed J-Tom's forehead and tucked her into bed.

"How is she?" AJ asked once Hugo reentered the living room.

"Resting." Hugo wasn't physically tired. But the last few days had left him spent. He blinked away the mental fatigue. "I'm keeping Jen here until I know she's okay." He kissed his mother's forehead. "Thanks for examining her."

"Sure." Mom's hawk-like glare followed Hugo when he sat heavily on the couch.

Hugo's thoughts revolved around J-Tom. The anguish of almost losing her hurt *everywhere*.

"I shouldn't have brought Jenny. She nearly..." The word "died" caught in Hugo's throat.

"Uso." AJ plopped beside him. "J-Tom looked great from what I saw on the news. But what happened to Spencer?" His eyes darted to Mom and he made a face.

Hugo stared at nothing. "Lady Liberty is searching." Spencer out there with Paxton-Brandt's backing put everyone he cared for at risk—especially J-Tom, Jordana, and Brie.

The TV displayed the Extreme Teens, Lady Liberty, and Battalion removing rubble and passing out foodstuff to survivors.

Mom stepped in his line of sight. "This Spencer issue is out of control." She folded her arms, which meant ultimatum time. "If she knows your identity, so does Paxton-Brandt."

Hugo glared up at her, already guessing her demands. *Hang up the suit.* Not happening. Then Hugo recalled Spencer's words. *Your identities are safe. For now.* "I don't think she's told anyone."

Mom's face contorted. AJ gaped at him as if he'd grown a third eye. "You believe that psycho?"

Hugo raised a hand to calm their understandable fury. "If Spencer had told anyone, something would've happened by now." He scratched his jawline, mulling over what else Paxton-Brandt could throw at him.

Mom was unconvinced. "Unless they're waiting for the right moment."

"Ms. Ortiz is getting her people to search for him," Hugo replied. On the flight back home, he'd told Ms. Ortiz everything about working with Dr. Michelman and the retired hero's disappearance. His former mentor had been rattled.

Mom relaxed, scratching at her neck. "Hopefully, he's not dead."

Hugo wouldn't accept that possibility. "I'm going back to Seattle tomorrow. Alone." No way was J-Tom going near Seattle. Or the field.

AJ rubbed his own arms. Something was on his mind. "But there are already tons of other heroes over there."

"Seattle and Tacoma still need help," Hugo said. Not returning never crossed his mind, even after Spencer's attack. He stretched his limbs, catlike. "But I got homework…"

AJ exchanged a look with Mom. "Oh…" He pulled his phone out. "We saw this." He played a video on the official Aegis YouTube channel. Haunting visuals of Seattle's and Tacoma's desolation were prominent during the thirty-second ad. This all came from Hugo's bodycam footage, sent to Annie Sherwood yesterday. No voiceover, just short sentences onscreen detailing stats about Seattle's disaster. Hugo's throat tightened, grief taking him back to the past tragic few days. At the video's end card were five charities Hugo had recommended to Annie. Damn, his PR Goddess was good.

Hugo liked the ad, dark memories aside. Hopefully, that encouraged people to donate. "Hey, Mom." He turned to her. "Don't you usually work Saturdays?"

Worry melted off her. "About that…" She wrung her hands nervously. "I got a job."

Hugo brightened at the news. "The nurse manager gig?"

She shook her head, bushy mane swinging back and forth. "Not exactly. It's a hybrid position. Part-nurse manager and part-philanthropic associate. The hospital was impressed how I connected them with your publicist." She grinned girlishly. "And moved me on to their philanthropic division. Community outreach. Food Drives. Fundraisers. In a few years, I'll transition into that full-time." She spread her arms, clearly anxious for feedback.

Hugo popped off the couch. "Mom, that's amazing!" He drew her into a firm hug. "Congratulations!

"Thank you, Bogota." She drew back, cupping his chin in both hands. "This is partially because of you."

Her eyes held such pride, Hugo had to glance away. Part of him felt unworthy. "Me?"

Mom let her arms drop. "You doing more than just fighting crime. But being a role model." Her eyes grew shiny. "I'm so proud."

Affection overpowered Hugo. "Well, I learned it from somewhere," he threw back, winning laughter from his family. The buzz of his work cellphone interrupted the moment.

"Hold on." He fished the cell from his pocket. Seeing the caller ID, he swiftly answered. "What's up?"

"Becky returned just now," Max replied. "She wants to see you."

Saracen. Hugo had forgotten about the terrorist with all this earthquake relief work. But Becky wanting to meet without prompting? Did she know he was onto her? Whatever the case, this was Hugo's chance to confront Becky about her Saracen connection. "Danger Room rooftop. Ten minutes."

Hugo suited up, then raced out of his neighborhood and took to the skies.

The late afternoon sun, low and red, was muted by the film of smog roaming down from Washington.

Becky was waiting on Danger Room's rooftop. The sunset flattered her hooded leather jacket and hip-hugging jeans. Her purple hair in a tight ponytail gave her a more youthful look.

Hugo floated a few yards away, just above ground.

Becky's eyes twinkled as she smiled. "Nice job up in Seattle."

Hugo wasn't here for banter. "Rebekah."

His brusqueness surprised Becky. She arched an eyebrow but said nothing.

Hugo realized any hostility would set off red flags. He hastily softened. "What do you got?"

Becky gave him another onceover. "This hits the news tomorrow. But I'm telling you first."

Hugo touched down on the roof. "About what?"

"The Washington earthquake." Becky pursed her lips. "There was nothing 'natural' about that disaster."

The import of her words cracked Hugo across the jaw. "Wait…Someone *did* this?" His interest in Saracen vanished.

"My thoughts exactly." Becky glanced away. "A massively powerful terrakinetic. Class-5…or higher."

Hugo silently digested this for several moments. A superhuman terrorist that powerful would spark backlash against all supers. That asshole Senator Huntley would have a field day.

But given her Saracen ties, Becky's word wasn't enough. "Is there proof?"

"How about a name and a face?" She produced a cellphone from her pocket, swiping a few times before handing to him. "Her name is Meteora."

Onscreen was a woman literally carved out of rock, her risqué clothes flaunting a sculpted frame. The snarl on Meteora's chiseled face exuded a vibe of there being no adversary she couldn't dominate.

With her powers, I believe it. Hugo suppressed a shudder, handing the cell back. "Never heard of her."

"Most haven't," Becky retorted. "She's contract. Low profile."

Hugo side-eyed her. "You call that earthquake *low profile*?"

Becky shrugged. "Her past contracts were. There's more."

Hugo rolled his eyes. "Really?"

Becky cough-laughed. "Meteora leads a crew of kinetic-type heavies."

Nausea filled Hugo as he thought about recent 'natural' disasters. The Gunnison National Park wildfires, the Carolinas' floods, the Montana tornadoes… "Does Meteora's crew have a pyrokinetic or hydrokinetic?"

Becky marveled at him, the winds ruffling her ponytail. "Hellfire and Alluvion. There's also an aerokinetic nutjob named Sirocco. They call themselves the Forces of Nature."

Anger rushed through Hugo. "I'd wisecrack under lighter circumstances." Four faces to beat down.

Becky smirked grimly. "They're part of a group that offers services to other criminal organizations. Like a temp agency for supervillains." She pocketed her phone. "The Vanguard defeated their first incarnation back in 2002. I've heard mutterings of their return for years now."

The specific year rang like a bell from a story Lady Liberty had shared. "What is this group called?" Hugo asked, brimming with dread.

Becky Knox's face was stony when she responded. "Villains for Hire."

CHAPTER 35

Greyson expected a tongue-lashing after returning to Shenandoah. And once he'd snuck away to his condo, Asher Martin delivered.

"What the fuck?" the Paxton-Brandt exec yelled, beet-red. Trying to act tough in his overpriced suit would've provided laughs if Greyson wasn't in the doghouse.

Connie watched from the couch in silence. Probably for the best.

"I'm sorry." Greyson didn't flinch from Asher's anger. "I lost track of time." The lapse in focus was embarrassing. But admitting the reason after Paxton-Brandt had forbidden him from engaging Aegis would only make things worse.

"Sorry? Sorry?" Asher tensed up like he was about to hit Greyson. Instead, he wisely backed up and squinted. "You're not going native on that team, are you?"

The accusation offended Greyson. "No. It was a slipup on a terrible plan."

Asher's eyes widened. Connie's warning look signaled that he'd crossed the line.

The Paxton-Brandt exec jabbed a finger at Greyson. "I worked with you," he said in low, acid tones. "Did everything you asked. Now you're blaming me?"

Greyson remained calm in the face of Asher's escalating anger. "I'm stating the flaws in your plan. Surrounded by that many heroes in a disaster area. Can you imagine if your plan had backfired?" Greyson shifted back to the reason why they were in this god-awful city. "We have a better chance defeating the Thrillers in Shenandoah, which is already distrustful of superhumans."

Asher opened his mouth, quivering from head to toe.

Greyson cut him off with a sharp hand chop. "I screwed up. That won't happen again."

"Like I should believe that?" Asher snapped.

"You have my word." Plain and simple.

The oath won more scorn from Asher. "Your word means shit. You're just a fraud gifted with powers."

He's trying to provoke me. Greyson searched for a response not involving expletives.

"We still have a backup plan," Connie blurted out, hand raised strangely.

Asher studied her like some insect, unimpressed "I'll devise the plans. Don't do shit until I say so, Damocles." He turned on his heel melodramatically and stormed out of the apartment.

"Guess I deserved some of that," Greyson admitted after several moments.

Connie rose and reached his side. "What happened up in Seattle?"

Greyson sighed, ready to confess. "Aegis was there," he whispered.

Connie staggered back. "What?"

Greyson nodded, eager and giddy. "He was forty feet away." He pantomimed the act of spearing a target on instinct, reliving the moment. "I had him in my sights, was about to skewer him—"

"Hirsch." Connie grabbed his face. "I know Aegis is your white whale. But you don't know what Paxton-Brandt is capable of. That scientist who betrayed them." She walked away from her husband, hugging herself tightly. "They tortured him and turned his own daughter against him."

That grabbed Greyson's attention. "Seriously?"

Connie looked shaken. "The editor-in-chief of some news site that went after Paxton-Brandt?" She stared at the floor. "They screwed with her pain medication until she OD'd, got her fired, and then had her 'disappeared'."

An intense cold spread through his chest. "Jesus," Greyson murmured.

"They're backing us now." Connie sounded so frail and sad. "But that ends if we stop producing results."

Greyson reached her in a few strides and pulled her close. "The only thing that matters is you and me. I won't let us down." He was just as afraid. But for his wife, he'd remain strong for them both.

Connie's eyes glazed over with affection. "I know." She draped her arms around his neck, dragging him closer. Greyson responded promptly, his mouth hungry for hers.

After they finished, he departed and snuck back to the Natural Born Thrillers' compound with hours to spare before dawn. As he settled into bed, he promised himself to follow Asher's new plan. *Unless Plan B works.*

The next morning, an insistent pounding on his door jolted him awake.

Greyson grumbled as he stumbled forward to answer. Bulldozer took up the whole doorframe.

Now what? Greyson kept his calm as he stared up at this man-mountain. "Hello," he replied stiffly.

Bulldozer sighed, as if offloading a massive burden. "Great work in Seattle, Levi." A grudging smile tugged at his lips. "Good job."

Greyson was confused. Bulldozer complimenting him? "Thanks." What trickery was this?

Before either could continue, Erika's voice blared on the speakers. "Everyone to the assembly room."

Erika calling an emergency meeting this early didn't bode well. The pair walked through the halls at a hurried pace.

Greyson sat amid the Thrillers, all in casual civilian wear. Brightburn yawned.

A puffy-eyed Erika sat at the table's head. "We'll tackle two other matters before addressing Bulldozer's behavior and Brightburn's vigilantism." Her glare raked over both teammates. "The goodwill from Seattle doesn't erase the bad behavior."

Bulldozer stared at the table guiltily.

"Now." Erika's features curdled. "News broke last night that a terrakinetic caused the Washington earthquake."

Greyson felt as nauseous as Erika appeared, barely hearing the outcry from the other Thrillers. What kind of sick fuck did this on purpose?

"What do we know?" Bulldozer demanded.

"Her name is Meteora." Erika's eyes burned. "Now the most wanted villain in America."

Homicidal psychopaths like Meteora made Greyson sometimes question his own methods. Most supervillains wanted money, power, or destruction. Greyson wanted a society free to protect itself. There was no comparison between him and them.

"But there's an incident that occurred in our absence." Erika gestured at the flatscreen on the wall. "A bomber targeting cells of Pax Humana." The burnt husk of a duplex appeared onscreen.

"Why is this a problem?" Reverb complained, hands behind his head.

"How many sites were hit?" Brightburn asked seriously.

"Three. We have to catch this bomber." Erika watched Shattershot pointedly. "I know," she spoke over the collective groan. "The bomber is a super, so we need to be involved."

Greyson furrowed his brow. Something about these attacks felt familiar. "Is there a suspect?"

Erika tore her gaze away from the empath. "The police have found a match." She pressed a button on a remote control, revealing a mugshot of a woman with pixie-cut green hair and a devious smile.

Bam-Bam. Superhuman. Conglomerate contract killer. Shattershot's girlfriend.

Shattershot turned deathly white. "Oh no…"

Oh yes… Greyson hailed. Plan B was in full swing.

CHAPTER 36

"I ran your evidence up the chain," Dawson professed over the phone.

Hugo sat in an empty classroom during Snack period, cellphone pressed to his ear.

"After news about the terrakinetic broke, everything started moving superfast."

Hugo stopped himself from scoffing in agreement. Two days had passed since he'd revealed to the detective what Becky Knox had told him about the Forces of Nature. The urgency had prevented him from confronting Knox about Saracen. Finding these criminals took top priority.

Immediately after, news had broken about the terrakinetic responsible for the SeaTac earthquake.

All hell had broken loose, with nationwide outcries for her capture. Anti-super advocates like Noah Huntley used this opportunity to demand more superhuman restrictions.

Scaring Hugo most was how many Americans agreed. Tragedy and fear were powerful drugs.

"What agencies are hunting Meteora's group?" he asked, a mobile app mimicking his Aegis cadence.

"The FBI, since they're domestic terrorists," Beale replied. "And the OSA, since they're supers."

Hugo adjusted his seated posture. "Does the company have more labs storing kaiju remains?"

Dawson sighed. "They're getting me that info today. The sooner the better." Wherever the two detectives were teemed with pedestrian traffic. "Again, thanks for your help."

"Sure." Hugo would be happier once the Forces of Nature were stopped. "Let me know when you've found these murderers." The call ended soon after.

Hugo adjusted his hoodie tee and hat before exiting the room. On the way to the Quad, where the Forces of Nature would strike next dominated his thoughts.

The usual kaleidoscope of sounds, smells, and sights flooded his senses once outside. He weaved through the jungle of Paso High's student body. Many overlapping conversations centered on the SeaTac quake and giving to the school donation site built by Simon.

Hugo welcomed the normalcy of the regular school day instead of the post-apocalyptic horror show in Washington. He spotted Jordana on a far side of the Quad with her softball friends. Hugo would deal with that situation eventually. Today, he craved his friends' company.

Brie and J-Tom sat together atop the group's table, in deep conversation. J-Tom seemed back to her normal lively self after visiting Ramon yesterday to upgrade her armor.

The rest of Hugo's friends gathered around Simon and Raphael, facing off while Grace filmed on her cellphone. Raphael dwarfed Simon in size, dressed in an oversized NFL jersey, jeans, and Timberlands, black du-rag covering his freshly cut hair. Simon faced him wearing the latest Aegis t-shirt (ha!). He'd been generating crazy videos for when SeaTac earthquake donations reached a certain level. When three thousand dollars in donations were reached, Simon and Raphael would rap battle each other.

Hugo inched closer, eager to hear more.

"Bogie." Simon waved him over. "Gimme a beat!"

The group offered warm greetings. Brie winked at him. J-Tom beamed. Grace ignored him. She was still angry, despite his apology attempts.

He'd try again in a few days and hopefully save their friendship.

On Simon's three-count, Hugo began beatboxing. The two friends battled back and forth, trading some fierce yet fun-loving verbal jabs and rhymes for the full five minutes of rap battling. Simon did better than expected, clever with his puns. Raphael countered with fierce braggadocious energy, gesturing with each verse. It was declared a draw, Simon and Raphael hugging it out afterward. Oohs, aahs, and laughs ensued. Personally, Hugo thought Simon edged out Raphael, but whatever. Trading high-five/side hugs with both competitors, he realized how much he enjoyed—needed—this normalcy.

Titan had no escape from being Titan. Knowing this, Hugo would never give up his secret identity. But Spencer could take that choice away whenever she wanted. Then there was Saracen…

Someone poking his ribs startled Hugo. Brie stood watching him curiously.

He forced a smile to hide his burdens. "Hey, Breezy."

"Hey, Bogie," She was glammed up as usual, high ponytail and a cropped polo shirt with baggy pants. Carrying her tennis bag instead of using her gym locker was odd. "Can we talk later?"

Hugo considered her request and his usual patrol after school. "Six-ish PM at Beach Bum Burger?"

"How about right after school?" Brie countered.

Hugo stared at her. The urgency in her voice was the kind a friend shouldn't ignore. "You alright?"

Brie offered a nervous laugh, but her heart raced. "I think so."

Hugo nodded. "We can meet then." Since the summer, Brie had climbed back to a good place mentally and physically. If she needed his help, he'd be there.

Right then, he caught sight of Baz Martinez sitting near the cafeteria with legs spread, holding court with his teammates. Natalie Rodriguez cuddled beside Baz, achingly pretty, giving his neck an occasional nibble. During Baz's final week at Paso High, the mood among his crew was bittersweet.

Hugo watched them, remembering Baz's request almost two weeks ago. Look after Brie. The request deserved an answer, especially after Saracen's stunt.

He marched toward the group of ballplayers. Harlan Mills and Cody Banks saw him first, immediately standing in alarm. By the time the other ballplayers noticed their change in mood, Hugo was already beside Baz. Natalie jerked away. Baz didn't turn, but his posture tensed.

Hugo's gaze swept over the now-silent gathering, all eyes on him. "Leave." One brusque word sent the gathering scattering, even Natalie. Only Baz remained.

Hugo sat beside him and leaned back.

Baz watched him expectantly. "Well?"

For the first time in forever, Hugo didn't hate him. "Okay."

Baz gawked, still uncertain. "Okay?"

Hugo nodded. "Okay."

Baz sagged in elation. "Okay."

Hugo rose and extended his hand. He felt eyes from all over the Quad watching them. "Good luck."

Baz stood, accepting the handshake. His disdain reserved for Hugo was gone. "Thank you."

Hugo turned and walked away. Within seconds, Baz's crew swarmed their friend and peppered him with questions. This didn't make Hugo and Baz friends. They could never go back after everything they'd done to each other. But ending the feud felt...right.

Across the Quad, Hugo's friends had questions in their eyes, Brie and Simon especially.

Jordana flagged him down first, so cute with her loose and kinky curls unbound and spilling down her shoulders. Jesus, Hugo hadn't realized how much he'd missed her until they were facing each other at the edge of the Quad.

"What was that about?" she demanded almost rudely, arms folded. "Peace in the Middle East?"

Hugo looked her up and down, enjoying the sight of those full lips, that face, the attitude in her stance. "You and I got more important shit to discuss."

Jordana shyly averted her gaze. "I know I've been weird lately, but—"

Hugo interrupted her with a kiss. He couldn't help himself. Jodie stiffened at first but quickly melted into it. Catcalls erupted around them. When he pulled back, she was blushing and swaying.

"I wanna be with you," Hugo declared. "Just you. If you don't feel the same, I understand. But let's stop treading water and move forward." That unplanned speech had spilled out of him. Being this vulnerable was scary as fuck but totally worth it.

Jodie stood dazed and wide-eyed. She opened her mouth to speak.

Hugo's breath caught, anticipation crackling through him—until the ground violently shook beneath him. It felt like giant hands were shaking the earth side to side in bone-rattling chaos.

The entire Quad freaked, screams ringing out as students clung to their surroundings for safety. Panic seized Hugo for a brief moment before Lady Liberty's training kicked in instinctively. He held a screaming Jodie close while gripping a support beam to stay upright. Within seconds, the ground stilled. Yet terror remained thick across campus.

Hugo checked on Jordana, who looked rattled but unharmed. Yards away, his friends were panicky and safe. Simon was holding a dazed Grace. J-Tom checked on the others surgically like Hugo had taught. Scanning the Quad, he could find no serious injuries or building damage. That did little to calm his nerves. "Oh no," he whispered.

"What the...!" Jordana looked around at the swarm of terrified teens. "That aftershock was CRAAZAY!"

"Wasn't an aftershock," Hugo retorted. A strong earthquake this far away from Seattle only meant one horrific thing. "They're here." They, as in The Forces of Nature. In San Miguel.

Jordana frowned at him, understandably lost. "Who's here?"

An alarm rang across school, followed by Principal Walker's voice booming on the PA system. *"Get to third period and await instructions. This is not a drill."*

No shit, Einsteiner. Hugo turned to Jordana as the rush of students became torrents. "Get to class."

Jodie nodded frantically and disappeared in the churning crowd to her third period.

Before Hugo headed off to find Meteora, he made sure they were safe.

Brent was toying with his phone near the English and Languages building while Simon and Groban gathered around. "Check this out..."

The N3 news app designated that quake a 4.7 magnitude—a warning shot. Hugo's main concern was the video Brent watched. "Oh shit."

Onscreen, the suburb of Atascadero was burning. Citizens screamed and ran from a quartet of menacing assailants. A flying man wreathed in gold flames streaked through the skies, hurling fireballs at anything in sight—Hellfire.

A black woman flew higher still, smiling maliciously. She gestured her hands to unload mini tornados at buildings, shredding the very foundations— Sirocco. On the ground, a man made of clear-blue water with a flattop rode a foaming wave through Colony Square—Alluvion.

In the center was Meteora, a chiseled rock statue animated to life. She motioned in several directions, nothing but contained anger on her face. Rock formations burst through the asphalt, ripping a path across Atascadero's streets. Hugo felt sickened guessing how many had died already.

"It's that terrakinetic bitch!" Brent exclaimed.

"And she's got backup," Raphael added.

"They call themselves the Forces of Nature," Hugo said.

That drew snorts and derision. "Seriously?" Groban mocked.

"Villains really need to stop naming themselves," Simon derided, eyeing Hugo. "Aren't most of the major heroes still in Seattle?"

Hugo ushered his friends along. "Not sure."

Groban brightened. "What about Tomorrow Man?"

"Now's not the time for jokes," Hugo chided. The number of students running about was thinning. "Get to your classes. Go!" The other boys jogged to their classes.

Simon lingered. "It's a distraction, right?"

Hugo nodded. "Which means something is getting stolen nearby." His heart was racing at the possibilities and fighting the Forces of Nature alone. He jabbed a thumb. "I gotta—"

Simon nodded, worry in his eyes. "Handle your business. I'll give the needed deflections." Since they shared third period, Simon could say that Hugo went home sick. His best friend was the best.

Hugo powerwalked across the Quad toward his gear stash location.

J-Tom fell in beside him. "What's our next move?" she asked, shouldering her backpack.

Hugo eyed her. "Go to your class." His focus had to be on the enemy, not her safety.

J-Tom gawked like a goldfish out of water. "My armor's ready. I'm fighting with you."

"Jennifer—" Hugo stopped himself from yelling. Every second lost meant another life lost. Now security guards were rounding up stray students. Maybe J-Tom could be useful while he fought the Forces of Nature. "Gear up and assist emergency services only."

"But—"

"Take it or leave it," Hugo declared.

When J-Tom reluctantly nodded, he headed for the storage facility.

There were too many people around to superspeed. Dammit! He turned a corner into an empty corridor to hide from security cameras when he sensed someone running from behind.

"Hugo, wait!"

Hugo almost punched a wall. This girl seriously had the survival instincts of a kitten. "Go to class, Brie!"

Briseis caught up to him, struggling with her tennis bag. "Have to...have to talk now." She panted while reaching inside her bag.

Hugo was about to erupt. "Get the fuck out—"

Briseis shoved something into his arms.

Hugo stared in confusion at his folded-up costume. The one supposedly in his gear stash location.

That hit Hugo like a truck, and he looked up. Brie's face was a study in calm. "You're gonna need that."

Briseis knows I'm Aegis. Hugo struggled to form sentences. "I...how?"

Brie waved off his stammering with surprising confidence. "Later. Go kick some ass."

Forcing his mush-brain into action, he glanced around to confirm the corridor was clear.

He raced off campus at blistering speeds, leaving a windblown Briseis in his wake.

CHAPTER 37

Greyson wasn't fazed staring at the carcass before him. *Should I be?*

Reverb and Brightburn had taken him to the crime scene to get him used to a hero's less sexy duties.

Their mutual shock at his indifference had been quite amusing.

This past year of violence and killing had numbed Greyson to seeing a dead body. Especially the charred and shriveled bodies strewn around another bombing by Bam-Bam.

Right on schedule. But Greyson had some more levers to pull before his plan came to fruition. He cast a dispassionate gaze at the blasted-out room while Brightburn and Reverb interfaced with uniformed cops at the scene. "How many dead?" the latter inquired.

The cop, a sturdy Filipino woman with her hair in a bun, sighed. "Eight. All top Pax Humana brass."

"Good lord," Brightburn whispered.

The officer cast a sullen look over the Thrillers. "This needs to be handled before more people die."

If the rudeness in the demand bothered Brightburn, she made no show of it. "I understand, Officer."

"We're working every angle," Reverb chimed in.

The police officer pulled something out of her pocket and handed it to Brightburn. "Check this out."

Brightburn took one look and slapped a hand over her mouth.

Reverb glanced at it and turned green.

Greyson peeked over Brightburn's shoulder. The paper, smudged in soot, detailed a factory layout. These were plans to bomb the Natural Born Thrillers' compound.

Greyson's mouth fell open. "Wow."

The officer nodded grimly. "Wow indeed. According to recovered phone and email chatter a few hours ago, they'd planned on doing this while your team was out of town until Bam-Bam attacked."

Greyson had to smile somewhat. Shattershot's girlfriend had saved the heroes hunting her down.

On the walk to their vehicle over the home's front yard, unwelcoming glowers from several cops onsite trailed the heroes.

It's only going to get worse, Greyson mused. He winked at one cop while stepping into the backseat.

Returning to the compound, Greyson remained silent while Brightburn and Reverb discussed the case. Their usual banter lacked its prior pleasantness thanks to a strained friendship. Good.

"I wonder what her motivation was saving the base," Brightburn wondered while driving.

"Guess we can ask her boyfriend directly," Reverb sneered.

"She wouldn't do this!" Shattershot protested after Greyson and the others stood in the common room and described the crime scene.

"Not helping," Bulldozer rumbled chidingly.

Greyson stood in the tension-riddled common room with the Thrillers debating Bam-Bam's fate. He watched in relish as the Thrillers' bonds continued to fray.

Shattershot spread his arms. "I'm being honest."

Brightburn seemed to reach some realization. "I get protecting you. But she's gone on a warpath."

Erika approached Shattershot with a haggard expression. "We need to find Bam-Bam. For her own safety."

Greyson added his two cents. "If it's not us, it will be law enforcement with a kill-order."

His words landed hard. All stares focused on Shattershot.

Warring emotions contorted the empath's face. "She'd never meet at our usual spots now."

"Then contact her," Brightburn pleaded.

Shattershot stepped back. "No."

A chill washed through the room, followed by Reverb's groan.

Greyson almost shouted hallelujah but opted for mock disappointment. The rejection seemed to strike Erika more deeply than the others.

"Then you'll sit this out," she replied coldly.

Shattershot turned pink with outrage, opening his mouth.

Greyson shook his head in warning, which curtailed the empath's outburst.

Shattershot then just stormed off down the hallways.

Bulldozer was the first to comment. "Can I say I told you so?" Other teammates voiced their agreement.

Greyson stiffened. All of them against Shattershot didn't serve his needs. "He's dumbstruck with love," he spoke over everyone. "Let me talk to him."

Erika responded with an oddly hostile stare, then nodded her consent.

Greyson found Shattershot in his own room, stuffing clothes into an open suitcase.

"What are you doing?" Greyson asked, concern brewing as he closed the bedroom door.

Shattershot glanced at him, shoving a pair of jeans into the baggage. "Can't stay here," he said, sickened.

Greyson didn't hide his surprise. "You're quitting?" This was too soon.

Shattershot stopped and looked at him sideways. "No," he scoffed. "I couldn't even if I wanted to." He sat on his bed, visibly beaten down. "Part of my parole is staying on an ERAT team for three years. I've been with the Thrillers for less than eight months."

"Then where—?"

"Joanie wouldn't do something this horrific," Shattershot blurted out, staring at the wall.

Greyson stared at him. "She's a criminal."

Shattershot popped off the bed. "Bam-Bam wants a new life." He shook his head, mystified. "Throwing what we have away makes no sense."

Greyson could see this young man was close to breaking. So he went to work as the sympathetic friend. "Do you know her full story? All her wants and dreams?" He searched the empath's face. "Even those closest to us don't reveal everything."

Shattershot raised his hands, only to let them drop in helpless anguish. "Maybe I don't. But I love her." The tears flowed then. "I have to find out the truth."

Shattershot leaned against a wall and sobbed for several moments. Greyson waited until he regained composure, and then articulated his decision. "Then I'll help you."

The empath sniffled in disbelief. "Seriously?"

Greyson smiled with genuine satisfaction. "Seriously."

Shattershot wiped away his tears. "Thanks. I owe you."

Hook, line, and sinker. Greyson raised one finger. "If she's guilty…"

"She's not," Shattershot assured.

Greyson rolled his eyes. Poor, lovestruck boy… "If she's responsible, we capture her." His words left no room for negotiation.

Shattershot's relief filled the room. "I'll contact her."

Greyson exhaled happily. "We'll sneak out later tonight." *Now we're in the endgame.*

CHAPTER 38

Hugo stopped at home first, switching into his Aegis suit, then raced back out at top speeds. Paso Robles flew by in colorful streaks and splashes of sunlight. Meanwhile, his mind was spinning.

Briseis knows my secret. Had she told anyone? Did Brie figure it out or had Hugo slipped at one point?

His worries vanished when another aftershock shivered the ground—almost throwing him off balance.

Hugo yearned to clobber the Forces of Nature, but two priorities took precedence. He banked a hard right for Lewis Middle School. He saw him outside on a corner, not in class like he should be.

Hugo stopped for a half-second, tossed AJ over a shoulder, and rocketed away. Next stop, Flamson Middle School. He spotted Zelda outside among her class, idly waiting. He slowed briefly, snatched her up, and then raced for the Clubhouse in Arroyo Grande.

Once beneath the main atrium's bluish lighting, he decelerated and placed his siblings on their feet.

"AH!" AJ almost faceplanted. He didn't travel often at superspeed.

Zelda spun around a few times, wide-eyed and bewildered. "Holy Moley! What the hellz!"

"Guys!" Hugo pulled his hood and mask back, then raised both hands to calm them. "It's me."

AJ and Zelda immediately relaxed. "Bogie?" his half-sister remarked gratefully.

Hugo straightened to his full height. "Sorry to scare you." He gathered Zelda and AJ into a firm hug. Them inside the Clubhouse gave him one less worry. But given Atascadero's proximity to Paso, who knew if his friends or Mom were safe? He let his siblings explore their location.

AJ seemed bewildered by the high-tech surroundings. "Where are we?"

Hugo gestured around his HQ. "My lair." That sounded corny, even with family.

Zelda scanned around in beaming recognition. "It's one of Geist's safehouses!" Of course, she knew this place. She whirled eagerly to face Hugo. "Did he gift this to you?"

Hugo nodded. "The walls are earthquake-proof. There's food for weeks. You two are safe here."

AJ looked somewhat impressed. "Where's Mom?"

Hugo winced. "The hospital. Helping people." Mom wouldn't stand for being cooped up instead of helping patients. But should an earthquake happen, they'd agreed that he'd put AJ in the Clubhouse.

AJ's demeanor improved after he'd heard this. "Is there a bathroom?"

Hugo chuckled, pointing left. "Around that corner."

Once AJ left the chamber, Zelda's mirth dimmed. "You need help out there."

Hugo furrowed his brow. She wasn't wrong. But Lady Liberty and the Extreme Teens were still up in Washington. And Hugo had faced greater odds than these clowns. "Tell your mom that you're safe so she's not worrying." He pulled the hood and half-mask over his face. "Be back soon."

"If not for my mom's combat rules, I'd be fighting beside you," Zelda blurted out, as astounded saying that as Hugo felt hearing it. "I love you."

His heart swelled. "Love you too." Rejuvenated, he turned and raced out of the Clubhouse.

Hugo flew over swaths of cityscape, Atascadero's skyline approaching rapidly, when he rang Dawson.

"Are you headed to Atascadero?" the detective asked.

"Yep." Hugo angled through puffs of clouds as another worry landed. "Who's in town besides me?"

"Justice Jones. Ballistic."

Hugo cringed. Not an encouraging number. And Justice Jones might still want to knock him out. "Ballistic can help with search and rescue. Arclight's coming too." He looked down at the urban sprawl. "Please tell me you have news on those labs."

"Salto Institute has two labs in San Miguel," Dawson replied. "Morro Bay and Cambria. With this earthquake, we can only spare a squad to Cambria. All other officers are stretched across the city."

Hugo understood, slowed by a brief updraft. Across the city, he smelled burnt flesh and heard terrified screams. "I'll check Morro Bay after handling these clowns." He couldn't wait to stomp all their faces in.

"Good luck," Dawson encouraged. Even he sounded doubtful.

Jeez... Hugo dropped closer to street level and gave another kick of speed toward Atascadero.

Hugo could hear the Forces of Nature's exchanges as the quartet came into full view. Police cars were overturned. Any cops still standing hid behind various structures, firing off rounds at these criminals.

Hellfire hovered above a row of small buildings, torching them in furnace blasts of orange flame. He was long-haired and rangy in physique, entirely wreathed in fire. His face bordered on orgasmic while citizens burned. "Have you ever seen such infernal delights?"

On the ground, Meteora gestured about like some maestro. "Hellfire. You know the deal." The streets reacted to her summons, asphalt twisting like snakes to impale any fleeing citizens. "Maximum damage and casualties while our associates do their jobs."

High above, a thick-bodied woman with buzzcut hair chuckled. "He's an artist, Meteora." Sirocco's green unisuit had a cape. Another reason for Hugo to hate her. As she soared overhead, citizens got blown off their feet with anything not nailed down. "Don't be a wet blanket." She winced. "No offense, Alluvion."

The final Forces of Nature member gave a throaty laugh. "None taken."

Hugo was seconds away, disgusted at how casually these villains chatted amid their slaughtering.

Alluvion was human from the torso up with a high-top haircut, but made of translucent bluish water. From the waist down his body was a tidal wave roiling down the streets. Judging from Alluvion's face, he was like a kid at a candy store. "Too bad the big heroes are in Seattle," he griped. "I was hoping for a fight."

"Seattle isn't that far for the fast fliers," Meteora remarked, directing a twisted spire of street to puncture the walls of Paragon's Pub. "If our partners aren't fast enough, you might get your wish."

Reaching downtown Atascadero, Hugo accelerated toward Hellfire. "How about now?"

He punched the pyrokinetic hard in the chest. Hellfire gasped and plummeted. Pouring on the speed, Hugo raced for Alluvion—plowing straight through the hydrokinetic.

Dammit. Did I get him? Sensing another foe advancing, Hugo whirled and unleashed a sonic scream at Sirocco. That knocked her head over heels for several meters. Annoyingly, the drafts keeping her airborne blunted his knockout blow.

Hugo would handle her later. He directed his attention on the other Forces of Nature members.

Meteora calmly waved a hand, raising a slab of street to catch an unconscious Hellfire.

"Holy shit!" Alluvion churned up next to Meteora, his watery frame unharmed by Hugo's attack. "Aegis!" He sounded more fanboy than supervillain.

Hugo jerked back. "You know me? I'm flattered." He measured the pair for the best attack approach. Even more jarring was the devastation now that the chaos had stilled. Atascadero had a large super population, but many lacked combat-ready powers. This made them as vulnerable as humans and just as dead. The corpses strewn about ranged between burnt, crushed by pavement, or drowned on the city streets. Hugo clenched both fists to curb his rage.

Sirocco floated to Meteora's side, worry on her pudgy face. "I don't like how public this is getting."

"Likewise," Meteora agreed. Her eyes glittered like diamonds. "But the money's worth it. Take him." She pointed. Pavement erupted around Meteora into spears of sharpened rock, snaking at Hugo.

He dodged and weaved around each spire, aching to kick Meteora's ass for what she'd done to his city.

From his right came the watery roar of Alluvion just as Sirocco's gale-force winds blasted down.

Hugo juked upward, watching Sirocco's winds bash Alluvion's liquid body sideways.

That was close. He checked for bystanders. Luckily, the streets had cleared for a good half-mile. Now Hugo focused on kicking this foursome's asses. He whipped about with another sonic scream at Sirocco.

She dodged last second as the ground beneath Hugo was clearing its throat.

He charged Meteora again. But she was ready, drawing all kinds of bedrock blockades from the earth.

Hugo punched through each barrier and the dust until he grabbed a startled Meteora by the throat.

He slammed the woman down, pasting her across the face with repeated, piston-like right hands.

Before a knockout blow could be landed, scalding fire raced toward him.

He soared upward, clutching Meteora by the neck. Hellfire's flames doused where he'd just stood.

Hugo cocked back to strike Meteora, when she slammed stony palms into his chest. Violent quakes quivered through Hugo's body to the bone. His muscles seized, forcing him to let go.

She landed several feet below, grinning. Sirocco, Alluvion, and Hellfire gathered around her. "Think you can win, Shield of Justice?" Meteora dared.

"Yes," Hugo countered and dove.

Sirocco climbed out of reach with startling speed, blasting him from behind with a wind burst. That sent him sailing into Alluvion's oversized fist, striking Hugo's chest so hard, he was seeing stars.

Hard water? Is that shit possible? he wondered. A cop vehicle broke his fall, crumpling under him.

Just as quickly, the ground lurched, sending Hugo tumbling down the street.

Shaking off the cobwebs, he climbed to his feet. The Forces of Nature had him surrounded. These guys were good. And Alluvion was definitely a threat.

"We're not the Elite," Meteora crowed, arms spread in challenge. "And you're just not that good."

Hugo itched to shut her up, just because. "You're a talker, aren't you?" Changing strategies, he flew up superfast. But a solid wall of wind slapped him back down so hard, he bounced after cratering the street.

Meteora waggled her fingers. Veins of gravelly pavement strapped around Hugo's limbs, pinning him down. He strained, but the formations over his arms and legs only multiplied.

Hellfire and Meteora held hands—melting together. Hugo gaped. "What the fuck?"

The outcome was a brawny rock monster well over seven feet. Orange fire pulsed from its pupil-less eyes, mouth, and every crack in its hide radiating heat. Hellfire and Meteora combined like a goddamn Transformer. Hugo strained against his manacles, which weren't splintering fast enough.

"Because of your arrogance," the beast boomed, Hellfire and Meteora speaking as one, "you will die!"

The rock monster dove down, slamming both hands into Hugo's torso. His body temperature skyrocketed. He arched his back and cried out, the heat nonstop and intensifying.

Even worse, his bones quaked more violently than before. He couldn't think straight, getting scorched inside out while his bones turned to jelly.

The rock monster's pupil-less eyes gleamed a sinister yellow as Hugo's world darkened.

Not...like this... He clung to what little consciousness remained and screamed, blasting the monster's face. It roared and stumbled back, clutching its disintegrating features.

Hugo struggled upright. He couldn't see straight, his legs wobbling. Smoke curled off his suit.

I'm hurt, Hugo realized after a quick self-assessment. *But we're not finished.*

He inhaled deeply for another sonic scream...and couldn't. Hugo tried again, unable to catch his breath. Then he saw Sirocco's wicked smile as ferocious whirlwinds encircled him, sucking the oxygen right out of his lungs. His muscles grew rigid, vapor cascading from his body straight toward Alluvion. Now Hugo's lungs and muscles were withering. He sagged, consciousness fading faster.

Fuck! To stay here meant defeat—and death.

Despite his arms and legs turning to lead, Hugo focused on that last iota of strength and rocketed down a street, smashing into a building or two. The impact sent him careening down a sinkhole opened in the strip mall parking lot. Several feet went on for forever, until he landed in a pile of grime and mush. Sucking in greedy breaths, he pushed up on wobbly limbs and dashed away into the darkness. Hugo fled, wounded and humiliated, hearing the Forces of Nature celebrate.

"Aegis bolted!" Alluvion crowed.

"I wanted to fill the sky with embers from his corpse," Hellfire whined.

"Aegis wants us to chase him, just like the Elite." Meteora sounded like herself again. She and Hellfire must've separated. "We hold positions and finish the job. Sirocco, give me some amplification."

Meteora spoke again, her voice carried by the wind loud enough for Hugo to not need superhearing.

"Your Shield of Justice is broken," Meteora boomed. "Your police repelled. Atascadero belongs to us. Further attempts to attack will cost you twenty lives every hour."

The world shook again. A stronger quake, caused Hugo to collapse in the gloomy sewers. *I failed.*

Exhausted, overcooked, and defeated, everything went pitch-black.

CHAPTER 39

Two days passed before Greyson found a realistic timeframe to escape the compound with Shattershot.

Erika departed for DC in the early afternoon to meet with Seneca International higherups. Greyson actually wanted her when his plans to dismantle the Natural Born Thrillers came to pass.

"Wherever your girlfriend is," Greyson instructed, "we need to meet her now."

Shattershot, eager and trembling, called Bam-Bam to schedule a meetup. Lower Shenandoah in an antebellum-style building on Avenue X, another casualty of the economic downturn. Greyson coordinated with Connie via text to arrive in advance and watch their location.

From there, the two snuck out when Bulldozer, Brightburn, and Reverb left on evening patrol.

"Should be a few hours," Reverb warned. "No house parties." He guffawed at his own joke.

Once they'd departed, Greyson and Shattershot headed out under a burnt-orange sunset in a smaller car. On the way, he texted Bulldozer through an encrypted line as Damocles, tipping him off to Bam-Bam's location and whom she'd be meeting.

Greyson had expected activity in lower Shenandoah this early evening. To his shock, the district was jam-packed with merrymakers in superhero costumes.

"Paragon Day." Shattershot had a sad smile as they roamed through dressed-up crowds. "His birthday. It's such a staple that the city kept celebrating, even after Paragon became persona non grata."

"No kidding," Greyson replied slowly. This was even better than he'd imagined.

The building sat in the heart of Lower Shenandoah, eleven stories tall with cracks running up the brick walls. Greyson and Shattershot found Bam-Bam pacing on the sixth floor, dressed in a maroon catsuit.

Bam-Bam's eyes widened. "Baby? Hi!" While embracing Shattershot, she watched Greyson warily.

Shattershot cupped her cute face in his hands. "Pax Humana? You didn't bomb their hideouts, right?"

Bam-Bam stiffened and stepped back. "Of course," she admitted, as if he should've known this.

Greyson allowed himself a smirk.

Shattershot looked like he'd been stabbed. "*What?*"

Bam-Bam got annoyed by his naïveté. "Babe. They were going to hurt you and your friends."

Greyson put on his best concerned face. "This doesn't look good, man."

Shattershot whirled on him heatedly. "I thought you were on my side!"

Greyson raised both hands in peace. "I am," he lied. "But she just confessed. There's an option, though."

"Wait." Shattershot faced Bam-Bam. "We can figure this out. I can take the blame."

Bam-Bam glowered. "Never. I did the crime."

While the lovebirds argued, Greyson's cellphone buzzed from a new text.

Hopefully, this meant Bulldozer was incoming. Once that hotheaded oaf saw Shattershot with a wanted criminal, his worst instincts would take over very publicly.

Greyson turned his back to Shattershot and Bam-Bam before checking his cell for new texts.

CIH: Incoming!

ME: Dozer?

CIH: Skye.

Panic tightened Greyson's chest. *Not her!* Erika was supposed to be away in DC until midday tomorrow.

Shattershot was holding Bam-Bam by the shoulders, desperation on his face. "We can run away together. Leave this behind." His hand swept their grim surroundings to stress his point.

Bam-Bam recoiled. "And look over our shoulders forever?" She shook her head. "That isn't living."

"It is for me when I'm with you."

"Guys," Greyson interrupted, mainly because this lovers' quarrel annoyed him. "We're running out of time. I have a way out of this before—"

"Before what, Hazard?" a female voice interjected. "Before I arrive?"

Shattershot staggered back. Bam-Bam gasped.

Greyson squeezed his eyes shut. "Something like that." Opening his eyes soon after, he saw the leader of the Natural Born Thrillers striding into the room in full costume. Erika Skye's presence was enough to own whatever spot she entered. Her sharp features were emotionless as she studied the room.

Her gaze landed on Shattershot's girlfriend. "Bam-Bam," she greeted with a smile that left her eyes cold.

Greyson slowly put several yards between himself and the couple. His thoughts raced on how to spin the surprise in his favor.

Shattershot raised his hands, casting puppy-dog eyes in Erika's direction. "Please let me explain."

Erika waved off his stammering with a lazy hand. "No need." She tapped the side of her skull. "And don't bother trying to sway me with your powers. I'm wearing a dampener."

Shattershot was trembling like a leaf, glancing to Greyson for instructions.

It would've been easy to take both heroes out. But Greyson's plan was to get Shattershot on his side to expose the Thrillers, not make them martyrs.

Erika's expression spasmed, as if she was near tears. "Guess I've been wrong about everything, huh?"

The catch in her voice forced Greyson to glance away. Guilt over his actions and what must happen hit hard.

Erika recovered and cleared her throat. "There is a way your girlfriend gets a lenient sentence." She pointed at Shattershot. "And keep you from going back to jail."

Shattershot was on his knees, to his girlfriend's disgust. "How?"

Greyson folded his arms, eager to hear this.

Erika spun and hurled three hot knives.

The energy projectiles plunged into Greyson's chest and stomach. "Ahhhhh!" Every nerve ending caught fire. Suddenly, Greyson lay on his side, paralyzed, black dots swimming across his vision.

"ERIKA!" Shattershot cried.

Erika Skye stood over him, bristling with hostile intentions. "Handcuffing this traitorous motherfucker." Four more hot knives sprouted from the fingertips of her right hand.

Greyson tried rolling on his back, sending waves of agony down his spine. If Erika had wanted, those knives would've sliced him up like butter. "Erika...what...are you...doing?" he gasped, barely conscious.

"Taking out the trash, Levi." Erika tilted her head. "Sorry, I meant Greyson Hirsch."

Hearing his real name collapsed Greyson's stomach in on itself. *How the hell?*

Shattershot was lost, watching Greyson. "What is she talking about?"

"Levi is an impostor." She jabbed an accusing finger at him, the tip burning with another hot knife. "Even creepier, Greyson Hirsch is supposed to be dead. Killed by Damocles."

Bam-Bam and Shattershot were beside themselves.

Shock and torment strangled Greyson's voice. Erika knew almost everything. Someone had betrayed him.

Erika aimed a kick to his stomach, shivering his ribs. He groaned.

"I thought you were one of the good ones." Erika's eyes sparkled with tears. "But when you fought Bulldozer at the compound, you could've fought back. You hesitated briefly before playing possum." She made a weirded-out face. "Couldn't shake it. Then I got proof."

Pain spasmed through Greyson from even tiny movements. And Connie couldn't reach him. "Who...?"

"Doesn't matter," Erika cut in contemptuously. "I know you leaked to Damocles about the Thrillers. You've been the poison infecting my team! A fraud gifted with powers!"

Those words seized hold of Greyson. *I've heard that before...*

Shattershot looked close to collapse. "Oh my God."

"What is this?" Bulldozer's voice thundered through the room, drawing everyone's attention.

His giant shadow blocked the entrance, with the smaller silhouettes of Brightburn and Reverb flanking him. Through hazy vision, never had Greyson been more fearful. His plan was falling apart.

Erika frowned at her teammates. "Why are you three here?"

Bulldozer stepped into the room, a dominating presence. "We got pinged from one of our Seneca contacts." His eyes darted from his leader to a trembling Bam-Bam. "Why are you with her?" His question was loaded with accusations.

Erika glowered at Greyson and then marched up to the metallic hero. "Dozer. You were right about Hazard. You were right about everything..."

Greyson, still barely able to move, watched his plans collapse.

Shattershot made furious movements toward him. "You were supposed to be my friend!"

"Shut up...and listen," Greyson hissed in desperation.

Bulldozer didn't look completely sold on Erika's apology, gesturing in their direction. Brightburn and Reverb were stone-faced as they watched the argument.

"The Thrillers seeing you with Bam-Bam...they'll never trust you."

Shattershot knelt beside him, pulling out power-dampening handcuffs. "Why should I trust you?"

Bam-Bam placed gentle hands on her lover's shoulders. "Because he can help us."

Greyson sagged. *Connie reached her.* God, his wife was amazing.

Shattershot whipped around and gawked up at his girlfriend. "What—you knew about him?"

Bam-Bam looked down in shame. "Not everything. But he and his partner can give us a new life."

Seeing Shattershot's indecision, Greyson pushed his advantage, pushing up to an elbow with great discomfort. "Erika will take her from you. Stand beside me...or fall before them."

In that moment, Shattershot chose. Pressing his fingers against his temple, the empath focused on Bulldozer, Reverb, and Brightburn.

The shift in the room's energy between the Natural Born Thrillers was palpable.

"This is on *you*, Erika." Brightburn looked disgusted. "For your failed leadership."

Erika stared back in disbelief. "Excuse you?"

"She's right, Erika." Bulldozer jabbed a meaty finger at his leader's face. "I told you not to trust either of them. You wouldn't listen. Blinded by your need to save every broken bird off the street." He gestured melodramatically with those massive hands.

Erika's jaw dropped. "Why? Because I have compassion for others, which you utterly lack?"

Bulldozer recoiled as if struck. "No." His thunderous voice bubbled with rage. "I just have a brain that can filter bullshit, unlike you."

Greyson realized what was happening. Shattershot was amplifying the team's negative emotions.

Now Reverb, all five-foot-eight of him, got right in the face of all seven-foot-three, four hundred pounds of Bulldozer. "I'm getting sick of your attitude, Dozer."

Bulldozer gave a deep belly laugh. "I'm sick of your happy-happy joy-joy asking to be kicked in the face."

Erika wedged between her teammates. "Guys—"

"Shut up!" Bulldozer palmed her face and shoved. She went skidding across the room into the shadows.

Reverb spread his arms in challenge. "Do something about it!"

"Gladly." Bulldozer backhanded Reverb with such force, Greyson felt it in his teeth.

And Reverb went sailing out of the room, and the building. A distant crash outside was followed by pockets of distant civilian screams.

Brightburn dove toward the powerhouse. "Assclown. Stop it!"

Bulldozer glared down at her. "You're with them?" He pointed in Greyson and Shattershot's direction. "Fine!" He lunged for Brightburn.

But the electrokinetic cocooned herself in lightning and hurled massive bolts at Bulldozer.

The attack launched him through the wall, obliterating it. Beyond the hole in the wall was an earthshaking thump followed by several screams. Brightburn then leaped through the opening after him.

Erika Skye rose and shook her head. "Stop it! All of you!" She hesitated when her gaze found Greyson. More shrieks from outside drove her toward her imploding team. She jumped out the wall opening.

Bam-Bam dropped to her knees. "Good God," she whispered as the battle commenced outside.

Shattershot was horrified by what he'd triggered. "The citizens…" he murmured in a daze.

Greyson smiled, feeling his aches subside. This was working out far better than expected. "That's the point."

Shattershot whirled on him sharply. "You wanted this." This wasn't a question.

Greyson didn't bother denying. The freedom felt amazing. "Took a detour, but yes."

Heartbreak cracked Shattershot's face. He backpedaled. "Why?"

Greyson struggled to his feet. The pain from Erika's hot knives was mostly gone. More shuddering impact from outside sounded. "Because…I am Damocles." Saying his name aloud filled him with courage. "I'm shedding light on The Natural Born Thrillers and their duplicity." He swept his arm around them. "Look how quickly they betray you." Greyson turned back to his flabbergasted friend. "These virtuous heroes are really dangerous hypocrites. Now the city of Shenandoah will bear witness."

Shattershot's face scrunched in revulsion. "You're a monster." He tapped this temple to employ his abilities.

Greyson offered a slow smile, feeling no different than before. Preparation paid off. "How will you stop me with my dampener?"

Shattershot gulped. "What…you—?" A blur moved from behind, cracking him over the head. He sank without a sound.

Bam-Bam stood over him, awash with regret.

Greyson nodded in gratitude. A deafening boom echoed from the streets, followed by the crackle of massive electricity. "Thank you."

Bam-Bam smiled. "The effects of Shattershot's power will last at least twenty more minutes," she advised.

"That's more than enough time," Greyson acknowledged. Erika couldn't stop all three of her rogue teammates. "Now kindly evacuate." He pivoted to face the gaping wound in the wall. Excitement washed away the last of his aches and pains. "There's work to be done."

CHAPTER 40

Hugo awoke to J-Tom at his side shaking him. He blinked and evaluated his situation, on some cot in a small and sparse room. Everything hurt from the beating the Forces of Nature gave him, but less than before. Oddly, the top part of his costume had been removed. Two other heartbeats were in the room.

Hugo jolted to a sitting position. "Whoa. Where—?"

J-Tom caught his shoulders. "Easy." Her freckles stood out on her pale skin, as did her short-sleeved black shirt. "You're in the Clubhouse."

Hugo glanced around and relaxed. No wonder the room seemed familiar. AJ and Zelda sat in chairs near the foot of the bed. His brother was relieved, his sister furious. That conversation won't be fun. The top half of his costume lay beside him, charred and blackened. Hugo looked down and shuddered. Dark-red blisters covered his chest. He turned again to J-Tom. "How—?"

"I found you and brought you here." She withdrew her hands from his shoulders. His friend ran fingers though her tight ponytail, nodding at the silvery suitcase by her seat. "When I mimicked the stealth mode in your suit, I also developed a way to track it."

Hugo nodded. "Smart." He fuzzily replayed the fight in his mind and felt incredibly foolish. That would have gone differently with backup. "How long was I out?"

"Brought you here twenty minutes ago." By how J-Tom pursed her lips, she had *lots* of thoughts.

"Geesh." Hugo swung his legs off the bed. His chest muscles spasmed at the sudden movement. But he forced himself to meet J-Tom and his siblings' stares. "Go ahead."

J-Tom didn't look pleased with whatever she wanted to say. "I'd say I told you so—"

"I will," Zelda popped up, coppery curls bouncing. "Dumbass!"

AJ rose and gently hauled her away before she could say more.

Hugo had no defense. He'd deserved it. "You're right, ZiZi." A new fear struck. "The earthquake!"

"5.6 magnitude," J-Tom replied. "Lasted seventeen seconds." She glanced away, as if recalling something. "Could've been worse. But the Forces of Nature are still trashing Atascadero."

Hugo noticed how quiet AJ had been. "You alright, uso?"

AJ's eyes were shrink-wrapped with tears. "They almost killed you." His voice was thick. "Like the Elite."

That was a razorblade of shame through Hugo's gut. The canned response would've been that risk was part of the job. *Say that to a boy who'd lost his father two years ago...* He bowed his head. "Sorry..."

"Hey, guys," J-Tom addressed the two kids. "Give us a moment?"

Once Zelda and AJ closed the door behind them, Hugo pushed upright. Every tendon ached.

Whatever wince he'd made must've been bad. J-Tom was at his side immediately, arms around his waist to support him. "I wanted to protect you," Hugo confessed. "After what happened in Seattle." Almost losing J-Tom— his trainee, his responsibility—still haunted him.

J-Tom's face emptied. "Hugo." She held him tighter. "Since summer, you've showered me with love. And I let you, because you make me feel special." She rolled her eyes and smiled. "And gooey. But if I'm going to be a hero, you have to believe in me. Like I believe in you." She held his gaze pointedly.

Hugo's shame deepened. For months, he'd only seen J-Tom as this fragile flower needing to be protected. Now Hugo saw only her inner strength shining bright. "Okay."

A cheeky smile slashed her face. "I got a big surprise for that Alluvion guy."

J-Tom's eagerness was infectious. A desire for payback against the Forces of Nature ignited through Hugo. But he couldn't deny the numbers disadvantage. "We're shorthanded."

J-Tom's smile broadened. "Well...not exactly."

Hugo raised his brow, dialing up his superhearing, and listened. AJ and Zelda weren't alone outside.

J-Tom stood on her tiptoes and kissed his mouth. "Gear up," she ordered in a low and sassy voice, nodding at the folded Aegis suit under Zelda's chair.

Hugo marveled at J-Tom bending over to activate the silver suitcase armor. The metal suit unfurled, shifted, and morphed over J-Tom as she stood—operating much faster than the last build.

Despite the many mistakes he'd made since becoming Aegis, telling J-Tom his secret had been the best. *I probably should tell her about Brie.* That still hadn't sunk in. But Hugo knew now wasn't the time.

He grabbed his spare costume, changing in seconds.

When he and J-Tom stepped out into the Clubhouse's main atrium in costume, Hugo saw his gaggle of visitors. All were bathed in the light of monitors broadcasting the devastation of Atascadero. Hugo could only glimpse the footage in quick glimpses. Watching the Forces of Nature drop more victims was salt in a gaping wound. His gaze landed on the nearest visitor. "Max."

The petite teen werewolf advanced toward him in a denim jacket and jeans, wild brunette tresses flowing down one shoulder. "You alright?" Concern filled her sun-kissed features.

"Been better—OW!" Hugo recoiled when Max slapped him upside the head. That actually hurt, given her immense strength. Some other guests chuckled.

Max's eyes glowed an eerie, angry yellow. "Why didn't you get backup?"

Hugo gave a sheepish shrug. "I'm stubborn."

"I like that girl," Zelda remarked from the corner she and AJ stood in.

Hugo ignored his sister and scanned the allies before him. Blackjack, a tall and brawny figure dressed in all-black with his bandana mask. His partner, Domino, had on her blood-red costume and goggles. The vigilantes flanked their pink-haired ward, Cherry Blossom, who surveyed her surroundings with wide eyes. Justice Jones nodded, wearing a cutoff hoodie that displayed his burly and tattoo-sleeved arms. He glared a hole into Hugo but no longer with disdain.

Shocking Hugo more was Jones's companion. Becky Knox wore a sleeveless leather romper, purple hair in a tight ponytail, built like an Amazonian. She had on her usual blasé face. This was the last person Hugo wanted here. "I thought you don't get involved."

Becky studied the Clubhouse with dispassionate sweeps. "A fistful of assholes attacked my city."

Hugo never got to question Becky about Saracen. And now wasn't the time either. On the monitors, another local business collapsed in flames thanks to Hellfire and his stupid-ass manbun.

Hugo glared daggers into Becky until she shrank back in discomfort. Then he faced Justice Jones.

The Outlaw Superhero shook his head. "You got your ass kicked, youngblood."

Hugo actually laughed. "No shit."

"I got your back." Justice Jones raised a fist, which Hugo bumped.

Blackjack chimed in. "Us, too, and we couldn't get a babysitter."

Hugo studied Cherry Blossom, shy and barely making eye contact. A total opposite of the raging tyke bomb from before. *Still, her powers could help*... "How much control does she have?" Hugo asked.

Domino exchanged a wary look with Blackjack. "Improving," she stated stiffly.

Cherry Blossom stared up at Hugo and rattled off something in sharp Japanese.

J-Tom stepped forward. "Sakura..." She continued...in modulated Japanese.

Cherry Blossom gaped, then nodded gleefully as if acing a pop quiz.

Heads turned, including Hugo's. "You speak Japanese?"

"Fluently," J-Tom replied. The eyes of her helmet pulsed blue. "Sakura means Cherry Blossom in Japanese. And she wants to blow these four away."

Becky looked impressed. "That's my kind of violence."

Justice Jones cracked his bull-like neck, cool as ice. "We roll into Atascadero guns blazing and beat the shit out of these punks," he summarized as if conferring a tailgating plan.

Max rubbed her hands together. Becky Knox cracked her knuckles.

Hugo winced, wishing things were that simple. "Atascadero's a distraction. Like Seattle, Colorado, Montana, and South Carolina," Hugo explained. "Someone's stealing kaiju remains from laboratories while the Forces of Natures create disasters." He paused, realizing how insane this sounded.

But from this crowd, the most extreme reaction was Max's exclamation of "Crazy."

"Hold on." Hugo needed to know if San Miguel PD had success at Cambria. He strode over to the consoles and dialed them up. They answered after the first ring. "Detective," he greeted.

"Aegis." Dawson's voice filled the chamber. "You had us worried for a sec."

Hugo cringed. Did *everyone* see him get owned? "I'll manage. What's the word on Salto's Cambria lab?"

"No intruders." Disappointment bled into Dawson's tenor. By the background sounds, Hugo guessed five other officers were present. "And with that new earthquake, police are spread all over the city."

Hugo glanced at his allies with a half-smile. "I got backup covered."

"How?"

"Text me the Morro Bay lab address." Hugo's mind landed on another ally. "Is Ballistic near Atascadero?"

"Yep," Dawson confirmed. "Evacuating civilians."

"Send me his number." After ending the call, Hugo turned to address his allies when another call pinged the console. He saw the number, bristled, but answered anyway. "Polymer."

"Hu—"

"Not alone!" Hugo interrupted.

"Sorry!" Polymer exclaimed. "Are you okay? Can I help?"

Hugo straightened in confusion. "Are you back in San Miguel?"

"I've been helping search and rescue with someone named Ballistic," Polymer admitted.

Hugo couldn't believe his luck. Bothersome or not, Polymer had EMT training and could be useful. "Perfect. Meet us at the borders of Colony Square in fifteen minutes."

After the call, Hugo turned to see all eyes on him. Justice Jones stood in front. "Whatcha thinking, kid?"

Hugo blinked. It took a moment to grasp that he was quarterbacking this mission. And *holy shit!*

Justice Jones would've been more qualified. But after his beatdown, Hugo needed redemption.

Thankfully, some form of a plan bubbled up. "We use two squads. I attack the Forces of Nature with Cherry Blossom, Ballistic, and Arclight," Hugo pronounced, containing his panic. "Blackjack and Domino help with rescue and watching Cherry Blossom. Justice, Max, and Becky stop the lab robbery. Arclight then joins them with Polymer." AJ and Zelda grinned proudly at him in the back.

Hearing no reaction, Hugo spread his arms invitingly. "Thoughts?"

Justice Jones scratched his stubble and gave an approving nod. "Damn good plan."

That settled Hugo greatly. He considered Max, still in human form. Completely shifting unlocked her full werewolf powers but had drawbacks—like clothing. "How good has your partial shifts gotten?"

Max's eyes lit up. "Funny you should ask." She vibrated, limbs extending, fur sprouting off her skin.

J-Tom gasped. Seconds later, Max was covered in a coat of dark fur with a more lupine face and yellow eyes. But she still resembled a humanoid in clothes. She whirled, hair whipping about. "What do you think?" Max sounded like herself, except for the growling undercurrent in her tone.

Hugo nodded. This just might work. "Perfect. Let's move."

Everyone dispersed and headed for the Clubhouse exit. Hugo's nerves were all over the place, leading a team into battle. What the hell? But he caught Becky by herself, adjusting her golden bracelets.

He walked up, grabbed her arm, and leaned close. "I know you're working for Saracen," he murmured, feeling Becky's heart skip. "If you fuck us, there will be consequences." He let the warning linger.

"*That's* why you're acting squirrely." Becky jerked out of his grip. "I'm on your side," she hissed. "So's he." Becky marched away, clearly rattled. Her gall was breathtaking.

Hugo forced himself to stay pokerfaced when addressing AJ and Zelda. "Tell your mom I'm handling this situation," he told his sister quietly. When Zelda nodded, Hugo high-fived both his siblings.

J-Tom lingered after the others left. Her helmet had no features, but her posture held a clear question.

"Watch Becky Knox," he whispered. "You see fuckery, you drop her."

"Done," J-Tom stated automatically.

Exactly the loyalty Hugo expected. The pair departed to join the team.

CHAPTER 41

The world beyond this building erupted while Greyson leaned against a paint-chipped wall to recover. Screams filled the night, combined with crackling electricity and the *thump-thump* of footfall.

Tears of joy filled his eyes after hearing this. His plan was coming to life.

"Hirsch?" Connie's voice sounded behind him. She appeared, carrying a bag.

Farther back, Bam-Bam dragged an unconscious Shattershot away.

Connie shivered. "It's World War 3 out there."

Greyson smiled as she reached for him. "As planned." Never had her nearness felt as nourishing.

She slipped a hand around his waist in visible concern. "You okay?"

Greyson smiled, brushing away the tears. "Could be better." He nodded at her bag. "Do you have it?"

Connie's reaction was reproachful. "Of course." She reached deep into the bag, pulling out his golden human-shaped Damocles mask. Now he was ready.

"Good." Greyson gazed upon the final piece in his mission. Another wave of screams followed by the sounds of colliding cars reached their attention. He nodded at Bam-Bam struggling to move Shattershot "Help Bam-Bam get Shattershot out of here."

Connie pulled Greyson into a fulsome kiss. When she stepped back, her eyes danced with want. "Do your worst."

Heady warmth refreshed Greyson. "Always. Be safe, love."

Once Connie moved to help Bam-Bam, Greyson pulled the mask over his head and negated his tether to the ground. He floated through the breach created by Bulldozer.

A smattering of burning overturned cars served as torches to illuminate the dark neighborhood.

Greyson took one sweeping stare up and down the street and swallowed a startled gasp. This couldn't be the same boulevard he'd walked down several minutes beforehand. All Greyson saw were people fleeing in every direction. Bodies lay everywhere, trampled or electrocuted or buried under rubble commemorating Paragon Day. Police cars were shredded in half, with officers injured or dismembered.

Greyson followed the screams and trail of destruction, easily finding the source.

Farther up the street, a mountainous metallic man was tossing cars and streetlamps with scary ease, a crazed glower in his face. Brightburn dove for cover, lobbing forks of blue lightning at her teammates without care for fleeing bystanders.

Reverb bounced toward his powerhouse teammate, a shimmery kinetic forcefield surrounding him. He unfurled both feet, drilling Bulldozer's face to stagger him back.

Shaking off the attack, Bulldozer punched Reverb so hard the smaller man sailed several blocks down the street into a building. Limbs splaying out, he slid to the ground.

"Time to intervene," Greyson murmured, floating toward the battle in progress. The closer he got, the higher the body count. Had these people no survival instinct?

Erika Skye stood in the middle of the ravaged street, several yards from Bulldozer between him and a group of fleeing people. Bright, deadly knives shone between her curled fists. She looked stricken facing her colleague. "Dozer! Please stop!"

Bulldozer roared, emotions amplified by Shattershot's powers, and charged full-speed.

Erika crouched, hurling her knives in a backhanded arc. Energy projectiles streaked toward Bulldozer, piercing his chest and abs and leg. He barely slowed, lost in rage. Brightburn lobbed another dose of lightning. That juddered Bulldozer, but he didn't stop. The screams grew louder.

Erika stood her ground, taking a traffic cop's stance with one hand raised like some traffic cop.

Greyson gasped, watching Bulldozer about to trample her. *And Erika becomes a martyr.*

He promptly reached out, tethering Erika's gravity to a building on her left.

That sent a surprised Erika staggering sideways.

Seconds afterward, Bulldozer stampeded over where she'd stood, each step shaking the ground. He accelerated his charge, overtaking the fleeing young people.

There was a series of sickening crunches. Greyson's stomach twisted, forcing him to turn away.

Horror erupted up and down the street's length, including Erika. "DOZER!"

Bulldozer finally came to a stop, looking around groggily as if roused from slumber. "What's going on?" He stared at his leader in confusion. "Erika?"

Despite Shattershot's powers wearing off, Shenandoah's citizens still fled, cursing his name. Greyson smiled beneath his mask. To them, these Natural Born Thrillers were now the villains.

Brightburn was sobbing amid the deafening chaos. "Dozer, what have you done?"

Bulldozer furrowed his metal brow, still not understanding. "What are you talking…about…?" His confusion died as he finally noticed the crushed and contorted bodies around him, some outright flattened.

Greyson relished in Bulldozer's bald-faced horror.

"No…Nonono." He clutched at his shiny scalp. "I didn't mean to! I'm sorry!"

Greyson couldn't let him regain his full faculties. He reached for a streetlamp, the long pole wrenched from the ground at his command. He made a throwing motion in Bulldozer's direction. "No, you're not. Not even close." The streetlamp accelerated in a downward blur, thirty-five times its normal gravity, and tethered to Bulldozer's body.

The jarring scrunch of metal puncturing metal caught everyone off-guard, especially Bulldozer. The hero seemed mildly stunned by the streetlamp impaling him from behind through his midsection, stabbing into the concrete.

"Bulldozer!" Erika Skye ran to him, sobbing.

Brightburn spotted Greyson hovering overhead. Her expression darkened. "Son of a bitch." She crackled from head to heel with electricity, a promise of violence.

"You don't know my mother!" Greyson responded insolently and pointed at a fire hydrant. Heavy gravity popped the cap off. A thunderous torrent of water spewed out, slamming Brightburn into an overturned car. Bolts of energy jumped out of Brightburn to spear several bystanders idiotically standing around. More electrocuted bodies dropped.

Brightburn spasmed then stilled, out of the fight.

That left one last Thriller. Greyson floated before a devastated Erika Skye, scattering more bystanders.

Any pity toward her went out the window the moment she'd attacked him.

Erika put herself between Greyson and a wounded Bulldozer. She looked so weary. "Who…are you?"

"Damocles," Greyson proclaimed, not using his vocal modulator. "But what's my real name, Erika?"

Her eyes widened. "Oh my God."

"That's right."

Bulldozer struggled and failed to pull the streetlamp out of his body.

Erika's face was inundated with conflicting emotions as everything clicked. "You did this," she said, sounding dazed. "You did this to the Thrillers. To Shenandoah."

Reverb leaped forward and landed beside his leader, stumbling. His kinetic forcefield shimmered so bright, it reflected off the battle-torn surroundings.

She still won't take responsibility. Greyson shook his head. "Correction," he calmly retorted. "All this was caused by you." He cast a sweeping arm at the wrecked neighborhood. "I truly hope you've enjoyed the ruin your team has inflicted on this city."

Erika seethed. Hot knives sprouted from between the fingers of her clenched fists. "I'm gonna kill you."

Greyson snickered at her useless wrath. "Language."

She made a hurling motion as if pitching a baseball. Ten scalding energy knives streaked at Greyson.

Brief panic came and went as he cocooned himself in anti-gravity.

The hot knives veered off at sharp angles, slicing harmlessly into buildings or cars.

Reverb gasped. Erika's jaw dropped. "How…did you do that?"

"Like I do this." Greyson let loose an invisible gravitational pulse with a swift hand chop.

Erika and Reverb got launched back, suspended briefly in mid-air. Both hit the ground in limp heaps.

Reverb's kinetic field evaporated.

"All too easy." Greyson floated to Bulldozer, who frantically yanked at the streetlamp speared into him. The pole was now warped beyond recognition. He roared in frustration at his own helplessness, swatting at Greyson.

But he remained an inch or so out of reach and slowly shook his head. Watching Bulldozer get his comeuppance was invigorating. "For the record, Dozer," he stated. "You were right about me."

Bulldozer's eyes nearly popped. "You're gonna die—"

Greyson lazily closed a fist. "Hush now." Heavy gravity pulled Bulldozer's lips together. Now his rage came across as muffled, wordless rage.

With the Thrillers lying defeated, frightened bystanders cautiously gathered. Most murmured and pointed while others sobbed at the casualties. But the growing anti-superhero sentiment was obvious on their faces and their words. Greyson spotted several people pointing camera phones. Two bystanders were hoisting up professional video cameras. Perfect.

Greyson beckoned them forward, switching on his vocal modulator. "Come closer. You'll want this recorded." He spread his hands once the cameramen were near, a preacher addressing his flock. Then he improved his speech. "People of Shenandoah, look at the wreckage these Natural Born Thrillers caused your city. And on a day of celebration, no less. Look!"

The demand startled many. But like sheep, they did as ordered. Their responses ranged from more grief to visceral anger. Good.

Greyson had them in the palm of his hand. "For centuries, we built our own prisons, organized and equipped our own enemies," he preached. "Licensed our salvation. All to fund our own oppression."

He pointed at a helpless Bulldozer, impaled to the ground by the streetlamp. "Each time we beg these heroes to save us, buying their merchandise, we fund our own oppression. The Thrillers are no different from murderers like Paragon, the Elite." His lip curled in disgust. "And the newest savior, the so-called Shield of Justice. Who are they to tell you how to live? The woman who beats citizens half to death? Or the leader who couldn't spot a mole within her own ranks?" Rage spasmed through Greyson as he thought of traitors. Someone who knew of his mission had betrayed him. *And I will rain down hell when I learn who,* he fumed.

"What makes you different from them?" a random woman shouted from the sea of faceless silhouettes.

Greyson grinned. "Because I, Damocles, am the cure." He jabbed at his own chest. "I am *necessary*." He paused, assessing his tone. "Melodramatic, I know. But some truths need pageantry to be digested." And by his rabid audience's reaction, they were listening.

In the background, sirens blared and grew closer. Greyson's time was nearly up. Shenandoah police cars moved in, slowed by streets littered with wreckage caused by the Natural Born Thrillers. Greyson squinted, noticing how these weren't, in fact, police cars. The familiar police Dodge Charger model and colors sported a Paxton-Brandt logo. This had to be their security forces to apprehend the Thrillers before actual cops arrived.

Greyson laughed freely, which sounded cartoonishly sinister with the modulator. "All yours, officers."

He soared into the velvety-purple heavens and away from the disaster area. Police drones attempted to follow, only for him to increase their gravity until each one plummeted.

Greyson rocketed off into the night, mission accomplished.

CHAPTER 42

The skies above Atascadero were stained by dirty smoke.

Bile rose in Hugo's throat as he watched the Forces of Nature's destruction moving farther into the San Miguel suburb.

Downtown Atascadero was a smoking, waterlogged ruin. Random pockets of flames hungrily licked at abandoned cars and local businesses. Paragon's Pub, a staple of Atascadero, burned brightly.

Meteora, Alluvion, Hellfire with his manbun, and Sirocco roved through the streets. The quartet lashed out at anything still alive, comparing kill counts. Hugo seethed in disgust.

Police had barricades around Atascadero. News choppers and drones soared overhead.

And here Hugo stood, hiding in an alleyway behind some roofless bistro. Fouled water sluiced around his boots, mixed with blood.

Every atom in him longed to race out and bitch-slap these four into next week.

That worked so well last time, right? Hugo grimaced. He couldn't screw up this second strike. Another Lady Liberty axiom bubbled up. *Fight with your head, not your ego. Lives depend on it.*

Hugo tapped the left side of his hood. "In position," he whispered. "Arclight?"

"In stealth mode and ready," J-Tom's modulated voice replied.

Hugo felt better having her here. "Ballistic?"

"Almost there." Scuffing noises detailed Ballistic scrambling to higher ground. "Step by step."

"Blackjack," Hugo hissed.

"Domino, Cherry, and I are moving into position," Blackjack replied, wind whipping in his location.

"Justice?"

"Becky and I are nearing Morro Bay's Lab," Justice Jones added, his motorcycle engine roaring.

"Polymer and I are at the city border. Waiting for pickup," Max informed.

"You need a codename, Max." Hugo sighed to calm the impatience. "Squad A. Wait for my signal." He peeked around the corner of a charred clothing store.

Sirocco hovered above an overturned Hummer. "Well?"

Alluvion swept over to his companions. Worry filled his translucent face. "The longer we wait, the shorter the escape window."

Hellfire spun around in a dazzling spiral of flames. "Why rush with so many splendors to paint?"

Meteora gave him an annoyed look, tapping a communicator on her collar.

"Bogie."

Hugo jerked back into hiding. The voice in his ear startled the shit out of him.

"Private channel," Simon continued. "You there?"

Hugo scanned around, unsure whether to be grateful or angry. "What are you doing?" he fumed quietly.

"School let us out after the second earthquake," Simon explained. "No one got hurt or anything. I'm home…and saw the fight. You okay?"

Hugo cringed. Of course, Simon saw him get his ass thoroughly kicked. "Mostly. I'm attacking again."

"Alone?" Simon asked disbelievingly.

Hugo scowled. "I got backup."

"Great! Well, I'm here too. For strategy."

Hugo chuckled. "Thanks, uso." Simon's support meant more than any superhero ally. Now he felt ready.

Currently, Meteora addressed her cohorts. "Myriad needs ten more minutes."

Alluvion wasn't calmed. "A lot can happen in ten minutes. What if Tomorrow Man shows up?"

His teammates laughed. "My first thought was who?" Sirocco mocked. "And my second was, 'oh'."

All four guffawed loudly, distracted.

They had to strike. "Guys?" Hugo asked, tapping his other comm channel.

"Ready," Blackjack confirmed.

"Ready," Ballistic added.

Hugo's relief preceded panic. *Game time.* He floated off the ground toward the Forces of Nature.

"We've never been caught," Hellfire singsonged, pointing a finger and torching letters on a store window, melting it to goo. "I'm not changing that narrative."

"Relax, children." Meteora waved him off. "We'll leave soon and get paid big bucks."

Hugo touched down in a crouch before them. Impeccable superhero landing.

Sirocco flinched away. Alluvion reared up like a watery cobra.

Hugo rose, heart aflutter. On the outside, he was cool and contained. "Not likely, Meteora."

Meteora's eyes glittered in disbelief. "You again?" Her scoff oozed pity. "Didn't we beat some sense into you?"

Alluvion grunted. "Someone's masochistic." He puffed out his translucent chest, growing three feet. Bright-yellow flames swirled around Hellfire. "I see a canvas ripe for graphic carnage." He rubbed his hands, sparks shooting out.

"Whatever." Sirocco floated her pudgy frame just over Alluvion and dropped into him with a splash-splash.

To Hugo's bafflement, a ferocious swirl of fog followed.

In their place was a towering monster resembling a cloudy Michelin Man born of nimbus clouds.

"This time," the cloud monster's voice was rolling thunder, "you leave in a casket."

Hugo didn't flinch from the threat. "This time…." He spied a ripple of movement behind the Forces of Nature. "I brought friends."

Meteora appeared baffled. "Friends?"

"Like me!" Ballistic appeared out of thin air in his gold-and-blue costume. He landed on top of a scorched sedan and tossed a fistful of kinetic-charged marbles.

"Who—?" Before Meteora finished, six marbles clattered among them and detonated on contact with the pavement. She went flying, pounded by successions of detonation.

Hellfire got thrown from the sky. The cloud monster stumbled into repeated discharges, roaring its displeasure.

Hugo inhaled and pasted the quartet with a rippling sonic scream.

Ballistic smirked from his perch. "Can't catch me! Whatcha gonna do about it?!" He backflipped over the Forces of Nature completely, kinetic energy boosting his speed and agility.

Hugo hung back, watching the assault unfold.

Meteora furiously struggled upright, rocky frame cracked.

"Alluvion. Sirocco. Separate and kill that bouncy asshole." She pointed at Ballistic cartwheeling away.

The cloud monster whipped and whirled. Abruptly, Alluvion and Sirocco were separate again.

The hydrokinetic rushed on his tidal wave in pursuit. "Gladly…WHAT?" A white spray doused Alluvion's arm, quickly coagulating into pasty cement.

J-Tom dropped stealth-mode, appearing in all her armored glory. "Still glad?" she mocked.

Sirocco dove at her. J-Tom swung her arm back without looking and fired a photonic blast. The aerokinetic yelped and dodged away from the slicing beam.

Hugo chortled, admiring her work. *Nice, Jenny.*

Meanwhile, Ballistic was dodging and flipping over every fireball Hellfire lobbed at him.

With one arm useless, Alluvion sailed in, wielding his other watery arm. "You—?"

J-Tom weaved out of the way, spraying Alluvion's other arm in that same fluid. Now the hydrokinetic keeled forward, weighed down by two leaden, useless arms.

J-Tom floated before him. "That looks uncomfortable."

Alluvion furiously jerked up, snapping both cement arms off. A fountain spewed out from his chest, embracing J-Tom like a lover. "C'mere…" He dragged her into his watery body completely.

Hugo almost raced to her rescue but stopped himself. *Let's see if Jenny can escape.*

Alluvion gloated at trapping J-Tom inside him. "Good luck not drowning…now…koff…koff." Alluvion's translucent body grew cloudy, slowing in movement. "What the…?"

Hugo smirked. "You look kinda stiff, Alluvion…." The pun was too obvious, even for him.

Soon, Alluvion froze into an alabaster statue of a human body and wave-like lower half.

J-Tom exploded out of him moments later. Alluvion crumbled into piles of brittle fragments.

Meteora screamed in wordless outrage.

Hellfire's eyes went saucer-wide before he got beaned in the chest by three rapid-fire marbles.

Sirocco clutched her head. "NOOOO!"

Hugo pumped his fist. "Three to go."

"That was awesome!" Simon exclaimed on comms.

"Right?" Hugo then turned to J-Tom. "Take Max and Polymer to the Morro Bay lab."

"Done." She zoomed toward the city border, her jet boots leaving a slight contrail. After hanging a sharp left, the armored hero disappeared.

Hugo tapped his hood for the main comm channel. "Justice. Arclight, Polymer, and Max are incoming." He recalled something Meteora had revealed. "Myriad is the thief at the lab. And she's a duplicator."

"I hate dupes," Becky complained.

Justice Jones chuckled. "Thanks for the warning, kid."

Hearing a rumble barrel his way, Hugo leaped straight up—evading a track of jagged earth ripping apart where he'd been standing.

Meteora came boiling forward. The hatred carved into her rocklike face was frightening. "I'm gonna make you my bitch!" She took a fighting stance.

Hugo clenched his fists eagerly. "Bring it on, *bitch*!" He flew headlong, erasing the distance between them in seconds. The collision shuddered down the boulevard. Hugo lifted Meteora clean off the ground and swung without restraint.

INTERLUDE: J-TOM

J-Tom hurtled up the winding coastline, crisp afternoon winds buffeting her armor.

The faint roar of her boots' thrusters trailed her flight. The round silhouette of Morro Rock loomed larger on a peninsula off Morro Bay's shoreline as she closed in on the coastal suburb.

The armor responded to her mental commands like another body part, thanks to its neural interface. On her helmet's viewscreen, the PCH below was packed and unmoving by mass exoduses and crashes.

She understood why. Meteora's seismic attacks triggered flashbacks of the 1987 SLO County earthquake. And the SeaTac quake had happened days ago.

The helmet viewscreen flashed loads of data on the many accidents or injuries below, including suggestions on how to assist. Countless people down there and across greater San Miguel needed help.

But she remembered her cargo, Polymer and Max Ochoa, and her mission. Or else the fight in Atascadero would be for nothing.

"Justice Jones." J-Tom beamed under her helmet at addressing the Outlaw Superhero. "We're almost there." She hung a sharp right inland with her passengers.

"So are Becky and I," Jones replied. "We're heading in from the back."

Within minutes, J-Tom found the lab's rear. One door happened to be open, which she soared through with Polymer and Max. Placing them down, she inspected her surroundings via her helmet's viewscreen. They entered a loading dock with four big rigs. Bodies of security guards trailed toward a violent commotion farther inside.

Justice Jones and Becky Knox stood in the center, punching and tossing swarms of attacking women.

J-Tom, via her helmet's viewscreen, counted twenty-five attackers.

Those are the thieves. J-Tom, Max, and Polymer dashed into the brawl without hesitation. Another notification pinged in J-Tom's viewscreen. "A silent alarm activated ten minutes ago," she declared. "San Miguel PD is twenty miles away."

"The thieves will be long gone," Polymer added, his fists ballooning four times their size. He had a weirded-out expression on his face. Max, fur-covered from a partial werewolf shift, glowered in confusion.

J-Tom's stomach twisted up, just like when she'd taken down Alluvion. *Here we go!* While firing photon blasts from the palms of her armored gloves, J-Tom now saw why everyone looked befuddled.

The women attacking Justice Jones and Becky had identical athletic bodies and matching black catsuits. All had bouncy gold locks and murderous glares as they threw themselves at the pair.

And by the quick calculations on J-Tom's viewscreen, more copies kept popping into existence.

Polymer's eyes bulged through his mask. "That's a duplicator!"

"No shit, pup." Justice Jones elbowed and kicked wildly to avoid getting dogpiled.

"God," Becky scoffed, visibly bored while knocking two copies' heads together. She fought well, each strike quick and smooth. "Duplicators are only useful for housework, cannon fodder, or orgies!"

Polymer was aghast. J-Tom laughed. Wherever Hugo had found this Becky Knox, she was a character—and insanely sexy.

J-Tom's mirth stopped as more Myriad copies appeared. She dropped to a knee and backhanded one Myriad copy away, wincing at the sickening crunch of its jaw. J-Tom blinked, recalling this woman's face. "She's called Myriad. Aegis encountered her a while back."

Max was a savage blur, her claws slashing any Myriad copies to ribbons. "I want an alias," she growled.

"She-Wolf," Polymer replied, kneeing a Myriad copy in the face. "I feel bad hitting women!"

Justice Jones snorted at his out-of-place chivalry. "Equal rights mean equal fights, pup!"

"I'll help with your *nom de guerre*," J-Tom blasted four Myriad copies with dazzling photon bursts.

"Children!" Becky barked, kicking a Myriad's face in. "Fight in progress!" Two more jumped on her back.

Polymer cringed while spinning around, hands morphed into enormous mallets. "Sorry!"

J-Tom kept blasting countless Myriad copies with their identical faces, her attacks set to heavy stun. But more Myriads kept popping into existence, more aggressive than before. So many identical attackers crowded J-Tom's space, pulling at her armor was suffocating—like almost drowning in Seattle. "They don't stop!" She didn't hide her desperation. "Trying to overwhelm us!"

Justice Jones was practically buried in Myriads but kept laying in bone-crunching punches. "There's no try, youngblood!"

J-Tom could no longer see Max or Polymer. Becky Knox barely fended off a horde of Myriad flanking her with several lightning-fast kicks.

"We need to find the prime!" Justice Jones yelled out nearby. "The Myriad directing the copies."

"But how—?" The idea popped into J-Tom's head so instantly, she almost high-fived herself. "Becky!" she called above the fray. "Can you track supers in this loading dock?"

Dozens of Myriads grabbed Becky's legs, leaving only her fists as weapons. "Yeah…" Her eyes glazed over briefly. She nodded at a van at the farthest end of the loading docks. "One in the van." Too many Myriads to count then dragged Becky to the ground.

Panic momentarily overwhelmed J-Tom. But she remembered Hugo's training and rocketed upward, three Myriads clinging on. The van at the far end of the loading dock tore out of hiding.

J-Tom twisted round and round, flinging the copies off, and zoomed past the van.

Please don't crush me! She cringed, landing in front of the speeding vehicle.

All kinds of alarms flashed on her viewscreen before the vehicle struck. Impact shivered through her armor. Driven several feet back, she braced herself and pushed forward to slow the wrecked vehicle.

She shoved the car off and approached the driver's-side window. Myriad slumped face-first in a bloodstained airbag. She groaned.

"Hi there!" J-Tom raised a gauntlet, palm burning bright. "Bye there."

One photon burst blasted Myriad out the car's other side. The duplicator flopped onto the floor, unconscious.

J-Tom turned back to her allies, who were beating down the now disorganized Myriad mob.

She jogged to the van's rear, her boots making *clomp-clomp* noises. She gave the back doors a huge tug, heart racing.

Inside were several cannisters with their own portable freezer to preserve the Tiamat remains.

J-Tom sighed in relief. Then she flew back over to the others.

Justice Jones, Becky Knox, Max, and Polymer all stood panting amid piles of Myriad's unconscious, maimed, or dead bodies. Only the ones still breathing vanished into nothing. J-Tom forced herself not to look too long at any of the corpses.

Polymer whirled about as bodies faded away. "The duplicates," he marveled.

Max, with her body fur and partial wolf muzzle, made even confused expressions menacing. "Did we win?" she asked.

Justice Jones adjusted his bandana. "We won this battle."

Becky approached, happily rubbing Max's shoulders.

J-Tom nodded, soaking in the rush of her first official battle. Then she remembered the battle still raging in Atascadero. "Aegis is still fighting the Forces of Nature." And she prayed to God that he would win.

CHAPTER 43

"Get OFF!" Meteora cried with a right cross to Hugo's mouth.

The rock-hard fist rang his bell and sent him skidding down the fractured boulevard.

Hugo rolled onto his side, cradling his jaw. "Oww."

"Ya gonna take that lying down?" Simon commented over their comm channel.

"Not on purpose!" Hugo hissed, almost missing the *whoosh-whoosh* spinning his way.

He popped up, a spinning full-sized truck just inches from his face.

Hugo braced himself, hands out, and caught the vehicle by the underside with ease. The momentum pushed him back a few feet. He glanced over to see the shock on Meteora's stony features. "Tag you're it!" Hugo tossed the vehicle right back into Meteora's face, sending her through a storefront.

The window shattered in an earsplitting *K-KEESH* of glass shards.

Hugo winced, not wanting that kind of collateral damage. He stalked through rubble toward his target.

Nearby, Ballistic kept somersaulting over cars to evade Hellfire's barrage of fireballs. The artsy pyrokinetic was growing more frustrated and reckless.

Sirocco was on all fours, shaking off the impact from Ballistic's attacks.

The truck ejected ferociously from the ruined storefront. Meteora emerged, her rocky exterior sporting several fissures. "Should've run." She knelt, placing her hands on the sidewalk. "What I do to San Miguel will make Seattle seem quaint." Small tremors shivered through the street, growing more potent.

Hugo's heart leaped, and he exploded forward. "No, you WON'T!" An uppercut to Meteora's chin launched her into orbit. Hugo flew in pursuit with a rapid-fire salvo of punches so fast, his arms blurred.

"No more deaths," he barked as they rose. "No more damage!" Hugo kept striking Meteora harder and harder with a reservoir of unbridled anger until she sagged.

Atascadero's buildings and streets now looked ant-sized this high up.

Not done yet. Hugo tucked his legs in, dropkicking Meteora's chest. She fell, arms and legs flailing.

And Hugo watched with relish…until the possible collateral damage dawned on him.

"FUCK." He dove at top speeds, raced past his target, and touched down as Meteora fell freely.

Right before she landed, Hugo drove a fist to her midsection. The shockwave mushroomed outward, rattling the ruined buildings and unbroken windows. The terrakinetic flopped to the ground, rolling to a stop a few feet away. She was out cold, her rocky skin shedding.

"Two out of four." Hugo cheered until an arid hurricane almost knocked him over.

Sirocco floated high above, arms spread like a prophet, her pudgy face enraged. "Not if I can help it." She poured on the winds, driving Hugo back, tossing vehicles and debris and any object not nailed down.

Hugo shielded his face, already having a plan for Sirocco. "Cherry Blossom!"

Moments later, the pixie-like Japanese girl floated behind Sirocco, bubblegum-pink hair billowing about. The girl's eager smile gave her the appearance of a demonic fairy. She tapped on Sirocco's shoulder, startling her.

"Who?" Sirocco frowned, turning to Cherry Blossom. "Know what? Don't care. You'll die, too—AAAAHH!"

Cherry Blossom cut her off with a bright, mushroom-like eruption.

Hugo turned away from the brilliance, the flareup heating his bones.

Just as quickly, the flash winked out. Sirocco dropped onto a BMW in a smoking heap.

Hugo did a quick listen, confirming a heartbeat.

Cherry Blossom floated to the ground and waved. Her grin might've been sweet in normal circumstances.

Hugo waved back, a little unnerved. Cherry Blossom had delivered. But something told him that she'd been holding back. *I got my hands full.* He scanned their surroundings. "Sirocco, Alluvion, and Meteora are down," he counted. "Three out of four."

Hugo didn't have to search far for Hellfire.

"Get AWAY from my muse!" A column of bright-gold fire veined in crimson torched down from above. Domino and Blackjack cried out, desperate to reach their ward.

Hugo ran, the world slowing around him, and snatched Cherry Blossom just in time.

Behind them, an upturned delivery truck, where he and Cherry Blossom had just stood incinerated.

Hugo checked first on Cherry, who was unharmed but shaking. He pointed at their location to say *Stay here.*

Cherry seemed to understand and nodded with fearful eyes.

Hugo zoomed out of hiding, to find Hellfire cradling an unconscious Meteora.

Ballistic also approached from the opposing end of the street with a slightly singed suit.

Hugo could've ended this fight but went with mercy. "Stand down, manbun." He inched closer.

Hellfire swiveled in Hugo's direction, eyes blazing. "An artist NEVER compromises!"

Hugo rolled his eyes. *Well, I tried.*

Hellfire hugged Meteora tighter. Their forms glowed—merging.

"Shit!" Hugo flew at them—eating a stiff backhand that nearly took his head off.

A lamp pole rushed up to catch him.

Hugo slid to the ground, dazed by the blow and what faced him.

The merged rock-and-fire monster stood, with fiery pits for eyes and a mouth.

"Now," the beast boomed in Meteora's and Hellfire's combined voices. "Feel the full scope of my power." The gestalt monster glowed brighter than before, heat oozing from cracks in its rocky skin.

Ballistic helped Hugo up. "Whatcha gonna do, about that?"

Hugo floated off the ground, watching veins of fire seep from the monster into faults along the surrounding street. The air swelled from escalating heat. He was drawing a blank on how to stop this.

"Titan's boomerang maneuver," Simon suggested on comms. "Like he did against Monstrosity."

"Ooooh." Hugo understood, then looked at Ballistic. "Be right back." He soared straight up.

As the rock monster bellowed its rage, Ballistic gaped after him. "Where are you going?"

"Trust me!" Hugo called back, banking left and then diving down until he hovered inches off the street. He rocketed forward. Atascadero zoomed past from quaint buildings to the ruins of downtown.

The distance between Hugo and the monster's backside shrank in seconds.

He smashed through its right leg, the limb bursting into a shower of flaming rocks. The monster roared and teetered on one leg, gigantic frame barely keeping balance.

Hugo flew seven blocks down the boulevard before making a tight U-turn.

"Now for the money shot," Hugo crowed, accelerating again. He punched through the monster's chest, the gaping hole belching flames.

Hugo soared up as the monster swayed and teetered. A sonic scream pummeled it for good measure. After a brief and blinding flash, Hellfire and Meteora lay unconscious beside each other.

Hugo floated to the ground. His team had won. The disbelief was dizzying.

Cherry Blossom stepped out from hiding, clapping excitedly. Blackjack and Domino moved to help Ballistic restrain Meteora, Sirocco, and Hellfire.

Hugo then noticed Alluvion, back in human form. His skin was light brown, flattop dark brown and kinky. He clutched his stomach, vomiting up whatever substance J-Tom had doused him with.

Hugo walked up and finger-flicked Alluvion's jaw. Head snapping back, he dropped without a sound.

"Four out of four." Hugo turned to the police barricade at the Atascadero border. Behind it, Superhumans Crimes Task Force was armed to the teeth and ready to strike.

Hugo motioned them forward. "Proceed."

The armed officers quickly swarmed the fallen Forces of Nature.

An incoming ping caught his ear, followed by an ID on his eyescreen. "Arclight. Good news?"

"The Morro Bay lab is secure,'" J-Tom's overmodulated voice replied. "And we caught Myriad."

Hugo's heart soared. "Nice!" J-Tom kicked ass without him. *We all did our part.* "Bring Polymer and Max back with you once she's arrested." He cast a pained gaze across the Atascadero's destroyed downtown. "We got lots of cleanup to do." Hugo called Dawson, telling him about what had happened at the Morro Bay lab.

A shadow overhead drew his attention. Hugo looked up to find Tomorrow Man far above, cape flapping in the wind. He surveyed the damage, features scrunched like smelling bad cheese.

"Godammit." Tomorrow Man flew off and vanished into the distance.

Hugo had to chuckle. Tomorrow Man was too late…*again*, and didn't even stay to clean up. Hugo shook his head and turned to Ballistic. "Let's get to work."

The group searched this war zone, finding some survivors within buildings that looked steamrolled. They also found quite a few dead. Hugo silently mourned each one, reminded again how damaging super-on-super battles were. Arclight arrived half an hour later with Max and Polymer. The five of them worked in concert to clear as much debris away for ambulances. Hugo had only experienced such effortless synchronicity with the Fab Phenoms. He enjoyed that immensely.

Once more, Polymer's EMT skills came in handy. Hugo knew the basics thanks to Lady Liberty and his mother, but more advanced training might be useful in the future.

By the time the sun began sinking into the hazy horizon, days of cleanup had been finished in hours.

Once certain areas were deemed safe, the news media came swarming in. "Aegis! Aegis!"

Hugo's instinct said to ignore them. But the damage and body count demanded answers. He grudgingly approached the throng of reporters, flashing cameras, and microphones jabbing at his face. "Speak."

"Robin Leffler. *Newsworthy.com*," one woman announced. "You just saved Atascadero but at a terrible cost. What do you say to the citizens tired of the collateral damage and scared of supers in general?"

Hugo considered this before answering. "People of San Miguel." He cast a sweeping stare across all cameras present. "I hear you. I see you. We heroes will do better in our roles to keep you safe."

More shouts arose before Hugo pointed at a skinny man with thick hair.

"Paul LaForge, *San Miguel Tribune*. In your brief career, you're usually more of a loner."

Hugo's stare made the reporter gulp. "When you phrase it that way..."

Laughter broke the tension. LaForge continued. "Is this alliance temporary or a new team?"

Hugo fought back a smile. "Should've seen that coming." He glanced at J-Tom in her armor, lifting wrecked cars onto tow trucks. Max, still in partial shift, dug through the ruins of Paragon's Pub.

Hugo's mirth dimmed as he faced the reporters. "It takes a community to protect a city. And this team belongs to that community."

"What is your team called?"

A moment ago, Hugo didn't know. He rubbed his chin, eyeing that wrecked pub. "The name is from a superhero active before my time." Hugo spoke boldly, digging into his vast superhero knowledge. That speech elective he took sophomore year was coming in handy. "The first superhero. The American Original. He set the standard for Titan, Lady Liberty, and everyone else." Hugo glanced down when recalling the tragedy that befell this icon. "Until a monster brainwashed him into committing atrocities beyond measure. His accomplishments were tainted or erased. Even his hometown disavowed him."

Hugo sensed discomfort washing over the reporters. Of course, since they knew whom he spoke of. *This could end badly*, a voice cautioned. Hugo steeled his worries away, solid in his decision. "This team will strive to live up to the best part of his legacy. Myself, Arclight, Polymer, Ballistic, Loba." Hugo pointed to each hero he proclaimed, landing last on Cherry Blossom. Not wanting to name her on camera, a possible codename came to mind. "And Sakura. We are...The Paragons."

That unleashed a cacophony of questions and flashing cameras.

"That's right, San Miguel!" Polymer marched up to Hugo's side. "Forget any build-a-team contests." He gestured at his lanky frame. "The Paragons stand ready!"

Hugo glared at him. "*Try* giving less of a shit," he hissed.

That wiped the gusto off Polymer's face. "Sorry."

Hugo turned his attention back to the media. "Now if you'll excuse us, there's a city to repair."

"The Paragons?" J-Tom inquired when Hugo approached. "You just came up with that?"

He shrugged. "Spur-of-the-moment choice." Hugo felt something click with that name. And trying to take back a declared codename or superhero team name after it got press coverage was very difficult.

J-Tom nodded her helmeted head in agreement. "I like."

Max, however, wasn't thrilled by her codename. "Since when am I Loba?"

"It's Spanish for 'she-wolf'," Hugo countered.

"I know that...oh..." Max paused and considered this. "I like!"

"You kids need help?" Lady Liberty floated several feet above like some benevolent goddess about to pass judgment.

Ballistic, Max, J-Tom, and Polymer turned to Hugo, who waved her over. "The more the merrier."

Lady Liberty's face gave away her joy at being accepted again. She landed, and gave him a glowing look before introducing herself to the mostly starstruck group.

Hugo felt eyes on him. In a corner away from view, Becky Knox leaned against a wall, arms folded while watching him pointedly.

She then disappeared into the nearby alleyway.

Hugo experienced various strong emotions at the sight of her. What these emotions were, he hadn't figured out. But Hugo had to confront Becky now. "One second." He zoomed toward that narrow alley.

Hugo braked in front of Becky. She was briefly startled before a lazy smile tugged at her plump lips. "You looked very iconic back there, Aegis."

Hugo got in her face. "What is your business with Saracen?"

Becky scoffed. "None of yours."

Her defiance didn't surprise him. "He came after people I care about, so I'm making it my business."

Becky was no longer amused. "Whatever you think you know is bullshit."

"And I should just take your word for it?"

That left Becky visibly stung. "If I wasn't on your side, why would I help you?"

Hugo wanted to believe her, but something in him resisted. "I've been burned before."

Her features hardened. No sentiment lived there. "Don't believe me? Fine. Just stop acting like you have the answers when you don't even know the questions." She pushed past him and stormed off down the alleyway.

Hugo watched her go, his mind awash with confusion.

CHAPTER 44

Greyson reclined on a couch, wincing as Connie inspected his lean and bare torso. A few aches from that bitch Erika Skye's hot knives lingered. Besides that, he'd come out of that confrontation mostly unscathed.

They didn't return to their condo. Too much exposure. Who knew if one of those surveillance drones had followed him? Luckily, Paxton-Brandt had a safe house in Fort Defiance deep in Shenandoah Valley outside city limits. And a dead zone with a twenty-mile radius extended around the facility.

"Better than expected," Connie murmured. She nestled against him while they watched the widescreen.

Ron Keaton, a *National News Network* anchor in a pleated black suit, graced the screen with a very serious news face. "Shenandoah's Paragon Day ended in tragedy when the Natural Born Thrillers superhero team incited an all-out brawl," Keaton went on. "No one knows what caused the blowup. But the toll on this city, which has already suffered over the years, was unimaginably high. Forty-one dead, over a hundred injured."

Satisfaction nearly burst out of Greyson. Push the right amount of pressure and The Natural Born Thrillers destroyed themselves. Just as planned.

Connie shuddered after the casualty count was read. Her face grew increasingly remorseful. Greyson studied this reaction, wondering if this would become a recurring problem.

Keaton continued. "Here's footage of disgraced hero, Bulldozer, trampling a crowd while his teammates did little to stop him. Be warned, this footage is graphic."

Bulldozer, roaring like a crazed beast, came charging forward down the street. College kids ran screaming. Yet Bulldozer gained on them with loping strides, running those civilians over. It looked almost as bad on camera.

Connie buried her face in Greyson's shoulder, while his stomach twisted. Luckily, the footage cut off before the full gory aftermath.

The screen returned to reveal Keaton's distressed news-anchor face. "If not for this Damocles person, who posted damning secrets online about the Natural Born Thrillers, the death toll would've been higher. No word on his current whereabouts. But I can safely say that most of the Natural Born Thrillers have been taken into custody and will be prosecuted to the fullest extent of the law. But Shattershot is currently at large." Keaton went on. "Public figures like Senator Huntley of West Virginia have already spoken up about their thoughts."

The US Senator appeared, a flat-faced man with curled red hair and piercing hazel eyes. "My prayers are with the people of Shenandoah." His expression turned incensed. "Once again, we had a preventable tragedy if not for the leeway we give caped thugs who are as big a threat as the villains they fight." Huntley's voice soared. "We, the people, are tired of being terrorized. But President Khan, or should I say the Superhero-in-Chief, will do nothing due to her obvious bias."

The screen returned to Keaton, suppressing his distaste. "These comments echo those made by Damocles. Below are his words."

Greyson felt odd watching himself spouting about the dangers of superheroes. It stunned him how many people were cheering. *I've started a movement*, he realized.

Connie gazed up at Greyson. "You're right, it was a melodramatic monologue," she noted dryly.

"It's a villain thing, I guess." Greyson sat with this newfound obligation. "But it got people's attention."

The Natural Born Thrillers were no more. Greyson rejoiced. He had nothing against them as individuals, except Bulldozer, just their corporate-sponsored heroics.

Connie's mouth pulled into a playful grin. "I loved it. It's just…the body count." She looked away. "I had Amarantha flashbacks."

Greyson let his shoulders slump. The visuals of this urban warzone had penetrated his hardened heart. "They had to see the price tag when a weapon of mass destruction becomes your guardian." He ran gentle fingers down Connie's back.

"Let's tone things down next time?" Her voice was hoarse with emotion.

Greyson couldn't promise a lack of casualties. But the amount this last time was more than expected. "I'll try, Con."

After some reporters spoke about Shenandoah's mood, the camera returned to Keaton. "In other superhero news, a similar situation unfolded in San Miguel. A group of four kinetic-type criminals called the Forces of Nature ran roughshod through the suburb of Atascadero." A smile cracked Keaton's features. "But thanks to Aegis and his new team, the Paragons, the group was apprehended." Keaton made an awkward face. "Maybe someone should talk to Aegis about that ill-timed name."

Him again. Greyson's mood plummeted upon seeing that hooded bastard, standing tall flanked by his allies. "We should've targeted him first," Greyson griped, popping up. "Now he has a team."

Connie curled up on the couch with equal disdain. "Aegis has to be next."

Greyson turned to his wife. "He will be," he guaranteed. No more bullshitting. Aegis had to be stopped while he was still a rookie.

The newscast vanished as an incoming video call appeared. Greyson's heart leaped when he saw the caller. "Olin."

Connie rolled her eyes. "How apropos." She clicked a button on the remote control to accept.

The Paxton-Brandt CEO appeared onscreen with that thick curly blond hair, wearing a dress shirt with the collar unbuttoned. "Congratulations, Greyson," he declared. "Are you well?"

"Great," Greyson remarked tersely.

If Olin noted his annoyance, he didn't react. "We have all five Thrillers in custody. Shattershot and his lover will get clean slates. The others..." His smile turned cruel. "We'll find appropriate uses for them."

The Natural Born Thrillers were no longer Greyson's concern. "What about Aegis?"

Olin nodded, expecting this. "In the future." He squinted. "But not immediately."

Greyson's rage was instinctive. "That's not acceptable, Steve," he retorted in sharper tones. "Aegis is selling his bullshit to everyone with a team behind him. We have to strike now."

Olin's stare was hard as steel. "No."

Greyson didn't flinch, but the churning power within begged for release. "I am *not* asking, Olin."

The two men glared back at each other for several seconds, the tension thick enough to choke on.

Then Olin softened by a hairsbreadth. "You made quite a public debut, Greyson," he reminded. "Which means Aegis, Lady Liberty, Freedom's Ring, and Battalion will be preparing for you. Is that what you want? To go after Aegis and fail?"

The explanation cooled Greyson's ire. Now he felt foolish. "I don't."

Olin's pockmarked features relaxed. "Same here. Which means we need to let Aegis and his group get complacent, lazy even." His smile became fatherly. "All the while, you're studying their moves, their habits, their connections. Let them forget about you. And when they are least expecting it, you will break them and be the sword of your namesake to lop their heads off."

Greyson had to laugh at that.

Behind him, Connie nodded in agreement. "He's got a point, Hirsch."

Olin studied her as if she'd made a dumb statement. "Of course I do. Why else would I be running a global conglomerate?" He winked.

Greyson couldn't dispute those facts. And against a hero lauded as the next Titan, power wouldn't be enough. "Alright, Steve," he acquiesced. "We'll play this your way. For now."

The bunker entrance slid open. Asher Martin entered in a designer suit with a roguish smile, like he owned the place. "Greyson! Your work tonight was sublime."

Greyson whipped around. In that moment, Erika's words filled his thoughts and why they held such familiarity. "You..." The concrete room suddenly felt very crowded.

Asher walked up, hands outstretched, too drunk on victory to read the room. "I had my doubts, but you came—AGGH."

He got launched back toward the wall on Greyson's right. The air rushed out of him as he slammed hard against concrete, limbs splayed like a starfish.

Connie leaped off the couch. "Greyson!"

"Hirsch, what are you doing?" Olin barked onscreen, outraged.

Dark fury eddied around Greyson's insides when he looked at Asher. "Tonight almost went south," he explained. "Because someone leaked my identity to Erika Skye."

The blood drained from Olin's face.

Connie eyed Asher. "Asher?"

Asher squirmed and struggled but couldn't free himself. "Why would I do that, you psycho?"

Greyson shrugged, the only person in this situation remaining calm. "Jealousy. Aggrievement. So many different insecurities."

Olin's squinted eyes darted to his subordinate. "Asher?"

Asher was fuming. "He's lying!"

Greyson went further. "Erika called me a fraud with powers—only one other person used those words. And I'm staring at him." He increased the wall's gravity, Asher's bones creaking under the strain.

After six seconds of increasing pressure, Asher cried uncle. "Okay, okay!" he wailed, and Greyson eased up. "Your mistakes almost derailed this project. I needed to protect Paxton-Brandt." He looked to the viewscreen beseechingly. "Mr. Olin, you have to understand that."

Greyson couldn't let Asher live. By Connie's expression, what she wanted was evident. But Asher was a Paxton-Brandt employee. The go-ahead could only come from one man. "How are we playing this, Steve?"

Olin adjusted his collar with a stony mask that revealed nothing. "I'll send a cleaner when you're finished."

Asher looked close to a heart attack. "Mr. Olin! Give me another chance."

The flatscreen went dark.

Greyson guffawed. "The same chance you gave me?" Many ways he could end Asher came to mind. Colorful and gruesome ways. Only one avenue resonated. He turned to Connie. "This man insulted you in front of me."

"I apologized!" Asher blurted out.

Connie tilted her head sideways, smiling wickedly. "I didn't accept."

Greyson waved her forward. "He's all yours."

Connie planted a firm kiss on his lips. "You complete me." She turned and reached out, passing intangible fingers through Asher's face.

Greyson didn't turn when the executive screamed, Connie going partially solid with her hand wrist-deep.

Just as quickly, she went intangible and yanked her hand back out.

Greyson negated the altered gravity, and Asher slid to the floor, eyes bloodshot, ears and nose leaking blood. He marveled at his amazing wife. *God, I love this woman.*

CHAPTER 45

"No fucking way!" AJ exclaimed on the living room couch.

"Angelo!" Mom barked from the kitchen. "Language!"

AJ scrunched his face. "Bogie swears a lot."

Hugo, seated with him and Simon, jabbed his brother in the ribs.

Mom responded with a reproachful side-eye that dared her sons to talk back.

AJ shrank away. "Sorry." He refocused on Hugo. "No frigging way."

"Yeah frigging way." Hugo yawned. Two days of clean up in Atascadero was exhausting. "The thefts were an inside job." He'd heard from Dawson last night. On TV, that charmless bag of farts, Senator Huntley, was on a talk show berating supers for the Atascadero attack. Added with news about the Forces of Nature causing the recent disasters, the Paragons hadn't grabbed as many headlines.

"How was it an inside job?" Simon asked.

Hugo recited what he'd heard. "Salto Institute owns nine labs across America. But employees from each lab need clearance to access physical stuff from other labs."

AJ scratched the back of his neck. "Like the Tiamat corpse?"

Hugo nodded. "Nina Smarts was one of few Salto employees with access to all labs. Salto's NYC branch went rogue, wanting to profit off designer kaiju. So they set up a black market auction to raise funds."

Simon looked as shellshocked as Hugo had felt. "What about Villains-For-Hire?"

"Hired to kill Dr. Smarts and rob Salto Institute's other labs," Hugo said, "using disasters to distract."

Simon and AJ were speechless. "Good lord," Mom murmured from the kitchen.

"The Myriad that got arrested went braindead within an hour." Hugo bristled. "She was a duplicate."

Simon went wide-eyed. "Again?"

Hugo furrowed his brow in frustration. "The real Myriad is still out there. She's a clever one."

Mom emerged from the kitchen in a blouse and slacks, frizzy curls styled in a low bun. She was starting her new position today. "Max? Angelo? Ready to go?"

AJ stood unhurriedly. Max emerged from the guestroom in a t-shirt, jeans, and her favorite denim coat. "Born ready." All San Luis Obispo County schools were closed the rest of the week while the district conducted seismic testing. Mom was dropping AJ off at Dallas Dunleavy's house and Max at Danger Room for a morning shift. Max was spending more time with Becky Knox to keep tabs on her for Hugo.

She looked at Hugo. "Patrol tonight?"

Hugo stood and grinned back. "You, me, and Ballistic."

Max clapped. "This superhero stuff is *fun*." Her mirth dimmed. "But I'll need to visit New Mexico in a few weeks and check on my family."

Hugo wasn't surprised to hear this. "When you go, the Paragons follow."

Max flinched from the offer, as if accepting showed weakness. "Bogie, you don't have to—"

Hugo waved off the protest. "Teamwork makes the team work." He held out a fist. "Paragons for life."

Max burst out laughing and fist-bumped him. "That's not a thing."

"I'm making it a thing," Hugo quipped. He wished his mother good luck before she left with AJ and Max.

He sat beside Simon. "So…" He put on a tight-lipped smile, tapping his foot. "Thanks for being there."

Simon folded his arms petulantly. "Glad you think I'm useful." His resentment was unmistakable.

Hugo opened his mouth to protest, only for a collage of recent incidents to skip through his brain. And his defense collapsed. "Yeah," he acquiesced. "I haven't been a great friend."

The admission appeared to surprise Simon, and he relaxed his posture. "I don't have superpowers or armor. But I don't deserve to get overlooked for being a normie or whatever."

Hugo winced. "I'm sorry I made you feel that. Things have been crazy, but that's no excuse," he said. "You've been my ride-or-die for years. That will never change."

Simon appeared satisfied by the apology. "What about J-Tom?" He nodded upstairs.

Hugo pursed his lips. She was currently asleep in his bedroom. They'd helped clean up Atascadero for two days, returning here each night. Lust kept overwhelming Hugo's fatigue. And J-Tom was always a willing bedwarmer. It happened many times last night...and this morning. Then there were the long, flowing conversations about anything and everything. Hugo could talk to J-Tom for hours and never get bored.

He leaned forward, sizzling pleasure dwarfing his guilt over Jodie. "It's nice, having someone in both sides of my life."

"And your bed," Simon snarked.

Hugo scowled at him. "That should probably stop now that we're teammates. And I want things to work with Jodie." Yet, Jodie hadn't answered his romantic gesture. And Hugo was still pondering how to wean off J-Tom's comforts without hurting her feelings. Drama. "Despite Jen's assets—"

Simon snort-laughed.

"Shaddup," Hugo snapped. "Despite that, you're fam." He held Simon's gaze. "I'll do better, I promise."

That reached Simon. "Thanks." He cleared his throat, and the tension. "You talk to G-Mama yet?"

"She's not calling or texting me back." Hugo feared that their friendship would never recover.

Simon's reaction was sympathetic. "I'll see what I can do."

With all the chaos these last few days, Hugo had overlooked another dilemma. "Another thing. And I'm telling you first." He lowered his voice. "Briseis knows I'm Aegis."

Simon stared back for a long moment, teetering between disbelief and anger. "You *told* her?"

"No!" Hugo denied. "She already knew." As calm as he sounded, his terror from earlier reignited. Who knew how long Brie had known or who she might've told? Hugo felt cold all over. "She handed me my fucking costume that was supposed to be in my gear stash site, right before the Atascadero fight."

Simon sank into his seat. "Jesus, Joseph, and Mary. How?"

Hugo slumped back with him. "Dunno." *Brie knows my secret.* He still hadn't digested this scary truth.

Simon dropped his arms, dawning horror on his face. "What are you going to do?"

Hugo had considered that. "I'm meeting Brie tomorrow morning to get answers and make sure she keeps quiet." And he had to make sure she kept quiet...unless she hadn't. Jesus.

Hugo rubbed his temples, filing that away in light of other priorities. "But today, I'm meeting Ms. Ortiz." Hopefully, they could settle their issues for good.

Simon threw his head back and laughed. "Your life is like a Korean TV drama, with superpowers."

Hugo doubled over, howling. "There are worse problems to have!" he managed between laughs.

After Simon left and breakfast in bed with J-Tom, Hugo showered before heading to Ms. Ortiz's house.

She greeted him at the door, wearing one of her ridiculous shapeless caftans, blondish hair in a long braid over her left shoulder. Strangely, he'd missed seeing her airy-fairy fashion.

"Hey, Hugo." She gave him a big hug, which he readily returned. Inside, energy crystals, rock formation photos, and esoteric paintings adorned the walls. One would never guess this was Lady Liberty's abode.

Zelda bounced up, bearhugging Hugo's waist fiercely. Clearly, she'd inherited Titan's strength. "Hey!"

Hugo chuckled and patted her back. "Hi, ZiZi."

Zelda then raced upstairs and out of sight. Her attitude had changed since Hugo had learned they were siblings. Almost like a cloud over her had cleared.

Ms. Ortiz gestured to her kitchen at the rear of the house. "Want anything?"

"I'm good." Hugo plopped down on a lounge chair. "Any word on Spencer and her dad?"

Ms. Ortiz's dismayed look spoke volumes as she sat beside him. "My contacts said that Ezra's stashed somewhere in San Miguel." Her face darkened. "Spencer's living with Steve Olin, Paxton-Brandt's CEO."

"So she's untouchable." Hugo swore. Now he couldn't do a damn thing to stop Spencer.

"I'm monitoring your house and your family," Ms. Ortiz guaranteed. "And I will find Ezra. I owe him."

Hugo preferred better news. But Lady Liberty's backing eased his concerns. "Thanks," he said wearily.

Ms. Ortiz brightened when changing topics. "You and your Paragons did so well in Atascadero."

Hugo waved off the praise. "Couldn't have done it without your mentorship," he deflected, and a lump formed in his throat. How asshole-ish must he have been. "I'm sorry if I came across ungrateful."

Ms. Ortiz shook her head, her thick braid swaying side to side. "I'm the one needing to apologize. I am so sorry for breaking that trust." She placed a hand over her heart, growing rather emotional. "I wanted to tell you about Titan after I returned from my trials."

Hugo looked down, struck anew by the dizzying weight of being Titan's son. "I appreciate that." He faced her. "Cuz I need your help. Apparently, I'm leading a team."

Ms. Ortiz smirked. "I thought teams weren't your thing," she teased, toying with her braid.

Hugo rolled his eyes. "It kinda happened once I started training my friend Jennifer." Thinking of J-Tom and how well she took to being a hero made him smile. "Almost like everything fell into place." *Coincidence or collusion?* he pondered, no longer smiling.

"I'm glad you gave Polymer a chance." Ms. Ortiz looked haunted. "He got bullied a lot on the Warguard." Her eyes refocused, whatever pain she'd let slip gone. "Teaming up will be good for you both."

Hugo might have felt the same, if leading his own team wasn't so scary. "I don't know what I'm doing," he admitted. "We got lucky in Atascadero." He mulled aloud his team's deficits. "Polymer, Ballistic, and I got field experience. J-Tom's still learning. But Max and Cherry have no formal training."

"Hugo…" Ms. Ortiz searched his face with doting eyes. "Are you asking for my help?"

He forced the words over this deep resistance within. "If you're able."

Her smile was like sunlight parting a cloud-filled sky. "I can whip you Paragons into a well-oiled team."

Hugo couldn't agree without a guarantee. "Promise that there will be no secrets about me."

Ms. Ortiz nodded before he'd even finished. "Deal." She studied him with maternal affection just like before. "Do you have any questions about your…about Titan?"

Hugo had plenty, one of which he wasn't sure he wanted answers to. "Are Zelda and I the only ones?"

By Ms. Ortiz's deep frown, she understood the question. "No. But the executor of Titan's estate has kept their identities sealed. If they choose to reach out, I gave consent for them to contact me."

"They?" Hugo blinked and let his head loll. "Wow." Titan had other children. After sitting with this a few minutes, he lifted his head and asked another question. "When did he tell you about me?"

"A decade ago," Ms. Ortiz said. "It was his idea to live in Paso Robles so you and ZiZi grew up together."

Hugo studied the way she shifted in her seat. "There's more."

Never had Ms. Ortiz looked so unnerved. "You never asked why I didn't sponsor you to attend superhero academies like Steinholt or Gainsborough."

Hugo scratched his chin, considering this. "I wanted to protect my identity."

"An academy would've worked," Ms. Ortiz pressed. "Learning with peers from different instructors."

Hugo couldn't figure out where this was headed. "So why didn't you sponsor me?"

"Titan asked me not to."

Hugo sat bolt upright. "Huh?" Now he was completely confused.

Ms. Ortiz closed her eyes a long moment. "Titan planned on training you himself when you manifested."

The revelation threw Hugo back. "Holy shit," was all he could muster.

Ms. Ortiz ignored the outburst. "Before his passing, he'd recorded videos for his will. I'd put off watching until late October last year." Her eyes tightened. "His death was still too fresh." She exhaled. "But once Morningstar got arrested, I found the courage to watch. One of his requests was for me to train you if anything happened to him."

Hugo's brain sagged. "But you said nothing." He sat up, anger blooming in his chest. "You attacked me!"

Ms. Ortiz was unremorseful. "I didn't think you could control your powers. And for Titan's sake, I would've preferred you lived a normal life." Her lovely features softened. "But your role in catching Morningstar and Titan's request changed my mind."

Goosebumps prickled Hugo's forearms. A nagging buzz built at the back of his neck. "Why was he against me attending an academy?"

Ms. Ortiz took a long, deep breath before answering. "Titan said…because Saracen warned him."

CHAPTER 46

"This city has been through enough," Gerald Sweeney, mayor of Shenandoah, declared in front of city hall. The older man was lean yet carrying a slight paunch, with buzzcut grey hair. He looked exhausted. But passion burned in his eyes as he spoke. "From this day forward, superheroes are banned from Shenandoah." That drew an eruption from the audience and officials behind him, like Senator Huntley, cheering him on.

Greyson reclined in his chair with a smirk. Sweeney *had* to denounce the Thrillers and heroes in general. He'd been the team's biggest advocate, so the press conference and lawsuit against Seneca International were damage control.

Connie clicked off the TV. The pair were at Paxton-Brandt's DC offices, in a fancy conference room. Her satisfaction was palpable and infectious. "They'll be the first."

"And not the last." Greyson spun in his chair away from the blank screen to the laptops before him. "On to our investigations. The Paragons."

Paxton-Brandt had been helpful in gathering intel on Aegis and his Paragons. He and Connie skimmed through Aegis's, Ballistic's, and Polymer's profiles. "We need more on these three," Greyson stated. Onscreen were images of pint-sized Sakura, ferocious-looking Loba, and the armored Arclight.

Connie made a disapproving face. "Sakura's a toddler. But from footage of that fight, she's insanely powerful."

Greyson nodded, eyes locked on Loba. "They all are." He'd never seen a real werewolf before. Most animal shifters stuck to rural parts of the Southwest, the Dakotas, the Louisiana bayous, or the Northwest forests. "Maybe Paxton-Brandt can investigate the Alpha Pack and see if she's connected."

Connie swiped the screen to the silver-and-blue armored Paragon. "Then we have Arclight," she remarked, running fingers through her sleek hair.

"Definitely not a robot," Greyson decided. "The armor looks like Ramon Dempsey's work." If Arclight was half as powerful as Dynamo had been, then that hero would be a formidable enemy. "There's clearly a close relationship between him and Aegis."

Greyson waited for Connie to chime in, like she always did. Silence. He turned to see his wife zoned out on the screen.

"I don't think Arclight's a he." Connie leaned in and jabbed at the screen. "See how slender the armor is? And the way they move?" She straightened confidently. "Arclight's a she."

Greyson had no dispute with that. "Maybe she's Aegis's lover."

Connie rolled her eyes. "Not everything is about sex."

They laughed. But Greyson's mind kept returning to why Paxton-Brandt kept stalling on Aegis.

Connie slipped an arm around his shoulders. "What are you thinking?"

Greyson pecked her cheek. While he wasn't a conspiracy theorist, this issue needed voicing. "Paxton-Brandt has been very…passive against Aegis," he murmured, scanning the room. "After he attacked their properties."

Connie nodded in agreement. "You know what else is odd?" she whispered. "I think the doctor who betrayed them was working *with* Aegis."

That blew Greyson's mind. "And might know Aegis's identity."

"Yeah..." Connie bit her lower lip suggestively, so cute when she pondered. "Why are they protecting one of their enemies from us?"

Greyson stroked her face with the back of one hand. "That's something I'd like to find out."

The door opened before Greyson could ponder further.

In walked Gwyneth Pierce with long strides. Olin's special assistant wore a tucked-in white blouse and wide-legged black pants, dark hair spilling down in lazy and liquid curls. "Good morning, Mr. and Mrs. Hirsch." Her smile warmed those cold grey eyes, giving her a more predatory appearance.

Greyson stood and shook Pierce's hand when she rounded the table. Connie did the same.

An odd rush of déjà vu filled Greyson's brain. He'd met with Gwyneth Pierce a handful of times. Today, maybe because of room lighting, her face jarred loose childhood memories—of The Vanguard. He shook the nostalgia off. "Ms. Pierce."

"I have news," Pierce announced. "Your actions in Shenandoah sparked quite a buzz." She tilted her head mischievously. "Mr. Olin was so impressed that he sent me here immediately."

Greyson didn't hide his displeasure. "A phone call would've worked."

Pierce continued. "We found excessive chatter on the dark web from certain elements of society." She arched an eyebrow pointedly.

Greyson had no answer, but Connie did. "The kind of elements not found on a periodic table?"

Pierce nodded. "From different parts of the country. Cincinnati. Tampa. Pittsburgh to name a few."

Recognition doused Greyson like cold water. Criminal organizations and supervillains.

"Weeks before," Pierce stated, spreading her arms wide, "most were sniffing for help with their superhero problems."

Greyson made a face. "Villains-for-Hire is a terrible name."

Pierce ignored him. "But now, most of them are requesting you."

Greyson had to laugh. His life had become bonkers. "They want me as a consulting supervillain."

Pierce's smiled turned greedy. "Wait for Aegis, or hunt these heroes now."

Greyson ogled. Where he'd seen Pierce before smacked him in the face.

Connie gripped his arm, regaining his attention. "You made a splash," she noted. "Now we can control the ripple effect."

Greyson forced himself to focus on the present. Destroying more heroes and refining his craft was alluring. "I want more intel on Aegis's crew and how they operate," he requested. "Too many unknowns right now. What better way to build up my experience than to strike where anyone least expects?"

Pierce clapped eagerly. "A wise choice. Olin will be pleased," she purred.

Once she left, Greyson faced Connie. "I know why she looks familiar."

"Where?"

Cold dread crawled down his back. "Gwyneth Pierce is Severine."

Connie was skeptical. "*Vanguard's* Severine? She died fifteen years ago."

"I know," Greyson realized. "But hasn't aged a day and works at Paxton-Brandt." Paranoia reared up again. A dangerous game was afoot. And Greyson had no clue what roles he and Connie were playing.

CHAPTER 47

"Everyone say cheese!" the nurse in blue scrubs called out, holding the cellphone camera up.

"CHEESE!" over a dozen young patients cried around Hugo, who remained stone-faced while cellphone cameras flashed. Aegis wasn't a smiler. And if Aegis smiled on camera, then someone might recognize Hugo Malalou's smile. And too many fucking people knew his secret already.

Hugo spent two hours at Atascadero State Hospital this morning visiting patients and doing vocal imitations for kids. Giving hope to residents of this suburb whose lives had been so affected was a trivial expense.

"I have to leave," Hugo said in his Aegis cadence when the clock neared eight. "You kids be good and be brave." He hugged many patients and thanked the medical staff present before zooming off.

Hugo honestly could've stayed for hours. But he was meeting Briseis El-Saden later.

After returning home, then changing from his costume into a tee with striped sleeves and jeans, Hugo raced off to the meeting.

Countless fears gripped him on the way to the old Liberty High campus.

Had Brie told anyone?

What did she want?

Was this a trap? Analyzing a friend this way gutted him, but he had to.

Crisp and chilly air tickled his skin on this semi-cloudy morning. The campus stood frozen as he cased it twice, checking every corner.

The parking lot was empty. A few vagrants were squatting inside the buildings. Satisfied, Hugo zipped toward the track field.

Briseis sat hunched forward in the middle bleachers, staring off at nothing. Her attire looked fit for a pep rally; white tank top, black short-shorts under a crimson and white Paso High letterman's jacket with the school logo. Brie wore no makeup, not needing it. Wavy auburn sheets spilled just past her shoulders as she puffed on a cigarette with shaky fingers.

Hugo wrinkled his nose at the smell and braked.

So zoned out, Brie didn't notice until he was a few feet away. She yelped and leaped up.

"Hey." She hastily stubbed the cigarette on the bleachers, then tossed it.

Hugo kept his distance. "Hey."

"I don't smoke." Brie winced at her self-contradiction. "Except I'm super-stressed. Now I'm rambling…"

Inside, Hugo tensed. Outside, he remained nonchalant. "Why so stressed?"

"Didn't know if you'd ghost me," Brie confessed. Those pale-green eyes could melt a soul.

Hugo narrowed his eyes, suspicion lingering. "You take a rideshare?"

"Yes," she replied immediately.

"Anyone know you're here?"

"My dad thinks I'm at your house."

A quick listen confirmed one electronic device on her. Hugo held out a hand. "Phone."

Brie bristled. "You're *not* destroying my phone."

Hugo rolled his eyes. "This isn't a spy film." He beckoned with his hand.

Brie pouted yet relinquished her iPhone. "I haven't told anyone about you if that's what you're worried about," she stated as Hugo turned the device off.

Handing it back, he glanced around. Liberty High was too exposed. "C'mere."

She advanced promptly. Hugo lifted her up in his arms, earning a squeal. Brie weighed less than a feather.

He got a grip around her waist and legs. "Hang on." Once Brie hugged his neck, he took off.

She swiveled her head, hair lashing wildly. Viewing the vast cityscape below put her fear and wonder on full display.

When they reached the cloud layers, he flew toward the looming pinnacles of Bishop Peak.

Soon, they were descending.

Goosebumps prickled Brie's slender legs, countless emotions playing across her face.

Hugo locked eyes with her the whole way down to the forest.

The tension went out of Brie, gazing back at him.

Hugo had seen this look before, but never so blatant.

Remnants of passions he'd forgotten seared down his chest until his sneakers touched loamy earth.

Sensing how close their mouths were, he shook off the stupor. He placed Brie on the ground and backpedaled.

Yet her dreamy, hypnotic gaze lingered a little.

Regaining composure, Brie noticed the maze of towering pinewoods surrounding them. Wildlife called out during normal morning rituals. A cornucopia of smells tickled Hugo's nostrils. Wispy fog seeped across the ground as sunlight burned it away. From here, the sprawl of San Miguel beside the sparkling sea was visible.

"Holy shiite!" Briseis exclaimed. "We're on the Bishop Peak summit?"

Her enthusiasm didn't quell Hugo's suspicions. "Needed a safe place to talk," he replied, hands in his pockets. "No one's up here this early."

Brie's face revealed nothing, but her heart was racing. "I have so many questions."

Hugo glanced at the heavens. "So do I." This was actually happening. He felt emotionally naked and scared, leaning on a pinewood for support. "How did you know? About me?"

Brie's breath caught, revealing her anticipation for this moment. "How did I know that you were Aegis?" she asked. "Or how long have I known about your powers?"

Hugo's brain nearly shut down. This was worse than he'd imagined. He turned. "Both," he answered in a small voice.

Brie's expression radiated love. "I knew you were Aegis when I saw you on TV fighting the Elite." She paced in a circle, brushing away windblown tresses. "I learned you were a super at Fall Fling."

Hugo leaned back on the tree, or else his legs would've given out. "You've known for a *year*?" His disbelief echoed throughout the forest.

Brie stopped pacing and faced him. "Yeah. It kinda broke my brain." The sun was doing some crazy stuff to her eyes, giving the pale green color an eerie luster. "Did you manifest after freshmen year?"

Hugo forced himself to focus as nightmare scenarios filled his brain. "A few days after."

Brie half-smiled as if deducing something. "You never left town that summer."

Hugo nodded faintly. "Spent the summer mastering my powers." This conversation was surreal. "You told no one?"

"No." Brie looked offended. "Why would I?"

"Things between us were ugly last year." Hugo couldn't avoid rehashing their past rift.

Brie hugged herself. "There were dark moments, when my life was a slow-moving train wreck. I wanted to tell everyone just to hurt you." Her stare was penetrating. "But something in me couldn't." She blinked. "Even when I hated you, I...still cared."

Heat cracked through Hugo's icy suspicion. "You almost said something before the library bombing."

Brie grimaced, clearly not proud of that memory. "I wanted you to confess. I couldn't wrap my head around what I saw at Fall Fling or if you were still the Hugo I knew."

Hugo zeroed in on her words. "What did you see at Fall Fling?"

"Our fight *destroyed* me." By her faraway stare, she was clearly reliving that night. "I ran into the bathroom and bawled my eyes out."

The immense guilt made breathing a challenge for Hugo.

"Then I heard a commotion and looked out the windows. I saw you." Brie's nostrils flared. "With that Asian punk princess you were dating."

"Presley." Hugo hadn't thought about her in ages, and didn't want to start.

"Yeah," Brie said. "You were consoling her with Baz, TJ, and DeDamien lying around you." She trembled again, hugging herself tighter. "Then you picked her up, jumped into the sky, and never came down."

Hugo wanted to kick himself for such sloppiness. "Oooh." Then he recalled his overwhelming panic that evening, barely hearing anything above his own heartbeat.

"Yeah." Brie nodded in agreement with whatever she saw on his face. "I was in shock. Being drunk didn't help. Next thing I know, I'm staring up at an EMT and J-Tom."

"Presley provoked Baz and them into attacking her." Hugo thought back on that night. The memories surfaced with crystal clarity. "I heard them from afar, thought they were beating her up. Almost killed them...which is what Presley wanted."

Brie searched his face. "What happened to her?"

Hugo opened his mouth to reply but then realized how he'd have to jump around to explain certain references and people. "Let me give you the full story, starting two summers ago."

For the next hour, Hugo walked with Brie through the mountain forest, filling her in on everything. Revealing Baz's beatdown and his pathetic suicide attempt evoked a Defcon Level 2 meltdown out of Brie. Hugo eventually calmed her and continued.

"Of COURSE, you told Simon," Brie whined when hearing who Hugo told first about his powers. Recovering mean girl or not, she remained petty as fuck.

"I'd thought you were just a speedster or flier," she explained after Hugo discussed the Paso High bombing. "Then the explosion happened, and I'm fading in and out. The last thing I remembered before waking up in the hospital...was you shoulder pressing the whole ceiling." Her smile was pure sunshine. "Between that and saving all those kids, I knew you were the Hugo I remembered." Other than those instances, Briseis said little throughout Hugo's storytelling. But he grew somewhat uncomfortable under her worshipful stare.

He didn't mention Titan being his father and only revealed J-Tom knowing his secret.

"I *knew* Jen knew!" Briseis looked relieved. "Either that or you two were fucking."

Hugo grimaced. "Well..."

Brie's jaw dropped. "Oh my GAWD!" She punctuated each word by smacking his arm, then recoiled in discomfort. "Another of my friends, why you...whoremonger!"

Hugo backed away. "I won't make excuses. But the whole Spencer drama crushed Jenny...and me." Familiar grief stabbed him. "We were there for each other, and just connected."

Brie reared up to angrily object, only to deflate. "I hate it, but I get it. But stop stringing Jodie along."

"I plan to." Hugo tensed for what he was about to divulge. "Another thing. Spencer's a super."

Brie justifiably facepalmed. "You're joking?"

"And…" Hugo steeled himself. "She's a legacy. December's daughter."

"*Vanguard's* December?" Brie went cross-eyed. "I swear I've stepped into an alternate universe."

Hugo waited a few minutes for her to recover. "I wanted to tell you in the summer."

Brie shied away from those words. "You don't have to say that."

"I mean it," Hugo pressed. There were few walls between them now. "My mom said not to since I couldn't control my powers yet."

Brie's smile turned curious. "How can you do normal stuff? Like…sex?"

Hugo laughed. "Lots of practice and self-control. Wait…" He sobered, recalling what started this. "How'd you find my gear stash?"

Brie smiled and glanced away. "You always come from that direction before lunch and first period," she said. "A week before the Atascadero quake, I walked over and found the storage unit but didn't enter."

Hugo thought back to the specifics of that day. "It rained. No wonder I missed your scent."

Brie stared at him blankly. "Scent… Oooh… Ewww!" She shuddered, then continued. "The day of the earthquake, I was meeting my counselor and heard a secretary say school maintenance got a call about rats in that unit. I ran over, searched for half an hour, found your suit." She massaged her right thigh. "And hurt my knee."

Hugo felt the stiffness bleed from his broad shoulders. He regretted ever doubting Brie's loyalty. "Thank you so much."

Brie lit up hearing that. "Anytime." She cleared her throat. "What happened with your robot duplicate?"

Hugo jerked back. Speaking with Brie about his double life was bizarre. "You said you only saw a blur."

"I lied," she retorted nonchalantly. "Didn't want anyone getting suspicious."

Hugo stared her up and down in amazement. She'd lied to police for him. Wow.

"That fucked me up." Brie looked up at him from under her eyelashes. "Kinda relapsed because of it."

"I noticed." Hugo vividly recalled Brie's glassy-eyed stupor in the days afterward.

"Oh." Brie hissed through clenched teeth and let her hands drop. "I'd had nightmares…since the Easy Breezy video came out and then after Black Wednesday." She nodded. "Was finally shaking them off when you got snatched at the carnival."

Hugo winced, innards twisting at the thought of hurting her again. "Sorry."

"After the Easy Breezy video." Brie's voice grew thick and wavery, her lower lip quivering. "I lost something. And I was…so sad." She fanned herself with both hands to dry the budding tears. "It made the bullying at school and online worse…. Even now, it still hurts so much sometimes I can't breathe."

Hugo knew where this led and cut the space between them in two strides. "You don't have to tell me."

"No, I have to—"

"No, you don't." Hugo looked into her eyes, taking her hands in his.

Brie stared back in bald-faced horror. "Baz."

"Yeah." Hugo drew her into his arms and cradled her flareup of grief.

Brie clung to him like a drowning woman. Hugo closed his eyes, surprised how much he'd missed this affection between them. Brie's body warmth and the thrum of her heart left him drunk and fuzzy. It wasn't until noticing the last of the fog burning away that he grasped how much time had passed. And by Brie's dopey smile, that hug was exactly what she'd needed.

"By the way," Hugo remarked when they reluctantly drew apart. "What's your problem with Aegis?"

Brie's grin turned cheeky. "Nothing."

"Then why don't you like him…me?"

"Aegis *is* my favorite, silly," Brie teased as if he should've known this. "But I can't go full Twihard over you. That might raise some questions."

Hugo burst out laughing. What had he done to deserve such great friends? "You're something else, Breezy."

INTERLUDE: SPENCER

The metallic ball whizzed past in a gleam of motion.

She blasted the target with a purple flash of ultraviolet energy. The sphere burst into tiny fragments.

Smiling, she wiped dribbling sweat from her forehead with the back of her hand. In black bicycle shorts and a sports bra, her hair up in a topknot, she stood ready for the next target.

A shiny blur flew up from the corner of her left eye. She whirled again, unleashing a UV blast from both hands. She undershot by an inch, the target floating higher.

She swore at the mistake and swept her UV blast upward in a scorching arc. The sphere got sliced and burnt to bits. Then she waited for another. That silvery sphere flew out from the ceiling of this sterile, steely training space. And she was ready to destroy that target as well.

Hatred gave her focus. Anger fueled her, even as her muscles were spent.

With each silvery sphere, she saw the faces of her enemies. Brie, her father, J-Tom, Hugo.

Spencer Michelman had worked on target practice for over an hour, testing her limits, pushing herself harder. And this had proceeded a hand-to-hand sparring session. This had become her life since Paxton-Brandt had freed her. She took this opportunity seriously.

After a scalding-hot shower, Spencer changed into a tank top and yoga pants, her long bob of black hair damp and lank down her upper back. She arrived on the third floor of her new home. This place was huge, sporting ultra-modern yet minimalist architecture. Exotic artworks from all across the globe decorated the walls, each with a story behind their purchase. She expected nothing less from Steve Olin, her current guardian. Living with a normal family was nice, but they still weren't *her* family.

She exited the elevator and headed past the glass walls between her and an open-air dining room. Usually, the Olin family ate breakfast here. Tonight,

Steve Olin stood in the center of an intimate gathering. Tallish and well-built with laughing blue eyes and whitish-gold hair, Olin looked like a CEO. The pricy suit was a costume, with no tie and his shirt collar open. By his jovial demeanor, Spencer never would've guessed that Olin was currently fighting to keep his job.

She slowed and did a double take at Olin's guests. "What the…hell?"

One guest was Noah Huntley. The US Senator had dominated the news of late, demanding restrictions on superhuman abilities and superhero identities to be public. Spencer knew many superheroes, so naturally she hated this stance. Most worrying was the growing support since the Forces of Nature's attack on San Miguel. By his skinny frame, bookish face, red curls, and kind hazel eyes, one would never guess this man's awfulness. Spencer gagged. Huntley made her skin crawl.

Also speaking with Olin was Rebecca Reyes, her red cocktail dress flattering that eye-popping figure. The news veteran's face looked somewhat waxy but that didn't diminish her beauty. Reyes's presence surprised Spencer, given her professional and personal relationship with OWE's Blur.

She couldn't place the handsome young man speaking with Olin and Huntley. But Spencer knew he was Brazilian, recognizing the complexion and features of her mother's people anywhere. Something about his carriage and designer suit revealed this was a man of importance.

Kai Bramble, the *Avngr* app founder, stood beside the dining table, with perfectly disheveled sandy hair and trimmed stubble. The lanky tech mogul's hoodie, frayed jeans, and "fuck you" flipflops, completed the Silicon Valley douchebro getup.

But Spencer's attention was drawn to the familiar face holding Bramble's attention.

Riva de León, longtime family friend, was in deep conversation with him while daintily holding a glass of red wine. The entrepreneur was glammed up with sun-kissed skin and glossy sheets of black hair. Riva's sparkly gold dress hugged her petite body, the *deeply* plunging neckline reaching her belt. No wonder Smith struggled to focus on her face.

Standing nearby was Lorna Zimmer, Riva's longtime friend and constant shadow. She cut a slim and dignified figure in her shimmering silver, one-shoulder gown with a deep side part to her pixie cut aquamarine hair. Lorna wasn't chatty or outgoing like Riva, usually sticking to the sidelines observing her business partner's interactions with those probing green eyes. Spencer had always felt somewhat creeped out in the woman's presence.

Riva usually gave a heads-up whenever she visited. Curbing the urge to grab Riva's attention, Spencer kept walking past the gathering.

She reached her bedroom, blandly taking in the surroundings. The Olins hadn't moved in all her clothes and furniture, but the large room had enough for now. She parked on her bed and began going through truckloads of homework. There was roughly two months to catch up on. But Spencer had always enjoyed academics.

Putting on her headphones with some music, she dove in headlong. Hours flew by like minutes before an insistent knock on the door reached through the music. Spencer looked up from her laptop, irritated. Was this Mr. Olin trying to play father figure again? But Spencer knew that would be rude. "Yeah?"

"May I enter?" The visitor outside wasn't Olin.

Spencer pulled off her headphones and popped to her feet, openly pleased. "Yeah. Come in."

The door opened to reveal Riva de León's face-eating smile. She slipped inside and closed the door behind her. Riva was shorter than Spencer without heels. But her charisma and that eye-popping figure dominated any room she entered.

Riva spread her arms. "C'mere, carina."

"Hi!" Spencer ran over and hugged Riva, the faint scent of alcohol tickling her nose. "Didn't know you were in town!"

"Last-minute trip…" Riva pulled back with a grim look. "Given the circumstances."

Spencer's enthusiasm dropped. "Yeah." Those "circumstances" surrounded her asshole father betraying Paxton-Brandt, and the company's woes. With Riva being a large investor, her direct involvement was understandable…and troubling. Spencer knew Paxton-Brandt was just one of many companies Riva had stakes in. But even before her mother had been jailed, this woman had been a surrogate mother since childhood.

Every so often, Riva let slip the side of which made her the successful entrepreneur she was today. The influence and generosity juxtaposed with ruthlessness.

Riva was Spencer's idol and spirit animal.

"So…" She steered her toward the bed, eyes alight with interest. "How are the Olins treating you?"

Spencer sat and gave a limp shrug. "I guess." She scanned the spacious bedroom indifferently. "It's not the penthouse, but I'll survive."

Riva seated herself beside Spencer, pushing stick-straight locks from her face. "Ask me anything."

Spencer blurted out her primary concern. "What's happening with my dad?" She hadn't seen him since Paxton-Brandt's rescue, didn't want to. She *hated* her father. Then Spencer thought of her sister, Daddy's favorite, and guilt trickled through. "I want him to suffer, but he's still my dad." She felt very exposed. "Losing him would destroy Rowan."

"And you." Riva watched her with affectionate eyes. "Your dad is still useful to Paxton-Brandt. And I've spent some of today making him more…agreeable."

Spencer recoiled. Riva and her father's business relationship had spanned two decades, starting before he'd retired from being a superhero. But these last couple years, Riva had made the lonely doctor her personal plaything. Spencer still didn't know how she felt about that. But if that kept her dad alive, she could accept the situationship.

Situationship… Spencer silently cursed Hugo Malalou's effect on her vocabulary.

Riva's laughter at her reaction was angelic yet eerie. "Your dad won't give us any more trouble."

Spencer changed topics as fast as possible. "What was that dinner with Senator Huntley and Kai Bramble? And who was that Brazilian guy?"

Riva glanced away impishly. "It was a meeting to discuss America's future," she intoned cryptically. "And that Brazilian guy is Rufio Braga, Brazil's vice president and its future."

By the curtness in that answer, Spencer expected no further explanation. "Sure," she remarked.

That touched on another side of Riva, this enigmatic mysteriousness wrapped in wisdom. The woman was barely north of forty years old yet dropped sage guidance like some ninety-year-old.

Riva brightened again and rubbed her hands eagerly. "Now I have questions. Steve said you'd make a great addition to Paxton-Brandt's new superhuman strike force." A questioning gaze crept into her face. "You used to scoff at your dad's previous career. Is following his footsteps what you really want?"

Spencer scowled, not at the question but her own reasons. Rowan had said she was too much like their supervillain mother to be a hero. Dad had suppressed her powers for years. The gross violation enraged her again like it'd happened yesterday. "I want to prove my family wrong."

"Is that why you're staying in San Miguel?" Riva queried, her Mexican accent slipping through.

Spencer gritted her teeth. "Oh. That." She'd figured that would come up, closing her laptop.

"Steve is as mystified as me," Riva continued, leaning closer to further inspect Spencer. "You could be at a European boarding school. Or attending Steinholt with Rowan."

Spencer made a disgusted noise. "I'm *not* going to school with those uppity super-twats."

Riva laughed again. "Or be privately tutored. Yet you're returning to Paso Robles High."

Spencer took a sudden interest in her lap. All kinds of emotions bubbled up that she didn't want to discuss. "I've got unfinished business."

"With Hugo and Jennifer?" Riva asked.

"Yes," Spencer hissed. She regretted telling Riva about them. "They betrayed me."

"I hoped you'd get your payback in Seattle."

Spencer gawked at Riva. "What?" She'd never mentioned Hugo being a super or J-Tom's delusions of superhero grandeur. Spencer had been extra careful when she'd snuck off to blindside Hugo in downtown a few weeks ago, even using one of her dad's silencer devices to blackout any nearby street cameras. Had she been caught? "How...?"

Riva cocked her head sideways. "Who do you think assigned you to Paxton-Brandt's earthquake recovery team on Mercer Island?"

Spencer couldn't stop staring at her. "You know who they are?"

Riva looked insulted. "I knew about Hugo months ago when you introduced us at that fundraiser for your school's new library. Your friend, Jen...call it a hunch." She tapped the side of her head. "Blessed with foresight, cursed with knowledge?"

Spencer leaned away, the implications leaving her ice-cold. "I…I…"

Riva cut her off by placing a warm hand on her shoulder. "Their identities stay between us…for now." Her reassuring smile morphed into a grim line. "So why are they still alive?"

The mercilessness in Riva's question paralyzed Spencer. "I couldn't go through with it. Jen's been my friend for years." A smile stretched across her face uninvited. "I loved being around her, soaking in her positivity." Her smile dropped with her mood. "Then Hugo turned her against me." The cocktail of emotions over Hugo fucking Malalou churned within.

Riva straightened in understanding. "The Malalou boy, again."

Spencer's thoughts drifted back to ninth grade. "I used to find that kid *repulsive*. Letting Brie treat him like trash yet coming back for more." She bristled. "Pathetic."

Her feelings changed dramatically after Hugo's growth spurt, which came with a spine. But last Halloween had changed everything when she'd learned that he was a super. "I tried seducing him to see if he might be useful to Paxton-Brandt." Spencer hunched her shoulders to curb the dizzying rush inside. "But he got under my skin…and I couldn't shake him."

Riva's gaze softened. "I remember," she said.

Recalling their good times made Spencer feel weak and vulnerable. She swayed, still desperate to be wrapped in the warmth of his hugs. "I felt more myself around him than anyone. He challenged me to not feel shame over my sexuality. I'd planned on telling him that I knew about him, then have him join Paxton-Brandt."

Riva frosted over. "On the Italy vacation that never happened?"

"Yep." Spencer began walling off those troublesome emotions.

"This is what happens when we fall in love. The object of your affection sometimes betrays you," Riva concluded. "But your plan for open hostilities won't end well…for anyone." Her gaze sharped. "Or Paxton-Brandt."

Spencer almost cursed in frustration. She'd had such nasty schemes planned for Hugo and J-Tom. "What should I do?" she complained. "Let them parade around like heroes?"

Riva grazed a finger across Spencer's cheek. "My plans to neutralize your friends was thwarted," she admitted with a touch of bother. "But I know how we can bring them to heel."

Spencer hadn't expected Riva's involvement. But the notion was encouraging. "I'd like that."

"Which brings me to what I really want to discuss." Riva stood, wringing her hands in unusual nervousness. "Paxton-Brandt's current situation has placed me in San Miguel for the foreseeable future."

Spencer perked up. "Great." Any length of time spent with Riva was a bonus. "How long?"

Riva tossed her sleek locks back. "For now, indefinitely. Even though you're staying with Steve Olin, I've known you since you were in diapers."

Spencer scowled. "Thanks for the reminder."

Riva grew serious. "How would you feel about staying with me? Either at my place in El Marquez or any of your father's homes around town."

For a long moment, Spencer couldn't speak or think. Riva de León, one of the wealthiest women in the world, asked to be her guardian. For once, someone in her life had chosen her.

"I'd..." Spencer paused to make sure she didn't get tongue-tied. "I'd love that."

The joy on Riva's face was like the sun parting through clouds. "I thought so."

Spencer rose from the bed and threw her arms around Riva's neck again. "Thank you."

The older woman hugged her back. "Of course, querida."

CHAPTER 48

Hugo never thought that he'd miss the sound of school bells. But stepping into Paso High's hallways today represented the normalcy he truly cherished.

He refused to become like Titan, whose life was a blur of battles, meetings, crisis aid, media events, public appearances, and one-night stands. Titan had no escape from being Titan.

In first period, Hugo's teacher announced a "Welcome Back" pep rally. Juniors and seniors had their rally during first period. Clearly the thought was that a "Paso High is awesome" speech with rah-rah cheerleading would wash away the terror of a super terrorist attack. Hugo was willing to be optimistic.

On the way from first period to the basketball gym, he weaved through herds of students to fall in beside Simon and Grace. He exchanged high-fives with his BFF. But Grace remained distant.

"Hey, G-Mama," Hugo greeted. "Been trying to reach you."

"Hugo…" Grace's tone was as unfriendly as her stare. "I'll be cordial for Simon's sake. But that's it."

That stung right in Hugo's chest. He hadn't expected outright rejection from her. A glance at Simon revealed matching surprise. "Grace. Can't we start over?"

"Not while you keep lying to my face." Grace quickened her pace to march ahead.

Hugo stared after her. The wound in his chest ached.

Simon gripped his shoulder, remorse in his eyes. "I'm going to fix this."

"No," Hugo begged off. Maybe some space would save their friendship. "I'll just back off."

"I'm not giving up," Simon persisted as they entered the gym. "By the way, I spoke with the newest member of our inner circle."

"Jesus." Hugo groaned. The last thing he needed was Simon and Brie feuding. "What did you say to her?"

Simon looked up innocently. "Just making sure that Brie knows her role," he said. "And keeps quiet."

"Just give Brie a chance," Hugo requested, climbing with Simon onto the bleachers to find seats. After he and Briseis had spoken, any serious concerns had vanished.

Simon wasn't swayed but said no more when they spotted Jordana and J-Tom near the upper rows.

"Hey, mami," Hugo greeted Jordana after saying hello to J-Tom. Simon parked beside him.

Jodie welcomed his arrival with a wet, sloppy kiss. "Papi." She caressed her finger along his warmed cheek. "You've been on a milk carton since the earthquake."

J-Tom stared ahead, a strange and stiff look on her face.

"Well..." Hugo missed her smile, her lips, her everything. "Been helping at shelters. Is your fam okay?"

"Eh." Jordana winced. "Big fight with the parentals about the SeaTac quake and who caused it." She shook her head in exasperation, ponytail swinging. "My mom wants outta San Miguel pronto."

Hugo's mood soured. *This shit again?* "Let me talk to them," Hugo decided, slipping his hands around Jodie. "I'm not letting you out of my sight yet."

She looked ready to refuse the assist, only to melt onto him. "Sure. I'm having no luck."

Just then, the crammed bleachers on both sides of the gym quieted. Principal Walker took the podium on the basketball court to give some speech about being "Paso Robles Strong," which wasn't a thing. Paso Robles had suffered minimal damage from the earthquake, much to Hugo's relief.

Then the football team, led by that bald maggot TJ Kim, charged out in Bearcats jerseys. The players took the mic, running around the gym like hyenas to hype Friday's game against Cayucos High, aka Cay-Useless, which Hugo would gladly skip. Afterward, the Songs cheerleaders performed an insanely sexy routine in their crimson-and-white uniforms. Every harmonized maneuver had Grace Misawa's fingerprints all over them, set against mid-2000s hip-hop.

Taylor von Stratton was front and center as Songs danced, channeling her inner Bad Bitch with each naughty spin, sashay, and hip gyration.

Hugo couldn't not stare, as did most boys in attendance. J-Tom was salivating. But Hugo's admiration ended at Taylor's dancing. Jordana was more than enough woman for him. *If she'll have me.*

After the pep rally ended, the upperclassmen headed back to first period. Hugo crossed paths with Brent, who'd given an update on his dating situation.

"I ended up not picking Marin or Karin," the basket ballplayer admitted dourly. "I didn't want to drive a wedge between them."

Hugo sighed, wishing he'd made the same choice. "You'll find the right one, Lefty. I promise."

While J-Tom and Simon were discussing riots in Shenandoah, Briseis skipped over to them. She wore minimal makeup with a tan leather jacket over a grey hoodie and jeans, big hoop earrings, hair up in a tight topknot.

"Hey, friends." Brie's gaze jumped from Hugo to Jordana. "Boy. Girl."

Jordana jabbed Brie's tummy, eyes alight. "Tell him about the thing."

"Ugh." Brie looked ready to stab Jodie. "Really?"

Hugo was lost. "What thing?"

Brie rolled her eyes ferociously. "I'm visiting Jodie at the Baywood Park store yesterday at the Five Cities Promenade. Some rep from their store was there." Her voice trailed off. She was embarrassed.

Jordana excitedly finished for her. "He wants Brie to model for Baywood Park!"

Brie reddened and shushed Jodie, glancing at students passing by as they entered a building.

Hugo smiled. "Awesome. You sure he's legit?"

Brie fished through her purse in frustration. "Here's his business card." She held up a typical stationery with the Baywood Park logo and contact info.

"DO IT, Breezy!" Jordana encouraged.

Brie stuffed the card into her pocket with such shame. "My life's getting on track," she said. "I don't wanna deal with the extra dumbfuckery around school."

Hugo watched Briseis shrink back. Before, she would've been bragging about this opportunity. "Do you want to model for Baywood Park?" he asked quietly.

Brie wouldn't meet his gaze. "Doesn't matter what I—"

"Briseis." Hugo searched her face, which always invited appreciation. "Do you want this?"

She stared down, nodding timidly.

Hugo let his smile broaden. "Then *fuck* what the haters think."

Brie looked upward with a captivating smile. That was the Brie he knew.

"Exactly!" Jodie glanced left, and her mood plummeted. "Speaking of haters…"

Hugo followed her glare several feet away to an intersection between corridors.

Brie paled. J-Tom flinched back. Simon murmured obscenities.

Baz Martinez cut a tall and striking figure with disheveled hair beside Natalie Rodriguez. He was hugging girl and guy friends, openly sad.

"Today's his last day," Hugo said. Tomorrow, Baz would leave for military academy.

Brie watched Baz mutedly. Conflicting emotions warred on her face.

"Good riddance," Simon grunted, earning smiles from Jordana.

J-Tom clutched Brie's shoulders from behind. "It's okay to miss him a little."

Brie shrugged off the comfort, annoyed. "I don't." Her resolve faded. "Maybe…"

Baz watched her with brief longing, then gave Hugo a subtle nod.

Hugo didn't respond. He was glad to close this chapter of his life.

Jordana's hand on his back snapped Hugo out of it. "You okay?"

Natalie abruptly punched Baz's arm to grab his attention.

He glared at her, annoyed. "What?" But Natalie's gobsmacked face prompted him to look where she was pointing. He went paler than milk, immediately gaping at Hugo. So did Natalie. Now many of Baz's congregation exclaimed a single name.

Hugo frowned. *No fucking way.* He strode closer for a better view, hearing the chitchat of a familiar voice cocooned by several girls laughing. His stomach roiled.

Simon called after him. J-Tom and Brie jogged to catch up. Hugo stood facing an alarmed Baz, wishing his senses were wrong. Then he looked.

Farther down this hallway, Spencer Michelman was surrounded by a gaggle of admirers. Her plaid skirt and white button-down top clung to her pleasing figure like skin, a blood-red tie hanging loose around her neck. She was freshly bronzed, sleek black hair at long bob length and slicked back. Sinfully pretty and in great spirits, she told her minions of some false trip to visit family in Rio de Janeiro.

Hugo's brain briefly turned to scrambled eggs. Spencer, back at Paso High. The prospect of his safe space becoming a warzone loomed above all else.

"Oh, good lord!" J-Tom exclaimed beside him. She and the others had caught up, now gawking.

"What the ever-loving fuck is she doing here?" Jordana demanded, hands on hips.

Brie looked terrified, given what she now knew. Simon's eyes bulged.

Baz turned to Hugo with a bitter beer face. "The real queen bitch is back."

At this point, Spencer noticed the commotion. She waved at Hugo and mouthed "Hello." Her mouth pulled into a sneer, dark eyes twinkling with pure malevolence.

From the corner of his eye, J-Tom made furious moves toward Spencer.

Hugo caught her arm. "Stay. PUT," he warned.

"Screw this!" Jodie beelined forward.

Hugo's heart stuttered. "Jordana!" he called out. But she kept walking.

Hugo swore, then eyed Baz. "Watch them." He powerwalked at normal speeds, hampered by crowds and the risk of exposure. He finally reached Jordana as she told Spencer off.

"You have some nerve showing your face here," she barked, head bobbing side to side. "What? You thought all would be forgiven after the shit you pulled?" Her Bronx accent grew thicker with her anger.

Most of Spencer's minions retreated from Jodie's wrath. A few more zealous types like Chloe Mendes and Kendall Caruso closed in to defend her.

Spencer waved them away, visibly tickled by Jordana's anger. "JoJo! Long time, no gossip."

Hugo blocked Jordana before she could respond. "Stop."

"But—"

"No." Hugo's answer was final. He spotted Raphael Turner trying to slink past the drama. But being a hefty six-foot-five made that impossible. "Get her outta here." He guided Jodie to his friend, to her dismay. Raphael silently steered Jodie away.

Hugo steeled his resolve before facing Spencer. But she was watching Jordana's departure blandly. "Jodie's so hot when she's angry. I see why she's your favorite." Spencer tilted her head, watching Hugo coldly. "Does she know Jenny's still your pet? Or is it Brie now?" She made a gagging face.

Hugo drew close until they were inches part, ignoring the growing stares and murmurs around them. None of these gossip-addicted teens realized how much danger they were in if Spencer lashed out.

So Hugo chose diplomacy. "What are you doing here?"

Spencer placed a hand on her chest in feigned surprise. "I go to school here, just like you."

"You know what I mean," Hugo growled quietly.

"Careful, Hugo." Spencer gave him a sidelong look, dark-blue eyes glittering. "You got so violent the last time we were alone together."

Hugo paused. The threat reminded him of her close ties with Principal Walker. He stepped back, barely lessening the thick, delicious tension between them. "Where's your dad?"

Spencer's eyes danced with amusement. "Ezra's getting what he deserves. Did you like my gifts?"

"The Instagram love letter?" Hugo bit back through gritted teeth, "or attacking me in Seattle?"

Spencer giggled softly, covering her mouth. "Fumigating your gear stash site."

Horror struck Hugo. "You tipped the school off," he breathed.

"Switch your gear stash regularly." Spencer wagged her finger in his face, then let it graze down his chest. "Rookie move, superhero."

Hugo pulled back from her reach, sickened. "Why are you doing this?"

Spencer's sneer became obnoxious. She closed the gap between them again. "Because it's fun."

Hugo glanced around nervously. Far behind him, he could hear Brie, Simon, and J-Tom's worried chatter. "Was it fun hurting J-Tom?"

"I'm just getting started." Spencer's stare was pitying. "Because I have so many plans for you and Jenny. When I said I'm gonna ruin your life, I wasn't joke... Oooh," She beamed at something behind Hugo, then looked to him again. "The way Brie's glaring? She knows about us."

Clenching both fists, he watched Spencer with deep vitriol. "Touch any of my friends, and you'll see plenty of me," Hugo promised menacingly. Whatever the price, he'd never let Spencer harm them.

She slid closer, standing just above his nipples, her stare venomous. "Then what?"

For a moment, Hugo had no comeback. Against Spencer, empty threats were unacceptable. After some fast thinking, the ammo came to mind. "I know which supers you've kidnapped for Paxton-Brandt." He leaned close, his whisper slicing through the hallway chatter. "I even saw a kidnapping in progress."

Spencer just stared. "You're such a bastard," she cooed. "Then again, you've always been a bastard."

The allegation behind her taunt landed on Hugo's chest like an anvil. "What did you say?"

Spencer's smugness returned. "Daddy let it slip after too much bourbon one night." She turned to leave. "Seems we're at a standoff. Can't wait to see who blinks first."

Hugo was sick of this conflict. Sick of the games. Sick of the risk to his friends and family. "It's not too late, Spence," he remarked. "You don't have to be the villain."

Emotion spasmed across her face. Whatever that brief lapse of humanity was, it vanished once she faced him fully. "What don't you fucking understand?" she scolded. "This is who I've always been." With that, she marched off with her entourage, which included Raphael's girlfriend, Karlee.

She's a spy. Hugo processed this, ignoring nosy stares while walking back to his waiting friends.

"Details!" Jordana pressed.

"What happed?" Simon asked.

Raphael looked heartbroken. "I had no clue Karlee was Spencer's friend."

Hugo jabbed a thumb toward an empty classroom. Brie, Jordana, Raphael, J-Tom, and Simon followed.

"Here's the deal," Hugo declared after closing the door. His friends had gathered around him. "Stay away from Spencer. Don't ever provoke her. She's dangerous." The mandate drew general agreement.

Jordana scoffed. "I can handle that sunburnt trust fund baby."

"No, you really can't," J-Tom blurted out, to Jordana's surprise.

"She's right," Hugo added. "I don't know Spencer like you do. But you don't know her the way I do. *Not* sexually," he added when Jordana gagged. Simon coughed to hide laughter.

Hugo went on. "Last summer, she physically attacked Jenny….and me. Not sure how bad it would've gotten if her dad didn't show up."

That caused open shock from Raphael and Jodie.

"Okay." Jodie raised her hands in surrender, disturbed. "I'll back off."

Hugo felt a modicum of peace and kissed her forehead. "Get to class, okay?"

Once Raphael and Jordana left, Hugo closed the door behind them.

J-Tom almost said more, then noticed Briseis. "Uh, what's up, Brie?" She looked at Hugo pointedly.

"It's okay," Hugo assured. "Brie knows."

Simon seethed in silence.

J-Tom's nostrils flared. "You *told* her about me?"

Hugo facepalmed. "No."

Brie was confused. "Bogie said you knew…" Realization filled her face. "OMGeezies, you're Arclight?"

J-Tom turned pink.

"Guys," Hugo spoke over them. "With Spencer back, we can't drop our guard until we figure out how to contain her." And he had no clue how without mutual self-destruction.

When his friends agreed, he nodded with a confidence he didn't feel. "We'll talk later today. Keep safe."

CHAPTER 49

The dispatch call came at the end of today's uneventful patrol. Hugo soared through the clear skies, the sinking sun the color of a peach. J-Tom was at his side in her silvery Arclight armor, with miles of greater San Miguel's orderly suburbia spread out beneath them.

A notification pinged on his half-mask's eyescreen, and he tapped on the side of his hood to receive it. "Dispatch. What do ya got?"

"Aegis," an older male voice replied. "Brawl breaking out at Gather Natural Market in Atascadero. Two supers, both heavy hitters. They're starting to cause some damage."

Hugo gave J-Tom an exasperated look. Since the Atascadero quakes, Gather Natural had been slammed with clients stockpiling like the end times were near.

"Who's closest?" J-Tom asked in modulated tones.

"Loba and Ballistic are patrolling Paso Robles," the dispatch agent replied. "Polymer and Cherry Blossom are off this evening." Cherry and Polymer were training with Lady Liberty.

"Arclight and I got this." Hugo hung a sharp left. J-Tom quickly followed, a faint afterburn trailing her.

Within three minutes, Hugo reached the front of Gather Natural.

Throngs of customers outside the grocery clustered around the fight. One man, bald and built like a truck, had skin resembling gold. The other was short and skinny, probably shorter than Simon. But his body emitted angry red light as he lobbed energy bursts at his larger foe. The big man staggered and dropped to a knee but quickly shook it off.

"That's my toilet paper, asshole!" The energy thrower raised both hands for another attack.

"You grabbed the last package yesterday, you selfish bastard!" the bigger man called back, reaching for a Dodge Ram to lift off the ground.

J-Tom made a disgusted noise.

Hugo was thankful to see the fight hadn't escalated…yet. He landed on one side of the conflict like a ballplayer after a slam-dunk. J-Tom touched down on the other side, her boots making a loud clank.

The crowd murmured in awe, backing away.

The big man dropped the car with a snarl. He was HUGE, easily clearing seven feet.

The skinnier man immediately powered down. "Whoa!"

Hugo straightened, hands on hips. "You know who I am."

"You've heard of me too," J-Tom echoed.

"You really wanna do this?" Hugo inquired, hoping for common sense.

The energy thrower wisely raised his hands. "Nope."

The big man wasn't so wise. "Stay outta this, capes!" He moved to charge at Hugo.

J-Tom's hand snapped up and blasted before he took a step.

One brilliant flash later, the big man slid to a stop at Hugo's feet, out cold.

J-Tom lowered her gauntlet, the circle in her palm dimming in illumination.

Hugo snorted and eyed the crowd. "When he wakes up, tell him if we catch him misbehaving again, he goes to jail." General murmurs and head nods confirmed.

Hugo turned to the energy thrower. "Take your toilet paper and go." He pointed toward the parking lot.

The man snatched his prize and scrambled away. The crowd was jockeying for photos and selfies.

"Move along!" J-Tom ordered, her helmet's eyes bathing the lot in floodlights. "Nothing to see here!"

A little later, Hugo and J-Tom returned to the Clubhouse, switching out of their costumes.

Hugo emerged from the shower, slipping on a t-shirt and jeans. J-Tom stood in the command center, cutting a lean figure in mustard-yellow capri pants and one of the off-the-shoulder t-shirts Hugo liked. Her ginger mane fell in lank and damp over one shoulder. She leaned forward, the wide monitors absorbing her full attention. One screen featured a grid-like map of Southern Africa.

"An easy night, thank God," Hugo remarked, running fingers through his still-wet hair. These past couple weeks between the Seattle quake and the Forces of Nature had been insane. "I have to get some studying in so I don't flunk another test."

"Sure," J-Tom mumbled, glued to the screen. "I'm staying a bit longer."

Hugo frowned. The monitor's glow highlighted her blank expression. "Jenny," he stated more seriously. "Everything okay?"

J-Tom closed her eyes. "No, it's just..." she insisted in brittle tones, "I got scolded by my volleyball coach for missing so many practices."

He reached his friend quickly, drawing her upright. "You should quit."

J-Tom stared at him, shocked and a little angry. "Why would I do that?"

Hugo shrugged. "I was watching one of your volleyball practices two weeks ago before we went to train." He shook his head, the memory floating in his mind. "You looked ready to stab your own eyes out."

J-Tom's eyes widened. "Was it that obvious?" she asked quietly.

Hugo gave a knowing nod. "Your poker face needs work."

J-Tom sighed and leaned back on a desk. "I used to enjoy stuff like volleyball and student council." She stared down. "But after becoming a superhero, those things feel like...meaningless."

Hugo understood her struggle, still paying a price for his choices. "Eventually, you'll have to choose."

"But should I?" She sounded so raw and sad. "You heard about the Natural Born Thrillers? They wanted to save Shenandoah. Now they're in jail, and Shenandoah just banned all superheroes." She lifted her hands, letting them drop limply. "What if all the good we do ends up meaning nothing?"

Hugo saw the light fading in J-Tom's eyes, knowing she desperately needed hope. "Let me show you something." He leaned forward, typing into a database their systems were linked to.

J-Tom sniffled but said nothing as he worked.

After a quick search, Hugo's target appeared onscreen. He still felt such pride from this save. "Darren Boggs." The screen revealed a bald man, young and well-dressed, happy. "Four months ago, he tried to commit suicide."

J-Tom made a face. "*That's* your lead-in?"

"Shush." Hugo waved off the snark. "I talked him off the ledge this past summer. I check in every so often." Warmth swelled in Hugo's chest. "New job. New girlfriend. Better outlook. Darren is why we do the job. So people like him can live."

He turned to J-Tom. "When I visited Atascadero State Hospital, you should've seen the young patients' faces." He was still confounded by his own popularity. "Because of me?"

That coaxed some laughter out of J-Tom.

Hugo draped an arm around her shoulders. "Part of me dreaded doing stuff like this at the start of my career. Now, I love it." His grin made both of them giggle. "Not just because it makes me feel better. It makes them feel better." Hugo turned J-Tom about, drawing her close. "Hope is our north star in the darkness. Hope is what we give to San Miguel."

He lifted J-Tom's chin, holding her gaze. "Being a superhero has fixed me in ways I still can't really explain," he admitted. "This job can do that for you."

J-Tom blushed. "I hope so." The pair hugged for a long and lingering while.

Minutes passed before Hugo spoke again. "I plan to work things out with Jodie."

He felt J-Tom wilt. "I figured." The bitterness in her words was sharp. "Guess we can't be lonely together anymore."

Hugo pulled back, cupping her face. "You deserve someone worthy of you. Don't forget that."

J-Tom shivered in appreciation. "Uh-oh. I'm about to cry, aren't I?"

Hugo kissed her forehead, then her lips. And she wrapped her arms around him.

A few hours afterward, he sat beside Brie in a Spyder. She was in tennis warmups, dark auburn hair falling loose and wavy. Brie had just parked in the driveway of her mother's palatial home when Hugo had called.

Two minutes after, he was in her car.

"Mumu's using a possible dog adoption to buy my affections," Brie explained, adjusting her driving glasses. "Figure it'll make a mother-daughter dinner semi-bearable." She focused on Hugo. "What's up?"

Hugo hesitated, already knowing what to ask. But should it be asked? "I need help with Jenny."

Brie's reaction was reproachful. "To break up with her?"

"Already did," Hugo countered tersely. It had been harder than expected, and not without one last sendoff. "She needs a Simon."

"Only *you* need a Simon, Bogie," Brie mocked.

"Briseis," Hugo warned.

"Sorry!" She gritted her teeth, instantly remorseful. "Old habit."

Hugo gave her a disapproving onceover before continuing. "Being a superhero will be much tougher than she realizes. J-Tom's going to need a confidante besides me to lean on. Somebody not in our world. Who better than one of her best friends?"

Brie seemed uncertain. "I'd be honored…but are you sure?"

Hugo nodded. "Positive."

Brie's fears fell away. "Thanks for trusting me." Her pale-green eyes sparkled in gratitude.

Hugo winked. "Always." After giving Brie a parting hug, he exited the car and zoomed back home.

INTERLUDE: BRISEIS

Moonlight spilled through the windows over two teens in bed, hands and mouths exploring each other.

Jordana's gonna kill me, Briseis realized, on her back and blissed out. But why did this mistake feel so good? Baz was on top, his lips roving down to her neck. Then came his soft kisses, his boyish grin when he looked at her, and that knowing touch. "Maybe we shouldn't," she murmured.

"Why?" Baz grunted, nibbling on her collarbone. His hands glided along her thighs, knowing all the familiar places to make her weak.

"My dad..." Brie panted.

"Not who I wanna think about," Baz interjected.

Brie giggled and shoved Baz off to behold his face. "He might come...home soon. And another thing." Buzzing off his hair emphasized his hotness. "I don't want this to be a thing again," she stated seriously.

In the dark, Baz smiled. "I leave for the academy tomorrow. I want to spend tonight with you."

That touched her in ways she wasn't ready for. "Well...when you put it that way." She dragged Baz down and kissed him forcefully, to bury everything that hurt, while his fingers unfastened her belt.

"Smart choice, Breezy."

Brie's eyes popped open. *That's my voice.* "Huh?" She turned her head left and recoiled.

Several feet away, she saw herself leaning back against a wall, triumph on her lips. This other Brie was a throwback from sophomore year. Custom trench coat dress, sleek auburn hair crowned by a bejeweled headband, too much makeup, and cheekbones that could cut glass. Her pale-green eyes glittered with superiority. And this Brie was worryingly thin from the binging and purging she once did.

Am I losing it again? Baz was oblivious as usual, focused on fondling her senseless.

Brie felt such sorrow watching this younger version of herself. The beauty and confidence were on display, with no genuine happiness. She longed to give that secretly miserable girl a hug.

"We always looked good together, right?" Younger Brie pushed off the wall. "And Baz is so pretty."

Brie shook her head and combed through memories of dating Baz, finding a harsh reality. "I think I loved the idea of us together more than I loved him."

Younger Brie scoffed at such introspection. "So? He's great in bed."

Brie measured her younger self's advice. "Good point." She grabbed the hem of Baz's shirt to pull it off.

A chuckle came from deep in his throat. "Let me handle that." He drew back, to Brie's brief dismay, and tugged his shirt over his head. She jerked back on her elbows.

Instead of Baz's upper body, Brie saw Hugo Malalou's browned torso. He looked carved out of stone, his hair spiky and tousled. Hugo casually tossed away his shirt. "Hey, Brie." His voice was crumpled velvet.

Brie couldn't move past her shock. "What happened to Baz?"

Hugo smiled in that cheeky way of his. "Who cares?" He wasn't pretty like Baz. But something about his roughhewn features and that body was so ruggedly beautiful it gave Brie the spins...

Baz who? Hugo looked as delicious as in that weird dream the day Mumu had dumped dad last year. He'd appeared when Brie was trapped in a crowded and colorless school hallway, kissing away her fears. The vision had driven her to Hugo's house, where she'd found that Presley skankbag at the door...

Brie snapped out of her daze.

"YES!" younger Brie cheered.

Briseis's body yearned for Hugo as much as her heart. "But...what about Jodie?"

"Not important." Hugo's dark eyes burned. "This is."

Brie ran a hand up the length of Hugo's six-pack...no, eight-pack, and that beautiful chest. "God, I've missed you." She sounded throatier than expected. His rock-hard abs beneath her fingers got Brie all tingly between her legs. Hugo was who she wanted...had always wanted. Now he was here in her bed.

Then the image of Jordana burst through the thick mental haze.

Brie yanked her hand off as if Hugo's flesh was scalding. Guilt landed instantly. "We shouldn't."

Hugo looked wounded, which knifed through her. The last thing she wanted was to hurt him again.

Younger Brie bristled. "Why not?" She gestured at Hugo. "He's right *there!*"

Every cell in Brie's body ached. "I promised Jodie—" she began fuzzily.

"*Fuck* Jordana!" Younger Brie's green eyes flashed with terrifying wrath. "She mocked you for being friends with Hugo, then dates him behind your back. Just like Spencer." Those last words stung.

Brie looked away. She'd wrestled with those truths, even after rekindling her friendship with Jodie. Still…

No…fuck! Brie shook her head. "That doesn't mean I should do the same thing." Caring only about herself no matter what had hurt people. "Jodie's my best friend."

Younger Brie rolled her eyes petulantly. "And you've forgotten who you are," she sneered. "You're Briseis Nefertiti El-Saden. Everyone at Paso High wanted you as a friend or a fuck. And you loved it!" Her lips stretched into a cruel smile. "You loved every second of it."

Brie flinched. She could lie to friends and family, but not herself. The power she'd wielded over her classmates had been exhilarating…and toxic. "I remember how awful I was to so many people." Tears filled her eyes.

"Because they were beneath you," Younger Briseis threw back. Cruelty somehow made her more beautiful. "Stop shrinking yourself to please your so-called friends." She let her arms drop. That callousness melted away, revealing a soft and youthful desire. "If you wanted, Hugo could be yours. You saw how he looked at you on Bishop Peak…how he *still* looks at you."

Hugo was watching her with such love, like before. Her heart threatened to burst. *My Hugo…*

A cruel smile pulled at younger Brie's lips. "There you go. Welcome back."

Brie grabbed Hugo's throat, dragging him down. Her vision blurred around the edges. Their lips touched…

Jordana… She shoved Hugo away, backing up on her elbows. "I can't." Her resolve steadied with each breath. "I won't."

Younger Brie shook her head, disgusted. "You're a sad shell of your former self."

Brie pushed silky locks out of her face. Had she always been this nasty? "I see why people hated us."

Younger Brie sighed in exasperation. "Fine." She approached, climbing onto the bed behind a saddened Hugo. "Since you have no guts…" Younger Brie grabbed his neck from behind. He gagged.

Brie gasped. Abruptly, her younger self swelled into a gargantuan creature covered in the midnight-blue armor of a medieval knight. The beast peered down at Brie. Its glowing blood-red eyes pierced through flesh and bone, reaching right into her soul.

She flattened herself against her headboard. Never had she known such deep-rooted terror.

And Hugo, despite his amazing powers, was getting choked out by this nightmare warrior. "If you won't have him," the creature rumbled. "Then I will!" The beast drew its other arm back, then rammed forward. A big, curved blade exploded out of Hugo's chest, spraying blood on Brie.

Hugo arched his back, the life leaving his eyes as if switched off.

"HUGO!" Brie felt like she'd been speared through the heart—and woke up screaming.

She swiveled her head. No sign of the beast. No blood on her shirt.

That was Brie's second dream about that…demon. Only this time, its name lingered in her thoughts. *Knightmare*. Brie trembled as she sat up.

Grace Misawa lay curled up and dozing at the foot of the bed. Inky hair pooled around the dancer's head.

Her presence mystified Brie, until she remembered. They'd scheduled a study date since both shared the same Spanish teacher.

"Must've passed out." Brie slumped back on her bed, calming herself with deep breaths.

She pushed up on her elbows and stuck out her bare foot to prod Grace.

That was when Brie spied the shiny blade tip to her right.

Where did that come from? She reached out cautiously to finger the bloody tip, one tank top strap slipping off her shoulder.

Her throat tightened. This matched the blade that stabbed Hugo in her dream.

Shaken, Brie tossed it away. Now blood stained her fingers. "What the hell is wrong with me?"

CHAPTER 50

Hugo observed San Miguel's financial district from several miles above. Between those corridors of steel-and-glass high-rises, a large crowd cheered.

"Are we ready?" Hugo shouted above the wailing winds.

"Launched this morning," Annie Sherwood confirmed.

Hugo smiled in satisfaction. Today had been bittersweet. His charitable site, The Shield Foundation, launched to help patients afford life-saving surgeries. But his friend Reggie Palmer's window for a heart transplant had shrunk considerably. Hugo's hospital visits weren't enough.

"Are you sure about this?" Annie asked yet again. "This could backfire."

"Or not." Hugo's plan was nuts. So he had to do it. "Guess we'll find out."

Annie sighed in amused frustration. "Fine. Johnny will have choices for the Paragons logo ready by tomorrow."

"Cool," Hugo replied. "Loba's, Cherry Blossom's and Polymer's new costumes will be ready in three to four days." Ms. Ortiz had agreed on this during their long conversation a few days ago. But as the Paragons established themselves, he wouldn't allow them to become some Disneyfied product like the Extreme Teens.

Annie brightened upon hearing about the costumes. "Great. Those three are in serious need of fashion upgrades." She then switched topics. "BTW, some people want to say hi."

"Hey, Hugo," a familiar voice greeted.

"Bonjour, mon ami," another woman added in French.

Hugo's heart sang. "Quinn! Therese! How are you?"

"Great," Quinn replied. "Therese is getting stir-crazy."

"Am not!" Therese jeered. "Quinn and I are finding plenty of adventures in Berlin."

Quinn made a rude noise. "Hopefully those adventures don't become a thing!"

"You soooo want it to become a thing," Therese teased.

Hugo chuckled. "You can always come back. San Miguel misses you."

"Depends on Ms. Bauer," Therese chimed in.

"Whatever," Quinn snarked.

Hugo loved how they sounded like an old married couple. "Love your *Q-Talk* podcast, Quinn."

"Thanks, Hugo," Quinn replied, noticeably flattered. "Annie says you're doing something reckless?"

Hugo rolled his eyes. "I'm gonna pick a fight. With Blur."

"Please…" Quinn implored. "Shut that pipsqueak up."

"Quinnie!" Annie gasped. Therese laughed uproariously in the background.

"Gladly!" Hugo ended the call smiling. The financial district was a sea of cheering humanity jam-packed within Sinsheimer Square.

Hugo zeroed in on a stage at the rear of Rockwell Financial Center with a massive billboard-like movie screen. Onstage, the Extreme Teens were in full force. Sunrider, Vendetta crouched and brooding, Cyberpunk, smoky-haired Starchylde, rock-skinned Roadblock. And last but not least, the speedster, Blur, in his costume tattooed by sponsors.

"Oh right." Hugo remembered this was an advanced screening of the Extreme Teens' new live-action film, *Extreme Justice*. All monies were being split between Seattle and Atascadero.

Before the film started, the Extreme Teens were indulging in spirited Q & A from VIP crowd members. Blur currently had the mic, ranting again about Aegis. "That Titan imitator saved Atascadero. But he needed help. Me?" The speedster pointed at himself. "I could've smoked the Forces of Nature easily."

"Why didn't you?" the young girl who'd asked the original question demanded.

Blur scowled. "Next question."

"Here goes nothing." Hugo plunged farther toward the massive gathering.

Within moments, several attendees pointed and marveled. Onstage, the Extreme Teens eventually noticed something was drawing attention from them.

Hugo slowed to a halt, hovering above ground like he stood on an invisible floor. The crowd erupted around him with an "AEGIS! AEGIS!" chant.

Hugo forced himself not to react at the insane cheers and women begging for Aegis to impregnate them. Wow. He locked eyes with a startled Blur.

By the time Hugo reached the stage and stepped onto it, Blur was barricaded off by four burly male bodyguards and his teammates.

Blur stepped forward from across the stage and waved his entourage away. "It's alright." Then he moved faster than comprehension.

A half-second later, Blur was in Hugo's face. The crowd ooooohed in scandalized anticipation.

Hugo never flinched, snatching a mic from an approaching Johnny Truelove. That excited the riled-up audience further.

Unlike his public debut, Hugo felt more relaxed in the spotlight. "Got something to say to me...boy?"

Thunderous cheers shook the gathering. Truelove was enraged. Cyberpunk and Roadblock exchanged angered stares. Sunrider was clutching her sides, howling. Starchylde turned to hide her delight.

Blur turned brick-red, until he suddenly relaxed. A smirk pulled at his lips. "You think you're the next big thing? Whatever." Blur pointed his finger in Hugo's face. "But acting like you're faster than me? Bullshit. I'm the world's fastest hero!"

The audience went crazy as Blur had fallen into Hugo's trap. "I never called myself faster than you. But that sounds like a challenge."

Blur glanced at Roadblock and Cyberpunk in smug amusement. "You don't have the balls to race me," the speedster retorted.

Hugo leaned in so they were eye to eye. "If you wanna race, then you *got* it!"

Now he could barely hear himself think. The crowd's reaction shook the surrounding buildings. Blur stopped smiling, no longer so confident.

Hugo raised a hand, and the crowd quieted. Jesus, that was awesome. "On one condition," he added. "If I win, all donations go to charities of my choosing. If you win, the donations go to your favored charities."

Blur looked up at Hugo as if he'd received the best birthday gift. "If I win? *When* I kick your ass, those coffers are coming to Big Daddy Quick, baby." He spread his arms, playing to the raucous crowd.

Hugo watched the speedster and shook his head. All that power wasted on a group of famewhores. "If you spent a fraction of this passion on being a hero," he remarked, "you'd be the greatest hero ever."

A cringing oooooooh rippled across the ocean of humanity beyond the stage as if a powerful punch had been struck. And it might as well have been.

Blur's cockiness vanished, leaving the expression of a young boy chastised by his betters. The rest of the Extreme Teens all got offended about the very true observation.

But Hugo had made his point. "My people will be in touch with yours." He tossed the mic to Johnny Truelove and flew off to the sounds of thousands chanting his name.

Now miles above the city, bathed in golden sun, Hugo banked left toward Paso Robles. Not a bad way to promote his charity.

Later in the day, Annie sent him stats from the overwhelming site and social media traffic to the Aegis Foundation. Donations were rolling in like an avalanche. Craziness. Annie's husband, Johnny Sherwood, would manage the day-to-day functions until a permanent site manager could be hired.

Hugo then received some alarming texts from Abbie Dunleavy.

AbbieD: FYI. Spencer wanted me to go public with our summer fling.

AbbieD: I said no and promised to deny it all if she ever said anything.

Hugo sucked in a horrified breath, gathering his thoughts before replying.

ME: Thank you.

AbbieD: I'm keeping my promise to AJ.

AbbieD: And you never slutshamed me like everyone else.

After a long patrol and then training with Lady Liberty and the other Paragons, Hugo changed into civilian clothes and headed to Jodie's house.

She looked sensuous in a gold trench coat-like top and matching belt, black pants, and heels, the J.Lo-style hoop earrings swinging as she sashayed. Her hair was up in a tight, sleek bun.

Once at downtown Paso Robles, they walked around holding hands. The streets were bustling with pedestrians enjoying Paso's many sights, sounds, and succulent tastes. But Hugo was more interested in Jodie as they discussed his meeting with her parents earlier tonight.

"Thanks for the stay of execution, Malalou." Jordana gazed up gratefully.

Hugo remembered how scared he'd been before talking with Jodie's parents about not leaving San Miguel before she finished at Paso High. The respectful yet fervent debate went how Hugo had wished.

"Like I said." He snuck in a kiss. God, Jodie smelled good. "I'm not ready to lose you yet."

"Yeah…" She flushed and turned her head, more out of shame. "What do you think of that Aegis vs Blur race? I mean, Aegis is crazy fast. But Blur's gonna smoke him. Brie felt the same way." Jordana wrinkled her nose. "She isn't a big Aegis fan."

Hugo snort-laughed. God bless Brie for maintaining the "I dislike Aegis" act. "I won't count Aegis out yet."

Jodie eyed him with a sexy smile. "Well, I wouldn't mind someone beating Blur so he'll shut up."

Hugo guffawed and draped an arm around her shoulders. He glanced at a billboard connected atop the clocktower broadcasting the evening news. Apparently, Jair Tentoria, President of Brazil, had died in a helicopter crash. How…sad. Hugo tore his eyes away, catching the time. 7:17 PM. He turned back to Jodie. "So we got an hour before the movie. Wanna get food?"

To his surprise, Jordana pulled away and stopped in front of him. There was a sudden shift in the energy between them. "There's something I need to get off my chest." She wrung her hands, heart thrumming fast. "And if I don't say it now, I might lose my nerve.

A growing dread crawled up Hugo's body. "Okay."

Jodie blew out a loud breath. "What happened with Spencer last summer hurt me. And I wasn't sure we could move forward."

Hugo's heart plummeted. But he kept calm. "I understand." He barely recognized his own voice.

Jodie shook her head. "No, you don't." She forced herself to meet his gaze, looking so stricken. "When you and I were working on us, I met someone from church. And we've been dating for weeks."

Memories of the Morro Bay Carnival filled Hugo. "The guy from the carnival."

Jodie gawked. "Damn, you *are* observant." She gave a puzzled smile. "Why didn't you say anything?"

Hugo kept his face blank while his heart cracked to pieces. "I'm in no position to get mad. And I figured you'd tell me if it's serious." He paused, studying Jordana's growing discomfort. "Which I guess it is."

She nodded with such guilt, as if she were in the wrong. "Things escalated so fast." Her voice wavered as the confession grew emotional. "He's sweet and attentive and wants to be my boyfriend. My parents LOVE him. He checks so many boxes it's like I created him at a build-a-boy shop."

Hugo swallowed hard. All he wanted in this moment was to run far, far away. Or just shut down emotionally. Somehow, he pushed down those selfish, cowardly urges and stayed present while Jodie spoke her truth. "Now you want to be with him?"

"I wasn't sure," Jodie admitted, fixated on the ground. "I wanted to talk about it after the carnival."

Hugo waited for her to put him out of his misery. "But?"

Jordana looked up at Hugo with dreamy eyes. "But...he's not you."

Hugo blinked, hearing but not processing. "Huh?"

A smile slashed Jodie's face. "The way you make me feel safe and loved when we're together. How you fought for me tonight. And you can unbraid hair." She took his large hands in her own. "I won't settle for anything less."

Waves of euphoria nearly knocked Hugo on his behind. *She chose me.* After everything he'd done to self-sabotage, Jordana had chosen him. There was no sweeter sensation.

Jodie pulled him closer, biting her lower lip. "You wanna be my boyfriend?"

"Hell yes," Hugo admitted before she even finished.

Jordana exhaled in relief, her shoulders sagging. "Good. As long as there's no one else."

"Not anymore," he confessed. No more Taylor. No more J-Tom.

"Same here. I love you." She stood on her tiptoes expectantly.

Hugo kissed her lovingly. Nourishing warmth spread throughout him. For a brief moment, he felt connected to everything. "I love you too," he said upon stepping back, hand over his thudding heart. "Jesus, you gave me a heart attack."

Jodie punched his arm. "You kinda deserved it." The couple kissed again, briefer but as passionate.

Hugo spotted SLO Grill Eats, one of many food trucks littering downtown Paso. His mouth watered. "This stand has some killer grilled cheese sandwiches." He eyed Jordana to gauge her interest.

She nodded eagerly. "Let's do it, papi."

Hugo eagerly approached the truck, which had a growing line. "What kind of bread do you want?" he asked over his shoulder.

No answer. Hugo turned back around. "Jodie?"

Jordana stood motionless, mouth open. Even more worrying, Hugo heard no heartbeat or breath.

Hugo reached her in one stride. "Jordana." Snapping his fingers in her face got no reaction. That was when he noticed the silence around him.

Bystanders were frozen in mid-stride, mid-conversation, living mannequins on sidewalks and intersections. Cars on the streets weren't moving.

Downtown Paso Robles halted, the freezeframe of a bustling city.

And Hugo was the only living person left. "What...the...hell?" he murmured slowly. Was this a supervillain attack? And why was he unaffected?

His growing panic got interrupted by the only other heartbeat for miles.

Hugo whirled around. A solitary figure slowly weaved through the frozen pedestrians, clapping. "You and Jordana confessing your love in realtime really pulled at the heartstrings."

When this new arrival stood about ten feet away, Hugo got a good look.

Travel-worn fatigues, obnoxious neck scarf, compact physique, shock of white hair, Asiatic features.

Hugo's throat felt constricted. "Saracen."

"Aegis." Saracen bowed melodramatically. "It's time you and I had a chat."

CHAPTER 51

Saracen's here. That thought sliced through Hugo's shock. Which meant Saracen had to be freezing downtown Paso Robles. Hugo clenched his fists, studying the pathway to knock out this bastard and not harm any citizens between them.

Saracen held up a finger in warning. "I'd reconsider that. Or else I'm gone and you'll get some awkward questions from Jordana."

He instinctively stepped in front of Jordana, hating feeling so helpless. "Let them go. Please…" He gestured to the frozen hostages surrounding them.

Saracen laughed, but not in a dastardly villain way. "Relax, Hugo." Walking to the grilled cheese food truck, he swiped the sandwich from a customer's hands. "They're now moving at one-trillionth of a second of our speed." He leaned back on the truck and began eating.

The wording shattered Hugo's theories of Saracen's powers. "You're a chronokinetic." The calm in his voice opposed his rising terror.

Saracen chomped on the sandwich. "I prefer time traveler."

Hugo's brain was close to imploding. "I thought chronokinetics didn't exist."

"You thought wrong." Saracen took another bite. "We're rare."

Hugo studied this odd little man with cool contempt. Saracen had a wiry build despite his stylishly mismatched attire. The best thing Hugo could do was get info to free Jodie and the people around him. "What do you want?"

Up close, Saracen's eyes appeared pitch-black. "A hot meal." He inhaled the rest of his sandwich and pushed off the truck. "Becky says you don't trust her."

Hugo bristled thinking about Becky. "Why should I trust your minion?"

Saracen wiped crumbs from his mouth. "Becky works for me." His humor dimmed. "But she's no minion." He brushed off his gloved hands. "I had her get your friend Max settled in San Miguel and send her to you."

"I knew that felt sketchy," Hugo exclaimed. Helping Max was too generous of Becky.

"Knox is a good, loyal person." Saracen's eyes narrowed. "And has tons of respect for you. Give her another chance."

Another incident came to Hugo's mind. "Did you send Cherry Blossom to Blackjack and Domino?"

Saracen's smile returned. "You're sharper than I expected." He raised, then dropped his hands. "I broke her out of prison…with help."

Hugo erased the distance between them in a heartbeat. "*You* helped Rainmaker?" The damage done by those escapees paraded through his mind. Hugo fought the urge to uppercut Saracen into orbit. "You let dangerous convicts loose on the public!"

Saracen never flinched or showed remorse. "That prison break would've happened a year later," he dismissed. "And it allowed me to free an orphan who'd been a lab rat most of her life."

The lies and manipulation were too much. But Hugo wanted—needed answers. "What about Jodie and Brie? You abducted them!" His anger soared. "And sent a robot to attack me!"

"I saved their lives," Saracen replied evenly.

"Bullshit!" Hugo seethed.

Saracen backtracked to put distance between them. "That night, your girlfriends would've been in a car accident while you were handling an apartment fire. One or both would've have died!"

That splashed water over Hugo's fury. He vaguely recalled a raging fire that night. Nothing else had mattered with Jordana and Briseis missing. Hugo calmed down and kept listening.

"That event changes you forever." Saracen shook his head of fluffy hair, sadly. "And not for the better. The Aegis robot was supposed to rescue them in your stead. But Polymer misconfigured the controls, causing its attack. So I had to involve myself." He adjusted his scarf.

Polymer again. Hugo frowned, still unsure about that choice. "Why him?"

Saracen shrugged as he meandered through the maze of human mannequins. "Polymer wanted your help in reviving The Vanguard." He looked over his shoulder, his expectant gaze beckoning Hugo forward. "In one future, you two would be teammates on the Young Vanguard. Just like you'd eventually teamed with Arclight."

Hugo went rigid. *"Jesus!* You got to J-Tom?"

"Indirectly," Saracen amended. "Decha Benjawan would've debuted as Arclight six months from now. You and he would partner up a year later." He smiled at something unseen. "But with so many shifts in the timeline, you needed Arclight as an ally now."

"So you created your own Arclight," Hugo said bitterly. Everywhere he turned, Saracen had tainted his career like slow poison. "One you can control."

"An Arclight for *you* to nurture and mold and groom into a hero." Saracen meandered through the motionless pedestrians. "Crashing two of Dynamo's training androids in the Thomas's backyard was part of my long game. For three years, I had Jen's 'Aunt' Stephanie Madden to foster her interest in robotics, even inspiring the Arclight codename."

"Madden," Hugo echoed. That last name felt too convenient.

Saracen clapped mockingly. "She goes professionally by her middle name, Helena. And she almost helped me expose the OSA's corruption."

"You let Paxton-Brandt kill her!" Hugo clutched his head as the consequences piled up. "J-Tom has no clue."

Saracen had the gall to look annoyed. "Only Quinn Bauer and Paxton-Brandt think Madden is dead. But she's alive in OSA custody."

Hugo recalled how devastating Helena's "death" had been for Quinn. "Why does the OSA still have her?"

"Before Madden worked at *SLOCO Daily*." Saracen treaded past Hugo. "She almost broke a story about America's failed regime change in Amarantha. OSA abducted Madden before it published. Then after torturing her for days to find the whistleblower, they mindwiped the detention and story from her memories." His expression softened. "I approached her years later to compile a bigger OSA exposé."

Hugo wasn't sure who disgusted him more, the OSA or Saracen. "When the going gets tough, Saracen gets going? And you're lecturing me on loyalty." He was over this coward. "Go *fuck* yourself!"

That rocked Saracen on his heels, but he recovered. "I protected her once, at great risk to the timeline." He circled Hugo with shark-like focus. "Saving her life again would've destroyed yours."

Hugo was lost. "What does that mean?"

Saracen smirked at his confusion. "Madden was jealous of Quinn Bauer's relationships in the superhero community. But after the bombing at your school, which Jen Thomas attends, Madden had impetus to investigate who helped Quinn solve Titan's murder." Saracen stopped in front of a riveted Hugo. "Thanks to Quinn's reimbursed lunch receipt the day of the bombing, Madden dug deeper until she learned all about you." He jabbed a finger at Hugo's chest. "Madden's piece would have exposed you, giving Baz's, TJ's, and DeDamien's families cause to press charges over Fall Fling. You would've gone to jail."

Horror flooded every inch of Hugo. One question came to mind: Did Quinn help her?

"Quinn knew nothing," Saracen said, as if reading his mind. "Nor would she betray you."

Fall Fling reared its ugly head again. Hugo had almost lost everything and didn't know it. "Oh my god."

"With the help of technology," Saracen went on, circling him again. "I erased you and the story from Helena's mind. Madden's capture was a setback. But she still plays a role in my plans."

Hugo shook off his stupor and faced Saracen again. The time traveler's obsession with him made no sense. "Why?" He grabbed Saracen's collar to hold him still. "What's this hard-on you got for me?"

The time traveler jerked from Hugo's grip, and not easily. "I've travelled as far into the future as the late twenty-third century. Earth goes through a lot of shit. Every probable future where humanity comes out on the other side or even thrives has one thing in common." He backed up, pointing at Hugo again. "You."

Hugo didn't—couldn't—believe such rubbish. "Me?"

Saracen spread his arms, baffled as well. "In any futures where you don't become a hero, your powers never manifest or you die prematurely." He paused at the choked reaction that last option got. "Humanity is doomed. Those hopeful futures where Aegis exists are more certain when you're part of the Paragons, Young Vanguard, or whatever. I could only position possible allies around you." Saracen gestured again at Hugo, his weathered face perturbed. "Joining a team had to be your choice, despite your stubbornness."

"Hey!" Hugo snapped. He was strong-willed.

"Jennifer Thomas was the most important piece." Saracen glanced at Jordana. "Training her opened you to being on a team."

Hugo was desperate to hear more. "But Titan. The Vanguard—"

"Remnants of a bygone generation," Saracen dismissed with a lazy handwave. "You inspire the next age of heroes who save this world. Titan understood that."

The last words Hugo's father had uttered to him in Alaska sprang up. *'This world's going to need you far more than it ever needed me.'* His throat tightened. "Is that why you told Titan to train me?"

Saracen's smile grew sad as he strolled ahead. "Had you attended Steinholt, in most futures, someone leaked your paternity to Titan's enemies." He turned sharply. "If that happens, they attack Steinholt, and you along with thirteen other students get slaughtered."

Hugo's legs gave out. He dropped to a crouch as the stock-still world swam. "I'm gonna be sick," he mumbled. So much of what Saracen revealed tied together like a cruel prank. Through his nausea, one question had gone unasked. "What happens in the future that's so terrible?"

Saracen chuckled without mirth. "As someone who grew up during the Sino Civil Wars, I thought I'd seen humanity's worst." Something on his face shifted. "Until five years ago, when I jumped to the end of the twenty-first century. Any supers who weren't killed or in hiding had been imprisoned. In most countries, superheroes had been outlawed." He spoke as if discussing some generic Hollywood film. "A coordinated attack on London and Washington DC by a superhuman terrorist ring in 2025 was the trigger. Titan or Lady Liberty training you prevented that future."

The cryptic tone spurred Hugo back to his feet. "What changed?"

"Instead of superhuman apartheid…" Saracen closed his eyes as if in pain, "a virus kills most natural-born supers by 2033. What follows is madness. America, Nigeria, Egypt, Saudi Arabia, Brazil, the French-Belgian Republic, and Southern China unite. They'll use surviving and manufactured supers as weapons to form a global dictatorship." He opened his eyes to reveal unmistakable fatigue. "My attempts to prevent this future keep getting overridden."

"By another time traveler?" Hugo realized he'd said "time traveler" unironically. *How. Is this. My life?*

"That's what I thought," Saracen said. "But as I studied what kept changing these last five years, I realized I've been battling a clairvoyant." He scanned his surroundings in helpless frustration. "Someone with enough power and resources to bend the future to their will."

The answer seemed logical to Hugo. "Then change the past."

Saracen's reaction was reproachful. "Too unpredictable. One of three things occur." He raised a finger. "Averting something like Martin Luther King's murder can cause worse events years later."

Hugo remembered how time travel dominated one season of the Battalion show. "A butterfly effect?"

Saracen nodded as if his lackwit student had finally caught on. "I know from personal experience. The SeaTac earthquake wasn't supposed to happen." He raised two fingers. "Two. Altering a past event can either delay or accelerate its occurrence. Titan was supposed to die in battle at least a decade later. But we both know why that changed."

Hugo clutched at his chest, struggling to breathe. Brie, Simon, Ms. Ortiz, J-Tom, and Max knew about his suicide attempt. No one knew that Titan sacrificed himself for Hugo. "And number three?"

Saracen watched him in silence for several moments. "Your change alters nothing." He gestured around him. "The present, however, is malleable until it has already happened."

Hugo blinked away the pain of never growing up with his biological father. But could he live up to Titan's expectations? "Who's this clairvoyant?"

Saracen shrugged. "Still looking. But from what every future consistently shows me, they chose the same agent of chaos." He gave the video billboard a solemn stare.

Hugo followed his gaze. Frozen onscreen was a man not large or well-built in body.

But his aura and featureless mask of mirror-like gold seized Hugo's attention. This was Damocles, a telekinetic or gravikinetic of terrifying power. Hugo gulped. "Is that who the clairvoyant is backing?"

"Sourdough."

Hugo almost jumped in the air hearing Jordana's voice. He spun to face his girlfriend, who was beaming at him and moving.

Immediately, the noises of Paso Robles assaulted Hugo. Cars driving by, overlapping conversations, pitter-pattering footfalls. A man nearby barked at his missing grilled cheese.

Hugo took in everything with panicked sweeps. Paso Robles was alive and back in motion.

And Saracen was gone. Dammit.

It took a moment for Hugo to regain composure. "Say what now?"

Jordana's confusion didn't dim her smile. "I'll like my grilled cheese with sourdough bread."

Hugo blinked, forcing himself to recall the blissful ignorance before Saracen's arrival. "Right. Sandwiches."

Jordana's smile dropped. "You okay?" She moved closer. "You look spooked."

Hugo wished he could've been honest. But he promised Quinn to keep her cousin out of this world. "I'm fine, babe." Forcing the jitters out of his voice was harder than expected.

Jordana leaned back, worry dominating her face. "You're not having…second thoughts about us?"

"Nonono!" Hugo grasped Jodie's shoulders. "It's just been a long week at school." Another lingering kiss eased her discomfort. He felt her smiling against his lips

Jordana relaxed, her bubbly mood returning. "Totally. Let's get in line."

She took Hugo by the hand as he looked again at the billboard.

The newscast showed Damocles fighting three superheroes in Cedar Falls, Iowa, laughing maniacally.

Hugo shuddered and let Jordana pull him along.

INTERLUDE: SPENCER

Spencer had no use for Idaho besides skiing in Sun Valley and Napoleon Dynamite. Sadly, Riva's private jet had taken them nowhere near Sun Valley.

She sat beside the entrepreneur in an Escalade, driving through the fringes of a town called Goldwater. Through tinted windows, a rural emptiness stretched on between pockets of hollowed-out factories.

Spencer turned in disgust, fixing her long-sleeved black dress with its white collar and matching cuffs.

Riva wore faded jeans and a white chunky turtleneck, her dark hair spilling down in wild and fluid sheets. She looked more like a ski instructor than an entrepreneur. Riva was chatting away on her cell. "Congratulations, President Braga," she gushed. "I told you Operation Dom Pedro would succeed."

"How long are we staying in this nowhereville?" Spencer whined once Riva finished her call.

"Check your privilege, Spencer." Riva's tight, reproachful expression had Spencer regretting her petulance. "Goldwater has its charms. In a few years, it will be like Sun Valley minus the crowds."

Now Spencer was interested. While she loved Sun Valley, the crowds had become insufferable. "That sounds appealing," She took another dispassionate glance out the window. "We're here on business?"

Riva nodded. "Visiting one of my labs." They arrived at a rundown barn several miles outside of Goldwater. Once inside, Spencer was startled by a platform lowering the Escalade underground.

When the ride stopped, the sterile walls surrounding them had no similarity to anything in Goldwater. From there, she and Riva exited their car and headed for an elevator, taking them farther underground.

Several technicians and scientists in lab coats worked in chambers of this laboratory on high-tech consoles. Despite her success, Riva warmly greeted her staff by name. She engaged the facility director Jimmy Drake, a sturdy man with a pockmarked face, like an old friend. That impressed Spencer.

They finally entered a smaller room with steel-grey walls except one wall-length window, a viewing room. On the other side of the window, four lab technicians fussed over a woman lying on a rectangular slab. Wide black cloth wraps over her chest and lower extremities were the only coverings on her doughy figure. A thin needle connected to a robotic arm pierced her navel.

Spencer stared at the scene, fascinated. The test subject meant nothing to her. But an experiment she had the privilege to witness was starting. Spencer paused on the woman's face. Sharp and approachably attractive features haloed by a pool of curly golden hair.

Spencer *knew* her. "J-Tom's aunt?" Her mind whirled. "But she died—"

Riva raised a hand for silence, and Spencer meekly complied. "The OSA staged her death and blamed Paxton-Brandt as an excuse to axe their contract." She tossed back her hair. "Since then, the OSA is putting on a pretense that Helena Madden is on some Eat, Pray, Love walkabout."

Spencer gaped at Helena's chest rising and falling on the table. "That was some Jason Bourne shit."

Riva kept talking. "She's not the first disruptor the OSA has disappeared for opposing them."

Those words shivered through Spencer. And these were the good guys? "Paxton-Brandt doesn't know?"

Riva's pitiless smile disturbed Spencer further. "This lab is separate from them. Paxton-Brandt is part of my kingdom, querida." She returned her attention to the window. "The OSA has mostly used Madden to train telepathic agents. Altering, suppressing, and erasing memories. Implanting false memories." Riva gave a harsh laugh. "Her mind's probably scrambled eggs."

Spencer didn't want to know this. Part of why capturing supers had been easy was never seeing them get tested on. But that long needle lodged in Ms. Madden's belly made her queasy. Spencer felt rock-bottom awful wondering how bad the OSA had scrambled Madden's brain. *Is Hugo right about me?*

Riva seemed not to notice her internal struggle. She pressed a button on the wall beside the window. "Are we ready, Dr. Kashanian?"

"Yes, Ms. de León," one masked lab worker stated through the viewing room speakers. "Starting now."

Spencer watched as the lab workers left the room, leaving Madden alone on the slab. A low hum sprang from the testing room, deep and droning.

At first, nothing happened. The hum increased. Madden's back arched, tendons and muscles in her neck and arms standing out. The woman's closed eyes tightened, her teeth clenching in agony.

While Riva watched expressionlessly, Spencer grew more uncomfortable. Was this necessary? The hum intensified.

Madden's eyes popped open, burning bright red. Madden's scream didn't sound human as crimson energy poured out of her eyes, pounding the ceiling.

Spencer backtracked from the window. "Holy shit!"

The hum stopped. Helena slumped on the metal lab, eyes rolled back into her head. Lab workers scurried into the room to examine the body.

Spencer gaped at this woman whom she'd met several times.

Riva tapped the speaker console eagerly. "Did you get blood samples?"

"Yes," Dr. Kashanian answered. "Plus, we know the EM radiation and dose that triggers her transformations."

"Perfect. Clean Ms. Madden up and return her to her quarters. Then start testing." Riva turned from the window.

Then Spencer unloaded. "You turned Helena Madden into a super?"

The businesswoman's eyes gleamed under the room lights. "Not quite."

Spencer was lost. "I don't understand."

Riva steered her to the room exit. "Back in 2003, Ms. Madden was a war correspondent during the Iraq War," she began. "She and several American aid workers got kidnapped by al-Thawra, a more forward-thinking terrorist group. They brutally experimented on the captives to create Titan-like sleeper agents. Al-Thawra had planned to unleash them on the Middle East posing as American supersoldiers and destroy its global reputation."

The vast conspiracy left Spencer gobsmacked. "Since I'm just hearing of this, I guess al-Thawra failed?"

Riva steered them to a hallway with no people traffic. "The project got stopped when a joint US and British military unit led by Lieutenant Noah Huntley located and rescued the captives."

The name seized Spencer. "As in Senator Huntley?"

Riva nodded. "Six of the fourteen captives survived the experiments. Including Madden. She and Huntley grew close afterward until she left Iraq." She winked. "But that's a story for another time."

Spencer almost vomited thinking of Huntley having sexy times.

Riva continued. "Since the survivors all checked out as normal, the incident was forgotten until 2010."

Spencer hated not knowing things. "What happened in 2010?"

Riva stopped and faced her. "An al-Thawra operative activated three assets to kill Titan, which brought Lady Liberty out of retirement."

Spencer felt a heady rush of nostalgia. That had been Titan's, Geist's, and Lady Liberty's first time teaming up. "I remember…"

"The OSA tested one survivor." Riva stated. "When his programming was deactivated, his DNA changed to normal, no memory of his crimes. He died two days later."

Spencer sagged under the weight of these revelations. "Wild…"

"The OSA kept tabs on Madden," Riva went on. "Obsessed with finding what triggers this change."

"The OSA failed?" Spencer asked.

Riva grinned again. "Yes. But someone has activated Ms. Madden many times in the last three years. The traces of excessive thyroxine in her blood are hallmarks of someone who's endured metamorphosis."

Spencer's inner nerd made the sin easy to ignore. "Who activated her?"

Riva grew somber. "A disruptor the OSA is hunting." Her eyes glazed over with lust. "The secrets within Madden's blood could provide a new way of protecting this world, rendering superheroes obsolete."

"Obsolete." Spencer wasn't sure how she felt about that, being an ex-superhero daughter.

Riva noticed this. "Does this scare you?"

"A little," Spencer confessed. "Maybe that's good?" The questioning tone was accidental but honest.

Riva gave a light chuckle. "Change frightens people, until they see the benefits a new world offers."

Spencer considered what her family and former friends might think. The same people who'd called her irredeemable. *Riva's the only one who chose me.* "Whatever you're doing, I'm all the way in."

Riva looked genuinely proud. "As I predicted, Spencer."

EPILOGUE

Hugo treaded through the drab, iron-grey halls in full Aegis gear, following the stocky bald man in a black suit. He hadn't known of this OSA Waystation in Creston outside Paso Robles. Then again, Hugo had learned how much he didn't know about the world around him this past week.

The stocky agent stopped at an open door near the end of the corridor, gesturing for Hugo to enter.

Inside were all the tenets of an interrogation room. Bland grey walls, steel table, and a mirror-like one-way window with four agents on the other side.

Hugo's attention zeroed in on the featured attraction. Devon Strauss hopped off the table, wearing dark slacks and a tucked-in white blouse with rolled-up sleeves. With the shiny badge and holstered gun on her belt, Devon looked every inch the OSA agent.

"Hey, Devon," Hugo greeted in his rumbling Aegis voice as the door closed behind him.

She approached, her loose ponytail putting her delighted face on display. "Glad you reconsidered." They shook hands. "After Atascadero, the Paragons will need our support."

Hugo expected such overreach. "I haven't accepted." He produced a small jet-black square from his pocket. The other side of the one-way window erupted in protest.

Hugo glanced their way and smiled. The silencer had been a gift from Dr. Michelman. That should scramble any recording/listening devices around this room, except in his costume's bodycam.

Devon rolled her eyes tartly. "Is that necessary?"

Hugo ignored her, twisting the cube once like a Rubik to activate and placing it on the table. "This meeting isn't happening, remember?"

"Fine." Devon pulled out a chair from the table and sat heavily. "What assurances do you need?"

Hugo faced her, buoyed by having something this agency wanted. He drew back his hood and half-mask. "Is Helena Madden in OSA custody?"

Devon was stone-faced, but her eyes widened a fraction. "Where'd you hear that rumor?"

"Choose your next words carefully," Hugo warned. *Or I'm gone.*

Devon turned a mild pink, temperature spiking. "Madden's being held at one of our black sites," she admitted after seconds of unblinking silence.

Hugo felt a jolt down his spine. "Jesus!"

"Madden possessed *stolen* classified data," she stated, defiant. "Were we supposed to let her disclose that?"

"By illegally jailing a US citizen!" Hugo couldn't mask his contempt. The OSA was just like Paxton-Brandt.

Devon looked away, having the humility to be ashamed. "Helena had to 'die' for OSA management to break ties with Paxton-Brandt. And she has to stay dead until Paxton-Brandt is destroyed."

Hugo scowled, realizing the position she'd forced him into.

"I maneuvered Quinn far away from Paxton-Brandt for months, until Helena dragged her into their line of fire," Devon stated, smoldering with hate. "She would go kamikaze on them if she knew her mentor's alive."

The passionate pleas reached beyond friendship. Hugo wasn't expecting that. Nor was he expecting Saracen to be right. "I'll help with Paxton-Brandt on three conditions," Hugo announced. "One. Hand Ms. Madden over to me afterward unharmed."

Devon pursed her lips, considering this briefly. "Done. Number two?"

Hugo breathed deep. "I know Dr. Michelman was working for you. Paxton-Brandt captured him."

Devon seemed almost bored hearing this. "We know. And we're searching. What are you asking?"

Despite Hugo's issues with Michelman, there was still good in the former superhero. "When he's found, please go easy on him. Michelman went against Paxton-Brandt to protect his daughters."

Devon's frown deepened. "Being a good parent doesn't make someone a good person," she lectured. "It just gives a predator one more reason to kill."

The hypocrisy left Hugo breathless. But he calmed and stood firm. "Immunity for him is nonnegotiable."

Devon softened. "I'll run that up the food chain. And three?"

Here we go. This ranked highest. "Damocles." Hugo caught Devon's face shift when that name was uttered. "The villain who beat the Natural Born Thrillers?" Hugo stated. "I need help finding him."

Devon held his gaze and lifted her chin a little. "That's a new name to us. But it's just new paint over an old vehicle." She moved past Hugo. "Remember Hurricane's murder last year?"

That jostled dark memories loose from Hugo's sophomore year. "A student betrayed him." He snapped his fingers. "Greyson Hirsch." Quinn's *Washington Post* article on Hurricane's murder came to mind.

Devon winced. "We tried capturing Hirsch in Mexico months ago, with Paxton-Brandt as a go-between. Yeah, big mistake," she added upon Hugo's angered reaction. "He slaughtered our contractors and escaped." She stared at the ground in resignation.

Hugo studied her body language. "What else happened?"

Devon looked up, incensed. "A computer virus struck several agencies this summer, ours included. Once we recovered, Hirsch and Constance Ishibashi's government files now said Damocles had killed them."

That floored Hugo. Was Saracen's clairvoyant behind this? "What about families, friends, coworkers?"

Devon was shaking her head before he finished. "All brainwashed to believe the same story." Her confusion was barefaced. "Whoever orchestrated this coverup leaked this fake story to the news media, added Hurricane as one of Damocles's victims. Now Hirsch is back in the US, hunting superheroes."

Terror surged through Hugo's veins. Damocles wasn't just dangerous, but well-connected. Saracen was right. Scared as he was, two months shy of seventeen, Hugo couldn't hide from this threat. "When you find him—"

"We'll tell you." Devon smiled for the first time this meeting, highlighting her attractiveness.

"I want everything in writing," Hugo demanded.

Devon nodded understandingly. "Yessir."

Hugo pulled his hood and mask back on. "Later." Grabbing the silencer, he disabled it and walked out. He didn't realize how badly his hands were shaking until he lifted off from the waystation.

The yellow sun had risen high enough to burn off the morning haze. Hugo waited until he'd soared miles away before tapping his hood. "Get all that?"

"Yeah." Simon sounded spooked. "Holy shit."

"Right?!" Hugo's insides were ice-cold, yet his nerves felt fried. "Saracen was right about everything." He slowed to a hover above Morro Bay. The coastline cut a jagged, foaming divide between land and sea.

"Can you trust the OSA?"

"Hell naw," Hugo snapped. "We recorded them admitting to illegally holding a US citizen." Hugo had another feather in his cap. "We also have that OSA dirt Quinn sent to Clint."

"Us against the OSA," Simon sounded thrilled yet scared.

"They're a temporary ally," Hugo corrected. To defeat his enemies, this devil's bargain was necessary.

"Should we tell J-Tom about her aunt?" Simon asked.

"Not until the OSA hands Ms. Madden over," Hugo shot down. "And the other Paragons can't know either. We tell Lady Liberty…and Becky Knox." But with Saracen's words being true, he'd give Becky a chance to prove her loyalty. He watched his city. San Miguel and its suburbs were still waking up.

"I watched what Damocles did to the Natural Born Thrillers." Simon's voice shook. "He's scary as shit."

"So am I," Hugo said to mask his own fears. Another call flashed on his eyescreen. "See you at school."

Hugo switched over to answer the new call. "Hey, Annie!"

"We have a problem," Annie replied, panic in her voice. "Something big is about to drop. On you."

Hugo instantly braked in mid-air. "What happened…"

Then he heard a cacophony of reports on TVs, mobile devices, and car radios all across San Miguel discussing Aegis. Hugo froze in mid-air, barely hearing Annie above what the broadcasts were declaring.

Many sources have confirmed that Aegis is Titan's son.

Only one response came to Hugo's mind. "Oh shit!"

Hugo and Greyson will return in UNITED WE STAND, coming in late 2020

Read on for a special note from the author

AUTHOR NOTES

That's a wrap for another volume of the Pantheon Saga! Big thanks to Carlos, Emmy and Corine for making this story pretty and coherent. Shout out to Ron, David A, David J and Jason for your feedback!

This book was an interesting challenge. I'd resolved a number of plot threads in *Gods of Wrath* and Quinn no longer being a POV character closed off that view of the larger superhero community. That's why we expanded Hugo's world much more. Plus, it was a naturally fit to integrate characters like Annie Sherwood, Helena Madden and Devon Strauss into Hugo's life as he seeks to build his own support team. And making sure that Quinn still had a presence in this book, even from afar, was vital. By the way, what are your thoughts on that trifecta of Helena Madden twists?? The J-Tom/Helena connection as well as her still being alive came to me during the plotting of *Absolute Power*. We'll see more of that in the future. Along with that, are you interested in exploring what Quinn and Therese's adventures in Berlin are?

Now that Hugo is a publicly known hero, keeping him confined to San Miguel/Central California didn't make sense. And that includes being on a superhero team. It was the next natural progression for his journey. However, I wanted to show that his earlier resistance was to joining an existing team. There was a level of trust he wasn't willing to relinquish, but now that he is mostly surrounded with people he can trust, Hugo can embrace forming his own team. The name Paragons was a nod to Hugo's respect for the veterans that came before him. Granted, I was annoyed when the Arrowverse called their team Paragons, but I was like "fuck it" and used the name anyway. Expect to see more team action in Book 6 as well as the normal growing pains a team might face. Hugo also is now in an exclusive relationship (finally). I know there have been issues with Hugo's bedhopping, but again its part of his journey. Now the struggle will be maintaining that relationship while juggling his superhero adventures and leading a team. Drama to come!

EKEKE

BTW, I was not expecting to enjoy his chemistry with J-Tom so much. They fit together much better than I could've anticipated. But their relationship was a bit codependent and a way to treat their mutual wounds. But now they can focus on being teammates on the Paragons. However, we have not seen the last of Spencer causing trouble for them both. She's just getting warmed up. Most importantly, Hugo finally knows about Greyson! It's been a long, slow burn. So expect for them to finally meet in violent fashion. And don't worry, this conflict between them will stretch out beyond Absolute Power.

Speaking of conflict. Ms. Riva de León! Now many people might wonder why do we need her when Steve Olin is around? Both oligarchs might be closely aligned on Paxton-Brandt business, but their larger goals differ greatly. This woman can bend foreign presidents to her will and replace the heads of state who don't serve her agenda. To say she's well-connected and dangerous is an understatement. And she has much more 'foresight' than Olin. Plus, there is the Michelman connection. More to come...

And how about Brie? I told ya she's worth the wait. I always saw Brie's arc as a rise and fall then redemption. Someone with flaws and dimensions who needed to grow up. I wanted to depart from the usually flat arc we see female love interests on, even though she did play damsel in distress more than a few times. And just for the record, Brie is not losing her mind. The creature she saw, Knightmare, is very real and very powerful. Knightmare will become a big problem for Hugo, Brie and their friends in Book 6.

For those of you confused who Max Ochoa is, she debuted in *Fright Night Frights*. Fun little novella.

As for Greyson, he has taken yet another step in his journey. Now he's got the backing of Paxton-Brandt and continues to build his reputation as a supervillain. In his mind, he's right and will do whatever it takes to rid the world of superheroes. But he's now confronted with the mystery of Severine and taking down a few more heroes before finally reaching Hugo. Strangely enough, Greyson is right about Hugo being the vanguard (ha!) of a new generation of heroes. Taking him down would be a very devastating blow given all the turmoil within the superhero community. But can he be patient and strike at the right time??

Greyson's relationship with Olin will be complex, with the CEO serving almost as a default father figure to this obviously unstable and powerful person. Another interesting avenue was Connie's reaction to the bloodshed. Granted, she is ride-or-die for Greyson but not as a mindless puppet. Will she have a breaking point when it comes to how far he's willing to go? And for Greyson himself, what will he have to do to defeat Hugo? The battle is coming and it won't be one-sided for either party. Which means, Greyson might have to go after people connect to Hugo to hurt him and throw the youngster off-balance. You ready for it?

As for when United We Stand is coming? I'm aiming for late 2020. Books 5 and 6 will also feature a 4 to 5-month time with a few of the characters in different situations than where we last left them. But before that even, I will release a new Pantheon Saga novella later in the summer to hold you guys over!

Until then, keep commenting, emailing and most importantly, **keep reviewing if you enjoyed these books!** Those reviews will help other folks discover the Pantheon Saga like you have!

CCE

PS. If you want to find out when the next Pantheon Saga book will be release, there are several ways you can stay informed.

1.) **Follow me directly on Amazon.** Head over to my Amazon author profile and click Follow beneath my picture. Amazon will now notify you by email whenever I release a new book. Easy, right?

2.) **Join my newsletter list at: bit.ly/pnthn-list.** This way I can stay in touch with you directly, and get notified of all my new releases.

3.) Follow me on BookBub. BB sends out New Release alerts to my followers the day of my new book launches with more punctuality than Amazon and features lots of good book deals.

Doing one of all three of these (recommended) will ensure that you hear about each new release in The Pantheon Saga. Go ahead and do one of them. I'll wait.

STAY UP TO DATE

For updates on new releases and exclusive promotions, visit my website to sign-up for my VIP newsletter. Email addresses are never shared or used for any other purposes.

I post book cover art and travel photos on Instagram. You can also follow me on Facebook and Twitter.

I also created a special Facebook group called "C.C. Ekeke's Supercool Readers" for all my readers to discuss my books, share interests and their lives, and talk directly to me (C.C.E.).

Mailing List: http://bit.ly/pnthn-list

Facebook Group: https://www.facebook.com/groups/CCEkekeGroup/

Facebook Fanpage: http://www.facebook.com/ccekeke

Instagram: http://www.instagram.com/ccekeke

Twitter: http://www.twitter.com/CCEkeke

BOOKS BY C.C. EKEKE

The Pantheon Saga

Age of Heroes

Monsters Among Men

Generation Next

Gods of Wrath

Absolute Power

The Pantheon Saga Short Fiction

Friday Night Frights

Star Brigade Series

Resurgent

Maelstrom

Supremacy

Ascendant

Star Brigade Short Fiction

Odysseys

Traitor

Forsaken

Inheritance

ABOUT THE AUTHOR

C.C. Ekeke is the bestselling author of the Pantheon Saga series and the Star Brigade series. When he isn't writing or daydreaming about outer space dogfights or battling dastardly supervillains, he enjoys reading, hiking, learning new languages, spending time with his family, and traveling the world. You can find him occasionally navigating the globe like Waldo (minus the red-striped sweater) or on www.ccekeke.com.

Absolute Power is Ekeke's ninth full-length novel and the fifth novel in his Pantheon Saga series.

Printed in Great Britain
by Amazon

45974852R00226